A SUMMER
AT WILLOWMERE

BY
ABIGAIL GORDON

MILLS & BOON

For David, with all good wishes

First published in Great Britain 2009
Harlequin Mills & Boon Limited,
Eton House, 18-24 Paradise Road, Richmond, Surrey TW9 1SR

© Abigail Gordon 2009

ISBN: 978 0 263 86860 9

Set in Times Roman 10½ on 13 pt
03-0809-46781

Harlequin Mills & Boon policy is to use papers that are natural, renewable and recyclable products and made from wood grown in sustainable forests. The logging and manufacturing process conform to the legal environmental regulations of the country of origin.

Printed and bound in Spain
by Litografia Rosés, S.A., Barcelona

Dear Reader

Having been brought up happily enough in a Lancashire mill town, where fields and trees were sparse on the landscape, I now live in the countryside and find much pleasure in the privilege of doing so. It gives me the opportunity to write about village life with its caring communities and beautiful surroundings.

So, dear reader, welcome to the third of my four stories about Willowmere, a picturesque village tucked away in the Cheshire countryside. During the changing seasons you will meet the folk who live and work there, and share in their lives and loves.

It is summer when Laurel comes to Willowmere with her broken dreams and aching heart, quite unaware that in this country paradise she will meet a man who stands out among men, who will mend her dreams and kindle in her heart the kind of love that is precious beyond belief. For Laurel and David, the past will be past and the future will beckon like a bright star in their skies in A SUMMER WEDDING AT WILLOWMERE.

Happy reading!

Abigail Gordon

The Willowmere Village Stories

Look out for James and Lizzie's story in
COUNTRY MIDWIFE, CHRISTMAS BRIDE, coming
from Mills & Boon® Medical™ Romance in November!

Abigail Gordon loves to write about the fascinating combination of medicine and romance from her home in a Cheshire village. She is active in local affairs, and is even called upon to write the script for the annual village pantomime! Her eldest son is a hospital manager, and helps with all her medical research. As part of a close-knit family, she treasures having two of her sons living close by, and the third one not too far away. This also gives her the added pleasure of being able to watch her delightful grandchildren growing up.

Recent titles by the same author:

CHAPTER ONE

LAUREL MADDOX groaned as the train pulled into the small country station that was her destination. She had two heavy cases to unload and there wasn't a porter in sight. Just two deserted platforms and an unattended ticket office were all that were visible as the doors began to open.

For someone used to the big city where platforms and staff were many and varied it was a depressing introduction to the place that was going to be her home for some time to come. Yet all was not lost as she prepared to heave the cases out onto the platform.

A voice said from behind, 'Can I help?' and when she turned the man it belonged to didn't wait for an answer. He moved past and swung the offending luggage out onto the platform, then turned and offered a firm clasp from a hand that was protruding from the cuff of a crisp white shirt.

As she thanked him Laurel was thinking that he was the only part of the scenery that she could relate to. Tall, tanned, trimly built, wearing a dark suit, he seemed more in keeping with the place she'd come from than the countryside that her aunt had described in such glowing terms.

'I need a porter,' she said. 'Is there such a person in this place?'

'Just one,' he replied. 'Walter does the job of porter, mans the ticket office, collects them when necessary.' He gave a wave of the arm that took in the spotless platforms and the tubs of summer flowers gracing them. 'And also keeps the place clean and attractive. Willowmere won the prize for best country station last year. But he does stop for lunch at this time of day.'

'So what about a taxi?' she asked wearily, obviously unimpressed by his description of the absent Walter's devotion to duty.

'There is one, but…'

'Don't tell me. Amongst all of that he drives the local taxi.'

'No. His brother does that,' he said with a smile of the kind not soon forgotten, 'but it doesn't look as if he's around at the moment. I have a car and it's parked just here. Can I give you a lift to wherever you're going? I know we're strangers, but I'm a doctor in the village surgery, if it helps.' He showed her his ID, which proclaimed him to be Dr David Trelawney.

'Well, OK. Thank you,' she said, trying to smile despite feeling weary and irritable and wishing she hadn't allowed herself to be persuaded to move to the Cheshire village of Willowmere. 'So you must know my Aunt Elaine. I'm going to stay with her for a while.'

'Elaine Ferguson, our practice manager? Yes, of course,' he said in surprise, and bent to pick up her cases. 'So you'll be wanting Glenside Lodge, then. If you'll follow me.'

As she tottered after him across the cobbled forecourt of the station on high-heeled shoes Laurel was feeling nauseous from lack of food and the journey It had been a month since she'd been discharged from hospital and she was gradually getting stronger, but at that moment she felt as weak as a kitten and was wishing she'd stayed put in her own habitat.

'There's a vacancy coming up at the surgery for a practice nurse,' Elaine had phoned to say. 'Why don't you give James Bartlett, the senior partner, a ring?'

'You mean live in the country,' Laurel had said doubtfully. 'I'm not so sure about that. It just isn't my scene, and I'm not sure I want to go back to nursing after what happened.'

Elaine was not to be put off. 'The air here is like wine compared to the fumes in the city, and with some good food inside you it will help to complete your recovery. You've done so well, Laurel, and I'm so proud of you. Come to Willowmere and carry on with your nursing here. You are too good at it to give it up. A country practice is a much less stressful place than a large hospital...and I want to pamper you a little.'

Elaine was clearly looking forward to her coming to live in her beloved village and the thought of her waiting to welcome her with open arms had been too comforting to refuse. As well as that, her aunt made the best omelette she'd ever tasted and if there was one thing her appetite needed, it was to be tempted.

There was also the matter of the job at the practice. Laurel had eventually phoned the senior partner, and having explained that she was coming to live in

Willowmere and was a hospital-trained nurse, he'd said that once she arrived he would be only too pleased to have a chat.

Returning to the present, Laurel thought that Elaine was going to be mad when she knew she'd come on an earlier train. She would have been there to meet her if she'd kept to the arrangements, but the opportunity had presented itself and she'd thought it better to get on a train that was there than wait for one that might not arrive.

'Is she expecting you?' David asked as he drove along a country lane where hedgerows bright with summer flowers allowed an occasional glimpse of fertile fields and their crops.

'Yes and no,' she told him. 'Elaine knows I'm coming but not on the train I arrived on. I caught an earlier one.'

'That explains it.'

'Explains what?'

'She won't be at Glenside Lodge at this time. Elaine will be at the surgery. So shall I take you there instead?'

'No!' she said hurriedly. 'She's told me where to find the key. I'd like to go straight to her place if you don't mind.'

'Sure,' he said easily. 'Whatever you say.'

At that moment she slumped against him in the passenger seat and when David turned his head he saw that she'd fainted. Now it was his turn to groan. What had he let himself in for with this too thin, overly made-up girl in sheer tights and heels like stilts, wearing cotton gloves on a warm summer day…and with the appeal of a cardboard box.

He stopped the car and hurried round to where she was

crumpled pale and still in the passenger seat. When he felt her pulse Laurel opened her eyes and sighed. 'I'm sorry,' she said listlessly. 'It's just that I'm hungry and tired.'

'And it made you faint?' he questioned, but the main thing was she'd come out of it quickly and in a very short time they would be at Glenside Lodge.

'So where is the key?' he asked when they arrived at the end of a long drive that in the past the carriages of the gentry had trundled along.

'Under the water butt at the back,' she told him weakly, and he observed her anxiously.

The moment they were inside he was going to phone Elaine and get her over here as quickly as possible, he decided, and in the meantime he would keep a keen eye on this strange young woman who looked as if she'd stepped out of a back issue of one of the glossies.

When she got out of the car Laurel's legs wobbled beneath her, and afraid that she might collapse onto the hard surface of the drive he put his arm around her shoulders to support her while they went to find the key and then opened the door with his free hand and almost carried her inside.

There was a sofa by the window and after placing her carefully onto its soft cushions he went into the kitchen to see what he could give her to eat and drink before he did anything else.

A glass of milk and a couple of biscuits had to suffice and while she was nibbling on them and drinking thirstily he phoned the surgery.

'What?' the practice manager exclaimed when he told her that her visitor had arrived and wasn't feeling very well. 'Laurel wasn't due until later in the afternoon. I'll be right there, David.'

With that she'd put the phone down and now he was waiting to be relieved of the responsibility that he'd brought upon himself by offering to help Elaine's niece.

'I'm not always like this, you know,' she told him languidly as she drained the glass. 'I'm known to be friendly and no trouble to anyone.'

'You don't have to explain,' he told her dryly as the minutes ticked by. 'I suggest that you see a doctor in case you're sickening for something.'

She managed a grimace of a smile. 'I've seen a doctor, quite a few of them over recent months, and lo and behold, now I've met another.'

Elaine's car had just pulled up outside and she became silent, leaving him to wonder what she'd meant by that. Maybe she was already suffering from some health problem as she didn't look very robust.

During the short time that he'd been part of the village practice David hadn't known anything to disrupt the calm efficiency of its manager. A petite blue-eyed blonde in her late thirties, Elaine Ferguson had accountancy qualifications and controlled the administration side of it in a way that kept all functions working smoothly. But when she came dashing into the small stone lodge that had once been part of an estate high on the moors, Elaine was definitely flustered and the young woman he'd picked up at the station wasn't helping things as on seeing her aunt she burst into tears.

'Laurel, my dear,' she cried. 'Why didn't you stick to the arrangements we'd made?'

'I know I should have done,' she wailed, 'but it was so quiet in the apartment and I felt so awful. I just couldn't wait any longer to be with you.'

David cleared his throat. Now that Elaine had arrived he wanted to be gone, but first he had to explain that her niece had fainted due to what she'd described as hunger and exhaustion and he was going to advise that she see a doctor *at the surgery* to be checked over.

'I hope you will soon feel better,' he said to the woebegone figure on the sofa who was sniffling into a handkerchief, unaware that her mascara had become black smudges around green eyes that looked so striking against her creamy skin and red-gold hair. The hair in question was quite short and shaggy looking and he presumed it must be the fashion back in London.

Elaine came to the door with him, still tense and troubled, but she didn't forget to thank him for looking after her niece and it gave him the opportunity to say his piece.

She nodded when he'd finished. 'I have quite a few concerns about Laurel and the first one is to get her settled here in Willowmere where I can give her some loving care. I've persuaded her to leave the big city for a while and come to where there is fresh air and good food.'

'Your niece isn't impressed with what she's seen so far,' he warned her whimsically. 'A station with just two platforms and no porter to hand.'

'So she didn't notice the shrubs and the flowers that Walter tends so lovingly, but she will,' she said with quiet confidence. 'Laurel just needs time to get a fresh hold on life. I'm taking what's left of today off and the rest of the week. I'd already arranged it with James so everything is in order back at the surgery.'

'I can't imagine it ever not being in order,' he said as he stepped out onto the porch.

'That could change,' she said wryly, casting a glance over her shoulder at the slender figure on the sofa, and as he drove to the practice on the main street of the village David was wondering what Elaine had meant by that.

'So you've met Elaine's niece already!' James Bartlett, the senior partner, exclaimed when he arrived at the practice. 'How did that come about?'

'I went by rail to collect the last of my things from St Gabriel's,' David explained. 'I thought it would be quicker than driving there, and when the train pulled in at Willowmere on the return journey I saw this girl about to get off and she had two heavy cases. So I stepped in and lifted them down onto the platform for her.

'She asked about a taxi but the one and only was nowhere in sight so I drove her to Glenside Lodge then rang Elaine and by that time she wasn't looking very well.'

James nodded. 'I know there is or was a medical problem of some kind. There was a period when Elaine was dashing off to London to see her whenever possible and it is why she has persuaded her niece to come and stay with her as they're very close.'

'I'm sorry for the delay on my part,' David said. 'I'd expected to be away only a short time.'

'Don't be concerned,' James told him. 'You couldn't leave a damsel in distress and Ben was here until midday. He's been on cloud nine ever since little Arran was born. It's a delight to see him and Georgina so bliss-fully happy.

'But getting back to practice matters, would you take over the house calls now that you're back, while I have a chat with Beth Jackson? Our longest-serving practice nurse is champing at the bit to hang up her uniform.'

'Sure,' David agreed. 'It's a delightful day out there and a delightful place to be driving around in. I'll get the list from Reception and be off.'

His first call was at the home of eighty-six-year-old Sarah Wilkinson, who had recently been hospitalised because of high potassium levels in her blood due to drinking blackcurrant cordial insufficiently diluted.

She was home now and due to have another blood test. Sarah had been quite prepared to go to the surgery for it, but they'd told her that the district nurse would call to take the blood sample.

Today his visit was a routine one. All the over-eighties registered with the practice were visited from time to time, and when it was Sarah's turn there was always an element of pleasure in calling on her because outwardly frail though she was, underneath was an un-complaining, good-natured stoicism that had seen her through many health problems of recent years.

One of them had been a sore on her arm that had refused to heal. It had resulted in visits to the surgery for dressings over a long period of time, but the old lady had never complained and of recent months a skin graft had finally solved the problem.

When she opened the door to him she said with a

twinkle in her eye, 'Can I offer you a drink of blackcurrant cordial, Doctor?'

David was smiling as he followed her into a cosy sitting room. 'Do you intend to put plenty of water with it, Sarah?'

'One can't do right for doing wrong in this life,' she said laughingly. 'I thought by taking the cordial almost neat I was building myself up, but no such thing.'

'I know,' he soothed. 'But we've sorted you out, haven't we?'

'Yes, you have and I'm grateful. So to what do I owe this visit?'

'It's a courtesy call. Just to make sure you are all right.'

'I'm fine. I'm not ready for pushing up the daisies yet. I'm going to enter my home-made jam and Madeira cake at the Summer Fayre at the end of July just to prove it. Are you going to be there?'

'Yes, now that you've told me about it. Although it's a while off yet, isn't it, as June is still bursting out all over. What time does it start?'

'Eleven in the morning until four in the afternoon. The café and the judging take place in a big marquee that Lord Derringham lends us. He's the rich man who owns the estate on the tops. One of your practice nurses is married to his manager and Christine Quarmby, who has that ailment with the funny name, is his gamekeeper's wife.'

'I can see that if I want to get to know what is going on in the village this is the place to come,' he commented. 'Do the people in Willowmere see much of His Lordship?'

Sarah shook her head. 'No, keeps himself to himself, but on the odd occasion that he does appear he's very pleasant and, like I said, he lets us use the marquee.

'On the night before the Fayre we have a party in the park that runs alongside the river. There's food and drink, and a band on a stage to play for dancing, with us women in long dresses and the men in dinner jackets. You must come.'

'Why? Will *you* be there?'

'Of course.' She had a twinkle back in her eye. 'Though I'm not into rock and roll. A sedate waltz is more in my line.'

'So can I book the first one?'

'Yes, you can.'

'I'm impressed.'

'Get away with you.' She chuckled. 'When the young females of Willowmere see you all dressed up, the likes of me won't be able to get near you.'

David laughed. 'Talking about young females, I gave one a lift from the station today.'

'Oh, yes? And who would that be?'

'She's called Laurel and is the niece of Elaine the practice manager.'

Sarah smiled. 'So that's another one that'll be in the queue.'

I don't think so, he thought, and returned to more serious matters by changing the subject. 'Right, Sarah. So shall I do what I've come for?'

He checked her heart and blood pressure, felt her pulse and the glands in her neck, and when he'd finished told her, 'No problems there at the moment, but before

I go is there anything troubling you healthwise that you haven't told me about?'

She shook her silver locks. 'No, Doctor. Not at the moment.'

He was picking up his bag. 'That's good, then, and if I don't see you before I'll see you at the party in the park.'

'So tell me more about Dr Trelawney,' Laurel said after David had gone. 'He told me that he's one of the GPs here.'

'He joined us just a short time ago from St Gabriel's Hospital where he was a registrar seeking a change of direction,' Elaine explained. 'David has replaced Georgina Allardyce, who has just given birth and tied the knot for a second time with the husband she was divorced from almost four years ago.

'Georgina is on maternity leave at the moment and may come back part time in the future. In the meantime, we are fortunate to have David, who is clever, capable, and has slotted in as if he was meant to be part of the village's health care.'

'He was kind and I don't think I behaved very well,' Laurel said regretfully. 'In fact, I was a pain. I'll apologise the next time we meet, but I felt so awful. I'm a freak, Elaine.'

'Nonsense, Laurel. You are brave *and* beautiful,' her aunt protested. 'The scars, mental and physical, will fade. Just give them time, dear.'

'Everything is such an effort,' she said despondently. 'I'd put on my war paint and nice clothes to make a statement, but didn't fool anyone, certainly not the Trelawney guy. He suggested that I see a doctor.'

'And what did you say to that?'

'That I'd seen plenty over the last few months and was about to tell him that I'm no ignoramus myself when it comes to health care, but you arrived at that moment.'

'Right,' Elaine said briskly, having no comment to make regarding that. 'Let's get you settled in. David said you fainted, so how do you feel now?'

'Better. He gave me some milk and biscuits.'

'Good. So let's show you where you'll be sleeping. Take your time up the stairs, watch your leg. I've put you in the room with the best view. It overlooks Willow Lake, which is one of the most beautiful places in the area.'

'Really,' was the lacklustre response, and Elaine hid a smile. Laurel was a city dweller through and through and might be bored out here in the countryside, but she needed the change of scene and the slower pace of life. Elaine wasn't going to let her go back to London until she was satisfied that her niece was fully recovered from an experience that she was not ever likely to forget.

'Is your fiancé going to visit while you're here?' Elaine asked after she'd helped bring up Laurel's cases. 'He will be most welcome.'

'It's off,' Laurel told her as she peered through the window at the view that she'd been promised. 'I'm too thin and pale for him these days…and then there are the scars, of course.'

'Then he doesn't love you enough,' Elaine announced, and without further comment went down to make them a late lunch.

She was right, Laurel thought dolefully when she'd gone, but it hurt to hear it said out loud. Darius was in the process of making his name in one of the television soaps and had rarely been to see her while she'd been hospitalised, and less still since she'd been discharged. When she'd said she was going to the countryside to assist her recovery he'd thought she was out of her mind.

'You're crazy, babe,' he'd said. 'Why would you want to leave London for fields full of cow pats?'

If his visits had been sparse, not so Elaine's. Her aunt had been to see her in hospital whenever she could and Laurel loved her for it. Other friends had been kind and loyal too. But Darius, the one she'd wanted to see the most, had been easing her out of his life all the time. In the end, dry eyed and disenchanted, she'd given him his ring back.

After they'd eaten Elaine said, 'Why don't you sit out in the garden for a while and let the sun bring some colour to your pale cheeks while I clear away?'

'If you say so,' Laurel agreed without much enthusiasm and, picking up a magazine that she'd bought before leaving London, went to sit on the small terrace at the back of the lodge. But it wasn't long before she put it down. It was too quiet, she thought, spooky almost. How was she going to exist without the hustle and bustle of London in her ears?

For the first time since she'd arrived, she found herself smiling. What was she like! Most people would jump at the chance to get away from that sort of sound, yet here she was, already pining for the throb of traffic.

The silence was broken suddenly by the noise of a car pulling up on the lane at the side of the garden and when she looked up Laurel saw that the window on the driver's side was being lowered and the village doctor that she'd met earlier was observing her over the hedge.

'So how's it going?' David asked. 'Are you feeling better?'

'Er, yes, a bit,' she said, taken aback at seeing him again in so short a time. 'You didn't have to come to check on me, you know.'

'I'm not,' he told her dryly. 'There are plenty of others who will actually be glad to see me. I'm in the middle of my house calls so I won't disturb you further.'

She'd given him the impression that she thought him interfering, Laurel thought glumly as he drove off. What a pain in the neck he must think she was.

Elaine appeared at that moment with coffee and biscuits on a tray and as they sat together companionably, she asked, 'Did I hear a car?'

'Yes. It was your Dr Trelawney.'

'David?'

'Yes, on his home visits. He saw me out here and stopped for a word. He doesn't look like a country type. How does *he* cope with it, I wonder?'

'The job?'

'No, the silence.'

'You ungrateful young minx,' Elaine declared laughingly. 'Lots of people would give their right arm to live in a place like this.'

'Yes, but what do you do for fun?'

Still amused, she replied, 'Oh, we fall in love, get married, have babies, take delight in the seasons as they come and go, count the cabbages in the fields…'

'*You* haven't done that, though, have you?'

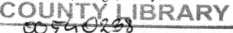

'Counted the cabbages? No, but I've been in love. Sadly I was never a bride. I lost the love of my life before our relationship had progressed that far.'

'Yes, and it's such a shame,' Laurel told her. 'You would have been a lovely mum. That's what you've been like to me, Elaine.'

'You are my sister's child,' she said gently. 'I've tried to make up for what she and your father lacked in parenting skills, but they did turn up at the hospital to see you, didn't they?'

'For a couple of hours, yes, because they'd read about me in the papers, but they were soon off on their travels again.'

'That's the way they are,' Elaine said soothingly. 'Free spirits. We'll never change them and they do love you in their own way.'

'I've lost *my* way, Elaine,' she said forlornly. 'I used to be so positive, but since it happened I feel as if I don't know who I am. My face isn't marked, for which I'm eternally grateful, but there are parts of the rest of me that aren't a pretty sight.'

'That won't matter to anyone who really loves you,' she was told. 'Like I said before, you're brave *and* beautiful.'

'I wish,' was the doleful reply.

David Trelawney was house hunting. Since moving to Willowmere he'd been living in a rented cottage not too far from the surgery and Bracken House, where James Bartlett lived with his two children.

So far it was proving to be an ideal arrangement. It wouldn't have been if his high-flying American fiancée had wanted to join him, but that was not a problem any more.

They'd called off the engagement just before he'd accepted the position at St Gabriel's, and though it had left him with a rather jaundiced attitude to the opposite sex, his only regret was that he'd made an error of judgement and would be wary of repeating it.

Yet it wasn't stopping him from house hunting. He didn't want to rent for long, but so far he hadn't made any definite decision about where he was going to put down his roots in the village that had taken him to its heart. He told himself wryly that he'd made a mistake in his choice of a wife and wasn't going to do the same thing when it came to choosing a house.

He'd spent his growing years in a Cornish fishing village where his father had brought him up single-handed after losing his wife to cancer when David had been quite small, and once when Caroline had flown over to see him he'd taken her to meet him.

'Are you sure that she is the right one for you, David?' Jonas Trelawney had said afterwards. 'She's smart and attractive, seems like the kind of woman who knows what she wants and goes out to get it, but I know how you love kids and somehow I can't see her breast feeding or changing nappies. Have you discussed it at all?'

'Yes,' he'd said easily, putting from his mind the number of times the word 'nanny' had cropped up in the conversation.

He'd met her on a visit to London. She'd been staying in the same hotel with a group of friendly Texans who, on discovering that he had been on his own, had invited him to join them as they saw the sights.

She'd made a play for him, he'd responded to her advances, and the attraction between them had escalated into marriage plans, though he'd had his doubts about how she would react to the prospect of living in a town in Cheshire, as at that time he'd been based at St Gabriel's Hospital.

It was going to be so different to the glitzy life that he'd discovered she led when he'd visited her in Texas. Yet she hadn't raised any objections when he'd said that he had no plans to leave the UK while his father was alive. But he was to discover that the novelty of the idea was to be short-lived as far as Caroline was concerned.

His uneasiness had become a definite thing when he'd been expecting to go over there to sort out wedding arrangements and she'd put him off, saying that she had the chance to purchase a boutique that she'd had her eye on for some time and didn't want any diversions until the deal was settled.

'I would hardly have thought our wedding would be described as a diversion,' he'd said coolly, and she'd told him that she was a businesswoman first and foremost and he would have to get used to that.

'I see, and how are you going to run a boutique in Texas if you are living over here?' he'd asked, his anger rising.

There was silence at the other end of the line and then the dialling tone.

She phoned him again that same day at midnight Texas time. It sounded as if she was at some sort of social gathering if the noise in the background was anything to go by, and as if wine had loosened her tongue Caroline told him the truth, that she didn't want to be a doctor's wife any more in some crummy place in Britain and wanted to call off the engagement.

As anger came surging back he told her that it was fine by him and coldly wished her every success in her business dealings.

He discovered afterwards that there'd been more to it than she'd admitted that night on the phone. A certain senator had appeared on her horizon and she'd used the boutique story as a get-out.

In his disillusionment David decided to make a fresh start. His father had once told him that his mother had come from a village in Cheshire called Willowmere, and shortly after his engagement to Caroline had ended he met James Bartlett's sister Anna in the company of a doctor from the village practice. They'd been involved in a near drowning incident in a village called Willowmere and the way they described the place made him keen to find where the other part of his roots belonged.

When he'd found his mother's childhood home the discovery of it pulled at his heartstrings so much that he decided he wanted to live in Willowmere, and as if it was meant he was offered a position in the village practice.

What was left of the house stood in the centre of a field on the way to Willow Lake, a local beauty spot, and as he'd stood beside it he'd felt that this was where he wanted to be, where he wanted to bring up his children if he ever married, and at the same time contribute to the health care of those who lived there.

All that remained of it was four stone walls, the roof

having long since fallen in, and he remembered his father telling him how his mother had left it as a bride and gone to live with him in Cornwall where *his* home had been.

David found no reason to regret his decision to move to the Cheshire countryside. He was totally happy there, but supposed it might not be everyone's choice. For instance, there was the girl he'd met at the station, he thought as the day took its course. She'd taken a dim view of the place.

So far he hadn't found a property that appealed to him and knew it was because every time he went back to the ruins of his mother's home the idea of restoring it was there.

Laurel and Elaine had had an omelette for their evening meal with chips and fresh green runner beans out of the garden, and when she'd placed the food in front of her niece she'd said, 'I know it's not exactly the fatted calf but it's something that I know you like.'

'I love your omelettes,' Laurel told her. 'I used to dream about them when I was in hospital.'

'Yes, I'm sure you did,' Elaine said laughingly. 'You must have had better things to think about than my cooking.'

'It was the only thing that cheered me up,' Laurel insisted. 'Darius was in the process of ditching me slowly, the skin grafts weren't a bundle of joy, and neither was my leg that they'd had to pin all over the place.'

'I know, my dear,' Elaine said soothingly. 'It isn't surprising that you're feeling low with all that has happened to you but, Laurel, it could have been so much worse.'

'Yes, I know,' she said flatly, 'and I really do want to like it here and get fit again. I look such a sight.'

'Not to me you don't.'

'Maybe, but your Dr Trelawney kept looking at me as if I was some peculiar specimen under the microscope. I wish my hair would grow more quickly.'

'Have patience, Laurel,' she was told. 'What has grown so far is still the same beautiful colour.'

'Yes, the colour of fire,' she said with a shudder as she ate the food beneath the watchful gaze of her hostess.

'I think an early night would be a good idea,' Elaine suggested when they'd tidied up after the meal, 'but how about a breath of good country air first? Perhaps a short walk through the village, past the surgery where David and I spend our working lives, and where you might be joining us when you feel like going to see James.'

'Yes, sure,' she agreed, 'and if that is where he works, where does he live?'

'David lives in a small cottage nearby. He's staying there until he finds a property to buy. I know that he's house hunting quite seriously but hasn't mentioned finding anything suitable so far.'

'And will he be living alone when he does?' Laurel asked.

'Yes, as far as I know, unless he has a wife tucked away somewhere, and I doubt that.'

David was returning from his usual nightly stroll to gaze upon his mother's old home when he saw them coming towards him. Elaine, trim as always in slacks and a smart top, and the strange young woman he'd met at lunchtime still in the same outlandish garb as before that looked totally out of place in the setting.

'Hello, there,' he said when they drew level. 'Have you been showing your niece the sights of Willowmere, Elaine?'

'Yes, some of them,' she replied, 'such as the surgery and your spacious accommodation.'

He smiled. 'It's all right for one, two at the most.'

'And are you still house hunting?'

'Er, yes, sort of. I've got something in mind but it won't be a fast solution.'

He was aware that Elaine's companion hadn't spoken at yet another unexpected meeting and thought that maybe now she was established in the village she was keeping a low profile, but he was to discover there was nothing wrong with her vocal cords.

'I don't remember thanking you for coming to my rescue when I was getting off the train,' she said in a less abrupt manner than the one she'd used then.

'Think nothing of it,' he said easily, as if the whole episode had been a pleasant break in the day. 'The main thing is how are you feeling now?'

She smiled and David was struck at the transformation.

'Improving,' was the reply, 'and once Elaine has shown me the lake it's off to bed for me. It's been a long day, but not as long as some have been recently.'

As they moved off in opposite directions David was thinking how pale she was. James had said there was a health problem of some kind regarding Elaine's niece, and he wondered what it was.

CHAPTER TWO

WHEN Laurel awoke the next morning she found herself looking up at an unfamiliar ceiling dappled by a summer sun and for the first few seconds couldn't think where she was, but not for long.

She was in Elaine's quiet backwater, she thought, with birdsong the only sound breaking the silence. Recalling how she'd asked her aunt what they did for fun in Willowmere, she wondered why she'd brought up the subject. *That* kind of thing wasn't going to be on her agenda with a broken engagement behind her and some unappealing scarring.

But now here she was and glad of it in spite of her lack of enthusiasm for country life. As sleep had stolen over her the night before she'd vowed she was going to make an effort to fit in and if she got the job at the surgery at least she wouldn't be moping around all day.

'Does anyone in Willowmere know what happened to me?' Laurel asked of Elaine as they ate a leisurely breakfast out on the sunny patio.

Her aunt shook her head. 'No. At the time I was too

distressed to talk about it, my beautiful niece caught up in the stupidity of others, and if anyone around here saw it in the papers they wouldn't see any connection.

'Right from the start I've felt it would be an invasion of your privacy to discuss you with others even though I've been bursting with pride every time I thought of what you did. But as far as I'm concerned, that is how it will stay, Laurel. If you should want to tell anyone, that is a different matter.

'And now what would you like to do today? If you're not over the moon with our lovely village we can go into the town and shop if you like, but I would rather we saved that sort of thing for when you've had some rest and relaxation, which could be in short supply when you're working at the surgery.'

'You mean *if* I'm working there. I'm not exactly spectacular at the moment with a gammy knee that sometimes lets me down and hair that looks as if it's been cut with a knife and fork.'

'Nonsense,' Elaine soothed gently. 'Your hair is growing back nicely and you're beautiful with your green eyes and lovely, curvy mouth.'

'And my rough red hands,' Laurel reminded her with dry humour. 'I wear the gloves all the time so that I won't be mistaken for a domestic drudge.'

'Get away with you,' was the response. 'People around here are very kind and if they knew how you'd got the scarring they would acclaim your courage and dedication to the job. But, as I've just said, that is entirely your affair, and as to how we are going to spend your first day away from London, what is it to be, the town or the village?'

'The village, I think,' Laurel replied. She would have preferred to go shopping but she knew how much Elaine wanted to show her Willowmere and they could always shop another day.

'So how about a leisurely stroll and then we'll have lunch at the Hollyhocks Tea Rooms? It may not be as upmarket as the places where you usually eat, but they won't be able to beat the food that Emma and her husband serve to their customers.

'Then if you like I'll take you to the surgery and introduce you to James. He will want to arrange a time to interview you. Beth Jackson, who is leaving, wants to go as soon as possible. She and her husband are opening a business next to the post office and if you feel the need, by all means wear the gloves, though I do think that you have no call to be so self-conscious about your hands.'

Laurel wasn't sure about visiting the surgery. 'Don't you think that David Trelawney might feel that since arriving here I've been continually in his line of vision?' she said dubiously. 'At the station, in the garden, when he was driving past on his way to house calls, and at sunset last night.'

'He'll be seeing much more of you than that if you're working at the same place,' Elaine said laughingly. 'And how do you know he won't feel that he can't get too much of a good thing?'

Laurel couldn't bring herself to share in Elaine's amusement. How long, if ever, was it going to be before she felt desirable once more? Each time Darius had visited her in hospital it had been clear that he wasn't keen on the damaged version, and as she'd fought her way through the pain it had been with her confidence at a very low ebb.

As they walked along the main street Elaine was greeted by everyone they met and Laurel was aware that some curious glances were coming her way, which was not surprising as she was wearing a high-necked sweater, a hat and gloves on a hot summer day.

This is so different from city life, she was thinking as she took in the friendliness of the people. She and her fellow nurses had often commented that in London people were always rushing about, and getting to know one's next-door neighbour was a rare event, but in Willowmere life seemed to be lived at a slower pace, as if each moment was to be cherished rather than passed quickly by.

It had always been Elaine who had been *her* visitor before this, staying at the apartment and enjoying every moment with the niece that she loved like a daughter, but now it was Laurel's turn to leave her natural habitat for a while.

And now here she was, happy to be with the one person who loved her unconditionally, yet feeling totally out of her depth amongst quaint limestone cottages and shops that had an individuality all their own.

'We passed the surgery last night if you remember,' Elaine said, indicating a large stone building across the way from where they'd just had an excellent lunch. Noting Laurel's lack of enthusiasm, she added, 'Are you sure you want to meet the people who work there?'

'Yes, of course,' she said with assumed heartiness, deciding that she may as well get it over with. At least it was only a place for local people with their ailments. There would be no rows of beds or doctors with sombre expressions looking down at her, and nurses treating one of their own with sympathy and efficiency.

She'd been introduced to the two receptionists, both of them middle-aged, pleasant and organised, met the two practice nurses and discovered that it was a delicatessen that Beth Jackson and her husband were going to open very soon at the other end of the main street.

At that moment the door of the nearest consulting room opened and an attractive, dark-haired woman was framed there, holding a baby in her arms. The doctor she'd been consulting was close behind and as she was about to leave he bent and kissed her tenderly.

Laurel's eyes widened and as Elaine steered her in the opposite direction she explained, 'That is baby Arran Allardyce come to see his daddy. Ben is helping out while Georgina, his wife, who is one of our regular doctors, is on maternity leave.'

'I see,' Laurel said, and wished that she had a man in her life to kiss her like that and a beautiful baby to go with it. Day would turn into night before that ever happened in the light of recent events.

James Bartlett, the senior partner, was all that Elaine had described him to be, pleasant, handsome, a very likeable man with two lovely children if the photograph on his desk was anything to go by, and when they'd been introduced her aunt left them to get acquainted.

She'd removed the hat by then, deciding that if she was going to be employed there it was only fair that the man sitting opposite should see what she really looked like, yet she needn't have worried. James didn't seem to see anything too odd about the young woman that Elaine had brought to the surgery. 'When could you come for an interview, Laurel?'

'Whenever,' she replied. 'My time is my own at present.'

'Then how about on the afternoon of the day that Elaine returns from the leave that she arranged in honour of your arrival? Say two o'clock?' As she got up to go he shook her hand and said, 'We'll look forward to seeing you then.'

She was missing nursing, but until Elaine had suggested she work at the practice had felt it would be too painful to go back to it. But there was something about this pleasant village health care centre that was reaching out to her...and of course there was David Trelawney. Where was he today?

Yesterday she'd been too frazzled to really register the man who'd come to her rescue when she'd been getting off the train, but now she was curious to see if he was as presentable as she'd thought. It would be nice to see him again now that she was in residence, so to speak, and it would give her the opportunity to express further gratitude for his assistance, but it seemed that it was not to be on this bright summer day, and it did rather take the edge off it.

If she and Elaine had walked a little further she would have had the answer to her question. David's car was parked outside the village hall. He'd been about to start his home visits when a call had come through and he'd gone straight there to find the chairlady of the Women's Institute, who were holding their usual monthly meeting on the premises, looking far from well.

She was experiencing severe chest pains, perspiring heavily, and her lips were blue. Before he'd even sounded her heart David was phoning for an ambulance and telling her gently, 'I'm sending you to hospital, Mrs Tate.'

She nodded. Maisie Tate was no fool. She wouldn't be chairlady of Willowmere's branch of the Women's Institute if she was. She could tell that the new doctor at the practice had her down for a heart attack and she didn't think he was wrong.

But if that was the case, who was going to look after her husband? Barry always had kippers for tea on a Thursday and she wasn't going to be able to call at the fishmonger's on her way home today.

David had finished examining her and as another stab of pain ripped across her chest he said reassuringly, 'The ambulance will be here any moment, Mrs Tate, and they'll take you straight to hospital when I've had a word with the paramedics.'

The rest of the Women's Institute was hovering around her anxiously and one of them, who must have known her routine, said, 'Don't worry, Maisie. I'll get your Barry his kippers.'

She nodded and David thought incredulously that this was the age group who'd been brought up to have a meal ready for the man of the house when he came in from work. But surely when he knew what was happening to his wife the absent Barry wouldn't have any appetite.

As he drove along the main street of the village on his way to the delayed calls he was surprised to see Elaine and Laurel walking slowly along the pavement ahead of him, and as he pulled up alongside them he saw that the short skirt, high heels and sheer tights had been replaced by jeans and sandals.

But the rest of her attire was still strange and he didn't think it was what the fashion-conscious were wearing for the summer in London. A soft felt hat was completely covering the short red-gold hair and she was still wearing the white cotton gloves.

'Hello, there, and what are you folks up to on this glorious day?' he asked with a smile that embraced them both.

'I'm showing Laurel around the village,' Elaine replied. 'We've just been to the surgery and she's been introduced to everyone there. Where were you, though? You were the only one missing, David, although you've already met my niece, haven't you?'

I have indeed, he thought, three times to be exact.

'Yes,' he replied with the smile still in place, and went on to explain with his glance on her so-far silent companion, 'I was out on an emergency call.

'And how are *you* this morning, Laurel?' he said easily, wondering if she was anaemic or something of the kind to be wearing that sort of jumper in the heat of summer.

'Much better, thank you,' she said flatly, and he sighed inwardly.

He turned to Elaine. 'I was called to the village hall where the Women's Institute are having a meeting and found their chairlady with a suspected heart attack.'

'Oh! No!' Elaine exclaimed. 'That would be Maisie Tate. Poor Maisie!'

'Yes, it was,' he replied, and thought he couldn't imagine her companion having much interest in the ills and ailments of the Willowmere villagers. There was an aloofness about her today and he was curious to know what lay beneath it as he never could resist a challenge.

'And so what do you think of our beautiful village?' he asked Laurel.

'I thought that you were a newcomer too,' she commented dryly, while comparing his clear-cut attractiveness to the wavy dark hair and fashionable stubble of Darius, who'd not wanted her any more because he'd seen the scarring and been revolted...

It wasn't a situation that would ever occur with this man, she thought with a rush of blood. There would never be an occasion when *he* saw her minus clothing and...where had such an idea come from anyway?

He was smiling at the comment and she thought how likeable he was as he said, 'I am a newcomer in one way, yet I feel as if Willowmere has always been part of me. Sometimes we find the place of our dreams and are given the opportunity to live there and that is what I intend to do when I've found a house.'

There was no mention of a woman in his life, Laurel noticed, which was incredible, but the odds were that there would be one tucked away somewhere, or relegated to the past for some reason.

'I must go,' he said, unaware that she was surmising about his love life. 'I have a few visits to make and am already late after the callout to Mrs Tate.'

'Yes, of course,' Elaine said, and to Laurel's horror she went on, 'Would you like to come over for dinner one evening so that I may show my appreciation for the way you looked after my niece yesterday?'

Ugh! Laurel thought, taken aback at the suggestion and its implications. It made her appear to be some sort of helpless, clinging vine, just as she'd been when they'd met at the station and afterwards. But she wasn't usually like that. It was just unfortunate that David Trelawney had been an observer of her moments of weakness.

If she was taken aback, so was he, she thought, seeing his surprise, but he soon recovered his poise and said politely, 'Er...yes...I'd love to.' He glanced warily in her direction. 'But please don't feel that you owe me anything for yesterday. It was just a matter of common politeness.'

As Elaine nodded understandingly Laurel thought wistfully that it would be, wouldn't it? The time was gone when she attracted admiring looks, or handsome men asked her out to dinner.

'When would you like to come?' Elaine was asking.

He gave a wry grimace. 'I'm free most nights. I spend most of my time house hunting or dreaming of renovating an old house I've seen.'

'And where would that be?' she questioned curiously, while Laurel stood by silently once more.

'It's a derelict building in one of the fields beside Willow Lake.'

'Ah! I know the one. It's called Water Meetings House. Why that one, though, when there are lots of nice properties in the area? It would need huge restoration work to make it habitable again. It's been like that for years.'

'Mmm, I know, but I do have my reasons,' he said, and without questioning him further Elaine returned to the subject of dinner.

'So how about one night next week?' she suggested. 'Say Friday when there is no surgery the following day?'

'Yes, fine,' he replied. 'What time?'

'Sevenish, if that's all right.'

He nodded and with a wave of the hand drove off.

As his car disappeared from view Laurel groaned openly and Elaine said, 'I know what you're thinking. That it is unkind of me to invite David to dinner when you want to keep a low profile, but Laurel, I'm not matchmaking. He is a stranger in the village, just as you are, and we in Willowmere are renowned for our hospitality.'

'I'm sorry,' she said contritely as the moment of gloom disappeared. 'The last thing I want is to become a me, me, me sort of person. Self-pity is a form of selfishness.'

'It can be,' Elaine agreed gently, 'but not in your case. And now let's take you home and put you to bed for a couple of hours and I guarantee that as each day passes you are going to feel more ready to face the world, and whatever you think of Willowmere you couldn't be recuperating in a better place.'

'You might be right,' Laurel said with spirits still lifting as she thought that it was more likely to be the village's inhabitants than its peace and fresh air that were going to help her take a hold on life again.

Yet as she looked out of her bedroom window before going to bed that night and saw a golden sun setting on the skyline, with the lake glinting in the distance amongst the drooping willows that had given it its name, it didn't all feel quite so strange as it had the night before.

Within minutes of placing her head on the pillows she slept and for once there were no smoke and flames turning her dreams into nightmares.

Beth called at Glenside Lodge for a chat in her lunch hour the following day and as the three of them relaxed over coffee she said, 'James must be feeling that it is one departure after another at the surgery. First it was Anna and Glenn going to work in Africa. Then Georgina and Ben had a blissful reunion, which resulted in them re-marrying and her giving birth to Arran in the spring, so *she* is going to be missing for quite some time too, hence David's most welcome appearance, and now I'm about to try a new slant on village shopping. You will be most welcome in the practice, Laurel, if you can sort something out with James, but are you happy that it might only be temporary?'

'Yes, it would suit me fine,' she replied. 'I'm rather at a crossroads in my life at the moment, so it would give me a short breathing space before I make up my mind what I want to do and where I'm heading.'

Elaine was nodding in silent agreement. Laurel was improving physically, but it was the mental scars that worried her. Her niece had been a bright and trendy twenty-five-year-old when it had happened, totally dedicated to the career she'd chosen and enjoying life in the big city when she hadn't been working, but now all of that had gone.

Her interest in the village surgery had been lukewarm

when she'd taken Laurel there, as had been her interest in life in general, but she wasn't going to sit by and let her stay in the doldrums. Her beautiful girl still had a lot to offer to those needing health care *and* to the man who would one day love her for who she was.

Willowmere in summer was a bright haven of colour. The new life that had come bursting through in fields and gardens in the spring was now established in abundant growth. Trees along the riverside, some of them hundreds of years old, were in full leaf, providing a background of fresh greenery against the flimsy craft of the canoe club as they sailed along on practice days, and bird life of every kind imaginable was to be found in cottage gardens and in the park that ran parallel with the river.

The charm of the village attracted walkers and visitors from miles around and as the days passed Laurel was aware that the Hollyhocks Tea Rooms were busy all the time with those seeking appetising meals to complement a summer day, and The Pheasant, its only pub, did much trade with others who had less discerning tastes but could guarantee a thirst.

Often it wasn't until late in the evening that the quiet that she'd been so dubious about descended. It was on one of those occasions that she went for a stroll in the gathering dusk beside the lake that was visible when she looked through her bedroom window.

Elaine had gone to bed and she'd been about to do the same when the urge to go out into the gloaming had overtaken her. The sunset had been magnificent and now it was still and sultry with a yellow moon above.

She'd been wearing a sundress in the house and instead of changing into something less revealing threw a light cardigan across her bare shoulders and sallied forth, minus the gloves.

There were still a few people about loath to be inside on such a night, but they thinned out as she drew nearer to the lake, and by the time she was only a field away she was alone, and looming up in front of her in the moonlight were the ruins of a big stone house. Could this be the place that David Trelawney had mentioned? she wondered. If so, what a mess it was in, yet what a position, just a hundred feet or so from Willow Lake, and on the other side of the house, not far away, the place where the two rivers that flowed through the village met. There was a tattered sign on the fencing that separated the field from the road and as she peered at it she saw that it said appropriately 'Water Meetings House.' She shook her head in disbelief. Was the man insane? It would take forever to restore this place.

'Hello, there,' a voice said from behind her.

She turned slowly and he was there, the village doctor who was considering rebuilding the shell of what must have once been a gracious home.

'Hi,' she said lightly, pulling the cardigan tightly around her shoulders. 'I came out for a stroll and stumbled upon this derelict house. It's the one that you mentioned the other day, isn't it?'

He was smiling. She could see his teeth gleaming whitely in the moon's light. 'Yes, it is. I expect you think I'm crazy to be considering restoring it.'

'Yes, I do as a matter of fact,' was the reply. 'Yet I can see why. It's in a fantastic position and so aptly named.'

She was a dedicated city dweller, but there was something about the moment with the two of them wrapped around by the silent night and the remains of the limestone house shining palely in the moonlight that was firing her imagination, and she thought whimsically that it was as if there were forces abroad that were out to entrance her, when she didn't want to be entranced.

As he observed her bemused expression David was thinking along similar lines. It was weird that Laurel of all people should be so much on his wavelength about this place and the ruins of his mother's old home. Meeting up with her out there in the moonlight was just as odd as on the other times they'd met.

It had come at the end of a very strange day. In the early afternoon he'd had a phone call from one of the Texan wives who'd been in Caroline's group when he'd first met her in London.

He'd been surprised to hear from her and even more so when he'd heard what she had to say. She'd rung to tell him that Caroline had married the senator that she'd been seeing at the time they'd ended their relationship.

'My Jerome said we should let you know,' she'd said gently in a soft Texan drawl, 'so that if you hear it from someone else it won't be such a shock.'

He'd thanked her and after chatting briefly had finished the call with no feelings of regret. There'd been just the relief of knowing that the big mistake he'd almost made had reached its final conclusion, and it would be a long time before he made such an error of judgement again.

He'd picked up the phone again and rung his father, and when he'd told him about the call from America and that it was definitely over with his ex-fiancée Jonas had exclaimed, 'Praise be! But I thought it already was?'

'Yes, it was, but now there is closure, Dad,' he said calmly.

'And are you sure you're all right with that?'

'Spot on,' he replied. 'It would never have worked. We had a different set of values.'

'One day you'll meet the right woman and when it happens you will know beyond any doubt,' Jonas said. 'When I met your mother I knew she was the only one for me, and it will be the same for you.'

'If you say so,' he agreed dubiously, with the old proverb about once bitten, twice shy in mind.

With the feeling of contentment still there he went to the local estate agent's while out on his calls and ended his uncertainties about the house by the lake by making an offer for it and the land it stood on.

In the summer twilight he'd gone to gaze upon what he hoped would soon be his and found that the strange day was not yet over. He'd found Laurel Maddox there, standing silent and alone in front of what had been his mother's childhood home.

CHAPTER THREE

HER eyes looked huge in the light of the moon. She was still clutching her cardigan tightly around her, and once again he wondered what it was with this strange newcomer to the village.

She was different from any woman he'd ever met. There was a sort of touch-me-not aura about her and yet he sensed hurt and vulnerability there too.

'I'll walk you home,' he suggested. 'We don't get much crime around here, but even so it isn't a good idea to be out on your own in the dark.' She didn't reply, but as he began to move in that direction she fell into step beside him.

As they walked along the road that separated the house from the lake she tripped over a loose stone and his arm came out to steady her. He felt her flinch at his touch and let his hold fall away as soon as she'd regained her balance.

She was happy enough when she was with Elaine, he thought, and no one at the surgery had had any adverse comments to make about her after she'd been introduced to them, so maybe it was him that she didn't care for.

Two in one day, he thought wryly. Caroline marrying her rich lover and Laurel behaving as if he'd got the plague, yet it didn't prevent his concern about her increasing.

When they reached Glenside Lodge and stopped at the gate he said, 'Take care, Laurel. If we don't meet before, I will see you on Friday.' Leaving her to go quietly up the stairs without disturbing Elaine, he strode off towards the village green and the cottage he was renting.

As she settled herself beneath the covers Laurel was wishing that she could act naturally when she was with David instead of being such a pain. She wasn't like that with anyone else, *but he wasn't like anyone else*. He was attractive and so likeable that he took her breath away, and the last thing she needed at the moment were those sorts of feelings.

It was Friday night. David had arrived with flowers and chocolates for his two hostesses and the three of them were having a drink before dinner in the sitting room of Glenside Lodge.

From the moment of his arrival his gaze had been on Laurel. She wasn't looking so drained, he decided, and though she wasn't saying much she looked happier. He wasn't to know that the moment he'd appeared again all her resolutions to keep her distance had disappeared.

He noticed that she wasn't quite so covered up tonight in the cream cotton dress she was wearing. It was full skirted and calf length, and revealed a slender neck decorated by just a fine gold chain. But the gloves were still on view, cream this time, and he decided that they had to be some sort of fad.

They'd taken their coffee out into the garden at the end of meal and were chatting about minor matters when Elaine said, 'I'm told that Maisie Tate is still in the coronary unit.'

'Yes,' he agreed. 'However, she is making good progress and could be home by the end of the week.'

'That's good, then,' she replied.

'Indeed. Plus Barry might soon be getting his kippers once more,' he said, and both women laughed.

As the night fell around them David asked, 'How long have you lived in Willowmere, Elaine?'

'Four years,' she told him. 'I was in business management in London and felt ready for a change. I'd always wanted to live in the countryside so applied for the post of practice manager at the surgery. Laurel was twenty-one at the time and didn't want to move out of her job, so she stayed behind.'

'And what job would that be, Laurel?' he asked, his curiosity about her unabated.

There was silence for a moment and then she said flatly, 'I was a nurse in a London hospital before I came here.'

David was taken aback. That was one for the book, he was thinking. 'So you were hospital based the same as I was,' he said, 'but aren't any longer?'

'Yes, that is so,' she informed him, and without giving him the chance to ask any more questions went into the kitchen to make more coffee. As she waited for the kettle to boil she thought wryly that he had done his best to hide his surprise but he couldn't see her in the role, and if the senior partner decided she was what he wanted at the surgery, David was in for an even bigger surprise.

He'd got her labelled as something and it wasn't a nurse. But, then, he hadn't known her before it had happened.

When she went back into the garden he and Elaine were chatting about the Summer Fayre that would soon be taking place in the village, and Laurel thought with sudden recklessness if he was going to be there, then so would she.

David had them smiling as he recounted his visit to the indefatigable Sarah Wilkinson, who was going to enter her home-made jam and cakes in the competitions and had promised him the first waltz at the party the night before.

'I hope you'll both be there,' he said.

Her moment of bravado had disappeared into thin air so Laurel steered the discussion away from the party and asked, 'Have you decided what to do about Water Meetings House yet?'

He smiled. 'Yes. I've made an offer and it's been accepted. The land and what is left of the house will soon be mine and then it will be action stations. I was brought up in Cornwall. My father still lives there, and will be coming shortly to see what I've bought. He is the only one who won't think I'm crazy because he knows why I'm interested in the place.

'I'd never seen it before until I came to this part of the world, though I knew about it. My mother lived in Water Meetings House until she married my father and they moved to Cornwall where he came from. She died when I was very young, so you see the desire to restore it and make it my home comes from that.'

'And is he coming to live with you when it's finished, or have you someone else in mind?' Elaine asked, and Laurel found that she was holding her breath.

'Not now,' he told her. 'I was engaged but it didn't last and the way of it ending has left a nasty taste in my mouth.' He was aware of Laurel's clear gaze upon him and now it was his turn to want to steer the conversation into other channels. The last thing he wanted to talk about was his love life, or the lack of it.

'With regards to my dad I can't see him wanting to leave Cornwall. He's a Cornishman through and through, but the offer will be there if he wants to join me. Otherwise I shall live there alone, but that is way in the future. I've got to rebuild the house before I can live in it.'

He rose to his feet as if talking about what lay ahead had made him restive and Laurel asked, 'Am I right in thinking that is where you intend going now? For a last look before you call it a day?'

He nodded. 'It would seem that you haven't forgotten our meeting there the other night. Yes, it might be. Do you want to come?'

If Elaine was surprised at the invitation she didn't show it. 'Yes, why don't you?' she suggested, and telling herself that it would seem ungracious if she refused after what her aunt had just said Laurel rose to stand beside him.

'Yes, all right,' she agreed. 'I've been inside all day and could do with some exercise.'

It sounded trite and she knew it, but maybe this time she might get the chance to show David something of the real her, the blithe spirit that until recently hadn't a care in the world.

As they walked towards the lake and the house nearby Laurel surprised him by saying, 'I think it's lovely that you want to rebuild your mother's home. Did you miss her very much?'

'I suppose I did,' he replied thoughtfully, 'but when she died I was too young to realise what was happening and my dad was wonderful. He brought me up on his own, but always kept her memory fresh in our lives. Where are your parents, Laurel? I haven't heard you mention them.'

'They're travelling around somewhere. Mum and Dad are free spirits, always wanting to be on the move. I see them from time to time but it is Elaine who has always cared for me. She is always there for me when they aren't.'

There was no condemnation in her voice, just a description of what *her* life had been like, and he asked, 'Has Elaine never married?'

'No. She was engaged once a long time ago but it didn't work out.'

Tell me about it, he thought, with the memory of Caroline's disparaging description of the future they'd been planning coming to mind.

The moon was on the wane but there was still enough light for him to see Laurel walking beside him in the cream cotton dress as they skirted the lake, and he felt instinctively that *she* wouldn't be deceitful. There was nothing devious about Laurel Maddox. What you saw was what you got and the more he saw the more he wanted to see, though it *was* just curiosity.

Aware that he was observing her, she asked, 'What?'

'You know that you puzzle me, don't you?'

'Do I? I puzzle myself sometimes.'

'You're a strange creature.'

'I'm what life has made me.'

'You mean your home life?'

'No, my working life.'

'I see.'

He didn't. Didn't see at all, but short of being intrusive there didn't seem much else to say, so he carried on moving towards the house, and when they were standing in front of the remains of it once more surprised her by saying, 'I have to rebuild it as it was before. It's a listed building, but when it's finished I'll be looking for some suggestions regarding the interior. Is that sort of thing in your line?'

'It might be if it was a smart apartment in the city,' she said slowly, 'but I don't think I would be much good at fixtures and fittings in a place like this.'

'Not to worry,' he told her easily, surprising himself that he was still persisting. 'I'll ask you again when I'm ready. I feel that you might have some original ideas, but it will be a while before I get to that stage. I've been shopping around for limestone to match the original structure and getting in touch with the kind of builders who could take on this sort of work, and have to admit that I'm finding it quite exciting.'

'I wish something as exciting would happen in my life,' she said with a twisted smile, and once again he found himself wanting to know more about her.

'Shall we make tracks?' he suggested before he started asking questions that she might not want to answer.

Laurel nodded and once again they walked side by side along the road that led back to the village, and said goodbye again at the gate of Glenside Lodge, but this time it wasn't so stilted.

'You are a good listener, Laurel,' he told her whimsically. 'I would never have thought so that day at the station when I offered you a lift, which only goes to show one shouldn't judge by first impressions.'

'Maybe so,' she agreed with the recklessness surfacing again, 'but my first impression of you hasn't changed.'

He faked a groan. 'That could be ominous.'

'It could be, yes, but it could also be the opposite.' And leaving him to make what he would of that she began to walk up the path, and on reaching the porch waved a casual goodbye.

Elaine's first hour at the surgery on Monday morning was spent with James, bringing herself up to date with surgery matters that had occurred while she'd been off, and at one point she asked, 'What did you think of Laurel?'

'Cool, composed—could be just what we want,' he replied, 'and the place where she was before doesn't take on inferior staff. We'll see how the interview goes this afternoon. By the way, I heard from Anna and Glenn over the weekend. They're coming back before Christmas and are going to settle permanently in Willowmere when they return, which I am delighted to hear.

'They were asking if there would be any vacant slots in the practice when they come back, which is why I only want someone temporary as practice nurse, so

Laurel would be perfect as she said that she would prefer that sort of arrangement.

'I've really missed Anna, and the children will be so happy to see her again, but Jess will still be their nanny.'

When David arrived back from his house calls James was returning from his at the same time and as the two men stood on the practice forecourt the senior partner said, 'Did you know that Elaine's niece is a trained nurse, David, previously hospital based like yourself?'

'Yes,' he replied, wondering what was coming next but having a good idea, 'though I only found out on Friday night when I went to have a meal with them.'

'I've asked her to come to the surgery this afternoon regarding taking her on as a temporary replacement for Beth and would like you to be present as I would welcome your input. Employing her would not be a major admin matter as it will only be for four months at the most, but you've seen more of her than I have, so do you think she would be right for us?'

'I can't say,' he said slowly. 'Laurel isn't the easiest person to get to know, yet I feel she could make a worthwhile contribution to the work here and although Elaine is her aunt she is also practice manager, and from what I've seen of her so far the efficient running of the practice is one of her top priorities.'

'You are quite right about that,' James agreed, 'so we'll play it as it comes.'

What next? David thought as he ate a solitary lunch in his consulting room. It seemed as if his curiosity regarding Laurel was going to be satisfied if she came to work at the surgery.

He was only just getting over the surprise of discovering she was a qualified nurse then she was being considered as a possible replacement for Beth.

When he went to the derelict house by the lake each night before turning in he kept expecting to see her there, but since Friday when they'd gone together there had been no sign of her, and each time he'd gone back to the cottage unaccountably disappointed.

He was standing by Reception when Laurel came through the main door of the surgery and her heart skipped a beat. She hadn't realised how much she'd wanted to see David again until that moment and here he was, smiling the smile that soothed her fractured nerve ends and making a pretence of being glad to see her, when all the time she felt he must be groaning inwardly at the thought of having her around the place all the time.

For his part David was noting that the high heels and the tights were back, but today they were matched by a black mini-skirted suit relieved by a white silk shirt.

All in all the outfit looked more fitting for an executive position than that of a practice nurse, but he wasn't to know that she'd dressed up more for him than the interview.

'So will I do?' she asked as she drew near.

His smile deepened and she felt her knees go weak. 'Yes, indeed,' he informed her, and ushered her into where James was waiting.

They were both attractive men, Laurel thought as she seated herself opposite the two doctors, but it was David who had her attention. She thought about him a lot, too much for her own good, but today it was business, not pleasure that she was there for.

This was her first move towards normality if there would ever be such a thing in her life again, and it had come from the unexpected source of a country practice in Cheshire. The last place she could ever have imagined herself working in at one time, but something like this was what she needed, small and friendly while doing nursing, the thing she loved best.

First, though, she had to convince those about to evaluate what she had to offer that she was up to it, and as calm descended upon her Laurel answered James's questions with a quiet confidence that David had to admire.

He would have admired it even more if he'd known the heartache that lay behind it. Laurel had thought she would never be able to face going back to nursing after what had happened, yet here she was, and it could only be the peace and tranquillity of Willowmere that was giving her the strength to be there.

David's first thought as she settled herself in front of them was that her gloves were missing, but for the moment Laurel's hands were tucked away behind a large handbag and he couldn't see much of them.

She was in control, he thought, calm and lucid. Yet she wasn't always like this. But James hadn't seen her when she'd first arrived and he was visibly impressed today. It was going to happen. Laurel was going to be working at the practice, temporarily maybe but there nevertheless.

'You can start immediately if you wish,' James told her after he'd offered her the position. 'Beth is keen to get away as soon as possible as they have much still to do before the delicatessen opens.'

'Yes,' she agreed and with a smile in David's direction, 'Elaine is going to have to get used to me cluttering up her working life as well as her home.'

'I don't think she'll mind too much,' he told her. 'After all, it was she who recommended you.'

'Which reminds me,' James said, 'if you ask her she she'll sort out your uniform for you. Unless you've still got the one from your previous position and would rather wear that.'

'No,' she said flatly. 'I haven't still got it.' With the comment came the terrible memory of being told how they'd had to cut it off her.

When she was ready to leave Elaine was closeted with a medical rep so she wasn't able to tell her the result of the interview and David walked to the door with her.

'So what have you been up to since Friday?' he asked.

'Not a lot. Why do you ask?'

'I thought I might have seen you up by the lake over the weekend.'

'And I thought you might think I was getting in the way,' she flipped back breezily. There was no way she was going to tell him that she'd forced herself to stay away from the place that had caught her imagination because if she wasn't careful, the lake, the house and the man standing next to her were going to take over her life...

'That sounds like an excuse.'

'Maybe it is, but does it matter?'

'Yes, it does. Why can't we be friends?'

She didn't want to be his friend, Laurel thought. She wanted to be more than that, but there was no way it was going to happen. Darius had shattered her confidence in her desirability just when she'd needed to find it again and as she met David's steady blue gaze she said, 'I already count you as a friend. How do you see me? As some sort of lame duck maybe who needs helping to the water?'

'Is that what you think?' he said in a low voice for her ears alone. 'I'm concerned about you, yes, but that's all. OK, you had a fall and injured your knee quite badly from what you say, but does that stop us from getting to know each other?'

He'd opened the door and now they were out on the forecourt of the surgery and she said, 'Yes, I had a fall and sustained a tricky fracture. I just wish that was all.'

'So what else is there?'

'Again, does it matter?'

'Yes, it does,' he told her for a second time, and thought it mattered a lot but he wasn't sure why.

'I'll see you tomorrow,' she said, clutching her bag to her, and he saw her hands. They looked red and rough, standing out against the rest of her pale, smooth skin.

Laurel had seen where his glance was and said abruptly, 'I haven't got anything catching.'

'I'm sure you haven't,' he said patiently, and thought, *You might not have, but I think I have and it isn't because I'm on the rebound.*

'I'm going,' she announced, breaking into his

thoughts. 'I'll see you in the morning, David. It's like a dream. I can't believe it, me Laurel Maddox, working in a country practice.'

He was smiling, his annoyance gone, 'Yes, indeed. I'm not sure which of us is the more surprised.'

She was good, David thought the next morning as he watched Laurel change the dressing on the leg of a tearful small boy. Her touch was deft and gentle, her manner reassuring, and by the time she'd finished smiles had replaced the tears.

It was the same later when he took a worried fifty-year-old farmer to the nurses' room for blood tests, having found changes in his prostate gland.

The other two nurses had gone for a break and it was Laurel who greeted John Price. He was a nervy type and almost before he'd closed the door behind him was voicing his fears. As David was about to return to his consulting room he stopped in mid-stride when he heard her say, 'I've worked on a men's surgical ward, Mr Price, and there are other problems besides cancer that can affect the prostate gland. So let's just take some blood, shall we, and see what our friends in the path lab come up with, and while we're waiting for the results put your fears to one side. Time enough to worry when there is something to worry about.'

David was smiling as he went to greet his next patient. Laurel had seemed alien in the dark blue nurse's uniform when she'd first presented herself, but she was settling in like a natural.

He was used to seeing her in high-necked jumpers

and buttoned-up cardigans, but as the morning progressed he was adjusting to the new image and liking what he saw, while Elaine was looking less anxious by the moment as Laurel slotted herself into the routine of the surgery.

It was Beth's last day. She was taking advantage of the chance to finish sooner than she'd expected and was only too pleased to welcome Laurel into the slot that she was leaving.

Gillian Jarvis, the other practice nurse, was also happy to have her there as it meant that she wasn't going to be coping alone when Beth had gone, and as Laurel looked, listened and learned, the new nurse felt the adrenaline start to flow.

She was acutely aware of David every time he appeared in her line of vision. When on one occasion he handed her the notes of a patient requiring a spirometry test with a hand that was protruding from the cuff of a smart white shirt, she was reminded of that day at the station when he'd lifted her luggage out onto the platform and then helped her off the train.

She'd thought then that he seemed out of place in the rural backwater where Elaine lived, but that impression was long gone. He fitted in perfectly, which was more than she was expecting for herself.

That occasion was a memory that kept coming back and when it did she cringed at the thought of what she'd been like. Did he still see her as the sort of useless creature she'd appeared then? If he did, this was her chance to show him that she wasn't.

'So how's it going?' he asked in the lull between surgeries and house calls. 'It must seem very different to hospital work. Did you not have any yearnings to go back on the wards? If you had wanted to, we have a big hospital not far from here called St Gabriel's.'

'I miss the bustle and thrust of hospital life,' she told him, 'but I'm really enjoying the change. The job satisfaction is great because it is so friendly and rewarding to be providing health care to people who say hello to you on the street and in the pub. It bridges the gap between doctor and patient.'

I wish I could be my natural self and bridge the gap between us, Laurel thought, but the chances of that were remote. David had just asked her if she wanted to go back to hospital nursing and could not be expected to know that the question had touched a very raw nerve.

'Working here is fine for now,' she told him, 'and by the time Dr Bartlett's sister comes back, I might have some clear idea of where I'm heading.'

'So why not join me for a drink in The Pheasant this evening to celebrate your first day in the village practice?'

There was silence for a moment as common sense battled with the longing to be with someone who actually wanted her company. David had already said he'd missed her at the ruins by the lake and now he wanted to take her for a drink. Could it be that he really wanted to be with her, or was he trying to be nice because for some reason he sensed her inner misery?

With colour rising, she said, 'Er, yes, all right. What time shall I be there?'

'I'll come for you in the car,' he said. 'You could be feeling the effects of your first day here by then.'

His consideration for her well-being brought a lump to her throat. Could it be that David guessed that as well as frailty of mind she also had frailty of body?

At that moment one of the receptionists called to him from the doorway. 'There's a firm of builders on the line wanting to speak to you, Dr Trelawney.'

As he took the phone from her, he said, 'I'll come for you about eightish, Laurel, if that's all right.'

She nodded and left him to take the call and for the rest of the day the evening ahead beckoned like a bright star on the horizon.

CHAPTER FOUR

WHEN DAVID RANG THE bell at Glenside Lodge that evening there was no answer, and his first thought was that Laurel had changed her mind. But if that was the case he would have expected her to let him know beforehand. Where was Elaine? Had they gone somewhere together maybe?

The door was unlatched and he pushed it open a few inches and called, 'Hello, anyone at home?' But there was still no sign of life and with sudden anxiety on their behalf he stepped inside and walked slowly towards the sitting room where he had laid Laurel on the sofa on the day of their first meeting.

It was as if the clock had been turned back. There she was again, curled up asleep with one hand pressed against her cheek and the other lying limply by her side, but this time there was nothing outlandish about her attire. She was wearing a long fluffy robe that covered everything except her feet.

Of Elaine there was no sign and remembering that he'd seen cars outside the village hall as he'd driven past he recalled her mentioning during the day that there was a meeting of the Summer Fayre committee planned for that evening.

As he stood looking down at Laurel he thought how defenceless she looked curled up on the sofa. It seemed as if her first day at the practice *had* taken it out of her and he wondered once again what it was with her.

The rough hands and short red-gold hair had a message for anyone involved in health care and yet she wasn't divulging anything regarding them and why should she? he thought. They were her affair and hers only, but he did wish she would let him share whatever the burden she carried might be. She was a mixture of many things, amongst them strong and positive one moment and the next frail and vulnerable.

She'd been adamant that the fractured knee was in the past and she seemed to walk normally, but was there something else, a more serious cause for concern right here in the present? He supposed he could ask Elaine what ailed her niece and could imagine the practice manager's expression chilling at what she would see as an intrusion into Laurel's life.

He pulled up a chair, settled himself beside her, and waited for her to wake up, but she slept on and the sun was setting on the horizon in the summer night when she sobbed in her sleep and lifted the arm that was lying beside her in a defensive movement.

In the same moment her eyes opened wide. 'Oh, no!' she groaned. 'How long have you been here, David? I am so sorry. I'd just had a shower, lay against the cushions for a moment and…'

He was smiling down at her, concealing his dismay

at her distress before she'd woken up. 'Don't apologise. You are so much less complicated when you're asleep.'

'And also less reliable, it would seem.' She was raising herself to a sitting position and was pulling the robe around her more tightly as she asked drowsily, 'Is it too late to go to the pub?'

'Not if you want to. Or we can stay here if you don't feel up to it. Where is Elaine, by the way?'

'She's at a meeting. If she'd been here she wouldn't have let me fall asleep so soundly,' she informed him, with the memory of her aunt's delight when she'd told her that she was going to The Pheasant with David.

'We are only having a drink together,' she'd protested, and had thought that after Darius she'd intended steering clear of relationships until she'd got her confidence back regarding her appearance. But out of the blue had come David and she could not stop thinking about him.

'Yes, well, enjoy your evening,' Elaine had said gently.

She was sliding her feet off the edge of the sofa and once she was in a standing position said, 'If you don't mind waiting a few moments while I get dressed, we'll stick to plan A—a drink at The Pheasant.'

It would be easy to suggest they stay where they were and to let the robe fall off her shoulders so that the damage to the smooth pale skin was visible. It would be one way of telling David why she wasn't always as happy as she would like to be.

He was a doctor and would have seen things a lot worse than the state of her back and shoulders, but not in this sort of situation would he have seen them. Once she'd done something like that it wouldn't be the same afterwards, no matter how he reacted. It could destroy the fine shoots of their blossoming relationship, so a drink at the pub was the safest option.

'Fine,' he was saying easily. 'I'll pick the car up in the morning before surgery. I don't mind what we do and once we've had a drink, if you feel rested enough we could go for my usual walk to the house of my dreams—or nightmares as the case may be. What do you say?'

'I say yes,' she agreed, and climbed the stairs quickly before the voice of reason said its piece.

She came down dressed in smart jeans, long boots, a pretty top and the inevitable cardigan and said, 'Let's go and forget about everything except that it's a mellow summer night and we are alive to see it!'

'You're on.' He smiled at her enthusiasm. 'I'll drink to that when we get to The Pheasant, but a couple of questions first.'

'Yes?'

'What are these things that we are going to forget? And obviously, we're glad to be alive—why wouldn't we be?'

'I was meaning such things as sick people and builder's quotes,' she said airily, 'and shouldn't we always be glad to be alive? I know that I am.'

Some of us are more grateful for it than others, she thought with the nightmare grimly remembered of the days and weeks after it happened when pain had been the enemy, and even as it had lessened she'd dreaded what lay ahead, feeling that there would never be any brightness in her life again.

But that was past, she was rebuilding her life in a new

place, with a new job to look forward to, *and* she'd met a new man. What would he say if she told him that being alive was something to be everlastingly grateful for when one had been so close to eternity?

By the time they arrived at the pub the moment of looking back had passed and as locals in The Pheasant smiled across at the two most recent newcomers to the village and others eyed them with mild curiosity, Laurel began to relax.

Maybe it was the friendliness in the atmosphere, she thought as farmers chatted to each other about their crops and parents about their children. When the landlord called time it wouldn't be a case of trying to flag down a taxi or going for the tube.

For most of them it would be a leisurely walk home, with the nearest of the two rivers that met beside Water Meetings House bustling along beside them, or taking a path alongside fields of ripening corn. For those in the limestone cottages scattered around the main street and on the lanes leading from it, there would be just a short stroll to the homes they held dear.

David was observing her thoughtfully and she wondered what was going on behind his steady gaze. She hoped he wasn't going to start asking questions that she didn't want to answer.

He did have a question, but thankfully it was one that she could cope with.

'So how did you enjoy your first day in the village practice, Nurse Maddox?' he asked. 'Was it up to expectations?'

'Yes, it was, Dr Trelawney,' she said with a smile. 'It wasn't until today that I realised just how much I was missing nursing.'

His next question was not so easily answered. 'So why did you leave it?'

'Circumstances,' she said in a low voice as clouds appeared on her horizon. He was unwittingly taking away the tranquillity that had wrapped itself around her while they'd been together, and before he said anything else she told him flatly, 'They are on the list of things that I want to forget about, so if you don't mind…'

'Sure,' he said levelly. 'Message received and understood. Shall we move on to plan B and take the walk to you-know-where?'

Laurel hesitated. She wanted to be out there with him, just the two of them in the warm darkness, but then what? If David came near her she would melt and another nightmare would have been born. This time of the senses, rather than the body that she sometimes felt was no longer hers.

She'd agreed when he first suggested it because she'd felt as if she'd needed to be near him as she needed to breathe, but she was aware that he saw her as an oddity and it was the last thing she wanted to be to him.

They'd known each other for only a short time, yet it was as if she'd always been waiting for him to come into her life. But why couldn't it have been before her world had come crashing down?

'I think I'll give it a miss if you don't mind,' she told him. 'I *am* rather tired still and I want to be at my brightest and best for my second day at the surgery.'

'Fine,' he agreed equably. 'In fact, I might do the same this once. Sometimes it can be frustrating only being able to stand and stare. The solicitor is pushing ahead with the sale and the builder I've appointed is raring to get started, but until the land and the house are legally mine there is nothing he can do. So I'll see you safely home and we'll call it a day, shall we?'

Laurel didn't want to be alone with him, he thought as they walked back in silence to Glenside Lodge. She'd been keen enough before, but the moment he'd asked why she'd left nursing she'd clammed up. If it was always going to be like this, what was the point of trying to get to know her?

He saw that Elaine wasn't back as they walked the last few yards to the gate and loath to let the evening finish on such a flat note he broke the silence by asking casually, 'Have *you* ever been in a serious relationship like I was, Laurel?'

He knew he was probably going to make matters worse by asking, but they couldn't deteriorate much further.

'Yes, I have,' she replied, 'but it is well and truly in the past, and before you ask yet another question, it ended because the man involved had lost interest. I didn't come up to scratch.'

He could see her face in the light of the lamp by the gate and was aghast to see her eyes bright with tears.

He took a step towards her and with arms outstretched said softly, 'Come here. The last thing I intended was to make you cry. Let me hold you for a moment.'

'No!' she cried, pushing him away.

'Why ever not?' he asked as his arms fell to his sides.

'I might get to like it and I don't want that to happen. I changed my mind about going to your house with you for the same reason.' As he stared at her in amazed dismay she ran up the path and into the house, closing the door behind her with a dismissive click.

Why couldn't he have let well alone? David thought sombrely as he crossed the village green to where the rented cottage stood small and compact. No wonder Laurel had wept if she'd been dumped by some moron who couldn't see any further than the end of his nose.

Yet it wasn't so long ago that he'd decided that she was the last woman *he* would ever be attracted to and it hadn't changed...or had it? If the number of times he thought about her was anything to go by, it had.

He was captivated by her mood swings, and by the frailty that was sometimes there, while at other times, as in her nurse's role, she was capable and energetic...

Cool it, he told himself as he stripped off and went to switch on the shower. *If you hadn't become involved with Laurel that day at the station you wouldn't have given her a second glance.*

So she's had an engagement that turned sour too. You can identify with that, but now leave it, get her out of your mind. Laurel has Elaine to look after her. It isn't as if she's on her own, and what you are doing borders on interference.

You have your answer now. She's been hurt by some guy and is wary of it happening again, and an accident where she fractured her knee badly at some time or other won't have helped.

* * *

When she'd closed the door behind her Laurel had stood without moving. There was perspiration on her brow and it wasn't due to the warm night or the sprint she'd done up the path.

To have stepped into David's arms would have been so easy, but the reasons for not doing so had been so clear in her mind that she'd made a scene instead of tactfully sidestepping the moment, which would then have passed off smoothly enough.

But there'd been the knowledge that they were on two different wavelengths to keep in mind. David saw her as some sort of mixed-up nurse-cum-city type who was as prickly as a hedgehog. To her he was like all her dreams come true and she'd nearly let him see how she was beginning to feel about him.

He'd probably gone home feeling totally embarrassed about the way she'd responded to what had been just a comforting gesture, but if he ever got the full picture of how she was beginning to feel about him it would take away what little confidence she had left since being disfigured, and she couldn't afford to go back to how she'd been then.

She'd ignored the voice of common sense by allowing herself to be committed to being with him every day at the surgery and if that wasn't a prescription for heartache she didn't know what was.

When she heard Elaine come in she pretended to be asleep because the first thing she'd want to know would be how she'd enjoyed her evening with David. She would feel better equipped to answer the question over breakfast when she was feeling less fraught.

* * *

As it turned out, it was a comment about David's car still being on the drive that was the first thing Elaine said the next morning. It had been there when she'd returned from the meeting and she'd expected to find him inside, but he hadn't been and Laurel had been fast asleep when she'd had a peep into her room. So he was going to have to come and pick it up before the day got under way.

'When did David say he was coming to get the car?' she asked.

'Some time before surgery,' Laurel said disinterestedly, and waited for what was going to come next, but Elaine felt she didn't need to ask. There was a glumness about her that told its own tale and maybe later in the day Laurel would feel like talking about it, but clearly not now.

As Laurel buttoned up her uniform in preparation for the day ahead, she heard his voice downstairs, mingling with Elaine's lighter tones, and she cringed at the thought of coming face-to-face with him at the surgery after her exhibition of the night before.

The morning was well under way before she saw him. He was dealing with both lots of patients because James had taken time off to go to the end-of-year concert at the village school.

Soon the twins would be on the long summer break and Helen, his housekeeper, and Jess, their nanny, would be kept busy keeping them fed and occupied.

The children both had speaking parts in the play that their class was presenting to mothers, fathers and other relatives, and while James had no qualms about

Pollyanna's performance, he knew that Jolyon's was another matter.

A more serious child than his sister, he didn't have much to say, but when he did the words issuing forth weren't the usual childish chatter and his father wasn't sure how he was going to perform on stage.

It was at times like these that he felt inadequate. The twins missed having their mother around, but the years came and went and he always managed to cope somehow. He didn't think he would ever find anyone to replace Julie but, then, he'd never tried to.

With James absent, Laurel saw David just twice during the morning when he came to the nurses' room to discuss the requirements of patients.

The first one was elderly Sarah Wilkinson and instead of asking her to wait on the chairs in the corridor he ushered her in personally and told the two nurses, 'Mrs Wilkinson needs some blood tests and I think we'd better have the full monty. I told her we would send someone to her home to take the bloods, but she is determined to save us time and has come to the surgery.'

The sprightly octogenarian was smiling as she told them, 'The doctor here is going to have the first waltz with me at the party on the night before the Summer Fayre, so I want to make sure I'm fit. I've told him that there'll be a queue wanting to dance with him when it gets around that he's going to be there.'

'I doubt it,' he told her with a wry smile. 'I'm not the flavour of the month in some quarters.'

That was one for her, Laurel thought, *and how wrong he was.*

An hour later he appeared again and this time she was alone, but as if the formal approach was still the order of the day he said briskly, 'There's a patient waiting outside, Laurel. He's come from a building site where they're doing demolition work and has an abscess on his forearm. It isn't bad enough to require hospital treatment, but it needs to be lanced. I'll leave him with you.'

'Yes, David,' she said with a similar lack of warmth, and then, in the pleasure of being in his company again, put to one side her decision to stay aloof and said teasingly, 'Not *your* demolition site by any chance, is it?'

'Are you referring to the one that you turned me into last night? Or the ruins by the lake?' he asked dryly. 'If it's Water Meetings House that you are speaking of, I wish it was, but as you well know I'm still waiting for the sale to go through.'

Leaving her feeling as if she'd been well and truly put in her place, he opened the door and called to the man seated outside, 'You can come through, Mr Peterson. Nurse is going to lance the abscess and put a dressing on it, and don't forget to take the antibiotics I've prescribed. Make an appointment to see me again in a few days' time before you leave the surgery.' The grime-covered building worker nodded and David went back to deal with the rest of those waiting to consult him.

How could Laurel be so flip? he thought as he waited for his next patient. A rapport had been developing between them, but last night it had disappeared in the strangest of moments and he was amazed at the hurt he felt at the way she'd rejected his offer of comfort.

James was back by lunchtime looking somewhat frazzled, though he was laughing as he told them how Jolyon had altered his lines in the play to his own version and refused to budge until the teachers had agreed he could.

'And the joke of it was that his was better than theirs,' he said. 'I did get a bit hot under the collar at the time, but Jess, who'd gone with me, was in stitches.'

While Laurel and Elaine were having a quick bite before afternoon surgery the practice manager said, 'You haven't told me how you enjoyed last night. Did you have a nice time with David?'

Laurel sighed. 'I did at first, but he asked if I'd ever had a serious relationship. I told him the basic details about Darius and made a fool of myself at the same time by weeping.'

'I think you could be forgiven for that,' Elaine said consolingly.

Having no wish to tell Elaine what had happened afterwards, she said lightly, 'I left David at the gate and went straight to bed.'

'He came for his car this morning while you were upstairs getting ready. Did you see him?'

Laurel shook her head. 'No. I heard your voices but was in the middle of getting dressed. He's been giving me the impersonal treatment all morning, which is fine as I keep telling myself that is how I should be with him.

But it isn't easy. After the Darius episode, and remembering my deficiencies, I know I shouldn't get any closer to him if I don't want to get hurt.'

'We are not talking about your actor friend now,' her aunt protested. 'David Trelawney is in a different class. He has integrity *and* compassion.'

'I didn't say he hadn't, but it isn't pity I'm looking for. I had lots of that when it happened and I'm not complaining. People were lovely, and their sympathy helped to get me through it, but when it comes to the crunch it's up to me now and I'm a mass of uncertainties.'

It was there that the discussion ended. The two doctors had gone on their calls, the surgery would soon be filling up with the second session of the day, and their separate functions awaited them.

As the summer evenings passed Laurel didn't go to the house by the lake any more. She felt that if she did it would contradict the way she was behaving towards David at the surgery.

When it came to health care they admired each other's application to the job, and as she absorbed herself into the routines and demands of the practice Laurel would have been content if there wasn't always a reminder of past happenings to take the edge off everything.

Because of that she was anxious to avoid any more incidents like the one where he'd wanted to offer comfort and she'd pushed him away, and it seemed as if David was only too keen to do likewise.

Yet he hadn't been able to resist mentioning that the sale had gone through, the stone had been delivered, and the builder was already on the job, and he'd been so upbeat about it she'd decided that she was flattering herself by expecting their faltering friendship to be casting any gloom in *his* life.

But what he'd said had made her curious, and one night in July she weakened and went to see for herself what was happening at the house by the lake at a much earlier time than when she'd gone before.

It was still daylight and she gasped with pleasure at the sight before her when she arrived at the building site. The walls were half-up, beautiful new limestone was rising out of the ruins, and she understood how David must have felt when he'd stood in front of what was left of his mother's old home and known that it was going to be his.

She was experiencing a similar sensation herself and so much for that, she thought as she turned away and began to walk slowly back to the village. It wasn't just wishing for the moon. It was wishing for the sun, moon and stars all rolled into one.

When she arrived back at Glenside Lodge David's car was on the drive, and when she went inside he was in the sitting room with Elaine.

'I was passing, Elaine was in the garden, and she invited me in for a coffee,' he said, as if he felt he had to explain his presence.

'So where did you go for your walk?' Elaine asked as she passed her a cup of the steaming brew.

'Oh, here and there,' she said vaguely.

'Not to the lake, then?' David asked casually.

'Yes, I went to the lake,' she said steadily.

'And?'

Knowing how dear the renovating of the house was to his heart she couldn't pretend that she hadn't gone that little bit further to where the building site was, and she told him, 'It's going to look fantastic. The stone that you're using is beautiful, so natural looking and enduring.'

His expression softened and Laurel thought if anyone had told her a month ago that she would be going into raptures over the rebuilding of a derelict property in the middle of a field miles from anywhere she would have laughed in their face. But that was what she was doing and it was all because of the man sitting opposite.

Elaine was about to leave them. 'The last meeting to arrange the party this coming Friday and the Summer Fayre on the Saturday is taking place tonight,' she explained, 'and I need to be there. So I'm going to have to leave you.'

When she'd gone there was silence for a moment and then David asked, 'So are we friends again, Laurel?' and for the life of her she couldn't say no.

'Yes, I suppose so,' she told him awkwardly, without meeting his glance. 'I've felt such a fool after the way I behaved that night.'

He shook his head. 'You mustn't. It was clear that the hurt in you that I'm always aware of comes from your broken engagement. That it must have upset you much more than mine did me and I will respect that, but it doesn't need to come between *us*…does it?'

She was looking down at the carpet as if the pattern on it had her mesmerised. So David thought he had her moods sussed. He wasn't to know it was something much bigger than being dumped by Darius that had blighted her life, even though it had been he who had delivered the final blow. But for the moment the easy way out seemed to be to let him carry on thinking that she wasn't over the break-up.

'No, it doesn't,' she told him, 'and, David, I'd love to be involved in helping you build your house…if you would let me.'

'Of course I will,' he assured her, his expression brightening. 'Didn't I say right at the beginning I would welcome your input? And by the way, are you going to the party in the park on Friday?'

'I wasn't going to but Elaine is insisting that I do so, yes, I'll be there.'

'So once I've done my duty with Mrs Wilkinson perhaps we could get together, us being the two new-comers to the village.'

'Mmm. Why not?' she agreed, and immediately wondered what she had in eveningwear that would cover her shoulders. It wouldn't have to be something skimpy and strappy like she'd always worn before, and thank goodness her hair was growing nicely again.

At that moment she wasn't to know that before Friday an occasion would arise requiring a united front from them, and it would have an appeal all of its own.

On the Thursday night they were the last two out of the practice. Gillian, the other nurse, had rung in sick and James had gone early because it was the twins' birthday and Jess and Helen had organised a special birthday tea.

They would be having a party for their friends on the

Saturday when he was free, but the two women who doted on them wanted to celebrate the actual day with them.

The last patient had left with the receptionists not far behind and Elaine had gone to keep a dental appointment, which left the two of them to clear away and lock up.

It was as they were about to shut the outer door and leave the premises that a man came running out of one of the cottages opposite in a panic. Seeing them, he shouted, 'My wife is pregnant! The baby wasn't due for two weeks but it's coming now. I can see its head!'

Even as he was speaking they were sprinting towards him. Turning, he led the way into a sitting room where a heavily pregnant woman was lying on a couch in a state of advanced labour.

'I can't hang on!' she screamed between contractions. 'I've got to push.'

'OK, Sharon,' David said reassuringly as he examined her. 'But I need to ask you to just hang on for a couple of seconds. I'll tell you when it's the right moment.'

Laurel was holding Sharon's hand and phoning for an ambulance at the same time, while her husband stood by looking as if he was going to collapse.

'Get a clean towel ready,' she told him to keep him occupied, 'and a bowl of warm water.'

The woman cried out again and David said in a low voice, 'She's been coming to the antenatal clinic at the surgery. Her name is Sharon Simpson. It's not her first, so that could be the reason for the speed with which the baby is arriving. She changed her mind about having it at home, and just after I joined the practice she transferred to the maternity clinic at St Gabriel's, so you won't have seen her before.'

He bent to check on progress again and then said urgently, 'Right, Sharon, now you can push.' As she obeyed with an almighty shout, they heard the first cry of the newborn as David gently eased it into the world.

'You have a daughter,' he told them as the man put down the bowl he was carrying and rushed to his wife's side, and as David carefully lifted the child for her to see, Laurel was there with the towel to wrap the baby in before he placed the little one in her mother's arms.

'Lizzie Carmichael was going to deliver my baby,' Sharon said as she looked down at her new daughter. 'She'll be disappointed when she finds out that she's missed the birth because this young miss was in such a hurry.'

'Or relieved that it's just one job less,' the happy father commented whimsically, touching his tiny daughter's face reverently.

'Not Lizzie!' Sharon protested gently, looking up tenderly at her husband. 'She loves what she does.'

'You were fantastic in there,' Laurel told David as they stood on the pavement afterwards and watched the ambulance drive off with mother, father and baby on board.

'Not really,' he protested laughingly. 'I've done quite a bit of gynaecology and obstetrics in my time, but not usually in such cramped surroundings. And what would I have done without *you* there?'

'Managed very well, I would say,' she said dryly, not

wanting him to guess how much it had meant, the two of them being there together at such a time.

He ignored that. 'All the excitement has given me an appetite. What about you? Do you fancy checking to see if the tourist trade has slackened off at Hollyhocks? It *is* climbing up to seven o'clock. Or will Elaine have made a meal?'

She shook her head, the red-gold of her hair catching the evening sunlight. 'Not tonight. She's had quite a lot of dental work done this afternoon and as she'd thought it would be, her mouth is sore. So either I go home and boil an egg, or take you up on your suggestion, and I'll give you two guesses which it's going to be.'

'Come on then,' he said, tucking her arm in his. 'Let's see if they've got anything left at the Tea Rooms.'

It so happened that they had, and as they relaxed in the cosy atmosphere of one of the most popular places in Willowmere, Laurel thought that she was asking for more heart-searching. Yet at that moment she didn't care because this was the first of three days that she and David were going to be around each other away from the surgery.

Tomorrow night was the party in the park, and on Saturday the villagers and the farming community would be combining their efforts at the Fayre, so what more could she ask?

One thing that she certainly wasn't going to dwell on was how she came to be getting so excited about country matters when in the past a movie or a nightclub had always been her scene.

CHAPTER FIVE

THE band was playing in the marquee in the park and as Laurel watched David performing a sedate waltz with Sarah Wilkinson, who was resplendent in dark blue brocade, the moment was taking hold of her.

There were lots of people there from the village and the surrounding countryside and there was an atmosphere of great good humour amongst them. Elaine was at the forefront of things as usual, smartly dressed as always in a long, strappy black dress that enhanced her fair colouring, and Beth and her husband had surfaced from the newly opened delicatessen.

Beth's daughter Jess, James's children's nanny, was there too with her boyfriend, but there was no sign of James himself, which Laurel thought was a shame. Yet she supposed that like most people the senior partner at the practice knew his own affairs best, though it was something she couldn't say for herself.

David had called for her and presented her with a corsage of orchids that went with her colouring perfectly. When she'd opened the door to him she'd seen that his glance had been on her outfit and had known that he was taking in the fact that she was not as well concealed as usual.

Anything strapless or low cut at the back would not have been suitable, but with the anticipation of the night ahead Laurel had chosen to wear a dress of dark green silk with cap sleeves and a short flared skirt, and the high heels were back.

He wasn't to know that the way she was dressed was another step towards the normality that she longed for, the freedom to be herself instead of the stranger that she had become during the long weeks of her recovery.

A sudden longing to tell him what it was all about had come over her as his glance had warmed at the sight of her, but it had been fleeting.

It would take more than a moment of admiration from him to make her lay her soul bare, or her shoulders for that matter. She sometimes dreamt that the scars had gone away, that she was whole again. Awakening to find that it was not so was heartbreaking.

Yet she was coping, mainly because she was learning to live one day at a time and by doing so was slowly getting some of her confidence back, the confidence that Darius had destroyed when he'd made it clear that he didn't want someone less than perfect.

The man who'd come to take her to the ball was playing a major role in the healing process, though he wasn't aware of it, and tonight she was happier than she'd been in a long time as she watched David escort Sarah to her seat when the music stopped.

As he changed direction and began to walk towards her with a smile that was for her alone she let the blissful moment wrap around her. As the band started to play the next number he raised her to her feet, and without betraying by word or glance that hers were not the softest hands he'd ever held David led her onto the dance floor.

It was a slow foxtrot, the most dreamy and romantic of ballroom dances, and this time Laurel thought she wasn't going to shy away from being held close in his arms. She was going to pretend that she had nothing to hide but her pride.

'Your perfume is like you,' David said as they glided around the floor with the short red-gold covering on her head resting beneath his chin. She smiled up at him, green eyes calm and untroubled for once.

'In what way?'

'Elusive. Hard to describe, but mind-blowing.'

She was aware that they were attracting curious glances from some of those there, the new nurse at the practice and the doctor who hadn't been there long himself so engrossed in each other, but she didn't care. Whatever life was like in the cold light of day, tonight was magical, and for the moment she wasn't going to think any further than that.

In the middle of the evening there was the unexpected appearance of Lord Derringham and his wife, who'd stopped by to make sure that all was satisfactory with the marquee that he'd provided, and as Laurel watched them chatting with Elaine and other members of the organising committee she thought that, wealthy though they may be, the Derringhams were very supportive of village life.

David and Laurel danced every dance and during any intervals dawdled outside with the scent of summer flowers all around them and trees festooned with fairy-lights twinkling like jewels beneath the night sky.

At the end of the last waltz Laurel sighed and David asked quizzically, 'Was that an expression of relief or regret?'

'I think you know the answer to that,' she said lightly. She could have said so much more that would have left him in no doubt about how much she'd enjoyed the ball and being with *him*. How the enchantment of it would stay in her heart forever.

But that would be running before she could walk. She had to move slowly in the new life that was opening up before her. She was not the catch of the century in anybody's eyes, far from it, and couldn't face the thought of being hurt again.

As they strolled home amongst the rest of the de-parting guests the centre of the village was full of noise and laughter, but by the time they reached Glenside Lodge there was just the two of them in the quiet night and as they stood at the gate once more David turned to face her and said softly, 'Are you going to run a mile if I kiss you?'

'No! Yes! I don't know!' she faltered, taking a backward step. 'Can't we just stay as we are?'

'What? In a situation where *I'm* never sure what you're going to do or say next, and *you* are happy for it to be that way?'

'Is that really how you see us?'

'How else?'

'It's been a lovely evening. Don't spoil it, David.'

'So are you still pining for the guy that you were engaged to?'

As *if,* she thought miserably and looked away, which brought forth a groan on his part.

'OK,' he said equably. 'Hurts of the heart are not as easily forgotten as some things, so let's change the subject.' Wanting to see her smiling again, he said whimsically, 'So are you any good at bricklaying?'

'Would you expect me to be?' she questioned lightly, relieved to be on safer ground.

'No. I was teasing.'

'My dad was in the building trade before he and my mum got hooked on travelling the world, and he would have liked me to show an interest as he'd always wanted a son, but I didn't want to risk breaking my nails. Why did you ask, though?'

'The builder I'm employing is short of bricklayers, or should I say stone-layers, but as I'm new to the area I couldn't help him on that, I'm afraid.'

'Ask Elaine or James,' she suggested. 'They know everyone around here. What about the fellow with the abscess that we treated? Did he ever come back for a follow-up visit? I wonder what *his* skills were.'

'I could find out, I suppose,' he said absently, 'but I do want the best, and it's late, Laurel. I'd better go.'

'Elaine hasn't come home yet,' she protested, reluctant for the night to end in spite of having behaved like a nervous virgin when he'd wanted to kiss her.

'She's on the committee, so will be helping with the clearing up afterwards, but that doesn't say she won't arrive any moment, so I'll say goodnight.' Their gazes met and he murmured, 'On second thoughts, I'm not leaving without this...'

Taken aback at his sudden change of mind, she didn't resist when he drew her into his arms. He kissed her lightly on the mouth and then putting her away from him said, 'That was merely to say goodnight, a less enthusiastic performance than I first had in mind, but better than nothing.'

With that comment he went, striding off into the darkness, leaving her drained from the mixture of emotions that the night had brought.

When he turned up at the Summer Fayre the next day David found Laurel serving soup and savouries to those strolling amongst the stalls and sideshows and looking anything but comfortable. She was dressed in a long black dress with a white apron and a white mob cap on her head, and when he stopped in front of the table that she was serving from and observed her laughingly she glowered at him.

'It's all right for you!' she muttered. 'Elaine talked me into this because the person who should have been on this stall had a family emergency that has prevented her from taking part.' She groaned. 'I'm supposed to be a serving wench.'

'You look really cute,' he told her, keeping a straight face, and she began to laugh. She'd wept after they'd separated the night before, tears of frustration and regret, but seeing him again in the light of another day was lifting her out of the doldrums.

'Can I offer you a bowl of mulligatawny soup, sir?' she asked, preening at him in the clothes of a bygone age from behind the table. 'It's the very thing to warm the cockles of your heart.'

'Yes, you can, wench,' he told her, his eyes dancing with laughter, 'though I can think of other ways of doing that which would be much more satisfying.'

Laurel gasped theatrically and tried to quell the spark of excitement she'd felt at his words. The queue for soup and savouries was growing and he said, 'Do you have a spare apron, plastic if possible, rather than starched white cotton?'

She pointed to a box in the corner and with ladle in hand said, 'Have a rummage in there.'

He found what he was looking for and within minutes was beside her, serving the soup while Laurel supplied the savouries.

There were smiles from those in the queue and one humorist shouted from the back, 'Can we get the flu jab while we're here?'

When the demand had slackened off they sat on stools beneath the awning that covered the stall and David said, 'When will you be free?'

'Someone is relieving me at two o'clock.'

'I'll circulate for a while, then,' he said, 'and when it's two o'clock I'll be waiting outside the refreshment tent.' She nodded, happy that they were friends again after their flat farewell of the night before.

As David went to explore the Fayre his thoughts were returning to the same moment as he wondered if 'waiting' described what lay ahead for him. Waiting for

Laurel to forget the past and its hurts, whatever they may be, and give *him* the chance to take care of her.

They'd stood side by side when Sarah had won first prize for her Madeira cake and a second rosette for her jam, and then wandered around the event that everyone had turned out for in full force.

It was clear to Laurel that this was a very special weekend for them and no one was going to miss it. Willowmere's tribute to rural living was 'times gone by,' which accounted for Laurel's attire.

As they moved amongst town criers, old-fashioned bobbies with handlebar moustaches and peasants, Laurel was amazed to see Lord Derringham amongst them, dressed appropriately as a country squire, and she said, 'I thought His Lordship wasn't seen in the village very often.'

'Me too,' David agreed absently, 'but it doesn't seem to be the case at the moment.'

He'd been trying to imagine Caroline at an event such as this and couldn't. In fact, he was having difficulty bringing her to mind at all since Laurel had come into his life.

Her thoughts were serious too, but very different. Soon she would have to take stock of what was happening to her, decide if she was really falling for David or was on the rebound, and she wasn't expecting it to be a difficult decision.

He was smiling across at her and she wished she'd met him before the thoughtlessness of others had made a mess of her life. Yet were she to be asked if she would do the same thing again, the answer would have to be yes. She'd chosen a career where the saving of life was the top priority whatever the circumstances.

David hadn't missed the fact that for the last few moments her thoughts had been far away, and if her expression had been anything to go by they hadn't been happy ones.

Yet he was not going to ask any more questions, even though he was curious to know why she dressed as she did. To keep probing was a sure means of putting the blight on their rekindling relationship. If it ever came to anything it would be because Laurel felt she trusted him enough to confide in him.

He'd wondered a few times if her obsession with covering herself up was because of something unsightly, like a regretted tattoo maybe, and had even let his thoughts run along more serious lines, such as domestic violence. Maybe she would open up to him when she was ready. He just hoped that day would eventually come.

When the Fayre was over Laurel and David walked Sarah home. They made her a cup of tea and settled her on the sofa with the prizes she'd won gracing a big oak sideboard, and turned their steps homewards.

He was going to ask her out to dinner when she'd changed out of her costume, and was about to voice the suggestion as his cottage came into sight. But the words hovered on his lips as he watched a taxi pull up outside the surgery, and of all people that he wasn't expecting to see, his father got out of it with a big suitcase and the morning paper tucked under his arm.

'I don't believe it!' he exclaimed. 'That's my dad. He never said he was coming!'

'I'll be on my way, then,' she said immediately. 'Enjoy yourself with your father, David. I'll see you on Monday at the surgery.'

'No, wait!' he protested, but she was moving swiftly in the direction of Glenside Lodge and his father was looking around him with interest as the taxi disappeared.

'You should have let me know you were coming,' he said delightedly as the two men hugged each other.

Jonas laughed. 'Why, so you could have hung the bunting out? It was a spur-of-the-moment thing. I suddenly knew I just had to see what you're doing with the house where your mother lived. How's it coming along?'

'Not as fast as I would like, I'm afraid. There seems to be a shortage of bricklayers. But let's go inside and I have to warn you, Dad, that my accommodation is not large. I have only the one bedroom.'

'Don't worry. I'll stay at the pub. Is it still The Pheasant?'

'Yes, it is, but are you sure? It feels rather inhospitable after you've come all this way.'

'Sure I'm sure,' he declared. 'I've come for the week and if there's anything I can do with regard to the rebuilding you have only to say the word. I'm not a bricklayer, but I'm no mean hand at dry stone walling.'

'You're on,' David told him. 'The walls around the site are in a dreadful state.'

'Lead me to them, then.'

'You won't be able to do much in a week, though,' he reminded him.

'We'll see. I can always come back again. Next time I'll close the cottage and leave one of my friends in charge of the boat so that I can stay longer. I can't believe what you're doing, rebuilding that house up by the lake. I can remember it as if it was yesterday, your grandmother telling me to wipe my feet before I stepped on her carpets. She always looked on me with a jaundiced eye when I went calling on your mother because I wasn't local.'

'There wasn't much of it left when I bought it,' David warned him. 'Just four crumbling walls in an overgrown field.'

'We'll soon have it shipshape,' Jonas promised. 'If nothing else, I'll be able to see to the perimeter walls.'

Instead of taking Laurel for a meal it was his father sitting opposite him in the small dining room of The Pheasant. The landlord had booked Jonas into a first-storey bedroom for a week and now he was absorbing all the sights and sounds of the place that he hadn't been near since he'd lost Rachel, David's mother. But the son so dear to his heart had changed all that, and here he was, back amongst the green fields of Cheshire.

'So are we going up to the house now?' Jonas asked when they'd finished their meal.

'Are you sure you want to after the long journey?' David questioned.

'Oh, yes, I want to.'

'Then, yes, by all means. I'll be keen to know what you think, but bear in mind the builder only started a couple of weeks ago. So far it's been a case of strength-

ening the foundations and laying the first few courses
of the fresh stone before the damp course goes in.'

Laurel had showered and changed, had a sandwich and
a mug of tea, and with Elaine still down at the village
green supervising the clearing-up process was wondering how she was going to get the evening over with.

She'd been with David for hours at the Fayre and
instead of being satisfied with that she was aching to see
him again. But if he was going to be entertaining his unexpected guest and showing him around the place that
he hadn't visited for thirty years or more, she could at
least go and look at the building site and dream a little.
There couldn't be any harm in that, and they wouldn't
venture so far after his father's twelve-hour journey.

It was quiet and very still as she stood by the gate that
led to the field, and on impulse she pulled it open and
went on to the site where an assortment of window
frames and door frames had already been delivered.

She was imagining where she would arrange everything if she lived there when she heard voices out on the
lane and froze. It didn't take two guesses regarding who
they belonged to, and she thought that David would
think that he couldn't even show his father around the
place without having her at his elbow.

'Hi,' he said as she turned slowly to face them, and to
the man by his side he said, 'Laurel is a nurse at the surgery,
Dad, and also my inspiration when it comes to this place.'

She was smiling as Jonas shook her hand, her com-
posure returning as she said, 'I don't think David needed
inspiring. He was captivated from the start, it being his

mother's old home, and now I must be off. I do hope that you enjoy your stay, Mr Trelawney.'

'I intend to,' Jonas said with a smile for the man at his side, and when she'd gone with a low-voiced goodbye to his son, he said, 'So what's with Laurel of the lovely green eyes?'

David laughed. 'Nothing, Sherlock, nothing at all. You've just seen her in an upbeat mood, but she isn't always like that. There's a sadness about her sometimes that worries me.'

'So she isn't the one and only that I told you would come along one day?'

'I didn't say that.'

'No, you didn't, did you?' his father said dryly. 'Now, tell me what your plans are for Water Meetings House.'

Elaine was sitting with a glass of wine and her feet up when Laurel returned to Glenside Lodge, and she said, 'I thought maybe you were out with David.'

'No, he's got a visitor.'

'Who would that be?'

'His father, a hale and hearty Cornishman with white hair and blue eyes, has turned up unexpectedly.'

'Really!'

'Yes. I've just met him at the building site.' Before Elaine had any questions about David and herself, she asked, 'Has it been a successful day?'

'Very much so,' she replied. 'Those kind of things are hard work, but well worth it because the community spirit is always there, and I kept getting glimpses of two people who seemed to "commune" very well indeed.'

'You mean David and I?'

'Who else? So when are you going to tell him what it's all about?'

'I'm not. I can't! I do *not* want him feeling sorry for me, or alternatively beating a tactful retreat.'

'You aren't being fair to him, Laurel.'

'Do you think I don't know that?' she cried. 'I'm allowing myself a month and then…'

'What?' Elaine questioned gently.

'I don't know. I wish I did.'

'You've heard about the tangled web we weave when we practise to deceive, I take it?'

'Yes, I have,' she said flatly. 'And have you seen my back and shoulders recently?'

Elaine nodded. There was no answer to that.

On Monday morning at the surgery, the two nurses were busy with the mother-and-baby clinic when Sharon and her newborn daughter appeared.

'She's beautiful,' Laurel said as big eyes looked up at her out of a smooth little face when Sharon placed her on the scales.

'I will never forget how you and Dr Trelawney looked after me at the birth,' she said. 'Is he anywhere around?'

'I'll see if I can find him,' Laurel told her. 'If he's with a patient I can't disturb him. But if he's free I'm sure he'll be delighted to see you both. What have you called her?'

'Elsey. It was my mother's name but we've changed the spelling.'

David had just finished a consultation and was about

to buzz for the next patient when she found him, and when she said, 'A young lady called Elsey is here to see you,' he observed her questioningly. 'You can spare a moment, can't you?'

'Er, yes,' he said, coming from behind the desk. 'Is she a patient?'

'Yes. With big eyes and skin as soft as silk,' she told him. She glanced down at her hands and thought to herself, *Unlike some of us.*

He saw the glance but didn't comment, and followed her down the passage to where the nurses' room was. When he saw Sharon sitting there with the baby in her arms he gave a satisfied nod.

'So this is Elsey!' he exclaimed. 'How have you both been, Sharon?'

'Fine, Doctor,' she told him. 'She's on the breast and is a very contented child considering what a hurry she was in to be born. I've just been telling Laurel how grateful I am for the way you both appeared out of nowhere and took care of me. It was as if you read each other's minds. I don't know what I would have done if you hadn't been there.'

His smile was still in place as he said, 'Yes, there is the odd time when we are in tune, but not always to that extent.' He prepared to go back to his patients and said, 'Take care, Sharon. If you let us know when you're having the baby christened, we'll try and get to the service.'

'That would be lovely,' she said, 'but it will be a couple of months before we can have it as my husband's parents are coming from New Zealand and they can't get away until then.'

'That won't be a problem, will it?' he asked Laurel.

'No, I shouldn't think so,' she replied, and could hear herself telling Elaine that she was going to allow herself another month around David and then it would be decision time.

She could feel the web of deceit that Elaine had talked about clinging around her, and as David left them to get on with the clinic after sending a puzzled look in her direction, the day continued to take its course.

'What was it this morning with Sharon and the baby?' he asked as they were leaving at the end of the day. 'Don't you want to go to the christening, or was it because I spoke for both of us without consulting you first? It didn't occur to me that you might not want to go, and if that's the case I'm sorry.'

Of course she wanted to go. They'd been magical moments when they'd been there for the birth of little Elsey. It had been one more lovely thing to remember him by, but if she kept to her resolve she might not be in Willowmere in two months' time and once she'd gone she wouldn't be able to face coming back, even for something as lovely as a christening.

She managed a smile, unable to bear the thought of David feeling guilty over something that he wasn't aware of. 'No, it wasn't anything like that,' she assured him. 'You just took me by surprise, that's all.' Eager to change the subject, she asked, 'How is your dad getting on with the stone walling round the field?'

'Great. All his life he's vowed he would never leave Cornwall, but I'm starting to feel he might have a rethink once the house is finished. I might add on a grandad flat, just in case the day ever dawns when I have children. But after the Caroline fiasco I'm wary of making another error of judgement. Do you have those kind of feelings about your broken engagement?'

She wasn't going to get involved with any more half-truths, she decided, and told him, 'I keep telling myself that any errors of judgement were on his part.'

'I'm curious. Who was he?'

'An actor called Darius Symonds. He's in one of the soaps.'

'So he's a household name?'

'Not in my house,' she said flippantly, and it was true. David's was the only name she wanted to hear, wherever she might be.

'I'm going straight to the site,' he announced, relieved to hear that she wasn't moping over the Darius fellow as much as he'd thought. 'Dad's meeting me there with a picnic meal from the Hollyhocks. Would you like to join us?

'I told him to bring enough food for three on the off chance you might agree to be our guest. I don't know how you feel, but I'll be glad to get out into the fresh air for a few hours after being at the practice all day.

'I'm anxious to see how the work is progressing, needless to say, then I'm going to have a go at the gardens and I use the term loosely. They are full of wild flowers, weeds and shrubs out of control.'

'I'll help you,' she offered impulsively, and immediately thought she wasn't going to get David out of her mind by working with him on the garden of what was going to be a beautiful stone house by the lake. But she had come to love the place almost as much as he did, and that was a straight course to heartache if ever there was one.

'I'd love to share the picnic,' she told him, 'but will need to go and change out of my uniform first and let Elaine know I'll be eating out.'

'I've got my working clothes in the boot,' he explained, 'and it's great that you're coming, Laurel. It doesn't feel the same if you're not around when I'm at the house, what there is of it!'

The walls that Jonas had been working on were rising out of the piles of fallen stone on the ground, and when she arrived he said with a twinkle in his eye, 'So is it the gardening you've come to do, my dear?'

She laughed and he thought she was an odd-looking young woman but there was something about her that caught the imagination, and without being told he could tell that was how it was with his son, but whether she was going to be *the* one was something yet to be revealed.

'Yes,' she told him. 'Though how much use I'm going to be, I don't know.'

David had been sprawled on the grass, propped up on his elbow with a mug of tea in his hand when she arrived, but now he was standing beside her and saying, 'I thought of getting rid of all the vegetation that has gone haywire and maybe leaving the rest of it half wild with a lawn here and there, a couple of water features and a gazebo overlooking the lake. What do you think, Laurel?'

'I *think* you're making me envious,' she said lightly, 'but, yes, that sounds great. So lead me to the food and then I'll get cracking. As you can see, I'm dressed for the job in a pair of old dungarees belonging to Elaine and a past-its-best sweater, and have borrowed some gardening gloves off her.'

'Yes, by all means take care of your hands,' he said, giving her the chance to explain why they were as they were, but in keeping with the occasion it fell on stony ground and he went on to say, 'There will be lots of brambles out there.'

They worked until the sun was ready to set, with Jonas back on the erecting of the walls and Laurel and David clearing the overgrown garden. It was hot work, the ground was hard from years of neglect, and he went across to where she was pulling out brambles by the roots.

When she looked up he said, 'That's enough for now. It will soon be dark. Why don't the three of us finish the night off at the pub? I don't know about you but I could do with a long, cold drink.' Taking off his gardening gloves, he reached out towards her and rubbed a grimy mark off her cheek with gentle fingers.

'Not like this, I don't think,' she said softly as their glances locked. 'I'll have to go home, have a shower and change into some decent clothes.'

It was a timeless sort of moment, the two of them in the garden of his mother's home, both of them hot and grimy, yet so aware of each other it could have gone on and on.

But they were not alone. There was a third member of the working party and he was calling from the bottom of the field, 'So what now? Is that it for today?' Smiling wryly, David signalled for Jonas to down tools.

'We'll drop you off at Elaine's house, then Dad and

I will go and get cleaned up at my place and we'll pick you up in an hour, say?' he said as normality returned.

'Yes, all right,' she agreed, knowing that she should call it a day when they arrived at Glenside Lodge, instead of spending any more time with David. Why couldn't she be satisfied with being near him all day at the surgery and working side by side with him in what would one day be a beautiful garden?

CHAPTER SIX

WHEN David was dropping Laurel off at Glenside Lodge some minutes later he said, 'Why not see if Elaine wants to join us at The Pheasant if she's available?'

'Yes, of course,' she agreed, and as soon as she was inside put the question to her aunt who had just come in from weeding her own garden.

'I'd love to,' she said. 'For one thing I'd like to meet David's father. My dad used to have a boat when I was small and we used to go sailing on the Norfolk Broads with him at every opportunity, so we will have something to talk about. But like you I need to freshen up and change my clothes. So who's first for the shower?'

'Huh?' Laurel said absently. She was back at the site in her mind, helping to make David's dream come true, and feeling that, after those spellbound moments in the garden, if he should appear at that moment she would be able to face up to telling him what it was that lay so heavy on her heart.

If the opportunity came later in the evening she would grasp it and clear the air between them. For once she felt strong enough to unburden herself to him.

She knew that Elaine was of the opinion she should have done so long ago and that perhaps she was making too big a thing of what had happened to her on a quiet night in the men's ward.

But only she knew how ugly she felt when she saw the bright red eruptions on her back and shoulders and the tight, unsightly skin of her hands. She was no different from any other woman in wanting to be beautiful for the man she was falling in love with, but the pleasure was being denied her.

They were seated at a table for four in the beer garden at the back of The Pheasant and as Elaine and Jonas chatted nonstop about boats, Cornwall and the Norfolk Broads, David said in a low voice, 'Those two are getting on famously, aren't they?' He smiled at his silent companion. 'You are very quiet, though. Are you all right, Laurel?'

'Yes. I'm fine,' she told him, and wondered what he would say if she told him she was trying to decide how to tell him what had happened to her before she'd come to Willowmere.

The best idea was to suggest they go for a stroll and leave the others to their conversation, and she was about to suggest it when David said, 'I noticed Sarah Wilkinson in one of the rooms back there. I'm just going to say hello. I won't be long.'

When he'd gone, Laurel went into the bar to buy another round of drinks. As she was about to step out into the garden, balancing a tray of full glasses, she paused as she overheard Jonas say, 'I suppose you know that David was engaged to be married to an American woman before he came to work in Cheshire and he broke it off.'

'Er, yes, I do,' Elaine told him uncomfortably.

He sighed. 'I don't know the full story but break-ups are never easy, are they? She was very attractive and they made a striking couple. I can't help but worry about him. Do you really think he's happy with his life here?'

'Yes, I think David seems very happy here,' Elaine butted in quickly as Laurel arrived at the table, knowing she'd heard and that Jonas's casual comments would be like a slap in the face to her niece. It seemed that she was not wrong in that assumption.

'I'm sorry, but I've got to go. Say goodbye to David for me, will you?' Laurel said as she put the tray down. Elaine watched in dismay as she left the beer garden by a side gate and began to walk along the main street at a brisk pace.

Laurel brushed away stinging tears. If she'd had any doubts about what she'd intended to do, David's father in all innocence had just made it very clear that it would be a mistake, and her newfound confidence was disappearing like water down a drain.

When David came back to the table he said immediately, 'Where's Laurel?'

'Oh…she left,' Elaine said awkwardly.

'Why?'

'I'm not sure. She looked tired so maybe she's decided to have an early night.'

'Without saying goodbye?'

'She asked us to say it for her.'

'Right, I see,' he said levelly, and thought nothing had changed. Laurel was still as unpredictable as when they'd first met and he was crazy to think he was beginning to understand her.

On a sudden impulse he said, 'Which way did she go?'

'Down the main street,' Elaine informed him.

'I need to make sure she's all right...don't I?' he questioned.

'Yes, you do,' she told him gravely.

When he'd gone striding off Jonas said wryly, 'And then there were two.' In a more serious manner he went on, 'Oh, dear. I didn't mean Laurel to hear me talking about Caroline. You must think I'm completely tactless. I did sense an affinity between my son and your niece.'

'Yes, you need have no doubts about that,' she told him flatly. 'But don't expect anything to come of it as far as Laurel is concerned.'

'Why not? She seems a sparky young lass.'

'Yes, she is, she has to be, and that is all I'm going to say.'

'So shall I redeem myself for spoiling the evening by walking you home before I turn in?'

'No,' she told him, managing a smile. 'It's still daylight and I've been doing my own thing for years. It's been great to meet you and hear all about life on the Cornish coast.'

Jonas flashed her a craggy smile as she departed in the opposite direction to the one that Laurel and David had taken, and commented to no one in particular, 'And then there was one.'

* * *

There was no sign of Laurel on the way to Glenside Lodge, which was not surprising as she'd had a few minutes' start on him, David thought as he drove to the old stone lodge at the end of the interminable drive that sloped up to the moors.

When he'd rung the doorbell several times and there was no answer he had to accept that either she didn't want to talk to him, had gone straight to bed and was already asleep, or she wasn't there, but if that was the case, where was she?

It was clear that in those few moments when he'd been chatting to Sarah something had upset Laurel and he hoped it wasn't something his father had said as Elaine would never do anything to cause her to leave so suddenly. With his hand on the gate latch, a thought struck him. Supposing she'd gone to the house? Yet surely it was the last place she would want to go to if it was his dad who had somehow put his foot in it.

One thing he knew, he had to make sure, and he drove off in the direction of the lake, relieved that he'd gone to pick up his car that he'd parked outside the cottage after giving Laurel and Elaine a lift to The Pheasant.

It was dark, lightless, with no moon shining in silver shafts between the willows tonight, and no slender figure standing where he'd found her on other occasions looking out over the building site. He turned the car round despondently and drove back to the village.

Laurel *had* gone home and when she'd let herself into the quiet house she'd gone straight up to her room and stood by the window looking down blankly onto the lane below.

She'd seen David drive up and come striding quickly along the path that led to the front door and had moved back out of sight, and each time he'd rung the doorbell she'd covered her ears with her hands.

She knew she should go down and apologise for the way she'd rushed off while he'd been talking to Sarah. It had been a selfish thing to do, making him suffer for her inadequacies, but she couldn't do it. Her legs wouldn't support her down the stairs.

Hidden in the bedroom she'd watched him leave and seen his momentary hesitation before he'd got back into the car and driven off in the direction of the lake, and the shame of causing him so much anxiety brought the use back to her legs.

She dashed down the stairs to flag him down, but was too late. All that could be seen were the taillights of the car driving off into the night.

In the absence of a war memorial in Willowmere a peace garden had been created by the locals and it formed an attractive centrepiece in the village. It was a circular arrangement made out of local stone and, whatever the season, was always a mass of flowers.

There was seating around it for anyone who wanted to stop and rest, and it was very popular with ramblers and others who visited the village or were stopping off en route to other parts of the Cheshire countryside.

It was only a short distance from where David lived and was always illuminated in the evenings once daylight had gone. It was as he drove the last few yards to the cottage that he saw her and relief washed over him.

Laurel was hunched on one of the benches that encircled the peace garden and when he stopped the car she got slowly to her feet.

He wound the window down and when she drew alongside asked levelly, 'So what's going on? You left the beer garden with not so much as a word. I was only chatting to Sarah for a matter of minutes. Surely you didn't object to that!'

'No, of course I didn't,' she said quickly, wondering what excuse she could come up with to avoid telling him that his father had made her even more aware of her shortcomings in those moments while he'd been gone.

'It was just that Elaine and your father were engrossed in their common interests, you had gone elsewhere, and I felt that I might as well leave you all to it and have an early night,' she explained in a low voice.

'And so why didn't you? If that was the case, what are you doing here? I've been chasing around looking for you like someone demented. You were happy enough before I went to speak to Sarah, so what went wrong in that short time, Laurel?'

'Nothing!' she cried. 'Will you please stop badgering me?'

'If the day ever dawns when I understand the workings of your mind there will be a flag flying over Willowmere,' he told her, still in the driver's seat, 'and now if you will get in the car I'll take you home.'

She obeyed without speaking and he drove to Glenside Lodge once more, this time with an easier mind because he'd found her, or more correctly she'd found him, but there was no joy in him.

Maybe he should ease off. Perhaps she felt suffocated by him. Yet she was the one who'd wanted to help with the garden, the one who was as interested as he was in the rebuilding of Water Meetings House.

But somewhere along the line she'd been hurt. He could sense it all the time and he didn't think it was just her broken engagement. She'd been in some kind of trauma that it seemed she didn't want to talk about and he had the choice of giving up on her or waiting until she was ready to open her heart to him.

She knew it was the moment to tell him where her hurts and fears lay, Laurel was thinking as he pulled up in front of the lodge, but she couldn't face it after the way his father had described his ex-fiancée. A striking couple he'd said they were, and a tear ran down her cheek at the thought.

As he switched off the engine David turned to observe her, saw it and, dismayed, fished a clean handkerchief out of his pocket. 'I can't bear to see you cry,' he said gently, wiping it away, 'especially when I'm responsible for your tears. Can you forgive me for being so unfeeling, Laurel?'

'I can forgive you anything and everything,' she told him on a sob, 'and in any case there's nothing to forgive.' She leaned over and kissed him fleetingly on the cheek. 'Good night, David.'

When he would have reached across for her she opened the car door, slid out of the passenger seat and said, 'I'll see you at the surgery in the morning.'

As she went quickly inside and closed the door after her, he thought wryly that her words of farewell were the only sure thing he could hold on to. He *would* see her tomorrow, and the day after, and the day after that, and would be thankful because he knew deep down that there was no way he could give up on Laurel.

Hard to understand or not, she had him enchanted and captivated, and he would just have to wait until she was ready to tell him what it was all about.

Elaine had returned and she said, 'I felt for you back there in the beer garden of The Pheasant. Jonas was upset after you'd gone. He didn't know you were there and realised he'd been rather tactless in bringing up the subject. It seems that he's picked up on the bond between David and yourself and I'm sure he would never have said what he did if he'd known what happened to you.'

'It doesn't matter anyway,' Laurel said flatly. 'I shouldn't have eavesdropped. But I was weakening—really he's done me a good turn.'

It wasn't true, of course. Jonas had inadvertently diminished her returning confidence.

After a brief greeting by Reception the next morning there was no time to talk even if Laurel and David had wanted to. The pollen count was high and quite a few asthma sufferers had arrived seeking relief. Added to that there was an incident in the waiting room when a toddler wandering around on wobbly legs toppled over and was knocked senseless as he hit his head on the side of a radiator.

The mother's horrified cries brought David forth from the middle of a consultation and Laurel flying out of the nurses' room to find patients crowding around mother and child and general chaos ensuing.

'Quiet, everyone,' he commanded as he bent over the stricken child, who was opening his eyes slowly and letting out a frightened wail.

'Don't try to move him,' he told his mother as she bent over him, 'not yet.'

The side of the toddler's head was beginning to come up in a soft, spongy swelling and both doctor and nurse were thinking the same thing—haematoma.

'So what's the situation?' the first of two paramedics asked when the ambulance pulled up outside the surgery where Laurel had gone to greet them.

'We have a small child who has fallen against the hard edge of a radiator and knocked himself unconscious for a few moments,' she said as she hurried them inside. 'There is swelling of the skull that needs checking out in case it's a haematoma.'

'What's that?' the anxious mother asked.

'Bleeding inside the head,' Laurel told her gently. 'It's just as a precaution, that's all.'

'Come on then, young fella,' the other paramedic said as they lifted the child carefully onto a stretcher, adding to his mother, 'They'll soon sort him out at St Gabriel's.'

'I do hope so,' she sobbed. 'I shouldn't have let go of him back there in the surgery. Oliver has only just started to walk and wants to do it all on his own. He doesn't like having to hold my hand.'

* * *

James hadn't been present during all the commotion. He'd driven up to the moors above the village in answer to an urgent request for a visit from one of the isolated farms up there and had arrived back at the surgery just as the ambulance was driving off at some speed, which meant that by the time he'd been put in the picture and helped David deal with the backlog that had arisen in the waiting room, it was lunchtime.

The delicatessen had opened officially that morning and when Laurel went across to buy a snack of some kind she found that David had done the same thing. When they'd been served and duly admired the new venture they walked back together in silence until he broke into it by saying, 'We're getting to be quite a good double act in a crisis, aren't we? First there was Sharon and the baby, then today little Oliver. I wonder what will be next.'

It was the last thing she was expecting him to say and she said the first thought that came into her head. 'Someone else's crisis maybe, but I'm not so good when it comes to my own.'

She'd coped with the emergency on the ward that night with speed and coolness, but the aftermath of it had become a personal crisis that went on and on. It wasn't going to go away, ever.

'Are you referring to a broken engagement?' he couldn't help asking.

'No, though that wasn't pleasant. You've been there yourself, haven't you? But at least you were the one who finished it. You weren't cast aside.'

'Not on the face of it maybe,' he replied. 'As for what

happened to you, sometimes there is no accounting for the stupidity of others. After my relationship with Caroline folded I decided to steer free of any other issues. That was until I met you, but having promised myself that nothing can be worse than making you cry, I'm staying on the sidelines, Laurel. Let me know if anything changes, will you?'

'So we are just going to be friends?' she said stiffly.

That made him smile. 'Yes, we are, Miss Prim. And would I be stepping out of line if I told you that your hair is looking very fetching?'

'No, not at all, I'll allow you that,' she replied, 'as long as you're not just saying it to make me feel better.'

He hadn't been wrong, he thought. It hadn't been a hairdresser who'd got carried away, and he'd seen her hands. Those two things were nothing to do with tattoos, but until she'd thrown off the protective clothing that she wore like a second skin he wasn't going to get any answers, and in the current state of their relationship that wasn't going to happen, not in his presence anyway.

When he'd eaten the salad he'd bought at the delicatessen David called in at The Pheasant to have a word with his father before he started his home visits, and discovered from the landlord that Jonas had gone to the building site once again. So it was a matter of having his anxieties of the night before brought back as he drove past the lake, though he didn't need any reminding.

'I don't usually see you at this time of day,' Jonas said when he pulled up on the overgrown drive of the house. 'Aren't there any sick people in Willowmere?'

'I'm only here for a moment,' he explained. 'I've

come to ask what you said to Laurel last night that made her get up and go.'

'You mean Elaine hasn't told you?'

'So you *did* say something, and what has Elaine got to do with it?'

'I didn't know Laurel was there—she'd gone to get more drinks. But I just mentioned that Caroline was attractive and how you'd made a striking couple. I also meant to say that she wasn't the right one for you, but Laurel was up and off. So I wasn't wrong when I thought there was something between the two of you.'

'Yes, well, for the record Laurel and I are just friends and that isn't going to change in the near future.'

'But you wish it would?'

'Yes, but she is a woman with a secret and until she's ready to tell me what it is, Dad, I'll settle for friendship.' He turned to set off. 'I'll see you about half six if you haven't already had enough.'

'I'll be here,' Jonas informed him stoutly, 'and I'm sorry for poking my nose into your affairs, lad. You know that your happiness means a lot to me.'

'Yes, but do please remember that I'm capable of sorting out my own life,' he said with a smile for the man who had been both mother and father to him for many years.

'Aye, I know,' Jonas replied, and ruffled his son's dark thatch with a soil-stained hand before turning back to his dry stone walling.

So had Laurel felt she was being found wanting in what his father had said? David wondered as he did the calls he'd set out to do. He hoped not, but the odds were that she had, and somehow, without actually putting it into words, he had to find a way to reassure her. It wasn't going to be easy as every time he tried to get closer to her she was on the defensive.

When he arrived back at the surgery she was chatting to Jess Jackson, the slender brown-haired girl who was nanny to James's children, and when she'd taken Pollyanna and Jolyon through to see their father Laurel said casually, 'Jess was asking me if I miss living in London.'

'And do you?'

'I did at first, but not now.'

Willowmere was casting its spell over her and so was he, but she wasn't going to tell him that. Instead she said, 'I'm going there for the day in a couple of weeks so it will be interesting to see if I have any yearnings.'

'Are you going for anything special?' he asked casually, breaking his promise to himself not to ask questions.

'I have an appointment to keep. Fortunately it's on a Saturday so I won't be missing from the practice at all. It will give me the chance to collect any mail that has been delivered to my apartment while I'm there. I've kept it on as it is always somewhere to go if I need a bolt-hole.'

'That is an odd thing to say. Why would you need somewhere to hide?' he asked quizzically. 'You haven't committed a crime, have you?'

'Not yet, and regarding it being an odd thing to say, I am an odd person, David. You've found that out already, haven't you?'

'Not odd, different maybe, but I like a challenge,' he

told her as the thought of her running back to London took his spirits down to zero.

When they'd both gone back to their respective functions in the practice Laurel wondered what he would have said if she'd told David it was a hospital appointment that she had to keep with the doctors who had done their best to repair her damaged skin.

They would decide if further grafts were necessary and if they were there might be no way of keeping her painful secret from David, but she would meet that problem when it came. If she had to be absent from the practice for a while maybe she could think of another reason for it, and then there was always the dismal alternative that she'd mentioned to Elaine, leaving Willowmere and moving back to London.

That evening she told Elaine that David knew she was going to London for the day and was curious why.

'And I don't suppose you satisfied his curiosity?' she said.

'Er…no…I didn't,' Laurel replied flatly. 'I said I had an appointment but didn't say where. After his father's description of the ex-fiancée I know I can't compete and have accepted it.'

Elaine shook her head despairingly. 'That doesn't sound like the gutsy girl who is the light of my life,' she protested. 'If you wanted David enough you would tell him what happened to you.'

'Don't you see it's because I'm so in love with him that I can't tell him?' she protested. 'When it happened I never thought that anyone would find me so unpleasant to look at as Darius did and that thought is going to stay with me always. In a weird kind of way I'm fortunate that all the scarring is where I can't see it. When I look in the mirror there is no sign of it. But that wouldn't apply to anyone I slept with, would it?'

There was only one answer to that, Elaine thought, and if Laurel would only give him the chance David Trelawney might provide it. *He* wasn't Darius.

Like others before it, the conversation wasn't getting them anywhere and on a lighter note she suggested, 'Why don't you go and give some help with the garden again on Saturday and when they've finished for the day invite David and his father back here for a barbecue? I'm sure the men would enjoy some freshly cooked food after their labours.'

'I suppose I could,' she replied with a dubious frown, 'but you know I'm no cook.'

'You'll be fine. It's just a matter of putting sausages, bacon and chicken drumsticks onto a hot grid and turning them over every so often. David will get the equipment working for you.'

'All right, I'll do it,' she said decisively. 'It's a nice idea just as long as it doesn't rain and Jonas is there to chaperon us so that I don't send out any wrong signals.'

He won't be there if I can help it, Elaine thought. She had plans for Jonas that would make him absent from the building site for most of the day on Saturday, leaving David and Laurel alone for a few hours.

There was a maritime exhibition on in the nearest town and she was going to ask him if he would like to visit it with her. It might seem a bit pushy as she'd only just met the man, but they had a few things in common, boats and the sea for starters, as well as the happiness of those they loved...

A big brown duck was waddling along the pavement in front of the practice when Laurel arrived the next morning. There had been a heavy shower shortly before, and each time it came to a puddle it stopped to drink.

As she watched it, fascinated, David came out of his cottage and on seeing what it was that had her attention he exclaimed laughingly, 'I don't believe it! There are lots of them on the river and this one must have come up the bank to investigate what lies on either side. It must be "quackers", drinking from puddles when it has all the river at its beak.'

As she joined in his laughter and left the duck to pursue its way, Laurel thought that only a few weeks ago the idea of being so enchanted at the sight of a duck waddling down the street would have seemed ludicrous, but she had to admit it, the countryside had taken her into its embrace. She was captive to its peaceful perfection, and even more so to the charismatic man beside her.

In the last few moments before the surgery doors opened she put Elaine's suggestion to David and he said, 'Are you sure? You've already discovered that it's hard work getting that garden to come out from under years of weeds and undergrowth without feeding us too.'

'Yes. I'm sure,' she said breezily, 'and if you are willing to risk the results of my cooking, the barbecue is on, as long as you'll sort out the technicalities of it for me.'

'Of course I will,' he assured her, with the thought of the approaching weekend becoming more appealing with every moment.

Clare from the picture gallery near the vicarage was one of the patients sent to the nurses' room for blood tests during the morning. She was still in remission from ovarian cancer and much happier for it, but James wasn't taking any chances, and as part of a routine check-up he'd asked for the tests to be done.

She was a pleasant woman in her fifties, unmarried, and ready to chat as she explained that she'd been Georgina Adams's patient until the dark-haired doctor that Laurel had glimpsed that first day with her baby had remarried her husband and given him another child.

'I'm little Arran's godmother,' Clare informed the two nurses with a wealth of affection in her voice. 'The Fates have lately been most kind to me. My cancer has disappeared, I was asked to be part of Arran's life, and my mother, who lives with me and can be difficult, has been a changed character since I was ill.'

When she'd gone Gillian, the other nurse, said, 'There goes a very happy woman and a brave one too. I've never once heard her complain about the cancer.'

Maybe there is a message for me somewhere in that, Laurel thought as she greeted the next person to be summoned from the chairs in the corridor, but it isn't ever going to stop the awful ache I feel inside when I think about David.

When she arrived at the house by the lake on the Saturday morning she gasped at the progress that was being made.

All the walls were up and the builder and his crew were on site, getting ready to put the slates on a new roof.

It was taking shape, she thought wistfully, and wished she could be a permanent part of it. As he went to greet her David was observing her expression. Would Laurel ever let him get near enough to tell her that Water Meetings House could turn out to be an empty dream without her there beside him?

There was one thing he was sure of. He knew that he wasn't going to be able to wait forever to discover what it was that always reared its head every time she was weakening in her resolve to keep him on the edge of her life. He told himself frequently that he could and would, and when they were apart the resolve was still there, but the moment he saw her again the longing to hold her close and tell her how much he cared was so strong he could almost taste it.

She was looking around her. 'I don't see your father. Isn't he here?'

'I thought you would know,' he said in surprise. 'Dad has gone to a maritime exhibition with Elaine.'

'No, I didn't know,' she said slowly, 'but it explains why she was out early and vague about how she was going to spend the day…and who with.'

'So it's just you and me,' he said. 'Do you think you can cope with that?'

'I'll have to, won't I?' she replied, and he gave her a long, level look and went back to his digging.

CHAPTER SEVEN

It was late afternoon. The workmen had gone home to relax for the rest of the weekend, and Laurel and David, hot and grimy, were about to do the same when he asked, 'What kind of a barbecue is it?'

'Gas,' she replied. 'One of those cylinder things has to be attached to it.'

He was laughing. 'Spoken like a true handywoman.'

She pulled a face at him. 'I'm a city girl, don't forget, an expert in fashion, take-aways and theatre tickets.'

'So you haven't fallen in love with Willowmere?'

She was admitting to herself frequently that she had. She'd fallen in love with everything about the place and him in particular, but it was a moment for evasions rather than honesty and she said casually, 'It's a nice place.'

His heart sank. He hadn't forgotten that she was going back to her roots in two weeks. Would she want to stay there when she'd renewed her acquaintance with the capital city?

They were back at Glenside Lodge, scrubbed and clean after their efforts at the building site, and it was time for the barbecue. David had used the main bathroom to shower and Laurel the one in the en suite in her room, and there'd been an awkward moment when he'd heard her lock the door as he'd been crossing the landing.

'You're quite safe, you know,' he'd said coolly from the other side. 'I'm not going to suggest that we shower together, or anything else that would be as remote from your thinking as the heavens above.' And when she hadn't replied, he'd gone on his way.

She'd closed her eyes in anguish. Yet there'd been no signs of distress when she'd reappeared in one of the inevitable high-necked tops and a long cotton skirt, and David's moment of rebuke seemed to have been just that because he was smiling as he said, 'The barbecue is up and running on the patio. I've connected it to the propane and the gas is lit. All we need now is the food. Are you sure you're up to this, though? You've had a strenuous day so far. I'll do the cooking if you like.'

'No. I'm going to do it,' she informed him. 'I know you think I'm pretty useless so it's time I showed you that I'm not.' She gave him a gentle push towards the garden chairs out on the lawn. 'Go and relax and I'll call you when it's ready.'

'All right,' he agreed, 'but be sure to adjust the flame if you think the food is cooking too quickly.'

It was all going to plan. The sausages and the chicken legs that Elaine had suggested were all sizzling nicely on the grid. Laurel turned away to prepare the bacon for cooking, not realising in those first few seconds that smoke was rising from fat that had dripped through. She turned around to see flames leaping up from the barbecue.

She was back on the ward, but this time fear didn't lend wings to her feet. She was transfixed, and David came leaping onto the patio and dampened the flames with water from the bucket they'd put nearby. The fire went out with a loud hissing sound, and at the same moment that he turned to reassure her that it was all right, just a minor hiccup, Laurel was swaying on her feet.

He caught her before she crumpled and carried her into the sitting room, thinking as he did so how limp and helpless she felt in his arms. For a few seconds no words issued from the mouth that had refused his kisses, no bright eyes looked up at him. There had been fear in them when the flames had appeared and now they were closed in a still, white face.

As he laid her down on the sofa, as he'd done on the day she'd arrived in the village, David was thinking that it *had* been a bit worrying, but it had soon been sorted. It wasn't as if the house had been on fire. It was such a shame that Laurel's intention to cook for him had been thwarted, but more important was for her to realise that now there was nothing to be afraid of.

She opened her eyes and the panic was still there. 'It's all right,' he said gently. 'Everything is sorted. You saw me put out the fire and I've turned the gas off. It was my fault. I should have stayed beside you while you were cooking the food.'

She turned her head into the pillow and said in a muffled voice, 'You must think I'm stupid. I just panicked.'

He shook his head. 'You're not stupid, Laurel. You

are bright and funny, clever and kind, but why were you so distressed?'

'It was probably because everything I touch is a disaster,' she said evasively. 'My engagement was a catastrophe, and now I can't even cook you a meal without almost setting the place on fire.'

He stroked her cheek gently. 'That's twice you've fainted on me. I hope you're not going to make a habit of it.'

'I'll try not to,' she promised weakly, and raised herself up on the cushions. 'I'm all right now, David. It was just the shock of seeing the flames leaping up, that's all.'

He nodded understandingly yet wasn't convinced, but if Laurel wanted him to think that he would go along with it for the present.

The sound of voices on the front path indicated that Elaine and Jonas were back and he sighed. So much for time alone with Laurel. 'Stay where you are,' he said. 'I'll go and explain what's happened to Elaine.'

'No,' she protested, getting off the sofa. 'I don't want to worry her. I'm fine now.'

'All right,' he agreed doubtfully, 'but…'

'I'm OK, David, I promise,' she insisted, and said with a pale smile, 'Thanks for being there for me once again. I'm sure you never expected to be lumbered with me in your life ever since you lifted my cases off the train that day at the station. I'm a nuisance, aren't I?'

He was smiling for the first time since she'd fainted. 'If being a top-notch nurse at the surgery, working beside me in that jungle I call a garden, and brightening my days with your presence constitutes being a nuisance then, yes, you are. And now, if you're sure you are up to it, I think we should present ourselves to Dad and Elaine, who are bound to have smelt the smoke and will be wondering where we are.'

He took her hand and as they went out into the hall together she wished that his firm, reassuring clasp could be there for her always in darkness and in light.

Elaine and Jonas had gone straight to the garden via the kitchen and were lounging with long, cold drinks in front of them when they appeared. Without any reference to lingering odours, her aunt said, 'Have you had a nice day?'

'The barbecue seemed to be cooking too fast and some of the food got overdone, so I'm taking David somewhere for a decent meal to make up for it,' Laurel announced, and met Jonas's shrewd blue gaze with, 'We'll see you two later.'

'Well done!' David said as they drove to the village. 'I couldn't have done better myself.'

'Oh, I'll bet you could,' she teased, happy that she had him to herself after all. 'Let's hope that they have a free table somewhere.'

'If they haven't, we can go to my place and I'll rustle up something to eat,' he suggested.

He was waiting to see her reaction to that idea and wasn't surprised when she said hurriedly, 'That wouldn't be fair. I'm supposed to be entertaining you. If they can't fit us in at the pub, Hollyhocks might still be open.'

'Sure,' he said easily. 'We'll just play it as it comes,' and wondered why Laurel had been keen for them to spend the evening alone before and now she was chickening out at the thought of him taking her to the cottage.

There wasn't a free table at The Pheasant, and Hollyhocks Tea Rooms *had* closed, so because of Laurel's reluctance to take up his offer of eating at his place David said, 'I think something is telling us to call it a day, don't you?'

'I suppose you're right,' she agreed, and on a crazy impulse that she knew she might regret said, 'But I *would* like to see where you live if you haven't changed your mind.'

'It will be my pleasure,' he said, 'but when I've made you a sandwich and you've sampled a glass of Helen's home-made elderberry wine, I *am* going to take you home. You did pass out earlier after your scare *and* you were helping me with the garden for a long time before that, so it's an early night for you, Nurse Maddox.'

'Who is Helen who makes the wine?' she asked, turning a deaf ear to his solicitations on her behalf.

'She is James's elderly housekeeper, who often sends round something nice when she has baked too much.'

As they walked up the path to the cottage David said, 'It's very small, compact in every detail but small. James offered me the annexe to the surgery when I moved to Willowmere. It's where his sister Anna used to live, but I saw this place and liked it and here I am, though hopefully not for long.

'I saw Lizzie Carmichael, one of the midwives at St Gabriel's, the other day. She'd heard about my building project and asked if I would let her know when I'm moving out of here as she's interested in coming to live in Willowmere and would like to rent the cottage if possible when it comes empty.

'She's a great girl but a bit of a mystery. Doesn't seem to be in a relationship of any kind, which is surprising, but I think that Lizzie is in love with the job. She's a born mother, so it must be a strange feeling to be delivering other people's babies all the time and never one of your own.'

He was turning the key in the lock and when the door swung back he stepped inside and waited for her to pass him in a hallway that was so narrow she couldn't help but brush against him as he pointed towards a sitting room that was attractively furnished but also quite small.

The brief moment of contact had made her blood warm, but Laurel controlled the urge to throw herself into his arms and looked around her. She could understand why David was rather cramped in this place and wanted his own space. It also explained why his father was staying at The Pheasant.

'Take a seat while I prepare something to eat and pour the wine,' he said, 'and if Helen's wine isn't to your liking, I'll make tea or coffee.'

When he brought in the food and drink he said, 'I'll be going from one extreme to the other when I move into Water Meetings House, leaving a tiny cottage for a large detached one. It can't come too soon, although I was happy enough here until I saw my mother's old home.' *And met you*, he wanted to tell her, but the thing she didn't want him to know lay between them as heavy as lead.

'Will you have a housewarming?' she wanted to know, and he shrugged the suggestion off as if it was of no account.

'It all depends on circumstances.'

'Such as?'

'Whether I want one.'

'Why wouldn't you?'

'I would have expected you to know the answer to that,' he said, stung by her casual questioning. He'd made his feelings for her clear enough. Did he have to express them in neon lights for her to take notice?

Laurel knew she'd upset him, and fighting an insane urge to take off her top and show him the reason why she was always holding back she got up to go.

'I can see myself home,' she told him. 'It's still daylight and you were right about me needing an early night, David. It *has* been a long day and I want to give the barbecue a quick clean before I go to bed after my catastrophic performance on it.'

'You're making too much of what happened,' he said gently, his good humour returning. 'It wasn't the end of the world.'

She gave a vestige of a smile. 'True, but one's world can end in a matter of seconds in some circumstances.'

'Are we talking about your broken engagement again by any chance?'

'Again…no.'

She was moving towards the narrow hallway. 'Thank you for a lovely day, David,' she said gravely. 'I'm sorry I'm so difficult to deal with.' And before he could reply she was gone, walking slowly in the direction of Glenside Lodge. Remembering how she'd made it clear that she didn't want him to walk her home, he didn't go after her.

* * *

Elaine was waiting up for her when she got there and her first words were, 'What happened with the barbecue, Laurel?'

'The food caught fire.'

'Oh, no, I should never have suggested it! That has never happened before. What did you do?'

'Froze to the spot, and while David was extinguishing the flames I fainted.'

'How awful that you of all people should have had such a fright.'

'Mmm, and I missed its only compensation. When I came out of the faint I was lying on the sofa, so David must have carried me there from the patio. He must rue the day he ever set eyes on me,' she said with droll regret.

Elaine had to smile in spite of her consternation. 'At least he must feel that life is never boring when he's around you, and so I take it that the food was spoilt?'

'Yes, it was burnt, then soaked. Before I go to bed I'm going to give the barbecue a good clean.'

'Too late, it's done and put away,' she was told.

'Thanks for that,' she breathed, and sinking down onto the nearest chair asked, 'And so how was your day with the ship's captain?'

'You are the cheeky one,' Elaine said laughingly. 'Jonas is a nice guy who loves his son the way I love you. He says he'll take me out in his boat if ever I'm in Cornwall.'

'And are you going to take him up on the offer?' Laurel asked curiously.

'Yes, if ever I'm in Cornwall, which is hardly likely.'

With a feeling that Elaine didn't want to pursue that topic Laurel headed off to bed. She paused on the bottom step of the stairs and said, 'It's been a strange day, full of peaks and valleys. It will be a relief to go to London to chill out when the time comes. I might even be looking forward to it if my reason for going wasn't my check-up.'

'I'm sorry I can't go with you for moral support,' Elaine said, 'but as you know it's the quarterly audit at the practice then and James and I will be bogged down with it all day Saturday.'

'I'll be fine on my own,' Laurel told her. 'If I have to have more skin grafts it won't be so soon.' With that she climbed the rest of the stairs and went to bed.

Sleep came fast. She was too tired to dwell on the day's events, but on awakening the next morning they came crowding back, and as she lay reliving them the worst thought that came to mind was knowing that it was going to be a long time before she ceased to see incidents like yesterday's as moments of terror…

She'd been involved in a nightmare happening not so long ago due to the duplicity and carelessness of others, and it was going to be etched in her mind *and* on her body for ever more. Now she was nervous at the drop of a hat.

The *best* part of the day had been coming out of the faint to find David looking down at her with his eyes full of concern. She didn't deserve him, she thought dejectedly. She was continually disrupting his life, blowing hot and cold and attracting catastrophes like a magnet.

Yet when the phone beside her bed rang and it was

him, every other thought was wiped out in the pleasure of hearing his voice.

'Just checking that you are all right after yesterday's trauma,' he said.

'Yes, I'm fine,' she told him. 'Are you all right?'

'Of course. I'm all right when you're all right.' She could tell from his voice that he was smiling. 'But promise me that you'll have a complete rest today. As your doctor I recommend no exertion. Dad and I won't be around. We're going to spend the day at the site as he's going home tomorrow and wants to get another day in on the walls. He's coming back soon, but for now he wants to make sure that his boat, *The Sea Nymph*, is all right. She's the woman in his life.' *And a lot easier to handle than the one in mine*, he thought.

Laurel's mind was moving in a different direction. Jonas's boat might be the love of his life, but it would be no good for holding close in the night. What if Elaine did decide to go to Cornwall?

When Laurel arrived at the surgery on Monday morning Georgina's husband, Ben Allardyce, and the father of baby Arran was in Reception, reading a poster that someone had put up over the weekend advertising a charity walk that was to take place the coming Saturday.

When she halted beside him he said, 'Georgina and I would love to take Arran on this walk, but the terrain gets a bit rugged out there.'

'So couldn't one of you go, and the other stay behind with Arran?' she questioned.

Ben's expression was sombre. 'I think not. We spent

years apart for reasons I won't go into, and now every moment together is so precious that we do everything as a family. What about you, Laurel? Are you into walking?'

'It would give you the chance to see more of the Cheshire countryside, should you want to,' a voice said from behind, and when she turned David was there. She watched as he added his name to the list of volunteers and then, raising a questioning eyebrow, passed her the pen.

It went without saying that she was going to write her name under his, she thought. Just the mere sight of him always sent common sense flying out of the window.

The patients were arriving and that was the end of the discussion, but when surgery was over she caught him as he was about to set off on his calls and asked, 'So where does the charity walk take us? Do I need to wear walking boots and suchlike?'

'I would say so,' he informed her, and then he re-membered the day when she'd tottered off the train in high heels. 'Whatever you do, don't come in your sti-lettos. Part of it is over rough terrain and if there has been much rain beforehand it can be boggy.'

'So you haven't forgotten the day I arrived in Willowmere?' she teased as he opened his car door and slid into the driver's seat.

'Of course I haven't,' he said in wry amusement. 'How could I? You were like a package that came without instructions or warnings.'

On that he prepared to drive off into the summer morning. Resisting the temptation to get in beside him,

Laurel went back to blood tests, injections and the rest of the duties of a practice nurse.

It was late afternoon and the second surgery was in full spate when David came into the nurses' room and said, 'I have the vicar's wife outside. Could I have an ECG, please?'

Gillian had some time owing and was due to finish early, so when Catherine Beesley presented herself it was Laurel who greeted her and explained the procedure.

'I came because I thought I had a hernia,' she explained as Laurel was positioning the rubber discs on her chest, stomach and feet, 'but when I mentioned to Dr Trelawney that for the first time ever I'm aware of my heartbeat all the time and it is quite fast, he said that must be dealt with first. I was amazed when he said the test could be done here in the surgery. I was expecting to have to go to St Gabriel's.'

'Just a short time ago that would have been the case,' Laurel told her, 'but not now. We're all high tech and will have the result of the ECG in a matter of minutes, printed out for Dr Trelawney to see.

'We will be in direct communication with the cardiology department at the hospital while you're wired up, and they will decide whether you have a problem or not.'

The vicar's wife was a sensible, homely sort of woman and as the equipment registered six level beats and then a hop, skip and jump, it didn't take a genius to work out that something was not quite right.

'The test has shown that you have two heart problems,' David explained when she went back into his room for the results. 'The first is that the electric impulses of it are not working correctly, and the other, which we do come across now and then, is that at some time in the past you've had a minor heart attack.'

'If that's the case, I don't know when!' Catherine exclaimed in disbelief. 'Are these two things anything to worry about?' she questioned. 'The vicar relies on me so much with his work in the parish, I haven't time to be ill.'

'I don't think either are anything too serious,' he told her, 'but I'm going to arrange for you to see a cardiologist, and now if you'll go back to the nurses' room I'll examine the area where you feel you might have pulled something out of place. The nurse will tell you what to take off and will be there all the time for reassurance.'

After the examination, he smiled reassuringly at Catherine. 'Nothing out of the ordinary there,' he said. 'Just a bit of muscle strain, but be sure to come back to see me if it persists.'

When she'd gone, looking somewhat dazed, Laurel said, 'Who would be a vicar's wife? In spite of being told unexpectedly that she has a heart problem, Catherine Beesley remembered to ask if any of us have put our names down for the charity walk.'

'And did you tell her that the best ramblers have signed up for it?' he quipped as he went back to the rest of his patients.

'I don't want to wear boots. They'll hurt my feet,' she said to his disappearing back.

He swivelled round. 'Strong shoes, then, and don't forget a hat in case there's a downpour.'

It all sounded wildly exciting, she thought as she went back into the nurses' room to tidy up.

Laurel awoke on Saturday morning to the sound of heavy rain and when she padded across to the window, sure enough, there was a downpour pelting out of dismal skies.

There was no pleasure to be had from the lake sparkling in the distance today, she decided, and was turning away when she caught her breath. Rising above the willow trees, some of them huge with age, were the sturdy grey slates of the roof of David's house.

It was a sight that she would have expected to be excited by, but instead she felt lost and lonely. She had dreamed that David had married the midwife, Lizzie, who was readily available, with a house full of babies that she'd delivered herself. In the dream, Elaine had laughed as she sailed into salt spray with Jonas out on the open sea, while she, Laurel, had fallen into the role of the perennial godmother-cum-maiden aunt with drawers full of high-necked jumpers.

As she caught a glimpse of herself in the dressing-table mirror she thought wistfully that at least she wouldn't end up wearing a wig. Her red-gold hair had grown longer and she rejoiced every time she saw it.

While she was in London she intended visiting her regular hairdresser and having it styled. Hopefully, when she came back, David might be impressed.

When she went down to breakfast, Elaine observed her expression and said, 'I know, the weather is dreadful, but it's early yet. By the time you are ready to leave, it might have cleared up.'

'I wish you were coming instead of going shopping,' Laurel told her.

'You won't need me around while David is there,' she replied. 'I'm not going on the walk because I don't want to cramp your style.'

'And what style would that be?' she enquired flatly, nibbling on a piece of toast.

Elaine's mind had switched to basics. 'Don't forget to make a packed lunch and take a bottle of water with you. Ramblers often stop to eat miles away from anywhere.'

Laurel was observing her in sudden consternation. 'A rucksack!' she exclaimed.

'I've got one you can use.'

'No, I don't mean that. I can't stand anything rubbing against my back.'

'I never thought of that,' Elaine said slowly. 'You'll have to carry it in your hand, so be sure to just take the basics.'

The weather had reduced the numbers of those who'd signed up for the charity walk and there were only a dozen or so stalwarts waiting outside the village hall when Elaine dropped Laurel off at the starting point.

The rain had eased off for the moment and a watery sun was filtering through the clouds as David came striding out of the cottage suitably clad in sensible clothes.

She saw that he was casting a dubious glance over her and when he reached her side he said in a low voice, 'The rucksack is made to be strapped on to your back for convenience.'

'Yes, I do know that,' she told him coolly, 'but I find it easier to carry it in my hand.'

He shrugged. 'OK. Just don't trip over it, that's all.'

'I won't,' she said sweetly, and he laughed.

'All right, I get the message, but at the risk of being told that you're quite capable of taking care of yourself, and knowing that not to be so, I suggest that you stay by me all the time. There are some dangerous places up there among the peaks, especially if a mist comes down, which it often does after rain.'

'Yes, all right,' she agreed meekly, having no intention of being anywhere else other than close by his side. After all, that was why she was there. It was to be with him that she was going to spend the day tramping around the countryside.

The vicar and his long-suffering wife were in charge and they explained that the route they were going to take was past Willow Lake, through the next village, up the hill road, and onto the moors for a short distance, eventually descending at the other side of Willowmere, having done ten miles in all.

'And in case any of you are apprehensive regarding minor injuries that you might sustain during the walk, Dr Trelawney has a comprehensively kitted out first-aid box in his rucksack,' the vicar announced jovially.

'So that's what we're here for,' Laurel whispered, 'to render first aid.'

'Not necessarily,' he replied. 'I'm here because I want to spend the day with you, and I hope that you feel the same.'

There was a mischievous twinkle in her eye. 'What? That I want to spend the day with me?'

'You know what I mean. Are *you* here because of *me*?'

'I might be.'

He rolled his eyes heavenwards and took her hand in his as the walkers set off on what was going to be the easiest few miles.

After a long dry spell the rain had brought freshness to the air. The green fields looked greener, raindrops sparkled on leaves and flowers, and as a grey squirrel climbed quickly up a nearby tree at their approach and disappeared amongst its branches, Laurel wondered how she could have been reluctant to come to live amongst all this.

As they passed the lake she and David exchanged secret smiles at the surprised comments of the rest of the party when they saw that Water Meetings House was rising out of the disrepair of years, and as the next village came into sight with the hill road just beyond, there was a happy camaraderie amongst those heading for the moors that lay beneath the shadow of the rugged peaks.

CHAPTER EIGHT

As THE walking party strode up towards the moors in no particular kind of order, the promise of the day was faltering again. The sky was darkening with rainclouds and all too soon it was pelting down on them.

They were on the edge of the moors now, with the peaks towering above them and steep gullies on either side of the path. Laurel and David were at the back of the single file of walkers. It was a time for care and caution, and even the two high-spirited youths who'd come along for a lark and were just in front of them were treading with caution when a moorland sheep, disturbed by the sound of heavy boots on the rocky path and the voices of those passing its grazing place, came careering out onto the path in a fright and ran straight towards one of the youngsters.

Startled, the lad stepped back to avoid the impact, teetering on the edge of the steep drop behind him for a second, then lost his balance completely and fell with a frantic cry into the gully below, where he landed beside loose debris that had fallen from the rock face over the years.

'Go and get the vicar!' David bellowed to the lad's friend, who was standing dumbstruck beside them as the sheep changed direction and went careering down the path they'd just come up.

Turning to Laurel, he thrust his mobile phone into her hand. 'Phone for an ambulance, but get our exact position from the vicar before you do. Better still, ask for a helicopter.' He looked down at the still figure at the bottom of the gully. 'They'll never bring him up on a stretcher. It's too steep and treacherous with bogs and dangerous overhangs of rock all over the place. I'm going down there while you direct operations up here, Laurel.'

'I'm coming with you!' she cried as the rest of the party came back after being told what had happened. 'Someone else can do that. I'm a nurse, for heaven's sake, and I'll be needed. Have you got the first-aid kit?'

'Yes, it's in my rucksack, and it would seem that I've got you too,' he said dryly. 'Do you ever do what you're told?'

'It depends on the circumstances,' she said, already taking note of what lay ahead on the way down to the unfortunate youth.

'Is an ambulance coming?' the vicar asked as he joined them at that moment.

'Helicopter,' David said tersely, as Laurel handed the phone to the panting clergyman and began to ease herself carefully down the steep hillside that in parts was made up of jagged rocks.

He was behind her in a flash and when she held out her hand to him David took it in his firm grip and together they began what was to be a perilously slow descent.

There was no way they dared rush it, no matter how badly injured the lad was, he thought as they picked their way amongst nettles in the undergrowth and stepped over fallen tree branches littering the place. There were rock falls everywhere and the overhangs above had a menacing atmosphere about them.

But there was no point in dwelling on things that might or might not happen. They had a life to save and if the frightened sheep had done the youth no favours in sending him careering over the edge, the Fates weren't being too unkind to him. They were sending him a doctor and a nurse—if he was still alive.

He was breathing but unconscious when they got to him and as David wrenched the rucksack off his back and bent to examine him, Laurel brought out the first-aid kit and prepared to follow orders.

'Breathing seems OK, pulse rather weak,' he said as the rain continued to fall in torrents, 'and from the odd angle that he's lying at I'd say that both his legs are fractured.'

Laurel was crouching over him to protect him from the rain, while trying to stem blood gushing from a head wound with one hand and unbuttoning the lad's shirt at the neck with the other to help his breathing, and David began strapping the boy's legs together.

He was pale and shivering, his skin cold and clammy from shock and the unwelcome downpour. David was taking off his waterproof jacket and then removing the thick sweater underneath it that was warm from his body heat and placing it over him, but they weren't enough to cover his injured legs.

Laurel knew that she had to do the same, whatever the

consequences, and followed suit, taking off her coat and removing the sweater underneath to provide more warmth.

David was bending over him, checking pulse and heartbeat again, and when he glanced up momentarily she'd replaced her jacket, but not before he'd caught a brief glimpse of scarring.

He made no comment, but as he bent to his task again she'd seen his expression and wondered what was going through his mind. Whatever it was he was halfway to knowing she'd received serious burns to the top half of her back and she wondered what he would have to say when or if he saw the full extent of them.

She could hear the sound of a helicopter approaching and in the relief of the moment everything else was forgotten as they waited to see if the pilot would be able to find enough space to land.

While he was hovering they continued to monitor the young victim and David gave a satisfied nod as his body heat began to rise and the shivering lessened.

She'd worked with a lot of doctors since she'd taken up nursing, Laurel thought, but there had never before been a situation as rewarding as this, working with David as they tried to save a life.

Maybe it was because she hadn't been in love with those other guys. Whatever it was, she wouldn't forget today. They were united in their professions, perfectly in tune. If only she was as sure of herself and him in the rest of their lives.

The pilot was flying as low as he could and bellowing above the noise of the engine, 'There's nowhere to land. We're going to have to winch him up. A paramedic is coming down to you now and one of the crew is going to follow him to supervise the winching.'

Almost as he spoke the door opened and the paramedic they'd been promised came swinging down on the end of a winch line, followed seconds later by a member of the crew.

When they landed beside them David explained briefly that there were suspected leg fractures, a head wound, cuts and grazes from the fall, and possible shock that they'd prevented for the moment with their own clothing.

'We've immobilised his legs to avoid further injury to the fractured bones,' he said as they prepared to winch the lad up to the helicopter, and the paramedic nodded.

'OK, Doc. We'll get him to A and E as fast as we can. He's had a bad fall but it was the kid's lucky day that you people were on the spot. I've seen you somewhere before, haven't I?' he said as they fastened the patient onto a lightweight stretcher and prepared to lift him upwards. 'Didn't you used to be at St Gabriel's?'

'Yes, that's right,' he said absently as the winch line began to work.

'And now you're a country GP,' Laurel said, as they began the slow climb back up to the road above.

'Yes, I am without any doubt,' he agreed. 'And what about you? Are you going to feel the pull of the city when you go back there next weekend?'

'I won't know until I get there, will I?' she said, grateful that any comments he was going to make about what he'd seen were being put on hold. 'But Elaine won't let me go back there yet. She says I have to stay here until I have roses in my cheeks.'

The top still seemed a long way off and when they stopped to rest David said, 'You are an amazing woman, Laurel. Do you know that?'

'Why?' she asked, acutely aware that her top coat was chafing her shoulders under the scarf. She was longing to throw it off but what would she wear then? Her jumper was stuffed inside the rucksack.

'Surely you don't need to ask! You faint at the slightest thing, yet in a situation as dangerous as this has been you don't bat an eyelid.'

'I only perform well when I'm centre stage,' she said with another shiver. 'Although I think you outclassed me on this occasion so I'll step back when they're handing out the medals.'

He sighed. 'I give up. Why are you always on the defensive when I say nice things to you?'

'It must be because I'm not used to it.'

The rest of the walkers were peering over the edge of the drop, watching them climb up, and before David could question that oblique remark someone shouted, 'Watch out, we're throwing you a rope. Tie it around your waists and we'll haul you up.'

When it came down she eyed it hesitantly, imagining the discomfort it was going to cause, but it was the lesser of two evils, she supposed, and let David tie it around her and then attach it to himself.

'I suggest that we carry on with the walk,' someone said when they had all reassembled beside the winding road. 'The lad's been taken to hospital faster than he could have ever dreamed. There's nothing else we can do.'

The vicar was about to comment, but as he was clearing his throat another member of the group said, 'You know who he is, don't you?' Turning to the injured lad's companion, he said, 'Tell them who your mate is, laddie.'

'Alistair's father is Lord Derringham. I'm staying up at the house with him while his parents are abroad on holiday. I'll have to let them know he's been hurt, I suppose,' he said gloomily. 'We only came on the walk for a laugh.'

'His Lordship's son? Oh, dear!' exclaimed the vicar. 'We must indeed let him know what has happened, but not out here. The reception is not good for imparting a message of such urgency. My wife and I will go back to Kestrel Court with you so that we are there for support when you make the call, or maybe we should put it into the hands of the estate manager?'

'That's Gillian's husband,' David told Laurel. 'He'll be the best person to break the bad news, and they can tell His Lordship to speak to us if he wants on-the-spot information, though the best plan would be for his parents to ring St Gabriel's for news of their son's condition.

'And now you need to go home for a hot drink, a bath and some clean clothes,' he said, still with no reference to what he'd seen. For the information of the rest of the party he added, 'We're off to get cleaned up and dried out.'

She nodded thankfully as her coat was making her back sore.

'Is Elaine going to be in when we get to the lodge?' he asked as they retraced their steps beneath a warm sun that would have been most welcome when they'd been at the bottom of the gully. At least it was helping them to dry out now.

'She said she was going shopping,' Laurel replied, hoping Elaine would be there so that the inevitable questions would be postponed, but her aunt was nowhere to be seen.

'I'll make hot drinks while you shower and change your clothes,' David said. 'Then we need to talk, Laurel, don't we?'

She nodded mutely and went to do as he suggested.

When he was alone, David's mind went back to what he'd caught a glimpse of on her shoulder when she'd been removing her jumper to cover the lad.

He was no fool, knew the scars left by burns when he saw them, and he wondered, as he'd done a few times, if she'd been the victim of domestic abuse. Was that why she was afraid of getting close to him? It was a likely theory. There was the fractured knee, the redness of her hands, the short hair she so clearly hated... Had it been caused by her ex?

The thought of anyone hurting her was too horrendous to contemplate, but he was a doctor and knew that kind of thing happened all the time, sometimes in the least expected relationships.

When she came down scrubbed, clean and dressed in dry clothes, he handed her a hot toddy and waited while she drank it before saying gravely, 'I got sight of the kind of scarring that serious burns leave when you were taking your sweater off down in the gully. How did that come about?'

'I was caught up in a situation that I couldn't get out

of,' she said in a low voice. 'The result being that I feel ugly all the time.'

So he hadn't been wrong. 'Domestic abuse?' he questioned gently, and watched her mouth go slack with surprise.

'No. Nothing like *that*!' she exclaimed, and as he waited for what was to come next he heard Elaine's key in the door and groaned silently. The moment that was going to bring clarity to their relationship had been there. Now it was gone and the way she greeted her aunt was proof enough that Laurel was relieved.

'What is this I hear about Alistair Derringham having a serious accident?' Elaine said as she came bustling into the sitting room. 'They were talking about it when I stopped off at the post office for some stamps, and I was told that the two of you risked your own necks to treat the poor lad at the bottom of some gully on the moors.'

'I'll let Laurel tell you all about it, Elaine,' he said, getting to his feet. He was accepting that he was going to have to wait a little longer to find out what had happened to Laurel in the past. At least he knew that the Darius fellow hadn't hurt her—well, physically at least.

She went to the door with him to say goodbye and as if the conversation that Elaine had interrupted had been about the day's events in general said, 'Shall I ring St Gabriel's to enquire after Alistair, or will you?'

'I'll do it,' he offered, taking note of how pale and exhausted she looked. It was making him think he should have waited until another time to ask about the scarring on her shoulder. He was aching to offer comfort, but he'd done that once before and Laurel hadn't wanted to know.

But after all they'd been through on the ill-fated walk he couldn't just stride off without letting her see that he cared, cared a lot, and would continue to do so whether she wanted him to or not.

Taking her limp hand in his, he bent and planted a kiss on the rough palm, then curled her fingers around it protectively and told her softly, 'Don't worry if you lose it. There are lots more kisses just waiting for their moment.'

Before she could reply he'd gone, tall and straight in the summer afternoon, and she had to hold on to the doorpost to stop herself from running after him.

She gazed at the hand he had kissed, aware that David had only seen a small part of the damaged skin of her back and shoulders. He'd known what had caused it, of course, but hadn't been aware of the extent of it. That was something he had yet to discover if ever she could bring herself to show him after Darius's unconcealed revulsion, but for now that was how it stood. Maybe when she'd been to London on Saturday to see the consultant, she might see the way ahead clearer.

When he phoned St Gabriel's, David was told that Alistair was conscious and had just come back from Radiography, where his leg fractures had been X-rayed. He would shortly be operated on. When he asked about the head wound he was told that no internal bleeding had been shown inside the skull, but the patient was still being monitored for shock.

'The lad's father is on the board of governors here,' the doctor in A and E told him, 'and has already been on the phone from some faraway place. He was ringing from the airport where he and his family were about to board the first available flight.

'I can't see roast lamb being on the menu for some time to come for that household,' he said. 'Or on the other hand that might be where they will prefer to see it, on a plate.

'He's got a lot of heavy bruising and cuts and scratches as well as the more serious injuries,' he went on to say, 'but it's amazing that a doctor and nurse were on the spot. At least it's one thing in his favour. There's no telling what would have been the outcome if the two of you hadn't been there.

'Alistair says that he's always being told off by his father for things that he is to blame for, but this time His Lordship can't complain as he did nothing wrong, *and* in any case it was one of his sheep. He owns that part of the moors.'

It was Wednesday morning and James had called David and Laurel into his consulting room for a quick chat.

He was smiling when they went in and Laurel thought with a sinking feeling that he was about to tell them that his sister and her husband were on their way home, which would be joy for him and the children but could mean an abrupt ending to her short stay as practice nurse if Anna wanted to take up her old job at the surgery. She accepted that she was employed on a temporary arrangement but had been hoping that it wouldn't be this brief.

She was wrong in her surmising and her eyes widened when James said, 'I've called you both in to give you some good news.' As she and David exchanged puzzled glances he said, 'Lord and Lady Derringham are calling in later this morning to thank you for what you did for their son, and while he's here he wants to discuss making some kind of gesture in a practical way connected with village health care. What do you think of that?'

'Amazing!' David exclaimed. 'We were only doing what we've been trained to do.'

'Maybe, but in very difficult and dangerous circumstances and His Lordship is aware of that.'

'The main thing is, how is Alistair?' Laurel said.

'He has both legs in plaster and the head wound will take some time to heal, but his parents are aware that it could have been much worse if it hadn't been for you two.'

'How about a complete makeover of the surgery?' she suggested.

'I'm not sure that His Lordship has something like that in mind,' James said. 'He might be thinking of just a plaque on the wall or something similar.'

'I hope not!' David exclaimed. 'Save that kind of thing for someone who deserves it, but we need to hang on until he's been and I think Elaine should be in on it.'

The Derringhams were in James's office for an hour, and afterwards they came out and thanked Laurel and David profusely for what they'd done for their son. To Laurel's surprise they'd had a toddler with them and Her Ladyship explained, 'Alistair is our eldest and Oliver, who is a year old, is our youngest. In the middle we have twin girls.'

'I wanted to do something for health care in the village to express our gratitude,' her husband said, 'and

I intend to be generous. So we've talked with James about funding a much-needed community midwife position based in the surgery.'

James nodded and smiled. 'This is a great chance to develop our antenatal care and is something we've wanted to do for ages. Rather than mothers from here and the surrounding villages having to travel to St Gabriel's, they can visit a midwife here and have the best of care on their doorsteps, so to speak. When Lord Derringham suggested the maternity clinic idea to the hospital trust they were all for it, especially if someone on their board of governors is prepared to fund it.

'They've already recommended a midwife for the position. What do you think about the idea?'

'Fantastic,' David said.

'Incredibly generous.' Elaine and Laurel echoed his sentiments.

'The midwife referred to would be Lizzie Carmichael, I think,' David told him. 'I've seen her at work and she would be an excellent choice.'

'So we are agreed, then?' His Lordship said, and observing their delighted expressions went on to say, 'I am also funding the refurbishment of a room for the clinic, and the equipment you will need. We have a young family of our own and both my wife and I are keen to see that mothers-to-be receive the best possible care.'

'That will be just what we need!' James exclaimed when the Derringhams had left to go and visit their son. 'We hope our brand-new maternity clinic will be up and running as soon as possible.'

* * *

When morning surgery was over James called all the staff into the big office below stairs and said, 'I'm inviting you all to Bracken House tonight to drink a toast to Laurel and David, who by being the kind of people they are have brought about this amazing offer from His Lordship.

'A community midwife in the village will be like a dream come true. He is a very generous man. So eight-thirty tonight if you can make it,' he concluded amid delighted applause.

Laurel's glance met David's deep blue gaze as they all went back to their duties and she knew that this was where she wanted to be, here in Willowmere with David and Elaine and the friends she'd made at the surgery, but with him most of all, in the house by the lake that was rising out of the rubble.

'What's wrong?' Elaine asked as they dressed to go to James's house that evening. 'You've hardly said a word since we came home. Is it the hospital visit on Saturday that is on your mind?'

Laurel managed a smile. 'No, whatever they say it won't make that much difference, will it? More skin grafts can only bring a slight improvement.'

'But you'll agree if they suggest it?'

'Yes, of course,' she replied flatly.

'It's the David situation that is really getting to you, isn't it? You are crazy, Laurel. That man is a king among men. If he loves you it won't matter to him that you have severe scarring. He will want you for what you are.'

'It sounds so simple when you put it like that,' she

protested, 'but suppose that he wants me for what *he* wants me to be and I don't live up to it. I know he isn't like Darius, but you remember what Jonas said, don't you? That the American woman was very beautiful and they made a striking couple. No one is ever going to say that when he's with me. An odd couple maybe, but never striking.'

CHAPTER NINE

IT WAS a merry gathering assembled there when they arrived at Bracken House, but as Laurel's glance went round the room she realised that there was no David. As if she read her thoughts, Gillian said, 'David has gone to collect his father from the station. He's back for another visit.'

'Oh, I see,' she said, and wondered if Jonas's return was connected with dry stone walling or Elaine, who was chatting to Ben and Georgina who had brought baby Arran along. Could it be that he'd returned to cement his friendship with the aunt who was also her loving friend?

More likely it was a bit of both, she thought whimsically, and was trying to work out what relation she would be to David if Elaine married his father when he came striding into the room. Now it was his turn to glance around those present until he found her standing by the window with a glass in her hand.

He came across immediately and said, 'Hi. Did they tell you where I was?'

'Yes,' she replied, smiling up at him. 'Your father has

come back, which makes me wonder what has brought him to Willowmere once more—whether it's the house or Elaine. If she is the reason, what would *our* relationship be if they tied the knot?'

He was observing her with raised brows. 'You are racing on a bit, aren't you? Elaine is a lovely woman, but Dad has never shown any interest in anyone else since he lost my mother and that's a long, long time ago. But going back to what you were thinking—' and he was laughing now '—if that ever happened, Elaine would be my stepmother, my dad your step-uncle, and we would be, er...I'm not sure, step-cousins maybe?'

He had ideas of a much deeper relationship than that for them, but the snag was did Laurel have the same yearnings?

But at least she was with him now, looking happy enough. He hoped she was beginning to trust him. That she was beginning to feel that whatever it was that she hadn't been able to discuss with him would be easier to bear if he was there to share it.

He loved her, wanted her as he'd never wanted anyone before, and if it took the rest of his life to convince her of that, it was how it was going to be.

He hadn't forgotten what his father had said when his engagement to Caroline had fallen apart. 'You will know when the right one comes along,' he'd told him, and it was true. It was as if he'd been hit by a bolt from the blue.

Even on that first day when she'd come wobbling off the train in her high heels he'd had a feeling that his life had changed, though at the time he'd thought it was for the worse as the strange female who was Elaine's niece had been everywhere he turned in the days that followed.

He often smiled when he thought back to when they'd first met. Laurel had turned out to be the most interesting and appealing woman he'd ever known.

She was observing Georgina's baby, he noticed, gurgling in his father's arms, and he thought he saw regret in her glance, yet why? Was it because she had no partner to make a baby with, or for some other reason that he knew nothing of, connected with the secret that was weighing her down?

'Let's go outside for a breath of air,' he suggested, and taking her hand in his led her into the garden at the back of the house and to a secluded gazebo at the far end.

'Why have you brought me out here?' she asked.

'It's not to seduce you, if that's what you're thinking,' he said lightly. 'I wanted to get you on your own for a few moments to find out what your arrangements for Saturday are, such as what train you're travelling to London on.'

'Why? Are you coming to see me off?' she teased.

'Do you want me to?'

'Er…yes, if you feel like getting up at the crack of dawn. I'm going on the quarter past seven train from Manchester.'

'No problem. I don't suppose it's any use my asking why you're going to London.'

'I told you. I have an appointment, a long-term one. I'll be back in the evening.' Steering the conversation away from her comings and goings, she asked, 'How is the house coming along? It's a few days since I was up there but I'll be back on the job on Sunday if you want me to continue helping with the garden.'

'Of course I do, but I think I should find you some thing less strenuous, such as choosing wall coverings, carpets and furniture. The builder has given me a completion date for the end of August.'

'So soon!' she exclaimed.

'Yes, the windows and doors are in, the plasterers have finished, and joiners and plumbers have taken over now. I have a decorator on hold so the end is in sight.

'The builder has quite a few contracts in the pipeline and hasn't let the grass grow under his feet, though that would seem to refer to the garden more than the house. And when it's all finished, *are* you still going to help me choose furnishings and fabrics?'

'I'd love to,' she said with a lump in her throat.

When he'd first suggested it weeks ago she'd been mildly surprised but had thought nothing of it, but now everything had changed and it would be a bittersweet experience if she never had the chance to live there with him.

As he watched the expressions cross her face David thought it would be so easy to tell her that the house would be empty and silent without her there. But first Laurel had to find the confidence to confide in him without any persuasion on his part, and, as he kept telling himself, he could wait a little longer.

And while that was happening he was going to buy a ring with emeralds to match her eyes and diamonds to sparkle as she sparkled when she was happy. As there was nothing wrong with *his* confidence he intended to see it on her finger sooner or later.

When he looked up Elaine was beckoning to them from the patio doors and they left the gazebo reluctantly and went back to join the others.

'James is going to propose a toast to Lord Derringham and the hero and heroine of the peaks and gullies,' she said, 'so be prepared.'

As they went inside the practice staff circled them and raised their glasses as James said, 'Will you all please drink a toast to the generosity of Lord Derringham?' And when they'd done that he went on to say, 'And to Laurel and David, who acted as true medical professionals.'

'I'm going your way,' David said as the gathering began to break up. 'I want to call at The Pheasant to make sure that Dad has settled in all right. We had no time to talk when I picked him up at the station with only minutes to spare before I was due here.'

When they were about to separate outside the pub he said, 'It's been a great day, hasn't it? A locally based midwife promised for the village, and the practice staff all together on a rare social occasion at James's house. I don't know about you, but I felt as if I really belonged as I haven't been here much longer than you.'

'The village has a timeless magic of its own,' she said. 'I never imagined I would ever hear myself say it, but if I had to choose it would be here that I would want to live.' Though only with you, her heart said. And before she proclaimed it out loud she left him to go and find Jonas and walked slowly back to Glenside Lodge.

Elaine was there before her and as they chatted over a bedtime drink she said, 'Georgina told me tonight that

when Ben first came to join us at the surgery she took
him with her on home visits to help him to get to know
the area. When they were driving along that same road
up on the moors, a sheep ran in front of the car and she
had to brake sharply to avoid an accident.'

'I don't suppose much can be done about that sort of
thing if they graze free up there,' Laurel commented,
'but that won't be much comfort to Alistair when he's
hobbling about with two legs in casts. The only solution
would be to have fencing along both sides of the road,
or for walkers to take less hazardous routes.'

Once they'd exhausted the subject of the lost
sheep, she said flatly, 'David has asked me why I'm
going to London.'

'And did you tell him?'

'No, I want to put what the consultant has to say in
perspective before I do anything else. David knows I've
got scarring, but not to what extent, and when I come
back I'm going to show him. I'm going to put my dith-
ering days behind me, even though we only can boast
half of a striking pair.'

'Put that comment behind you,' Elaine insisted.
'Jonas didn't mean anything by it. David will have seen
worse scars than yours, bad as they are.'

'Maybe, but not on someone he might want to make
love to.' And with that dismal thought the last thing in
her mind she went up to bed.

On the Friday night before she was due to go to London
there was to be a barn supper at Meadowlands, a farm on
the edge of the village, and when Laurel asked what it

would be like she was told that there would be lots of wholesome food in the form of crusty bread, various cheeses, home-made pickles and sauces, savouries, apple pies and lots of fresh fruit from various orchards, along with country and western dancing to work up an appetite.

'So are you going to go?' Gillian asked when the vicar's wife came in, selling tickets. Catherine Beesley had had the cardiogram that David had arranged and was waiting to see the cardiologist for the result. In the meantime it would seem that she was still busy with parish work and would continue to be so.

'I suppose so,' Laurel said half-heartedly. She knew that Elaine would be there and maybe Jonas as the light was beginning to fade earlier in the evenings with mid-summer's day having been and gone some weeks ago, and he wouldn't be able to see to carry on with the task that he'd set himself up at the house.

Every time she thought about what *her* input was going to be in the resurrection of it she couldn't help but feel pleasure at the prospect of being asked to make suggestions about the interior, but there was always the feeling behind it that she was going to be on the outside of things.

Yet it didn't stop her from pretending that she wouldn't be, and she would conjure up visions of children with their mother's odd colouring or their father's dark handsomeness playing in the garden, or sleeping in one the spacious bedrooms, but always the memory of a certain night on the wards, its aftermath, and the undeniable evidence of it came to spoil it.

On the morning after they'd all gathered at James's

house David said, 'Have you ever been to a barn supper, Laurel?'

She laughed. 'No. Until I came to Willowmere I didn't know what a barn was. There is going to be one on Friday in someone's actual barn, I believe.'

'Yes, and from what my patients tell me it is not to be missed, so are we going?'

'I don't know,' she replied, as if the question hadn't made her heart beat faster. 'I have an early start on Saturday morning.'

'I am hardly likely to forget that, but we don't have to stay late, do we?'

'No, I suppose not, and it will be an experience.' She couldn't pass by the chance of spending extra time with him before the day of revelation approached.

The reaction of Darius when he'd seen her back was imprinted in her mind and she knew that whatever David felt he would conceal it. He would never be so unkind, yet she wasn't expecting him to be the same afterwards.

There would be lots of people at the barn supper so there would be no opportunities for heart-to-heart talking on *that* occasion, and in any case she was going to wait until she'd been to London to see if there was any chance of improvement of the damaged skin in the future.

Once again Elaine was helping with the arrangements for the occasion that everyone seemed to be looking forward to and had gone on ahead when David called for Laurel on the Friday night and found her waiting at the gate dressed in jeans, a checked shirt and high boots.

He smiled when he saw that her outfit was almost a

replica of his own and offered her one of the two Stetson-type hats he was carrying.

'I found these in a cupboard at the cottage,' he said, 'and thought we may as well go the whole way for the country and western.'

'Why not?' she said, sparkling up at him. He was such a joy to be with and he cared for her, she thought mistily, though she sometimes felt that his feelings were more protective than passionate.

They had a wonderful time in the huge barn, which was clean and fragrant. The atmosphere was relaxed and friendly, the food plentiful and good to eat, and the music foot-tapping and rhythmic.

Jonas wasn't there and when she questioned David about his absence he said, 'I tried to get Dad to come, but I think he was a bit shy. He's more at ease with boats than a lot of people. I'll take you to Cornwall some time if you like. It's a small fishing village where I was brought up and it has its own particular charm, like the rest of the county.'

When there was no reply forthcoming he said wryly, 'You're not exactly bubbling over with enthusiasm at the suggestion.'

'That's because I'm not sure what the future holds,' she told him awkwardly, 'but it's nice of you to offer.'

In one of his rare moments of irritation he replied, 'I'm not trying to be "nice", Laurel. I can't think of a more inane word to describe me. I have much stronger motives in suggesting it. For one thing I'd like to show you where my mother is buried, as you are taking such an interest in her old home. It's on a headland looking out to sea, not far from Dad's cottage.

'It would seem that between us we have a triangle of locations that mean a lot to us. Willowmere, Cornwall and London, and I have to say that it is this village that comes top of the list.'

She couldn't agree more, Laurel thought, but she wouldn't want to live there without him in her life. She could tell from the way he was talking that David had his own ideas about that. He was wanting to be with her more and more and it was so hard to say no when it was what she wanted too…

But she had nightmares about saying yes if he asked her to marry him and then him finding out on their wedding night that she was less than desirable.

It was why she had to tell him soon, before it went any further between them, and not having changed her mind on that score she made the most of the night in the barn. She danced every dance with the hat on her head and the boots on her feet, until David protested he needed a drink and went to get them glasses of cider on tap from a wooden cask.

They left before it was over with the early start in mind, and as he walked her home David thought wryly of the number of times they had separated at the gates of the old stone lodge.

The day couldn't come soon enough when they lived in Water Meetings House, together for always. He didn't care how much Laurel shied away when he asked her to marry him. He would woo her until she had no refusals or doubts left.

He held her close for a brief moment as they parted, releasing her before she had the chance to wriggle out of his arms, and said, 'So I'll see you at the station at what time in the morning?'

'I need to get the six-thirty local train to get me to Manchester in time for the inter-city connection,' she told him, 'but you don't have to come, David. Why not have a lie-in?'

He shook his head. When was Laurel going to get the message that he wanted to be with her every minute of the day…and in the night too?

Reaching up, she brushed her lips against his cheek but he kept his arms by his sides, and as he strode off down the lane she watched him without moving until he was out of sight.

He was waiting for her in early sunlight when she arrived at the small station that Walter looked after so painstakingly, and as she walked towards him he said, 'So you didn't oversleep?'

'Does it look like it?' she parried. 'Though I don't mind telling you it was an effort to get up after all the dancing and the cider.'

'I'm coming with you as far as Manchester,' he told her. 'I want to do some shopping.'

'Fine,' she said, and went to book her ticket in the small office at the entrance to the platform.

'Aren't you the young lady who helped the doctor take care of His Lordship's son?' Walter asked from behind the glass that separated him from the travelling public.

'Er…yes,' she replied, and thought if she'd been in London she could have been the Queen of Sheba for all he would have known.

'The village folks have really taken you to their hearts after that,' he informed her, and as she prepared to join David, who was standing just a few feet away, he said, 'Have a nice day, my dear.'

'That is what it's all about, isn't it?' she said as she and David walked along the platform. 'People around here take the time to get to know each other.'

'Mmm, that is so,' he agreed as the train came chugging into the station. When they were settled in an almost empty carriage he said, 'Are you glad that you took the time to get to know *me*?'

'Yes and no,' she told him. 'Life was less complicated when I didn't, but I wouldn't have missed it for the world.'

'There is an element of the past tense in what you've just said,' he remarked, observing her keenly, 'but I'll try to keep an open mind.'

They arrived in Manchester after a short time and when she would have left him at the barrier he ignored it and walked to the door of the carriage with her. As she turned to say goodbye with one foot on the step he said gravely, 'Take care, Laurel. Come back to me.'

She nodded and without speaking boarded the train. When she'd found a seat by the window she flashed him a half-smile and thought if David was under the impression that she was looking forward to the day ahead he was mistaken. The only impetus that was taking her away from him was the hope that there might be some way she could be made to look less un-attractive than she did now.

'Are you creaming the affected area regularly and keeping the skin out of direct sunlight?' the consultant asked when he'd examined her back.

'Yes, of course,' she declared. 'My back rarely sees the light of day. It isn't something I would ever want to flaunt. It still looks dreadful.'

'I know,' he said sympathetically, 'but you have to remember they were third-degree burns that you received. We did everything possible at the time to repair the damage, but it won't ever completely disappear. It will become less noticeable as time goes by, but the scars will always be there. We could try plastic surgery. We've gone the limit with skin grafts. Would you consider that?'

'Yes, anything,' she said flatly.

'We're pretty booked up at the moment. It could be a while before we get round to it, yet I will certainly put you on the list if you're sure, but again there is no certainty that it will be other than a small improvement. That is all I can guarantee.'

His words stayed with her all the time during her homeward journey and she asked herself dismally what she had expected. A promise of perfection, hardly, but she'd hoped for some joy to come out of the visit to the burns unit.

When she got off the local train at Willowmere her eyes widened. David was waiting for her on the platform.

'How did you know which train I would be on?' she questioned, and he smiled.

'I didn't. I've just been meeting each one as it came in and finally hit the jackpot. What sort of a day have you had?'

'Average,' she told him wearily. 'It's good to be back.'

'Let me take you for a meal,' he suggested, 'or if you want I'll cook for us at my place. Would you like that?'

'Yes, I think I would.'

She was going to keep to her vow of telling him about the full extent of the damage to her skin and the sooner the better, she was thinking. If they went to Glenside Lodge Elaine might be there, and Jonas maybe, and she would lose her nerve.

David was watching her as they ate the food he'd prepared and the thought of the ring he'd bought was uppermost in his mind. If she was in agreement when the meal was over, why didn't he take Laurel to see the progress that had been made with the house and then surprise her by asking her to marry him in the place that meant so much to them both?

He'd vowed to wait until she showed that she trusted him, but did it matter? She would do in time, he would make sure of that.

She was tired, but when David suggested they go to the house Laurel couldn't resist, even though it was putting off the moment of truth. There would always be another time, she told herself.

'The electricity supply was connected today,' he said as he turned the key in the door, 'otherwise I wouldn't have suggested we come.' And when it swung back he flicked on a light switch and the hall was flooded with light.

As she looked around her at oak panelling and a domed ceiling Laurel didn't have to say anything. The expression of delight on her face was answer enough if he'd had any doubts about her reaction, and as they went from room to room he watched her pleasure increase until they were back in a sitting room that was waiting to be enhanced by some furniture.

'The house is beautiful, David,' she breathed.

'And so are you,' he said softly. 'Will you marry me, Laurel, and live with me here?'

He saw her expression change. 'I'm not beautiful!' she cried. 'And I can't marry you. It wouldn't be fair.'

'Why not?' he exclaimed, unaware that his proposal had taken away her one chance of showing him that she trusted him. If she told him how scarred she was now he was going to think that she'd saved it until she was sure of him, and it wasn't like that at all. Over recent months she hadn't been sure of anything, least of all the reactions of others.

'I'm waiting,' he reminded her in a flat tone. 'If nothing else, you owe me an explanation, Laurel.'

Suddenly it was all too much. She was wearing an outdoor jacket and clutching her handbag in a clammy hand, and almost in one movement she flung the bag to one side and wrenched off the jacket. Then as he watched in stunned disbelief she took off one of the high-necked sweaters that he'd seen her in so often, and turned slowly to present her back to him.

She heard his sharp intake of breath like a death knell

about to toll. 'So this is what you couldn't bring yourself to tell me. Who or what did that to you?'

'Does it matter?' she said dismissively. 'It's there and isn't going to go away. I've been to London for a check-up at the burns unit where I was treated, hoping there might be a chance of some sort of cosmetic improvement, but didn't get much joy out of the visit.'

'And you couldn't tell me any of this,' he said in a low voice. 'You thought so little of me that you couldn't share your heartache. What kind of a person do you think I am, Laurel?'

She didn't answer the question. Instead she had one of her own. 'Would you want to wake up to this patchwork quilt every morning?' she asked flatly, still with her back to him. 'Take me home please, David,' she begged as she replaced the clothes she'd taken off, and after switching off the lights and locking the door he did as she'd asked in the silence that had fallen upon them.

CHAPTER TEN

WHEN they arrived at Glenside Lodge she opened the car door and was out of it before he'd had the chance to break the silence, and he thought dismally there would be no lingering under the streetlamp tonight.

The lights were on so he waited until she was safely inside and then drove home to the cottage and sat staring into space. Every time he visualised what Laurel had gone through he felt sick inside. He still didn't know what had happened, but he was a doctor and knew that it must have been something terrible to have done that to her skin. No wonder his father's comment about Caroline had sent Laurel running for cover.

If he'd been there he would have made sure that she'd also got the message that there hadn't been much else to commend his ex-fiancée, but he hadn't been and she'd fled to hide her hurt.

When he'd found her she could have told him then, but she hadn't. He hadn't been entirely convinced by her reaction with the barbecue and had thought there was more to it than just a scare. Now he knew that it had been with just cause on her part and his heart ached when he thought of the pain she must have suffered. He wished he could turn the clock back and wipe out the times he'd told her she was unpredictable and difficult to deal with.

She'd asked him to take her home, and his dismay at what she'd revealed to him had been so acute he'd done as she asked instead of telling her that he loved her as she was and wanted her in his arms, in his bed, in his life for always.

The midnight hour was long past. Dawn would soon be breaking over the sleeping village, and he thought determinedly that he had to make things right between them before another day took its course.

When Laurel let herself into the house there was no sign of Elaine, and a note on the hall table said, *Have gone to mind Arran for Georgina and Ben. They're dining out with a Swedish colleague of his and have suggested I stay the night as they might be late back. Hope all went well with the check-up. See you soon, love Elaine.*

She breathed a sigh of relief. She had the place to herself, thank goodness. If Elaine saw the state she was in she would want to know what was wrong, and she felt as if she would choke on it if she had to explain.

Sleep wasn't swift in coming, which was not surprising as her thoughts were going round and round in a miserable circle, and eventually she slipped on the fleecy robe that she'd been wearing on the night David had found her asleep on the sofa and went to sit out in the garden.

It was hot and airless with only a sliver of moon up above, and as she sat alone in the silence Laurel thought she'd behaved like a crazy woman, throwing the words she'd longed to hear back in his face. So much for dignity. She'd intended telling him calmly and without drama so that he could walk away without embarrassment if he felt the need. She hadn't expected him to be as cruel as Darius had been, but neither had she expected him to be so hurt and condemning when she'd finally shown him the scars. He hadn't said a word after that. It was as if a shutter had come down between them and she doubted it would ever be raised again.

When the car swished to a halt at the gate in the light of the streetlamp and David came up the path to where she was huddled on a wooden bench Laurel remained motionless.

He stopped in front of her and beckoned for her to rise. 'Come with me and don't ask questions,' he said in a low voice, and she obeyed.

When he'd tucked her into the car she found her voice. 'Where are we going?'

'You'll soon see,' he said, and she lapsed into silence again.

When the lake with the house behind it came into sight she shrank down in the seat and pulled the robe more closely around her, and he smiled across at her.

'I don't think anyone is going to be around to note your strange attire at this hour and there isn't any need to cover yourself up any more, is there?'

He'd stopped the car in front of the house, but instead of taking her in that direction he took her hand and walked her down to where the waters of the lake lapped against a small stone landing stage.

'It was here that you cast your spell over me,' he said, embracing the lake and the field where the house stood with a sweeping gesture, 'and it is here that I want us to be for ever and always, loving and living in the house back there once I've convinced you that I love everything about you, including the scars.

'I love you for your spirit that must have been almost quenched by what happened to you, for the forthright person that you are in everything except the thing that you mistakenly thought set you apart from other women.

'It is what I should have told you when you showed me your back, but I was so taken aback I said the first thing that came into my head. Can you forgive me, Laurel?'

'I've told you before, David. I can forgive you anything,' she said softly as dawn began to lighten the sky, 'and I do so want to live with you in Water Meetings House.'

'And you shall,' he promised, 'because I'm going to ask you again. Will you marry me, Laurel?'

'Yes, I will,' she told him with sweet gravity, and this time she went into his arms knowing it was where she belonged.

Later, as daylight began to slant across the water, he said gently, 'So are you going to tell me what happened?'

She nodded, with the dread having left her. 'Yes. It is long overdue.' She held his hand tightly. 'I was on night duty on Men's Surgical along with another nurse who had gone for a break when it happened.

'I was settling in a patient who had been brought up from the high-dependency unit when I smelt smoke and saw that the door of a small side ward was shut, which was against regulations.

'When I flung it open I was horrified to discover that the bed was on fire with the patient still in it. The curtains nearby were also on fire. Smoke was filling the room and I knew I had to get him out of there fast.

'The fire alarm had gone off and help would soon be arriving, but there wasn't time to wait so I ran across and half lifted, half dragged him off the bed and began to carry him towards the door in the choking smoke.

'It had swung to behind me and as I opened the door the draught turned the blaze into a flash fire and caught my back as I staggered out into the corridor with him. I collapsed with one leg crushed beneath me and the patient on top of me.

'I could hear raised voices and pounding feet but they seemed a long way off and I remembered nothing else until I surfaced two days later with a doctor looking down at me sympathetically as he was about to explain that I'd got third-degree burns on my back, that my hands were all blistered, and my hair was burnt.

'The only good thing to come out of it was that the fire had been contained to the one room. No other patients had been hurt, just myself and the old guy who hadn't been able to resist lighting a cigarette. He too had severe scarring but amazingly made some degree of recovery.

'They told me when I surfaced for those first few moments in the burns unit that I had some painful times ahead of me and that skin grafts might be required once the extent of the damage to my skin had been calculated, but I was so heavily sedated not much of what I was being told registered. Though it registered fast enough when at last I was conscious enough to see for myself what the fire had done to me.

'There were no-smoking notices all over the hospital, but the old guy had pleaded with his visitors to leave cigarettes and matches, and aware that they were breaking hospital rules they'd closed the door after them when they'd left.

'He'd confessed afterwards that he'd lit up as soon as they'd left and after the first few puffs, weak and ill, he'd dozed off and let the lighted cigarette fall on the sheets, then panicked and threw it away, setting light to the curtains. It changed my life for ever.'

Overwhelmed with tenderness, David had listened without interrupting as she'd told him what he'd wanted to know ever since they'd met. And now, as she turned towards him, he said, 'You are so brave and so beautiful it takes my breath away. Don't ever be afraid of the reactions of others, Laurel.'

Her smile was rueful. 'They wanted to give me an award but I didn't want one. I just wanted my skin back, and it was Darius who made me lose confidence about the scarring. I showed him my back on one of his infrequent visits to the hospital and he couldn't take it, said it was nauseating. I finished with him soon after.'

When he would have expressed his disgust she told him gently, 'Shush, David. It's forgotten. If he hadn't been like that I would never have met you.'

She couldn't believe it was happening. The black despair of the last few hours had disappeared. He really wanted her, she thought joyfully. David wanted her as much as she wanted him and he wasn't fazed by what he'd seen on her back, even though it did look like a map of the Pennines.

He was taking a small jeweller's box out of his pocket, and when he opened it and she saw the emerald surrounded with diamonds glowing on its velvet bed she turned to him with eyes wide with amazement.

'When did you get that?' she breathed.

He laughed. 'Do you remember me saying that I was going shopping in Manchester?'

There were tears on her lashes as she told him, 'After Darius I didn't think any man would ever want me. Then I met you when I was looking a sight and hating the thought of living in the countryside.

'When I discovered that you were a local *and* a doctor in the village practice it all became so much more bearable, though it didn't make me any more confident regarding my appearance or eager to expose my disfigurement.'

'I'm not "any man",' he said steadily. 'I'm the one who will love you no matter what, through thick and thin, in sickness and in health. I want you to wear this ring on your finger to show that you belong to me and soon I hope, very soon, I'm going to place a gold wedding band next to it. How soon do you think we can arrange a wedding? A week? A fortnight?'

'And you're sure that this is what you want?' she asked, with the feeling that it was all a dream.

'I'm sure all right,' he said softly, 'and will be happy to demonstrate how much whenever the opportunity occurs.'

The emerald was on her finger, and the first of the demonstrations that David had promised was so satisfactory they repeated it several times

As Willowmere basked in glorious September sunshine, Edwina Crabtree and her fellow bellringers were out in full force. The vicar had raised his eyebrows at holding a wedding at such short notice, but for David and Laurel he was happy to make an exception.

Their families and friends were gathered in the church to share in their special day. Everyone from the surgery was there to wish them well, along with Pollyanna and Jolyon in the charge of Jess and Helen, while their father was occupied with his duties of best man.

Sarah Wilkinson had brought out the blue brocade again, and Clare, proudly holding baby Arran, was there too.

The Derringhams had also put in an appearance and there was much sympathy for Alistair on his crutches.

A newcomer to local health care was also one of the guests—David's acquaintance from St Gabriel's, Lizzie Carmichael. She'd been appointed as the new community midwife and had introduced herself to James. Lord Derringham's plans for the maternity clinic were taking shape and everyone was very excited.

At that moment the organist began to play the wedding march and as everyone got to their feet she was there, his bride, breathtaking in a white satin gown, wide-eyed and beautiful with Elaine beside her.

Unknown to Laurel, Elaine had discovered the whereabouts of her parents and that morning they'd turned up at Glenside Lodge to watch their daughter marry the man who held her heart.

They would be off again the next day if they ran true to form, but she'd long learned to live with that and it was good to see them, though they would never hold a place in her affections like Elaine did.

So it was Elaine who walked Laurel down the aisle, proud and happy to be giving the niece she loved so much to the man of her dreams. David waited at the altar, tall and handsome in his morning suit. James stood next to him, equally tall and handsome, as best man.

Jonas, as happy as Elaine because his cherished son had found the love of his life, smiled at them from the front pew, and passed Elaine his handkerchief to dab her eyes.

The reception was to be held at the completed Water Meetings House, and when David carried Laurel over the threshold it would be the moment that their hopes and dreams became the reality that he had promised. Maybe, somewhere in the ether, his mother would be smiling down on them as they began their life in what had once been her childhood home.

The day was finally over and the newlyweds were alone. They walked hand in hand to where Willow Lake, beautiful and timeless, would always be there to enchant them, and then wandered blissfully back to Water Meetings House. At last, Laurel lay in David's arms, and as he kissed the scars that she'd tried to hide from him she knew beyond doubt how much he loved her.

MIRACLE: TWIN BABIES

BY
FIONA LOWE

All the characters in this book have no existence outside the imagination of the author, and have no relation whatsoever to anyone bearing the same name or names. They are not even distantly inspired by any individual known or unknown to the author, and all the incidents are pure invention.

First published in Great Britain 2009
Harlequin Mills & Boon Limited,
Eton House, 18-24 Paradise Road, Richmond, Surrey TW9 1SR

© Fiona Lowe 2009

ISBN: 978 0 263 86860 9

Set in Times Roman 10½ on 13 pt
03-0809-50861

Harlequin Mills & Boon policy is to use papers that are natural, renewable and recyclable products and made from wood grown in sustainable forests. The logging and manufacturing process conform to the legal environmental regulations of the country of origin.

Printed and bound in Spain
by Litografia Rosés, S.A., Barcelona

Always an avid reader, **Fiona Lowe** decided to combine her love of romance with her interest in all things medical, so writing Medical™ Romance was an obvious choice! She lives in a seaside town in southern Australia, where she juggles writing, reading, working and raising two gorgeous sons with the support of her own real-life hero! You can visit Fiona's website at www.fionalowe.com

Recent titles by the same author:

THE SURGEON'S SPECIAL DELIVERY
THE DOCTOR CLAIMS HIS BRIDE
THE PLAYBOY DOCTOR'S MARRIAGE PROPOSAL
A WEDDING IN WARRAGURRA
A WOMAN TO BELONG TO

To Serena, for her eagle eyes,
her hard questions and her enthusiastic support.
Thank you!

CHAPTER ONE

OXYGEN stats are dropping! Tube him!
More blood, he's bleeding out!
Flatlining. Stand clear, now!

A lone kookaburra's raucous laugh vibrated the hot, torpid summer afternoon air, mocking Nick Dennison's thoughts. Thoughts that were firmly fixed in the past, over one and half years ago before everything in his life had gone pear-shaped. Back in a time when being a doctor had defined him and life had been work, and work had been his life.

Resting back on his haunches after being bent over pulling weeds, he pushed against the trowel and stood up, stretching his back. Sweat ran down his cheeks and he wiped his face against the tight sleeve of his T-shirt, leaving a trail of rich black earth against the soft cotton.

Through the shimmer of the eucalypt-oil heat haze he could see in the distance the small fishing town of Port Bathurst, affectionately known by the locals as Port. Snuggled into the curve of white sand and turquoise water, protected on one side by a treacherous reef and on the other side by a granite-flecked mountain,

Port was a glorious work of nature and far from the man-made inner-city life he'd always known.

A wet nose nuzzled his ankle as a ball dropped next to his foot. He glanced down at the intelligent and loving eyes of his blue heeler. 'Have you rounded up the chooks yet, Turbo?'

The dog cocked his head to the side, picked up the ball and sat down, hope and expectation clear in his expression.

Nick rubbed the cattle dog's black ears. 'I take it that's a yes.' He accepted the saliva-covered ball and hurled it off into the bracken, watching the dog tear after it. He had once talked to a hundred people a day—now he was conversing with a dog and talking to his vegetables. He'd craved solitude and simplicity for a long time. Now he finally had it.

He heard the phone ringing through the open window of his cottage and instinctively glanced at his watch. Tuesday. Five o'clock. His mother would have just got in from her midweek ladies' tennis match. He let the phone ring out. Being asked a hundred questions about his health and his lack of future plans wasn't conversation.

He grabbed a shovel and started spreading manure, losing himself in the joy of being able to do physical work again, closing his mind to everything except the rhythm of the movement.

Dr Kirby Atherton jogged down the long Port Bathurst pier just as the last tinges of orange faded from the cloud-studded sky. Another hot day was on its way, which would make the holidaymakers visiting town happy, but distress many of her elderly patients. She'd only been in town a few weeks but her early morning run was part of her routine. She lacked control over many things in her life, but keeping fit—*that* she could control. Running both exhausted and exhilarated her and helped keep the demons at bay.

'Morning, Doc.' A wide grin sliced across a weather-beaten face.

Kirby jogged on the spot next to a stack of crayfish pots and looked down at Garry Braithwaite, sluicing his fishing boat. 'Morning, Garry.'

'Everyone calls me Gaz, love.'

She noted his request for next time she greeted him. Acclimatising to Port was a lesson in letting go of city ways and shortening every long name and lengthening every short one. 'Good catch?'

'Not bad.' He indicated a large white plastic trough filled with crawling crustaceans. 'These beauties will be in Japan before you're in bed tonight.'

'That's amazing.' She glanced behind her at the fish co-op which was ablaze with lights. This was its busiest time of day as it accepted the catches of the local fleet. She turned back, a wistful tone in her voice. 'Are they all going to Japan? Not even a few to the farmers' market?'

'Just the ones the co-op rejects. I've got about five.' He started to wind up the hose, his expression cheeky. 'Do you have a special dinner guest tonight, Doc? Perhaps you should talk to Deano and get some abalone.'

Kirby ignored the inference. In some ways coming to Port had been like stepping back in time. It appeared to be the small town's opinion that no matter how qualified, successful or independent a woman was, if she

was young and single she must be looking for a
husband. A few months ago Kirby might have agreed.
'Save me a small cray, Gaz, and I'll catch you at the
market in half an hour.'

She turned and switched on her MP3 player, and with
her feet matching the thumping bass beat she ran toward
the aroma of freshly brewed coffee, the sweet smell of
fruit muffins straight out of the oven and the scent of rich
brown earth clinging to freshly picked produce.

She'd been trying to get to the market for the last three
Saturdays but each time a sick patient had derailed her
plans. Coming to Port was supposed to be the commence-
ment of her GP training but within a week of starting as
the town doctor, her mentor had fallen ill. Without supervision, Kirby was flying by the seat of her pants.

It was still early in the season but if the last weeks
had been a typical Port Bathurst summer then she really
needed some extra help as well as a mentor. She didn't
want to have to move again and find another GP pro-
gramme, and returning to Melbourne was *not* an option.
Surely there was an experienced doctor with a family
who wanted to have an idyllic summer by the sea?

But Port Bathurst wasn't Lorne or Sorrento, it didn't
have designer clothing shops, the mobile phone coverage
was intermittent and the dial-up internet was really more
down than up. The glory days of it being a gold-rush port
had faded. Today it sat at the end of a very long road, with
a large chunk of wilderness between it and the nearest
town. Although all these things had been part of the charm
that had drawn Kirby to the historic town, it seemed to put
most people off. No one had answered her advertisement.

Kirby surveyed the slowly building crowd. It was still early so there was a marked absence of teenagers but plenty of empty-nesters clutching well-planned lists, examining the fresh produce and enthusiastically haggling over prices. Toddlers and preschoolers full of energy zipped up and down between stalls, way ahead of their half-asleep parents. A man in his thirties walked past, pride radiating off him as he held his wife's hand and wore a baby sling on his chest, his newborn snuggled against him fast asleep.

Family is everything. She steeled herself against Anthony's uncompromising voice but it wasn't enough to stop the ache that throbbed inside her whenever she glimpsed such a scene. She swallowed against the tight-ness in her throat, rolled her shoulders back and kept walking. Forget eating healthy—right now she needed hazelnut coffee and a hot jam donut.

She unexpectedly paused, derailed in her quest by the sight of an old wooden trestle table groaning under the weight of bountiful vegetables. Arranged in groups for effect, the vivid colours of nature demanded attention. The red and green skins of the capsicums shone, the plump white ends of spring onions contrasted stun-ningly with the healthy dark green tails, and the ruby tomatoes promised an old-fashioned, rich flavour. The vividness of the colours astounded her and she was struck by how lush and enticing everything looked. These vegetables glowed with good health and were positively sexy.

'Can I help you?'

The deep voice vibrated the air around her, moving

it across her skin like a silk caress and leaving behind a tingling trail of unmet need. Completely stunned by her body's reaction to a disembodied voice, she glanced up.

Emerald-green eyes, the colour of the bay, gazed down at her, swirling with hints of blue and dancing with undiluted charm. An indistinct memory stirred.

'Anything take your fancy?'

You. She bit off the word that thundered hard and fast through her head and found her voice. 'I've never seen vegetables like this before. The colours are amazing.'

He smiled and dimples carved into his cheeks, seeming to darken his early morning stubble. Surprisingly deep lines for a man who looked to be in his early thirties bracketed a wide mouth, and unexpected fine lines radiated from his eyes toward short dark hair streaked with silver. 'Thanks. They're my first crop of organic vegetables so I feel like a proud dad with his children.'

She raised her brows. 'Except you're selling them.'

He grinned. 'Every kid has to go out and make their way in the world.'

She laughed. He was the most gorgeous farmer she'd ever met. Not that he really looked like a farmer despite the fact he had a cattle dog sitting quietly beside him. There was no sign of a battered hat and his pressed stone-coloured shorts contrasted with a fresh blue-and-white-striped short-sleeved shirt—smart, casual weekender clothes, the type that a man of the city would wear. A gym-buffed man of the city.

Working out in a gym could have given him his broad chest and wide shoulders but not the sun-kissed skin.

Skin stretched over taut muscles and was covered by a smattering of golden hair which was in stark contrast to his darker head hair. No, this man's body emanated a base power generated by sheer physical hard work.

She studied his face. Something about him seemed familiar and yet nothing about him prompted recognition.

His brilliant green eyes danced at her. 'If you tell me what you're thinking about, perhaps I can suggest a vegetable to match?'

Horrified that he'd caught her out staring at him as if he was on display like his stock, she randomly pointed to a stack of vine-ripened tomatoes. 'I'll take two, please.' She noticed small white scars on the back of his hand as he reached across the table.

Long, tanned fingers picked up the red, round fruit and placed them lightly against her palm. 'I recommend you spread hot, grainy toast with the local goat's cheese in virgin olive oil, and then top it with thin slices of tomato covered with freshly ground pepper and some of my basil. You'll be licking your lips and fingers to soak up every last wondrous morsel.'

An image of him languorously licking her fingers spun through her, making her dizzy. She'd obviously been working way too hard if her mind could just shoot off on dangerous tangents like that. She'd come to Port Bathurst to start over and to protect herself, and that didn't mean melting into a puddle of lust at a stranger's feet.

'Right, thanks. Organic food and recipes, too. Awesome!' *Can you hear yourself? You sound inane.*

He shot her a crooked smile. 'Enjoy. It's the small things in life that are worth holding on to.'

'A farmer *and* a philosopher?'

A shadow flickered across his gaze for a moment before being absorbed by a world-weary smile. 'Something like that. Enjoy your weekend.' He accepted her money and turned to serve his next customer.

A flash of something akin to rejection spiked her, which was illogical and ridiculous. This wasn't a social situation. He was a stallholder and she was a customer and he had a line of customers behind her waiting to be served. *No man is worth it, remember!* Her indignant and wounded subconscious kicked her hard, reminding her of Anthony's betrayal.

Reminding her of why she'd come to Port Bathurst in the first place. A new start—keep moving forward and never look back.

But repeating her mantra didn't stop a deep line of disappointment rolling through her. A disappointment which was completely out of proportion to the situation. Man, she must be tired, but then again, working flat out for a month would do that to a girl. She tucked some flyaway strands of hair behind her ears and took a deep breath. *Just keep moving forward.* She turned and walked toward the coffee cart, needing the java jolt and sweet taste of hazelnut more than ever.

The queue for coffee was long and congenial and she chatted to people about the weather, signed a petition to save the old bridge, and listened to concerns about how the new fishing quotas would affect the town's main industry. Getting to know Port was all part and parcel of being a country GP.

'There you go, Doc. One skinny hazelnut latte, super-sized.'

'Thanks, Jade. It smells divine.' Kirby gripped the cup and headed toward a free table. She put her tomatoes and coffee down and slid into the chair. Carefully easing the tight-fitting plastic lid off the top of the cup, she admired the foamy froth, took a deep anticipatory breath and lifted the coffee to her lips.

The frantic barking of a dog and yelling voices stalled her sip and she turned sharply toward the commotion.

Jake, Gaz's ten-year-old son, came running toward her, his chest heaving and his face pinched and white. 'Dr Kirby, Dad can't breathe!'

She leapt to her feet and yelled out to Jade in the coffee cart, 'Get the St John's kit from the hall.' Then she ran, following the boy back toward his father. The crowd opened up around them, easing their passage through the closely lined stalls. She hurdled some packing cases and in the distance she could see Gaz leaning forward, coughing violently and trying to breathe.

His solid height and weight obscured the person who was helping him. Someone had his right arm around Gaz's waist and his hand pressed firmly against the fisherman's chest. Thankfully someone who obviously knew first aid. Kirby hoped he was giving a sharp blow to Garry's back at chest level.

Kirby ducked around the craft stalls, concentrating on her feet missing cables and desperately wishing for a more direct route to get to her patient. She looked up again. Gaz continued to cough, but his colour was fading from bright red to white.

As she got closer she saw the first-aider was her farmer. He'd just placed both his hands under Garry's armpits and thrust inwards. Surprise washed through her that he knew this newer and less damaging technique. Most first-aiders still used the older Heimlich manoeuvre. She prayed that whatever was choking Garry would be projected out of his mouth soon.

Just as she reached them, Garry slumped forward, his face blue. Instinctively, Kirby threw herself at him, her shoulder catching him on the chest, preventing him from falling. 'I'm—'

'Help me get him down.' The farmer's voice held an unexpected authoritative command and a tone that brooked no argument. 'I'm a doctor, just do as I say.'

Kirby staggered under the unexpected words and Gaz's weight as she tried to grab his arms. A farmer-cum-doctor? But she had no time to think about that strange combination. All her concentration was on the fisherman who struggled for every life-sustaining breath.

'Doctor!' Jade ran up clutching the first-aid backpack which Kirby immediately put on the ground and opened.

'I need the pocket mask,' the doctor and Kirby both said at the same time.

Questioning green eyes framed with thick brown lashes appraised her as she helped him lower Garry onto the ground. 'I'm Kirby Atherton, the town's doctor.'

'Excellent. I'm Nick. Let's get him onto his side and I'll try more lateral chest thrusts.' He knelt next to their patient, placing his hands firmly over the ribcage. Using his weight, he pressed with a downward and forward movement.

'I'll check his airway.' Kirby rolled a now blue Garry onto his side and put her finger inside his mouth, hoping desperately to feel a foreign object.

'Anything?' The word held hope and dread.

'Nothing.' She rolled him back, checked his carotid pulse and chest movements, and called out to Jake. 'What was Dad eating when he started choking?'

The trembling boy tried to speak. 'St-stra-strawberry. He threw it in the air and catched it in his mouth.'

'It will have lodged in his trachea.' Nick voiced her exact thought.

'Starting mouth-to-mouth.' She applied the pocket mask over Garry's mouth and lowered her head. He needed air but she had no idea if she could she manage to force any past the obstruction.

'Find me something I can put down his throat that will grip. Try the jewellery stall.'

Kirby heard Nick's mellow voice instructing Jade as she counted and puffed five breaths into the uncon-scious man.

The moment she raised her head, Nick applied the same pressure again over Gaz's ribs, thrusting down-ward and forward.

Kirby rechecked Gaz's airway, hoping to feel the firm fruit. Her stomach rolled. 'Still nothing.' She gave Gaz another five breaths, panic starting to ripple through her. If they couldn't secure his airway soon, he'd go into cardiac arrest.

'I've got these.' Jade came running back and handed Nick a pair of long, thin pliers.

Kirby's fingers detected a faint beat. 'Pulse, weak

and thready. He's going to need an emergency tracheostomy to bypass the blockage and avoid arresting. Jenny, pass me the scalpel blade.'

'Hang on a mo.' Nick spoke quietly but decisively. 'Give me half a minute with these sort of forceps and see if I grab the strawberry.'

Kirby didn't want to waste any more precious time. 'But we don't have a laryngoscope for you to visualise the trachea.'

Green eyes flashed with ready understanding. 'I've done it before in EMD.'

A blurry image played at the edge of her mind but immediately faded, overtaken by her focus on the emergency. 'What do you need me to do?'

'Steady his head for me.'

'Will do.' His confidence reassured her and she placed her hands over her patient's ears, two fingers still resting on his carotid pulse.

The scream of the ambulance's siren broke over the tense crowd, the sound both urgent and comforting as it brought the medical equipment they really needed.

'Here goes.' Nick shot her a look that said, *Nothing ventured, nothing gained*, and lowered the thin, silver pliers into the slack throat of the unconscious man. 'Can't feel anything, damn it.' His long fingers carefully controlled all the minute movements with stunning expertise.

Kirby kept her gaze on Nick's hand, willing it to find the obstruction. Time spiralled out, each second an agonising wait. Garry's pulse suddenly faltered under her fingers. 'No pulse. Get out now. I'm starting CPR.'

Nick immediately pulled his left arm back, and a

soft, half-dissolved strawberry hung limply from the tip of the forceps. 'Got it. Roll him over.'

Kirby moved her patient's head to the side as he started coughing violently and vomited up a stream of pale pink liquid onto the ground.

Relief surged through her as she checked his pulse. 'Pulse back, patient breathing.' She looked up into Nick's face, as the worry lines on the bridge of his nose faded. She experienced a sense of déjà vu. 'Lucky save.'

He nodded, a slow smile appearing through the stubble on his jaw. 'Very lucky.'

'Kirby!'

She turned to see Theo and Richard, the ambulance officers, running toward her. 'Great timing, guys. We need all your gear.' She grabbed the black oxygen cylinder with its distinctive white top and quickly unravelled the pale green tubing. Gently, she lifted Garry's head and looped the elastic over his ears, adjusting the Hudson mask. 'This will help you breathe.'

The sick and bewildered man gripped her arm. 'Thanks, Doc.' His voice rasped out the words. 'I couldn't breathe… It scared the hell out of me…worse than being on the boat in a storm.'

She smiled down at him. 'I'm glad I was here, but really it was Dr…' She realised she didn't know his surname. 'Nick? I didn't catch your surname.'

He finished attaching the Lifepak electrodes and scanned the ECG tracing before looking up and speaking straight to Garry. 'I'm Dr Nick Dennison, and I'm just glad I was two stalls over.'

Nick Dennison. Kirby did a double-take so fast she

almost cricked her neck, the name having instant recognition in her brain. But the man in front of her looked
nothing like how she remembered Melbourne City
Hospital's up-and-coming emergency care specialist.
What on earth was he doing in Port Bathurst, selling
organic fruit and vegetables?

CHAPTER TWO

Nick concentrated hard, keeping his gaze firmly on the cannula he was inserting into Garry's arm, immensely glad of the distraction. Kirby Atherton's sky-blue eyes sparkled hypnotically, like light dancing on water. It had been the first thing he'd noticed about her when she'd walked up to his stall, quickly followed by her willowy height and the way her running gear clung deliciously to every feminine curve.

But it had been her eyes that had really drawn him. He had the craziest sensation that if her eyes were deep pools of water and he dived into them, he would emerge changed somehow. He tried to shrug the irrational feeling away. Not even on his worst days last year, when he'd hardly been able to get out of bed and the drugs he'd been taking had made him despair, had he experienced such foolish thoughts.

And prior to being sick, when life had consisted of work and a revolving door of beautiful women, he'd *never* thought twice about a set of eyes. Perhaps his mother was right. Maybe he had been out of social circulation for too long.

Brushing away the unsettling thoughts, he released the tourniquet, watching the flow of saline, checking for problems, and refocusing on far more straightforward things. 'We're going start you on antibiotics, Garry.'

The exhausted patient just nodded from behind his mask.

The two burly paramedics lowered their stretcher in preparation to transfer Garry from the ground to the slightly more comfortable but narrow gurney.

'Do you need a hand?' Nick taped the drip firmly in place.

'We'll be right, thanks, Doc. We do this all the time so we're in the swing. Best help you can give us is to just step back out of the way.' Theo locked the brakes of the stretcher with his foot.

He stood up and moved to the side at the same moment as Kirby. Much of her fine blonde hair had escaped its pink elastic hair tie and strands blew across her flushed cheeks. Her scent tantalised his nostrils, a blend of exercise and glowing health overlaid with a swirl of flowers and berries. He breathed in deeply.

'I'm going to ring through to Barago Hospital.'

Her words brought him back to the task at hand and he caught her sideways glance—the look quick but questioningly intense—as if she thought she should consult with him.

Her mouth opened ready to speak and then her teeth suddenly dragged across her bottom lip, momentarily flattening it before the skin rebounded into shape—full, soft and rose red.

Blood pounded through his veins with an unexpected

rush and it took every ounce of concentration to stay connected to the conversation. Hell, what was wrong with him? Had he stepped back so far from his previous life that he'd disconnected from things and lost the ability to focus? He ran his hand though his short hair, missing the satisfaction of being able to tug at its length. Once he'd been known for his single-mindedness and right now he wanted that back.

She spoke again, this time her words less certain. 'I think he should be evacuated and have a bronchoscopy.'

She reminded him of a resident who knew her stuff but lacked confidence in her judgement. It was a scenario he was used to but today it surprised him because as a country GP she must be used to making decisions all the time. Glad to be back on familiar territory, he moved to reassure her.

'It's a good call. The choking might have been an accident but he's at an age where you need to rule out multiple sclerosis or other muscular conditions.'

'Let's hope it was just an accident, Nick *Dennison*.' She raised light brown brows at him. 'You are *the* Nick Dennison, youngest appointed head of Emergency Medicine in Australia?'

He studied her pretty features, looking for something that would spark his memory, but nothing did. Surely if they'd dated or worked together he would never have forgotten those eyes. He shoved his hands in his pockets, knowing there was no point denying the truth. 'That's me. I'm sorry, have we met before?'

She shook her head. 'Not really. I attended one of your lectures when I was a resident at Prince William

Hospital. I was on duty that night and wasn't able to go to the dinner afterwards, but I think you met a friend of mine, Virginia Charters.' She shot him a knowing look. One that said, *You didn't call.*

He had no recollection of Virginia Charters but then again, that entire lecture tour had been a blur of cities, lecture theatres and women eager to date him. He loved women and he loved dating. He just didn't love or date one woman.

He took a punt on the type of women he'd accepted invitations from, women he'd wined, dined and satisfied before his world had imploded. Before he'd lost complete interest. 'Ah, Virginia…brunette and vivacious?'

He caught the surprised and almost disappointed look cross her face that he sounded like he'd remembered.

'Yes, that's Virginia. I'm sorry I didn't recognise you but you look very different from how I remember.'

He grinned, wanting to keep things light. He had no intention of telling her what had happened to him. He had no intention of anyone in Port ever knowing. His time here was all about wellness and no way was he looking back. 'It's the lack of a suit, a lectern and the slide presentation glowing behind me.'

Her mouth immediately widened into a broad smile that soared to her amazing eyes. Eyes that filled with coloured prisms, the many hues of blue which spun and twirled like the shards in a kaleidoscope.

His heart jolted hard in his chest and his breath stalled as a flicker of almost forgotten heat surged deep inside him.

Lust?

Yes! He wanted to whoop with delight.

His libido had vanished the day his world had changed but today it was back, albeit dusty and creaky. Four months of opting out of the mainstream and concentrating on his health was paying off. His body was back.

Suddenly his fascination with her eyes, her mouth and her curves made sense. It wasn't Kirby Atherton per se. She just happened to be the first pretty woman he'd come across that coincided with his recovery. He relaxed into the knowledge as his world came reassuringly back into kilter.

Kirby briskly went through the motions of handing over Garry's care to the Barago Hospital and organising Jake into the care of his aunt. Four phone calls and an hour later she had it all sorted but throughout the process her mind had buzzed continuously with the fact that Melbourne's most well-known ER doctor, the man aptly dubbed 'the playboy doctor', was in sleepy Port Bathurst.

The stories about him said he worked hard and played hard and he was well known for hitting the trendy clubs and bars until the early hours. He and her friend Virginia had shared an intense twenty-four hours and Kirby had been the shoulder Virginia had cried on when he hadn't called afterwards. She'd also been the voice of reason, pointing out that Ginny had virtually thrown herself at him and to give the man credit, he'd never promised her anything other than a good time. That he'd apparently delivered.

At the time, Kirby had had the advantage of distance because she had been cheerfully engaged, blissfully happy and busy planning her future of marriage, motherhood and medicine. Although she could appreciate the model good looks of urbane and sophisticated men like Nick, she'd always fallen for the guy-next-door type—the home-town handyman slash family man.

Anthony only talked about fixing things, remember? Then he hired someone else to do it.

She shoved away the unwanted thought that reminded her of how blind she'd been and refocussed on the memories of her friend. Ginny had been the one to go for tall dark and handsome. Except Nick hadn't been dark then, he'd been blond, which was part of the reason she hadn't recognised him. Today his hair was shorter and darker and physically he was thinner but more toned.

She ran her fingers through her hair. Nick Dennison and Port Bathurst just didn't match. Port didn't have a cutting-edge emergency department and as for nightlife, well, the recent crazy whist night at the tennis club had pushed the envelope. Lasting until midnight, the hall had rocked because someone had brought along their CD player and got people up to dance after the cards had finished. Nick in Port was like the translated instruction booklet that came with her new bookshelves—it made no sense. Her mind went round and round, stuck in a loop.

Who cares why he's here? He's a doctor with a wealth of experience.

The truth sliced sharply through everything else, stripping away all irrelevancies. Nick was a doctor and she needed a doctor *and* a mentor. The equation balanced perfectly. Nick working in Port alongside her meant she could stay in the town.

It didn't matter that he was a party boy, a smooth-as-silk charmer and heart-stoppingly gorgeous. She'd given up men and men like Nick had never been her type anyway. No, this would be a professional association only and keep her GP training on schedule.

The only thing left to do was ask him if he would work the summer season with her. Rolling back her shoulders, she headed toward the market to professionally proposition Dr Nick Dennison.

She arrived at Nick's stall and her heart skipped a beat as she watched him in complete control but cloaked by a lazy charm. Out of his suit and white coat he looked much more like the sort of guy she'd once been attracted to. *Breathe. This one is not for you. No man is for you.*

He was serving a customer, his amazing green eyes and his total attention completely focussed on Phyllis Gutherson, Port's resident naysayer. But her usually sour expression had vanished and in its place was a girlish smile. She looked twenty years younger.

Waiting her turn and shaking her head in wonder at how he'd achieved such a miracle, Kirby bobbed down next to Nick's dog and scratched his ears. 'Your master could charm diamonds from jewel thieves, couldn't he?'

Large brown eyes gazed adoringly up at her as the dog laid his head in her lap.

'Turbo, stop it.'

At the sound of the deep, commanding voice, both the dog and Kirby looked up.

A smile met her gaze. A smile that fizzed intoxicatingly through her like the bubbles of champagne. Her bent knees liquefied and she wobbled slightly as she rose to her feet.

He leaned casually against the stall table. 'That dog will turn on the charm if he thinks it will get him something.'

'Gosh, and I wonder where he learned that from.' She shook her head, laughing. 'You just managed to make Port Bathurst history by getting Phyllis Gutherson to smile, and charming her into buying your last item of produce. I mean, who eats radishes?'

This time his grin had a tinge of guilt to it, not dissimilar to that of a kid caught out sneaking biscuits too close to dinner. 'I will concede I might have used a well-placed compliment or two to move the radishes but, hey, I just sold everything I harvested for my first market.' He raised his hand as his eyes danced with elation—joy, pure and simple.

Without thought, she raised her hand to meet his, drawn completely by his enthusiastic aura that seemed to wrap around her, pulling her in. Her palm connected with his in a slap of celebration.

Heat tore through her hard and fast, ricocheting from skin to muscle to deep tissue and fanning out until every cell vibrated with its legacy and she tingled all over. Tingled in a way she never had before, not even with Anthony, the man she'd loved and thought she'd be spending the rest of her life with. Horrified, she jerked her arm back to the safety of her side.

Remember why you're here. She swallowed hard and cleared her throat. 'That's fabulous. Congratulations. Can I buy you a cup of coffee to help you celebrate and to say thank you for your help with Garry?'

'Thanks for the offer, but I have to pack up here first

and I don't want to hold you up.' He picked up some boxes and stowed them into the back of a ute.

Kirby hauled her gaze away from his rippling biceps and tried to keep her focus on why she was actually here. She didn't just want to blurt out, 'Please work with me.' The situation needed more finesse than that. 'How about I give you a hand and then we go for coffee?' *Don't sound so needy.* 'If that suits you.'

Emerald eyes studied her for a brief moment. 'OK, it's a deal.' He tipped over the wooden trestle and grabbed the old metal supports, his broad palm wrapping deftly around them.

Kirby had a sudden image of a leather tool belt sitting flat across his washboard abdomen and him fixing all her sticking sash windows. *Stay focussed. He's a doctor, not a handyman.*

'Excellent.' She passed him boxes and watched him stack them as if they were a mathematical problem. 'How long have you been in Port?'

'Technically, I'm not in Port because I don't live here.' He slid the long trestle into the ute.

Kirby's gut went into freefall. With his vegetable selling she'd assumed he lived here. Her plan depended on him living close by.

He paused in his stacking and extended a muscular arm out toward the mountainous rainforest area behind the town. 'My property's Riversleigh, thirty K out, near Sheep-wash Corner.'

Her gut steadied. She was still in the game—just. Sheep-wash Corner was pretty isolated, even more out of the way than Port. Nick Dennison hadn't just left

Melbourne for Sleepy Hollow, he'd gone bush, a tree-change. But why? The situation got even more intriguing. 'How long have you lived out there?'

His cheerful open face suddenly closed, and the dimples in his cheeks smoothed over. 'Four months.'

He handed her one end of a tarpaulin. 'What about you?'

She caught the deft change, the power switch in the conversation, and she pulled the tarp tight, just like her mother had taught her as a child when she folded sheets. He didn't want to talk about why he was here. 'I've been here since the start of the month.' She walked up to him to match her corners to his.

'Is this a long-term plan for you?' His fingers slid over hers as he moved to accept the tarp.

The sharp tingle of sensation almost made her drop her corners and she found herself gripping them instead of releasing them into his hands. The moment she let go, she flexed her fingers, willing the shimmering away.

Since the age of twelve Kirby had been tall and she was used to being a similar height to many men. But she had to tilt her head to look up into Nick's face. It disconcerted her. *He* disconcerted her. 'It's a summer plan to start with. I'm doing a six-month GP rotation.' *Six months to pull herself together.*

'A summer by the sea. Sounds relaxing.' His dimples reappeared, deepening as he smiled.

Her heartbeat seemed to skip. How could one man's smile make her feel almost dizzy? *This is your opening—grab it.* The practical words broke into the haze that enveloped her brain. 'Actually, apart from a run along the pier in the mornings, that is as close as I've got to the beach.'

He slapped his palm down on the tailgate of the ute and Turbo immediately jumped onto the tray, turned around and lay down. 'Quiet Port Bathurst been keeping you busy?'

'It's hardly quiet! Between the residents, the work with Kids' Cottage and now the tourists arriving, I can barely get to the laundrette on a Sunday to do my washing. I had easier days back at Royal William.' She stared straight up at him. 'I'm surprised the hospital board didn't approach you when you moved down here.'

His hands stilled for a fraction on the tailgate. 'Until this morning, the hospital board didn't know I was a doctor.' He slammed the back of the ute shut and wiped his hands on an old towel. 'No one did.'

His words stunned her. 'Why on earth not?'

A shadow passed through his eyes, like a cloud scudding across the sun. 'Because I didn't come here to practise medicine.'

Her plan, so clear and perfect in her head, took a massive broadside hit, but she wasn't letting go just yet. 'But you're a talented doctor and Port needs you.'

Dark brows drew together, causing a crease at the bridge of his nose. 'No, it doesn't, Kirby. Port's got you. Besides, I'm an accident and emergency specialist, not a GP, and right now I'm really not interested in working.'

She wanted to stamp her feet. She had the ideal mentor in front of her and he didn't want to work. She chewed her lip as her limited options ran through her head. With a deep breath she played the only card she had left in her deck. Honesty. She raised her gaze to his and spoke from the heart. 'Without your help, I can't work here.'

Over the last couple of months Nick had said an enthusiastic 'No' to five job offers from hospitals around the country with barely a second thought about his decision. But one glance from Kirby's blue eyes, swirling with honesty and tinged with pleading, and suddenly every reason for not working was teetering on unsteady foundations. 'What do you mean, you can't work here without my help?'

'How well do you know Port?'

'I don't really know it at all. I come here for the market but I use Barago as my centre for supplies as it's bigger.'

She laced her fingers, moving them back and forth against the backs of her hands. 'Soon after I arrived in Port, Christopher Grayson, the town's GP, fell ill.'

Ignoring the wavering feeling, he stuck firmly to the facts. 'When is Grayson due back?'

Her gaze held his with a steady look. 'He's not. Unfortunately, he had a stroke and he's currently in rehab.'

He shoved his hands in his pockets, empathy weaving through him for a man who had a battle on his hands. But this wasn't his problem and there was another solution. The foundations steadied. 'So you advertise for another doctor to help you with the workload.'

She sighed, tucking stray hair behind her ear. 'It's not just the workload. I came to Port as part of my GP rotation.'

The image of her tugging at her bottom lip when she was deciding to send Garry to Barago beamed against his brain. His chest tightened. Suddenly her hesitancy and lack of confidence made sense. 'Please don't tell me this is your first six-month GP rotation.'

'It is.'

Damn it. He slammed his right fist into his left hand. 'So without supervision you can't practise?' But the question was rhetorical, he knew the answer.

'Not in Port, no.'

He wasn't ready to work in medicine just yet. He'd promised himself six more months, just savouring being well. Hell, surely he deserved that after everything he'd been through. He ran his hand across the back of his neck, trying to sort out his thoughts. He had no connection with this woman, no reason to turn his plans upside down to help her. The obvious solution shot into his head. 'You could go elsewhere to do your rotation or back to Royal William.'

A shudder of tension moved through her. 'Royal William isn't an option I want to pursue. Look, Port has already lost one doctor, so it can't afford to lose me.' She tilted her head and the brilliant blue of her eyes flickered over him, pulling hard at his sense of duty. 'And you wouldn't do that to a rural community who's so enthusiastically embraced your organic vegetable venture, would you?'

The words hit like a flyball, hard and unexpected. The woman in front of him with her long, blonde hair, honey-gold skin and an air of vulnerability had suddenly transformed from a pleading porcelain doll to a steely blackmailer. He could turn down large hospitals where there were plenty of other contenders for the job but she had him backed into a corner where his 'no' would impact on many hard-working people.

He wanted to kick the tyres on the ute, he wanted to be back on the farm digging over beds filled with fragrant soil, he wanted to be anywhere but here, dealing with an unwinnable ethical dilemma. He crossed his arms and took in a deep breath. 'That's true, no town deserves to be without a doctor.'

'So you will work in Port this summer?' Expectation and enthusiastic anticipation filled her voice.

A flood of heat collided with frustration. Well, she wasn't getting everything her own way. 'I'll mentor you and give you the supervision you need, but I'm warning you now, I'm a tough teacher and I'll expect one hundred and ten per cent.' The words came out on a growl—the one he'd perfected to keep his interns on their toes. 'But as for working, well, it will be with *strict* conditions.'

He waited, expecting to see signs of anxiety at his mild threat about being a tough teacher, and he certainly expected to see both disappointment and hear questions about the conditions he planned to impose.

But her mouth widened into a smile that raced to her eyes and seemed to dance around her like the white light of sparklers. 'That's fantastic. You won't regret this, Nick, it will be a fabulous summer.'

But every single part of him regretted it already.

CHAPTER THREE

KIRBY sat and stirred her coffee at an outside table, looking down and watching the white foam of her latte blend into the hot milk. Nick sat opposite her. Usually she chose this table so she could admire the view of the bay and enjoy gazing at the pelicans, fascinated by the way they lowered their feet in preparation for a water landing.

But today she'd caught herself admiring the way Nick's thick brown eyelashes almost touched his cheeks when he blinked and how the new streaks of silver against his temples gave him a look of authority. Unwanted tendrils of attraction had tightened inside her and she'd glanced away. It was a lot safer to stare at her coffee.

Nick moved the straw of his smoothie up and down through the dense blend of fresh fruits. Apparently he didn't drink coffee. This was yet another surprise as every doctor she knew considered coffee a vital part of their day, but absolutely nothing about this man fitted the picture of the doctor she'd expected. However, despite everything being at odds with expectation, he'd offered to help her and that was all that mattered.

'You're missing out on an amazing flavour just for a

superficial caffeine buzz.' He winked at her as he drank his fruit concoction, his Adam's apple moving rhythmically and hypnotically against his taut muscular neck.

A rush of heat burned her cheeks and she dragged her eyes away. 'It's not just the buzz, it's the flavour of hazelnut.' She already had a buzz and she hadn't even taken a sip of her coffee. It had started simmering inside her from the moment he'd said he would mentor her. It felt oddly strange and yet deliciously wonderful and she was pretty sure it was relief.

You can call it relief if you want to.

She immediately took an indignant sip of her coffee and turned a deaf ear to the voice inside her head. Of course it was relief. Her search for a doctor was over and now she could stay in Port for her full six months. *Stay a long way from Anthony and Lisa.*

'Tell me about the demographics of Port Bathurst.' Nick pushed his large shake container off to the side, his eyes fixed firmly on her and filled with businesslike intent.

Kirby relaxed under his professional gaze. This was the working relationship she'd anticipated when she'd asked him to mentor her. 'Fishing and farming are the main industries but life is tough in both. Many young people are leaving town, although the mayor was telling me that recently there's been a push to increase tourism. A new diving business has opened in the main street, along with charter fishing trips, "Surf the wave" classes and catered cycling holidays.'

He nodded. 'I sold vegetables from the farm gate to a family on a Gypsy Caravan adventure the other week. They'd started out from Port and were taking the back roads. Regeneration is really important for rural communities like this.' He leaned back in his chair. 'So, how does all of this impact on the medical services?'

'It keeps us busy. The clinic is attached to the hospital and there are six acute beds and a small emergency centre plus midwifery. Major traumas get airlifted to Melbourne after being stabilised here and elective surgery goes to Barago. We have a large elderly population and the hospital has a nursing-home wing which is currently full. Oh, and then there's Kids' Cottage.'

His eyes darkened slightly. 'What's that?'

She leaned forward as her enthusiasm for KC spilled out. 'It's a fabulous holiday camp for children. They have camps for sick children with chronic illnesses, they have camps for healthy kids who have siblings with chronic illnesses or disabilities, and they have camps for kids whose families are struggling emotionally or financially and just need a bit of breathing space.'

Nick's fingers started to unroll the rim of the shake container. 'But Kids' Cottage would have their own medical staff, right?'

She shook her head. 'No, the town has always provided medical assistance since it started one hundred years ago. It's something that the locals are very proud of.'

A muscle twitched in his jaw. 'That's one of my conditions.'

Laughter bubbled up inside her. 'Are you going to fight me for first dibs on working with the kids?' A nurturing warmth filled her, tinged with regret. 'But I know what you mean, the cottage was a big drawcard for me to come to Port.'

His mouth firmed into an uncompromising line. 'There'll be no fight. I don't want to work at the camp so you can happily keep all that work for yourself.'

She blinked, completely startled. 'But the camp is so much fun. Why on earth don't you want to work there?'

The waxy cardboard unravelled in his hands, pulled apart by rigid fingers. 'I said I'd help you but there'd be conditions. This is one of them.'

His usually mellow voice was suddenly brusque and for the first time she caught a glimpse of the 'doctor in charge', the doctor used to issuing orders and being instantly obeyed without question. It caught her by surprise and a jolt of anger speared her. She tilted her chin—she wasn't a green first-year resident. 'What do you have against working with children?'

A streak of something she couldn't really define flared in his eyes for the briefest moment, before being cloaked by a spark of irritation. 'I didn't say I had anything against working with children, I'm just exerting my right not to.'

His arrogance astounded her. 'I suppose you had a paediatric registrar to save you from such work.'

'That's right.'

The blunt words hit her, their uncompromising tone harsh and decisive. 'Well, there's no paediatric registrar in Port so what about children who come into the clinic?'

His mouth flattened into an obdurate line. 'On the unlikely chance you're not available, I'll see them.'

'Well, that's reassuring.' The sarcastic words leapt off her lips as a fizz of frustration spread through her. 'Do you have any other demographic groups you refuse to work with? Any other conditions I should know about before we start?'

His eyebrows rose in a perfect arch at her mockery, but when he spoke his tone was all steely business. 'This is how I see it working. Each weekday morning I'll meet you at seven a.m. for the nursing-home ward round and I'll work half-day clinics Monday to Friday with lunchtime case-review sessions as part of your supervision. I'll be unavailable on Saturdays because I'll be at the market.' He extended his arm toward her, every part of him vibrating with tension. 'Deal or no deal?'

She recognised the adversarial glint in his eyes as a thousand questions hammered in her head and poured into her mouth, demanding instant answers. She couldn't understand why he wouldn't work at the camp. Why he would prefer not to see the children at the clinic—none of it made sense, but she swallowed hard against every single question, forcing them down deep. If she quizzed him too closely on why he wouldn't work at KC he would walk, and she couldn't risk that. He had her well and truly cornered and she had no choice.

Slowly, she stretched out her right hand and slid her smaller palm against his. Work-hardened calluses scraped gently over her softer skin in a tantalising caress as his fingers wrapped around her hand. His heat poured through her, racing along her arm, radiating into her chest, tightening her breasts and then burrowing down deep inside until every part of her had liquefied with desire. Yet a dangerous vixen-voice betrayed her, demanding even more.

No, no, I'm not doing this. I am immune to men. But

her body disagreed. His touch was unlike any hand-shake she'd ever known and she breathed in sharply, trying to grasp control of her wayward and wanton body which longed to drape itself over the chair and purr with pleasure. She finally found her own voice and hoped it sounded firm and businesslike. 'Deal.'

A smile roved across his face, creating twinkling dimples in his cheeks, sparking emerald lights in his eyes and completely eliminating all signs of his previous tension. 'Deal it is, then.'

'Wonderful.' The word came out horrifyingly breathy, the vixen having gained control. Suddenly the deal that would keep her in Port, well away from Anthony and her shattered dreams, was no longer the 'get-out-of-jail-free card' that she'd expected.

'But, Doctor, are you sure you've seen enough?' Mrs Norton's rheumy blue eyes sparkled as arthritic fingers fumbled over the pearl buttons on her crocheted bedjacket.

'Let me help you with that.' Nick smiled as he quickly buttoned the jacket on the elderly woman who would have been a stunning beauty in her younger days. 'If you can flirt with me, Mrs N. then you're doing just fine, but I have adjusted the diuretic so that should make breath-ing a little easier.'

'Thank you, Doctor.' She touched his hand as he finished latching the last button. 'And when will you be in to see me next, dear?'

'Tomorrow morning.'

'I'll be ready.' She gave him a wave as he left the room. Mrs Norton was the last nursing-home patient on his morning round's list and over the last hour he'd met all the residents. Every female patient had held his hand and flirted with him as well as showing him pictures of their granddaughters and great-granddaughters. *'She's a wonderful cook, Doctor, and you could do with some fattening up.'* The male patients had gruffly given him fishing tips, shaken their heads at his choice of football team and told him the 'sure-fire' solution to aphids— *'garlic and soapy water, Doc.'*

After working in emergency medicine for years, he'd expected to find a nursing-home round slow and boring work. He didn't know if it was because he hadn't worked in almost two years and today he was just enjoying being back in the field, but he'd been surprised at how much fun he'd had chatting with them all. The moment he got home he was going to make up that aphid-fighting mixture and use it on his tomatoes this afternoon.

He glanced at his phone and read a text from Kirby asking him to meet her at the clinic. She hadn't made it to rounds, having been called out at six a.m. to Kids' Cottage.

He'd had no idea the town had a kids' holiday camp dating back a hundred years. When he'd initially said he would have conditions attached to working here, he'd been thinking about how he would juggle the farm with practising medicine and still have precious time for himself. He hadn't realised he would need to use the 'conditions' banner for anything else, but no way was he going to be the medico for a kids' camp.

He shuddered as the memory of his father's voice suddenly sounded in his head. *You have to go, mate. You'll enjoy it if you give it a chance.*

He'd hated the enforced time he'd spent at camps as a kid and he sure as hell wasn't spending time there as an adult. This time he had a choice and he was choosing to say no.

Suddenly the vision of Kirby's wide blue eyes aimed squarely at him and full of disapproval shoved his father's voice out of his head. Damn it, *he* was the experienced doctor and he had the right to say where he would work without giving a full-on explanation. He was so *not* revisiting his childhood, especially not with a woman whose eyes threatened to see down to his soul.

Better that she thought him a jerk than to go there.

Yeah, right. You go ahead and think that if it makes you feel better.

He ran his hand across his hair, short spikes meeting his palm, and he grunted in frustration. Hell, he didn't even have to be working in Port! This time here was supposed to be all about wellness and focussing on himself. He was the one doing *her* the favour.

Shaking his head to clear it of unwanted images, errant thoughts and the eminently reasonable voice of his father, he strode toward the clinic, which was attached to the small emergency department of Port Bathurst Bush Nursing Hospital. Pushing open the door, which was covered in healthy-lifestyle posters, he stepped into the waiting room.

'Good morning. You must be Dr Dennison. Welcome!' A woman who looked to be in her early fifties with spiked, short red hair walked toward him, extending her hand. 'I'm Meryl Jeffries, the practice nurse, and it's wonderful that you're here.' She pumped his hand firmly and didn't draw breath. 'The whole town is talking about how you used Cheryl's jewellery pliers to pull that strawberry out of Garry's throat, and thank goodness you were there. Anyway, Kirby is just giving Theo the scoop on young Harrison, who thought that he'd start the day by jumping off the top bunk and fracturing his tib and fib so she'll be here in a minute and, well, here she is now so I'll let her give you the tour as I've got my baby clinic.' She threw her arm out behind her toward the reception desk. 'But if you need anything just ask because Vicki and I have been here for years.'

Vicki, who looked a bit older than Meryl, glanced up from the computer and smiled at him over the top of her bright purple glasses. 'Lovely to have you here, Dr D., and, like Meryl said, just yell. My only rule is that you bring the histories back to me as you greet your next patient so they can be filed or else things get lost. Oh, and I made you a ginger fluff sponge and it's in the kitchen so help yourself to as much as you like because you do look a bit on the thin side, dear.'

He opened his mouth but words escaped him. It was like work had just collided with his mother—instructions and praise all rolled into one with a slightly disapproving look thrown in. 'Ah, thank you for the welcome and the cake.'

They both nodded and smiled and then Vicki returned to her computer screen and Meryl disappeared down the corridor.

'I see you've met Meryl and Vicki.' A familiar tinkling laugh sounded behind him.

He turned around to find a smiling Kirby walking

toward him. Her hair moved in sync with her body, brushing across her shoulders and floating around her face. On Saturday she'd been wearing Lycra running gear. Today she wore a summer dress with a close-fitting scoop-neck top that hugged her waist before opening out into a short full skirt that showcased her shapely long, tanned legs. Bright red painted nails peeked out of strappy sandals.

Heat poured through him and zeroed in on his groin, making him dizzy. His reaction to her was so much stronger than two days ago and that made no sense at all. On Saturday she'd had a bare midriff and figure-hugging clothes on so of course his body had reacted. Hell, he'd been pleased it had because it meant things were finally getting back to normal despite the fact he'd always preferred brunettes.

But today far more clothes covered Kirby's body and yet the hidden curves tantalised even more. He dragged his gaze up from the hint of creamy breast back to her face and prayed she hadn't noticed his lapse of profes-sionalism. He might have been known for dating many women but he'd *always* kept work and pleasure dis-tinctly separate. He never dated someone he worked with directly so he definitely needed to get back into the work saddle again if those lines were blurring.

He rubbed his jaw. 'Those two are like a hurricane. Are they always like that?'

'Always.' A more serious expression played around her mouth. 'But don't be deceived—they really know their stuff and the clinic runs like clockwork. Vicki's children are adults and living in Melbourne now so I think she's missing mothering and she's making up for it with us.' Her eyes danced, softening the indignant look that streaked across her face. 'Although I've *never* had a cake made for me.'

He answered without thinking. 'You can have as much as you like. I really don't eat cakes.'

'First no coffee and now no cake?' She tilted her head enquiringly, a glint of interrogation in her eyes. 'Next you'll be telling me you don't drink.'

He smiled, falling back into old habits in an attempt to deflect her. 'I do drink but only top-shelf wine on special occasions.' He didn't really want to talk about why he'd given up cakes and cream. 'So how about you show me around the clinic and the emergency department of the hospital and then I can get started.'

Work. After all, that was why he was here. He itched to throw himself into a busy day because working seemed a heck of a lot safer than talking about himself or ogling a colleague's décolletage.

'Can I run something past you?' Kirby caught Nick between patients.

'Sure. What's up?' His eyes darkened to the colour of moss as he swung around on the office chair, his gaze fixed firmly on her.

A gaze so intense that her skin tingled. *Get over yourself. You asked the man a question and he's giving you his undivided attention, just as a colleague should.* She gripped Melinda Nikoloski's history and focussed on the facts. 'I've got a thirty-five-year-old woman with general fatigue, enlarged glands, persistent cough, raspy voice and episodes of shortness of breath.'

'On bare facts alone it sounds like summer flu.' His mouth tweaked up on the left in a thoughtful smile. 'But you wouldn't be running it past me if you thought it was flu.'

She slid into the chair next to his desk, grateful for his intuition. Grateful that he was here. Leaping into this job a year before most people started a GP rotation had stretched her, but she'd been desperate to leave Melbourne, desperate to distance herself from everything that reminded her of what she'd lost, and Port had been desperate enough to accept her. 'The previous doctor saw her a month ago, made a diagnosis of flu and prescribed bronchodilators for the shortness of breath.'

He tapped his silver pen on a notepad. 'So how is she now?'

'Not much better.' Kirby chewed her bottom lip in thought. 'She could be anaemic, like many women in their mid-thirties are, so on Friday I ordered a routine full blood examination and those results should be back shortly, but even so, I have a nagging feeling about it. Totally non-scientific, I know, but nagging none the less.'

Understanding lined his face. 'Listening to your gut feeling is an important part of being a good doctor. Out here you don't have access to the full weight of diagnostic tests that you get in a large hospital.'

He sat forward, his hands flat on the spun cotton of his summer trousers which so casually covered what she imagined to be solid, muscular thighs. 'A persistent cough and shortness of breath can too easily be attributed to asthma. As we've got an X-ray machine, let's do a chest X-ray. It's a simple test and hopefully we can rule out a lung mass.'

'But she's not a smoker and has no other risk factors.'

He shrugged. 'There are *other* masses that can be found in the chest. But that said, it's important to remember that non-smoking females are dying from lung cancer because it's being missed in the early stages of the disease. Granted, the air down here is cleaner than other places but you don't know what she's been exposed to.' He tugged on the hair just behind his ear, his voice rising slightly. 'Hell, we don't know half of what we're exposed to in the air or in our food.'

His heartfelt reaction surprised her. He sounded more like an environmentalist than a doctor. But, then again, he did grow organic vegetables and he didn't drink coffee. Two things she knew he hadn't done two years ago because Virginia had basically told her everything about this citified man who'd loved the good things in life. 'OK, I'll organise a chest X-ray. Thanks.'

'No problem, it's what I'm here for.' He spun back on his chair, his attention returning to the article he'd been reading when she'd walked into the room.

Familiar disappointment slugged her and she tried to shrug it off because there was *no* reason to feel like this. Nick had done his job well. Very well. *He's the mentor, you're the student. That's what you want and that's what you're getting.*

She continued to remind herself of that against the strange hollow feeling in her gut as she walked back to her consulting room. Glad of something to do, she picked up the phone and called Melinda, asking her to come in for a chest X-ray.

Melinda sat in the chair, her face pale with black smudges under her eyes. She rubbed her knee. 'I think I should have got an X-ray of my knee as well as my chest. It's been sore for the last week.' She sighed. 'I really hope the chest X-ray will tell you what's wrong with me because I'm sick of feeling like this and I think I'm getting worse, not better.'

Kirby silently agreed with her patient—Melinda had the pasty pallor of someone extremely unwell. She slid the black and white film onto the light box and flicked on the light. Using her pen she outlined the image. 'Your heart is here and it's the normal size, and if there was any fluid on your lungs or infection that would show up as white on the film. But your lungs are pretty clear, which is why they look black.' *And you don't have a tumour, thank goodness.*

'But I feel so awful.' Tears welled up in the woman's eyes. 'I'm so grumpy, the kids and Dev are avoiding me and all I want to do is sleep but I keep going hot and cold and my joints ache.'

'Just hot at night?' Piece by piece she tried to match up the vague symptoms. She rechecked the X-ray but there was no lower lobe consolidation, no sign of pneumonia.

Melinda wrung her hands. 'Sometimes during the day too.'

'Are you still menstruating?' Menopause was unlikely but Kirby had learned the hard way that some- times the unexpected happened.

Her patient grimaced. 'Oh, yes, I'm doing that too well—flooding, in fact.'

Which led Kirby back to her initial thoughts from Friday. Menstruating women were often anaemic—lacking in iron could make you feel pretty low. *But not give you hot flushes.* The words nagged at Kirby. Perhaps she needed to run a test for hormone levels and do blood cultures as well.

She glanced at her watch and picked up the phone to speak to Vicki. 'The courier should have arrived with the results of your blood test and hopefully the results will say I need to prescribe you my famous orange-juice-and-parsley iron-boosting drink.

'If that's the case, in two weeks you'll feel like a new woman and we can discuss your options to reduce your menstrual bleeding.' She smiled, trying to reassure her patient despite an enveloping sense of gloom that Melinda's condition would not be that simple and neither would it have such a straightforward solution.

But she *had* to be wrong. Right now she didn't trust her gut at all, given the way her body melted into a mush of pulsating need at one smile from Nick. How could one smile from a man she knew to be a woman-ising charmer undermine everything she'd learned at the hands of Anthony? *Face it, Kirby*, he'd said. *You can't give me what I need.*

She knew better than to get involved again—this time she knew in advance what the outcome would be and she wasn't putting her hand or heart up for another brutal and soul-destroying rejection. No, now she was a lot wiser and she knew better than to let attraction blind her to a handsome man. But her body wasn't listening to her brain and it betrayed her every time she clapped eyes on Nick. No, she definitely didn't trust her gut, because right now her radar was really out of whack.

A knock sounded on the door and Nick walked in, holding a printed piece of white paper with the familiar logo of Barago Hospital's pathology department. The smile on his face didn't quite reach his eyes and the lines around his mouth looked strained.

'I brought you this.' He handed the report to Kirby and immediately turned his attention to Melinda. 'I'm Nick Dennison. I hope you don't mind me barging in like this but as I'm working with Dr Atherton I thought I'd introduce myself.'

Recognition moved across the sick woman's face. 'Oh, you're from the market. When I bought those strawberries from you on Saturday I didn't realise you were a doctor. Mind you, I didn't get to taste any of them, the kids ate them all before we got home!'

Kirby heard the warm burr of his voice reply to Melinda but her whirling brain didn't decipher the words. At first astonishment that Nick had brought in the report drowned out the conversation then shock rocked through her, muting everything around her, and finally aching despair obliterated all sound. She read the pathology report three times and finally closed her eyes against the words. But they lingered against her retina as if burned there. Melinda had leukaemia.

Slowly the conversation between Nick and her patient sounded in her ears again and she sucked in a deep breath, turning to face them both. Nick had pulled

up a chair, his casual demeanour tinged with an alert-
ness she hadn't noticed before. She realised he'd read
the report and that was why he'd brought it in.

She shot him an appreciative look—she hated giving
out bad news. It wasn't something a person got better
at with practice and it certainly never got easier.
'Melinda, the results of your blood test are back and I'm
afraid it's not good news.'

Melinda instantly stiffened, fear clear in her eyes.
'What do you mean?'

Nothing Kirby could say would soften the truth. 'Your
white blood cells—the ones that fight infection—are
abnormal and that means you have a form of leukaemia.'

Melinda's hand shot to her mouth before falling back
to her lap. 'You mean cancer of the blood?'

Kirby nodded slowly. 'That's right. We need to get
you to Barago hospital this afternoon for a series of
tests, including a bone-marrow biopsy so that we can
get an accurate diagnosis and start chemotherapy.'

But Kirby knew Melinda hadn't heard a word since
she'd confirmed leukaemia was cancer.

The petrified woman started to breath quickly, short,
shallow breaths, her hands gripping the sides of the chair.

Kirby reached for a paper bag but Nick grabbed it first.

'Melinda.' He squatted down in front of her and took
her hand. Looking straight into her eyes, he spoke
slowly. 'I need you to breathe into the paper bag and try
to slow your breathing. I'm going to count to help you.'

Melinda's gaze fixed on Nick like a drowning woman
seeking a life preserver in a choppy sea. Her hands
trembled against the paper bag.

The timbre of Nick's voice vibrated reassuringly. 'Breathe in…breathe out… Breathe in…breathe out. That's fabulous, you're doing really well.'

Kirby stood up, needing to do something, and gently touched Melinda's shoulder. 'The dizzy feeling will fade with the deep breaths.' She felt so inadequate. This woman had just been told awful, life-changing news and her battle was only just beginning.

She caught Nick's steady gaze, filled with empathy, but she couldn't see any trace of her own feelings of powerlessness and frustration there. Had he given bad news so often that it no longer got to him? She immediately dismissed the uncharitable thought but she couldn't fathom the rock-solid determination that took up residence in his eyes.

Slowly Melinda lowered the brown paper bag onto her lap, her pupils, large and black, almost obliterating her hazel irises. 'I'm going to die, aren't I?'

Nick kept his hand on Melinda's arm as he sat back in his chair. 'You're about to start the biggest challenge of your life but many people successfully go into remission and go on to lead long and happy lives.'

A sob escaped Melinda's lips. 'But you can't tell me I'm not going to die.'

Nick spoke quietly, his voice steady and firm. 'Right now we don't know enough about your condition to tell you any more than what Kirby already said. This is why you're going to Barago for an accurate diagnosis and then probably to Melbourne for treatment.'

He leaned closer and the dappled sunshine streaming through the window caught his profile, emphasising the silver in his short hair and the unusually deep lines around his eyes and mouth. 'But I can tell you this—leukaemia will test you and force you to dig deep to release a strength you never knew you had. It will make you question everything about your life, force you to prioritise and give you the opportunity to truly know what is important to you.'

Kirby watched Melinda visibly calm under Nick's words and she wished she'd been able to express herself so eloquently but she was still back at 'It's so not fair'. She'd never heard any doctor speak about cancer like that. Usually, it was sticking to the bare facts about treatment.

As he picked up Melinda's hand, sunlight struck the backs of his hands, making the scars whiter than ever. 'I know you didn't put your hand up for this and it's a journey you don't want to take, but I can guarantee you there are parts of the trip that you won't regret.'

'Can I hold you to that?' Melinda's pain-tinged words sliced through the air.

Kirby's heart hurt and anger surged through her that a young mother of three had to deal with this illness and all the unknowns a disease like cancer generated.

'Absolutely, and I'm here to talk to any time.' Nick smiled but, unlike his usual charisma-laden grin, this smile simply conveyed serenity. 'And once you're home, I'll be keeping you supplied with vegetables.'

How could he be so calm? She railed against the unjust diagnosis. Melinda had leukaemia! How on earth could he be talking about vegetables?

Organic vegetables.

Something urged her to really study him while his attention was fully fixed on Melinda and slowly information started to slot into place. He was an experienced city doctor now growing vegetables in the country and avoiding talking about why. His shorter than expected hair grew darker than the blond it had been two years ago and the premature streaks of silver in his hair matched up with the deep lines around his eyes and mouth. White marks on the backs of his hands matched the type of scars left by an intravenous cannula.

Her lungs emptied of air and a shard of pain cramped her heart as all her unanswered questions about Nick lined up. She'd just solved the puzzle. She'd bet her last cent he was talking to Melinda not as a doctor but as a fellow traveller. Nick Dennison had experienced cancer.

The only question still needing an answer was what type of cancer. *No, there's one more. Has he won the battle?*

The thought that he might not terrified her more than it should.

CHAPTER FOUR

NICK bit into the sweet nectarine, savouring the complex but delicious summer flavour on his tongue, and marvelling at the taste. Once he wouldn't have given that a second thought.

'That looks good.' Kirby walked into the staffroom, her usual cheerful demeanour completely absent, dented by the morning's work and Melinda's diagnosis.

This woman confounded him. She lurched from being in charge and confident to needing more reassurance than he would have thought necessary. She reminded him of a junior resident, which was nonsense as she must have far more experience than that if she was doing her first GP rotation.

'Catch.' He tossed her a nectarine and pulled out a chair.

'Thanks.' She bit into the fruit she'd neatly caught and juice dribbled down her chin. Her pink tongue darted out, stroking her skin and licking at the sweet juice.

The image of her tongue against his chin, against his lips, in his mouth, beamed in 3D depth. Colours exploded in his head as blood drained to his groin. He silently started chanting the names of all the bones in the body and blood slowly and regretfully returned to his head.

Now fully back in control, he risked looking at Kirby with the eyes of a colleague. Right now she needed a mentor and that was his job. He sat down and gave her an encouraging smile. 'If you're going to take everyone's problems on board like this then you're not going to last very long as a GP.'

Her large doe-like eyes reflected sadness, and a sigh rolled over her plump bottom lip. 'But it's just so unfair.'

He took in a thoughtful breath and wondered if she was one of those people who had lived a charmed life untouched by misfortune. 'Life isn't fair, Kirby. Surely you've worked that out by now.'

Her sparkling eyes, always so fill of vibrant colours and movement, suddenly filled with pervading emptiness. The change both startled and disturbed him and something inside him ached.

A moment later she shook her head and gave him a tight smile. 'I know I'm a hopeless case but when something happens outside the realm of what is expected in the circle of life, I find myself railing against it. If Melinda was seventy-eight I'd feel sad but she would have raised her kids and lived a full life.'

Memories of a parade of eyes filled with resignation and expressions of grief and fear hammered him. 'She still can.' His words sounded overly firm but he hated the way people assigned a death certificate to a diagnosis of cancer, which was why he refused to talk about what he'd been through.

A flash of understanding and purpose streaked across

her face. 'Oh, don't get me wrong, of course she can and I hope she will, but I wouldn't wish that *struggle* on anyone.' Her gaze hovered on him for a moment, her expression intent. 'Would you?'

The hairs on his arms rose for a moment as he met her unsettling stare. He leaned back casually and placed the pit of his nectarine on a plate that sat between them, striving not to give anything personal away. 'Of course not. But although her treatment will be tough, she'll appreciate parts of the process.'

'Really?' Her brow creased in lines of confusion. 'How so?'

'She'll learn a lot about herself.'

'More than if she wasn't sick?'

He relaxed as the discussion stayed centred on Melinda. 'Absolutely. In general, human beings don't like change and most of us don't put our hand up to experience it. Cancer barges in and railroads you so you have no choice but to meet it head on and change.' He learned forward, warming to his topic. 'You drop the non-essentials and you see things with a clarity not everyone gets the opportunity to have. It's probably the only advantage of the disease.'

'That's an interesting perspective.' Kirby put the pit of the nectarine down on the plate and then leaned forward on her elbows, her chin resting on the palms of her hands, her gaze fixed directly on him. 'I've never heard it explained like that before but that's because it's happened to you, hasn't it? That's why you're here in Port, growing vegetables, instead of slaying even bigger career dragons in Melbourne.'

His chest tightened at her soft-voiced but accurate assumption. Damn it, he'd walked right into her question and he didn't want to answer it. He wanted his time in Port to be free of everything he associated with illness. He didn't want to see sympathy for him shining from those large bluer-than-blue eyes, and he didn't want her to start tiptoeing around him like people had in Melbourne. He just wanted things to be as they had been right up until this point. Shrugging, he bluffed. 'Perhaps I just wanted a tree-change.'

She shook her head. 'I *might* have believed that on Saturday. After all, growing veggies and living in the bush could have been because you'd burned out from years of fast-tracking up the professional ladder, but even then it was a stretch. Now too many things add up—your hair, your vice-less diet.' Her fingers reached out toward his hand and with a feather-soft touch they traced a jagged white scar. 'The marks of an infected IV.'

A fire-storm of sensation detonated under her touch, rolling through him fast and leaving smouldering desire in its wake. Desire he could no longer pretend didn't exist. 'Why is this so important to you, Sherlock?' He trapped her hand with his free one, sandwiching hers between his.

Her pupils dilated into inky discs and a pulse fluttered in her throat as she took a long deep breath, making her breasts strain against the fitted bodice of her dress. 'Because you're a puzzle.'

He recognised her body's response to him, the marks of desire matching those of his own. Their attraction for each other ran between them like a vibrating wire.

It had been months and months since he'd held a woman's hand, hell, since he'd really held a woman. Like so many things in his life, he'd taken for granted the touch of a woman. He loved women. He loved their company, their scent, their curves—everything about them—and now his body craved to hold a woman in his arms again. He ached for it. These feelings he understood. Mutual attraction. Undiluted lust.

And he read them in Kirby's pink cheeks, her slightly open mouth and in the lift of her breasts. He read enough to want the buzz of the chase.

But without warning the heat from her hand surprisingly morphed from scorching fire to cosy heat, warming him, swirling around in sweet tendrils, licking at his self-imposed silence.

'And I can't resist solving puzzles.' She smiled a long, slow, knowing smile, which wound across her face, bringing it alive, the way colour invigorated a black and white canvas.

A smile that promised something good, something wonderful. A smile that called to him unlike any smile ever had. Right there and then, not telling her became harder than keeping his own counsel.

'So you can't resist me?' He traced a circle on her hand with his thumb.

Kirby's body shivered as his caress sent waves of delicious need pounding through her. *Remember Anthony, remember the hurt.* She forced out a laugh and pulled her hand out from under his, ignoring the chill that followed. 'See, this is the puzzle. You're known for flirting charm.'

'But not for growing vegetables. Fair enough.' His guarded expression unexpectedly melted. 'I can see why me being in Port is a puzzle because for years I worked hard and played hard.'

'So what changed?' She tried not to sound as if she was interrogating him but she badly wanted to know what had happened more than she probably should.

'Just under two years ago I couldn't shake off a virus. I felt like I had treacle running through my veins and I was constantly tired and my skin seemed to itch like mad. Then I discovered a pea-sized lump just behind my ear.' He tilted his head, his deep green eyes questioning. 'What do you think, Doctor?'

He'd just turned his story into a teaching session. She ran the symptoms through her mind. 'A type of lymphoma?'

'Well done, Dr Atherton. I had stage-one non-Hodgkin's lymphoma so I stepped down from Melbourne City and started seven months of IV chemotherapy.'

She schooled her face not to show any emotion but to keep it focussed on a teaching session, as that was obviously the way he wanted to go. 'How was that?'

'What do you think it might be like?'

She spoke from the heart. 'Bloody awful.'

He laughed a rich, body-shaking laugh. 'That pretty much sums it up.' He flattened his hands out against the table. 'And you're pretty observant, Sherlock. I did have problems with infections on my hands so I ended up with a chest tube and a natty scar.'

He raised his brows and shot her a look of pure, unadulterated flirtation—a classic Nick Dennison look.

'But you didn't know that because you're *yet* to see me with my shirt off.'

Her mouth dried at the thought of all that exposed golden skin but despite the fog of lust that encircled her brain she managed to see through his ploy. She rolled her eyes. 'You can't derail me that easily.' *Liar!* 'I want to hear the whole story. Did you have radiation therapy as well?'

He ran his hand through his hair and frustration raced across his face. 'Yeah, I did and losing my hair really sucked, not because I minded being bald for a while but because I realised that when things get to me I run my hand through my hair. When there is no hair to tug on there's no satisfaction in it at all.'

'You could have invented a new action.'

He smiled, his eyes sparkling and dimples scoring his cheeks. 'Ah, but old habits are very hard to break.'

Just like flirting. It was second nature to him—see a woman and flick into flirting mode. 'It won't be long before you can really bury your fingers in your hair.' Her fingers tingled, wanting to do that very thing, and she quickly laced them together. 'But generally treatment takes about seven months. How come you didn't go back to work?'

He pushed back his chair, walked to the water filter and flicked on the tap, pouring two glasses of water. 'I went onto oral chemotherapy and I felt awful. If I'd worked at a desk job perhaps I could have managed it, but not A and E.'

She stood up and walked over to him, calculating the elapsed time since his diagnosis, still confused. 'Are you still on chemo, still battling the lymphoma?'

He immediately stiffened. 'No. The chemo is finished and I'm in remission. I'm not battling non-Hodgkin's lymphoma. I'm surviving it.'

His words shot out harsh and uncompromising and at that moment she understood exactly why he hadn't wanted to talk about being sick. He was focussed on his future, not his past. 'And Port and growing vegetables is part of that?'

He passed her the glass of cold water and leaned back against the bench next to her. 'When you spend a year feeling like death warmed up, you get sick of yourself and you get sick of the role of being a patient. You also get weary of well-intentioned people asking you how you are.' His eyes narrowed slightly, as if willing her to understand and warning her at the same time. 'I wanted some time out between being a patient and going back to work, time to just enjoy being well.'

'But why did you decide to grow vegetables?'

'When you're faced with the possibility of dying, you make changes you never expected to have to make. Taking a break from work was one, changing what I ate was another. Until I got sick it was easy to dismiss the link between food and illness but I can feel the difference in myself. I couldn't do "nothing" for nine months and I was growing my own veggies so I just extended it, and the markets are fun. I came out there because no one up here knew me—' He gave a wry grin, resignation clinging to him. 'Well, almost no one.'

She bit her lip, realising that by pushing him back to work she'd interrupted his plan. 'Sorry.'

He leaned into her, his shoulder nudging hers in a

friendly bump and his arm lingering against the length of her own. 'No, don't be sorry, it's all good. I'm enjoying myself and in six months' time when I go back to the city I won't be rusty.'

His body warmth swam through her, making her dizzy. *In six months' time.* At least he had a plan. She'd rushed to Port so fast she really couldn't see past tomorrow. All she knew was that everything she'd expected to be happening in her life right now wasn't. Every plan she and Anthony had made lay scattered in a million irreparable pieces and her love for him had been returned, stamped unacceptable.

Her world spun on an unsteady axis and the only thing about her future that she truly knew was that it would not be happening with Anthony. *Not happening with any man.*

'You OK?' Penetrating eyes bored into her.

She shoved her gloomy thoughts of heart-breaking loss back down where they belonged, plastered a smile on her face and spoke the first thing that came into her head. 'I'm still having trouble seeing you as a farmer.'

'Come see me in action, then.' He pulled his keys out of his pocket and walked toward the door. 'I'm working in the veggie patch every afternoon.'

The unexpected invitation was tantalisingly tempting. She strove for feigned interest and casualness. 'I'll keep that in mind if I'm ever out that way on rounds.'

He nodded. 'You do that. Around three is a good time to drop by.'

'Is that when you take a break?'

He stared straight at her, his eyes shimmering like

sunshine on water, backlit with teasing intent. 'It's the hottest part of the day and usually the time I lose the shirt.' He gave her a knowing wink and disappeared.

Indignation at his perceptive wink, the one that said he knew she enjoyed looking at him, floundered against the surge of hot, delicious longing that shook her to her toes and left her wanting more.

He's your colleague and mentor. But the words sounded hollow. She dragged in a deep breath, determined to make the words count. They had to mean something. They had to protect her because, no matter how much she wanted to see where he lived, no matter how much her body craved to see him shirtless, she wouldn't allow it to happen.

She couldn't. She refused to allow herself to get close to another man again and have him find that her perfect body was so internally flawed. No way was she going to expose her faulty body to any more derision and heartache. She lived with the heartache every day already.

Nick took a long slug of water from his water bottle and then took off his hat and squirted some over his head, enjoying the coolness of the liquid against his hot skin. Turbo gave him a baleful look from under the tree. 'Hot, mate, isn't it? Only mad dogs and Englishmen go out in the midday sun, eh?'

Turbo barked.

'Sorry, I see what you mean. It's three o'clock and you're under the tree so you don't qualify as mad.' He jammed his hat back on his head and toyed with the idea of stopping but he needed to get this fertilising done now that his mornings were taken up with the clinic.

He caught himself glancing down the dirt track that doubled as his driveway. Heat haze hovered, making the metal of the closed gate look crooked. It had been four days since he'd issued his invitation to Kirby, suggesting she visit the farm.

Four days since she'd sat opposite him, her cheeks flushed, glistening lush lips and a sultry voice that rumbled through him every time he thought about it. She hadn't been able to hide her attraction to him and he'd expected her to drive up the track the following day. But she hadn't shown up and she hadn't mentioned the invitation since he'd extended it.

It was probably a good thing. *I don't think so.* He ignored the voice, overlaying it with reason. He'd been high on the joy of lust when he'd issued the invitation and had broken his self-imposed requirement of keeping work and play separate. Two years of celibacy could do that to a bloke.

The professional colleague part of him was pleased that at least she was the one being sensible but despite knowing that he still glanced at the gate each afternoon. It niggled that he did that. It niggled even more that she hadn't come. Two years ago he'd never been stood up and he wasn't that sure he wanted to get used to the feeling.

Two years ago and for years before that he'd dated women—lots of women. He loved the chase, the variety, the conversations and the sex. Unlike his parents, who'd been high-school sweethearts and had married each other at twenty-two, he'd avoided anything that came close to a committed relationship.

And cancer hadn't changed that. A committed relationship meant marriage and children. He didn't particularly have anything against marriage per se, but children, well, no way was he going to be a parent. Not when he'd lived through his parents' unresolved grief—he had no intention of reliving that same nightmare or exposing himself to that sort of loss again.

I just want a normal sister. His twelve-year-old self jetted up from the depths he normally kept sealed.

Plunging his shovel into the enormous pile of mushroom compost, he threw himself into the work and pushed his childhood back where it belonged. But he couldn't get the usual buzz of satisfaction that hard labour gave him because Kirby kept dogging his thoughts. Kirby with a mouth designed for kissing and a body made for pleasure, but who'd been professionally friendly at work and had kept every conversation strictly about patients. No matter what topic he tried to bring up she always neatly brought the conversation back to work. The level of supervision she was demanding bothered him.

By now in her career she really should have a lot more confidence in her diagnostic ability and treatment options, and only be using him as a sounding board for difficult cases. Instead, she seemed to want his review of all her cases. He needed to talk to her about that.

He lifted the shovel, dumping the contents into the wheelbarrow. He'd do it tomorrow but he'd have to be ready because every day this week, at the end of their lunchtime meeting, Kirby had jumped up and said, 'You'd better head off so you can enjoy your afternoon,' and she'd walked briskly out of the staffroom door, back toward her office.

His body absorbed the rhythm of the shovelling, his mind unravelling and roaming free. He suddenly realised that all week Kirby had been leaving the meeting abruptly the moment the last case had been discussed. She never lingered just to chat. No chatting and she hadn't visited. Was it possible she didn't want to spend any time with him?

Nah, not possible.

Laughing at the resurgence of his now healthy if misguided ego, he laid his shovel across the wheelbarrow and lifted the handles, ready to push his load to the vegetable garden.

Turbo barked and jumped up.

'Rest time's over, is it?'

Instead of running over to Nick, Turbo stood stock still, his black ears standing up, alert and listening. He ran part way down the track and then returned, barking all the time as if to say, *Come on.*

Nick put the barrow down and listened. Faintly in the distance he could hear the vroom of an engine. Using his hand as a shield against the sun, he saw a familiar, once-white, now red-dust-covered four-wheel drive round the bend and pull up at the gate.

Everything comes to those who wait. The gorgeous Kirby had arrived and for the first time ever they were going to be truly alone. He couldn't stop the broad smile rolling over his lips.

CHAPTER FIVE

YOU'VE still got time to turn around. Kirby braked at Nick's gate, already regretting the impulsive decision to drive along Nick's road in the hope of checking out his house. Why hadn't she just kept driving straight back into Port? Checking over her shoulder, she threw the gear stick into reverse, anxious to get back to the safety of the main road. With a quick, final glance around to check all areas were clear before she pressed down the accelerator, she looked up—straight into lush-green smiling eyes filled with a wicked glint.

Nick. Her mouth dried, and her tongue automatically moistened her lips. He'd seen her and now there was no turning back.

He moved forward with the easy grace of a panther and with a practised hand lazily swung the gate open and walked toward her car, his gait easy and rolling—a farmer's walk complete with a faithful dog trotting by his side. This time he really did look like a farmer from the tip of his battered hat down to his worn elastic-sided boots. Thankfully a shirt still covered his chest but as he got closer she realised it was wet.

Damp cotton clung to well-defined pectoral muscles and solid biceps, outlining them in perfect, taunting detail. Her heart thundered so hard in her chest that she could hear it. Could he? For all that the shirt didn't hide, it may as well have been off. *Why* had she pulled the wheel hard right at Sheep-Wash Corner? After all, her concern about a patient could have waited until tomorrow morning.

But that's not really why you're here, is it? You caved in and gave in to wanting to see where he lived. Gave in to wanting to see him.

Her palm connected hard with the top of the steering wheel and she welcomed the jarring sensation thudding painfully all the way to her shoulder. She was really starting to hate that challenging voice. She knew she should have just kept driving but she hadn't so now she needed to salvage the situation.

Wanting to be on the front foot, she flicked the switch that operated her window and watched it wind down, determined to get in the first word. 'Hello.'

He leaned forward, his arms resting casually on the door. 'G'day. Glad you could make it.'

His slow, drawling delivery stroked her skin, stoked the banked heat inside her. She swallowed hard as his scent of rich earth, hard work and soap washed over her, tugging at a basic need. In her search for control she blurted out, 'I was on my way back from visiting Tom Lenders and I wanted to ask you something.'

Dark brows rose, overriding the first crease of a frown as a flicker of disquiet appeared in his eyes. He pushed back from the door, the corded muscles in his arms thick like rope. 'Put her in gear and I'll meet you up at the house.'

'Are you sure?'

He nodded and slapped the cab of the vehicle with his hand as if to say, *Go through now*.

With her gut churning she drove through the gate, but Turbo soon had her smiling as he bounded forward, racing the car up past an enormous fenced vegetable garden. Glancing in the rear-view mirror, she saw Nick swing and latch the gate shut before turning and jogging back along the track. Pulling her eyes back to the road, she took the curve and a house came into view.

Wonder chased by regret immediately poured through her. A freshly painted weatherboard miner's cottage with a corrugated-iron roof stood in front of her, its plain Victorian lines offset by the simple decorative carving at the top of each veranda post. She slipped out of the four-wheel drive, her feet crunching on gravel, and Turbo immediately dropped a ball at her feet, panting at her in enthusiastic anticipation.

Distracted, she patted his head, her gaze still fixed on the house. *Whatever you want, my darling. Nothing will ever be too much for my wife and family. You know family is everything to me.*

She swallowed hard against Anthony's duplicitous voice and walked slowly up the box-hedge-lined path that led to the centre of the veranda and the front door flanked by matching aloe vera plants in heritage green wooden planters. Her shoes sounded loud on the hardwood boards as she stepped up from the worn blue-stone step. Two wicker chairs sat invitingly on the veranda, with a low table in front of them. A sheaf of papers had been weighted down by a jug covered with an old-fashioned doily that kept flies from touching the contents. A well-thumbed novel lay face down, its spine deeply creased down the centre.

If there'd been a discarded scooter or skateboard nearby and some balls and a chalkboard, it would have been exactly as she'd pictured the house Anthony had promised her. The one she'd envisaged sharing with him and raising their family in.

Don't go there. Anthony doesn't want you. It's over, you know it's over.

Taking a deep breath, she plastered a smile on her face and turned at the sound of Nick's footsteps on the crushed white-rock path. 'Great house.'

'Thanks. I like it, although I wouldn't want to spend a winter without installing some heating.' He grinned at her. 'Open fires are all very romantic but they don't keep you very warm. It's definitely a summer house.'

He pulled off his work gloves, dropped them onto the table and poured two glasses of what looked like lemon cordial from the jug and passed her a glass. 'Grab a seat.'

Tendrils of warmth flicked through her veins as she lowered herself into the wide, comfortable chair. 'Is that the plan after this summer? To use it as a holiday house?'

He leaned back in his chair, his long legs stretching out in front of him, his left arm hanging down the side of the chair as his fingers rubbed Turbo's head. 'Probably. I love it down here but, like you, it's just a short-term plan.'

She stiffened as the horror of returning to Melbourne

merged with all her insecurities. 'Why would you assume my plan is short term? Don't you think I can cut it as a country GP?'

He levelled a prosaic stare directly at her. 'You said this was your first GP rotation. That means you have to do a second one somewhere else.'

'Oh, right.' *Dumb, dumb, dumb.* She really should learn to think before she spoke. She took a slug of her drink and changed the subject. 'This is delicious—what is it?'

'Home-made lemon cordial.' He trailed his finger around the rim of his glass. 'You said you wanted to ask me something about Tom Lenders?'

Thankful to be back on safe territory she grabbed onto the topic with enthusiasm. 'Tom is a seventy-five-year-old man with hypertension and has recently been complaining of shortness of breath.'

'Any history of asthma?'

'No, and his chest X-ray is clear. There's no sign of cardiomyopathy or congestive cardiac failure but he has an audible wheeze and his peak flow is lower than expected.'

He tilted his head, intelligent eyes scanning her. 'So, what are *your* thoughts?'

She sat a bit straighter, feeling confident of her answer. 'I'm thinking that he has a form of asthma precipitated by the betablocker he's been taking for four years.'

Frown lines formed across his brow. 'And you brought this case to review why?'

She caught the slight tone of censure and was puzzled by his reaction. 'I wanted to be sure I didn't miss anything.'

He nodded, his lips pursing together firmly. 'You

haven't missed a thing *but* I think you're missing the hospital system.'

His words sailed far too close to the truth for comfort and she smiled tightly. 'It takes a bit of getting used to but, no, I wouldn't say I was missing it.'

One black eyebrow rose enquiringly. 'Really? You've come from an environment where every decision made by a resident is reviewed by the registrar and every decision made by the registrar is reviewed by the consultant.' He put down his glass. 'Although by the time third year's over, most consultants are giving registrars a large amount of free rein.'

'Hmm.' She nodded and tacitly agreed. After all, what he said was true even though it hadn't actually happened to her.

He leaned forward. 'You would have found that?'

His gaze seemed to rivet itself to her mouth and she realised she was gnawing her bottom lip. She *so* didn't want to talk about this. Didn't want talk about how her life had fallen apart and she'd left her position at Prince William's way too early.

She tried a politician's tactic. Nodding, she gave another 'Hmm' and raised her arm. 'What do you call that tree over there?'

His head didn't move and his eyes didn't even flicker in the direction of the solid tree with the unusual seedpods. 'A banksia.' His gaze narrowed and his jaw tightened. 'You did finish third year?'

His accusatory tone lingered between them and his razor-sharp investigative look not only cornered her, it pinned her to the wall. Every instinct had her wanting to flee and she willed her phone to ring, wanting something, anything, to happen that would get her out of here. Adrenaline poured through her, the fight-and-flight response going into overdrive, and her body responded violently with a flush of non-sexual heat.

Horrible, unwanted heat washed through her, starting in her toes and building in intensity until all her skin burned so hot and tinder dry it felt like it would peel. Sweat immediately followed—drenching her, running in rivulets under her breasts, settling in the creases of her skin, threatening to soak her vest top. She gave thanks it was a hot summer's day and the flush and sweating would go unnoticed.

You're twenty-seven! What did you do to make this happen? Anthony's bitter voice boomed in her head. She downed her drink, forcing away the unwelcome voice, willing the hot flush to subside and steeling herself against the painful reminder of what it really meant.

Nick rose in one fluid movement and silently refilled her glass before settling back into his chair. His quiet voice rumbled deeply around the veranda, laced with tough resolve. 'As I'm acting as your mentor, I need to know how much experience you really have. You need to be honest with me, Kirby. I need the truth.'

The truth. Her heart pounded in agitation. He'd caught her out. She'd been double-checking everything because she hadn't had enough experience as a senior medical officer. But the moment she told him she'd left Prince William's early he'd ask why and the truth involved so many things she didn't want to tell.

The truth, the whole truth and nothing but the truth.

The words read to a witness in court echoed in her mind. Suddenly a tiny shaft of light pierced the darkness and she knew she could tell Nick the truth. She sent up a silent vote of thanks that he hadn't asked for the whole truth. That she wasn't prepared to give.

Nick waited, watching a battle of emotions on Kirby's oval face. She really didn't want to tell him but he wouldn't let her get away without telling him. He would have to write up a report on her and for an accurate assessment he needed to have a starting bench-mark. But he didn't want to sound like an inquisitor.

After all, she'd come out here to visit and he wanted it to be social more than work. He wanted a chance to be alone with her. He stood up and extended his hand. 'How about we walk and talk? There's a place I'd like to show you.'

Her already large eyes seemed to expand and her pale face flickered with gratitude mixed with resistant resignation. 'If you insist.' Her hand slowly slid into his.

'I do.' He pulled her to her feet and her reluctance seeped slowly into him, tagged by slowly building heat.

The moment she stood, she eased her hand out of his and walked toward the veranda steps.

Inexplicable loss streaked through him and he forced down every desire to grab back her hand. He strode after her. 'This way—the path goes from the back of the house.'

They walked in silence for a few minutes and he finally broke it. 'Come on, Sherlock, fill me in.'

She ducked under a low branch of a casuarina tree, her footfall hushed against the pile of dropped needles.

'You're right. I didn't finish my third year. In fact, I only completed seven months.'

He held up another branch for her and gave in to his need to breathe deeply, inhaling her wildflower scent as she passed by. 'That goes some way to explaining things.'

She gave a tight smile. 'Good.'

With the set of her mouth and the line of her shoulders he knew she was holding back more than she was giving. He took a calculated gamble to get her to tell him the story. 'Were you asked to leave Prince William?'

She came to an abrupt halt, indignation streaking across her face. 'No, I was not asked to leave. In fact, I was asked to reconsider my resignation.'

'But you didn't.'

'No.' She sighed and kept walking. 'I left for personal reasons.'

The path ended as they arrived at a creek lined with vibrant green tree ferns. Large fronds bent low toward the water, which burbled and rushed over and around granite boulders worn smooth by its action. Getting Kirby to tell him her story was like getting blood from one of the creek's stones. 'They must have been pretty big reasons if you left a job to come to this one before you were one hundred per cent ready.'

Her hands balled into fists and hung by her sides. 'If breaking off an engagement constitutes big, I guess it was.'

Her words surprised him, mostly because he hadn't expected her to have been engaged. He'd never considered marriage, it wasn't part of his life's plan, but he could empathise. 'At least you broke it off before it involved the full catastrophe of property and children.'

She swung away from him, an agonising sound starting to break from her lips.

The sound stopped abruptly but not before it tore at something inside him. He reached out and touched her arm. 'Hell, Kirby, I'm sorry, I just assumed it was you who broke it off.'

She turned back slowly toward him, her expression so full of hurt that it was the most natural thing in the world to pull her into his arms. With his forefinger he traced a line down her cheek. 'He didn't deserve you.'

As she looked up at him her voice cracked. 'He didn't want me the way I am.'

More than anything he wanted to banish the look of empty desolation that hovered in her beautiful eyes, haunting him. He tipped his head forward, feeling the caress of her breath on his face. 'More fool him.'

She stared straight at him and snagged her bottom lip with her teeth.

Desire thundered through him so hard it almost knocked the breath from his lungs. With his hand gently cupping her jaw, he lowered his mouth to hers, fusing his lips against her waiting softness and claiming what he'd dreamed about for days. She tasted of sugar tinged with citrus, of searing heat and need, and he lost himself in her, like a parched man stumbling into an oasis.

He trailed his tongue across her lips, touching, tasting and seeking entry, needing to bury himself in her heat and tang. Needing to absorb her essence, feel it in his veins.

Her mouth opened slowly under his and with a moan of need he accepted her unspoken invitation and deepened the kiss. Like an early voyager he explored and then he plundered, eagerly taking everything and still not getting enough. His arms tightened around her, moulding her soft curves to his toned body, treasuring the feel of having a beautiful, supple woman in his arms again. Stunned by how it far exceeded any memory.

Pulling away the loose band that barely held her hair in place, he breathed deeply, taking his fill of the aroma of cinnamon apples. His fingers splayed through her silky strands, revelling in the way their softness caressed his skin. As his mouth played over hers, he explored all the contours and dips, the peaks and hollows and left behind a firm imprint of himself.

The sound of the racing water of the creek, the songs of the birds and the rustling of the breeze through the ferns slowly retreated. All that existed was the feel of Kirby in his arms, the touch of her mouth against his and the way his blood pounded through him until every cell vibrated with the bliss of being alive.

'Nick.'

Her voice seemed a long way away. 'Hmm?' He started to trail kisses down to her jaw.

'Nick.' Her voice sounded louder, insistent, and her hands gripped his upper arms.

The pressure acted like a brake. He lifted his head and looked at her through dazed eyes, her image slowly coming into focus. Her fine hair cascaded around her face in complete disarray, her lush lips were wet, pink and swollen, but it was the startled look in her eyes that centred him with thudding brutality.

What the hell had he just done? He'd always prided himself on his finesse with women, of giving rather than taking, and yet right now, without any thought for her or her comfort, he'd kissed her senseless like a frustrated and randy teenager. He pulled back, mortified. 'I'm sorry, I shouldn't have done that. I shouldn't have kissed you.'

She stiffened slightly and her eyes, normally so clear, suddenly clouded, but then she shook her head. 'Please don't feel bad, it's not you, it's me. I just can't do this right now.' She drew in an unsteady breath and rested her palm on his forearm. 'I know it sounds really clichéd but what I really need is for you to be a colleague and a friend.'

A friend.

His blood drained from his groin and tried to perfuse his brain. A beautiful woman stood in front of him asking for his friendship. He'd never really done friendship with a woman and every part of him recoiled. He wanted her in his arms, he wanted her naked, and he wanted her wrapped tightly around him. Hell, he just wanted her.

He silently cursed the complete irony of the situation. His body had finally come roaring back to life, pulsing with virile good health, and the one woman he wanted didn't want him.

Somehow he managed to smile. 'Sure, I understand.'

Relief streamed across her face. 'You do?'

'I do.'

The hell you do, he told himself.

But he had to pretend he did. He had no other choice.

CHAPTER SIX

'HEY, Dr Kirby, I bet you I can race you to those big trees.' Cooper pointed to the large Norfolk pines at the far end of the big asphalt car park at the back of Kids' Cottage.

'You're on.' Kirby stooped down and tightened her shoelaces, smiling to herself. Three days ago Cooper had been withdrawn and sullen but the Port sunshine and the fabulous staff at KC had drawn him out. 'But do I get a handicap?'

Cooper flexed his fingers which extended from gloved palms. 'Nah, that's mine and today I'm not sharing.'

She grinned at the determination on his face. 'You're a tough opponent.' She put her left foot forward on an imaginary line as Cooper dropped his hands. 'Ready, set.'

'Go!' Cooper thrust forward, the wheels of his wheelchair spinning quickly as he propelled himself down the slight incline and toward the trees.

Kirby ran hard, needing to put in some serious effort to keep up, and she arrived at the pines seconds after him, panting for breath.

A beaming boy full of the flush of a win gave her

faint praise. 'You did OK, Doc, better than my camp counsellor. I beat him by heaps!'

Too breathless to laugh, she rested her hands against her thighs. 'Thanks, Cooper, I like to keep fit.' She caught her breath and then headed back toward the main building, leaving Cooper at the archery range. Glancing at her watch, she increased her pace as she'd promised to do story time for the younger campers.

She loved spending time at KC and couldn't understand why Nick didn't want to do any work here. Why he really preferred not to work with children at all. She wondered if it was because Melbourne City was so very close to the Royal Children's Hospital so not many children came through Emergency. Perhaps he hadn't worked with many kids and paediatrics put him out of his comfort zone. But that reason didn't quite gel with her because Nick Dennison had a bring-it-on attitude to life and nothing seemed to faze him.

It really shouldn't bother her but it nagged at her because it was yet another part of the unsolved puzzle that was Nick, and she hated to admit it but the man fascinated her. He shouldn't because he wasn't her type at all. No man could be her type now.

Still, Nick not wanting to work at KC meant she didn't have to share the kids with anyone. She treasured that, visiting most days, even when she wasn't needed for her professional services. Although there was a large group of diabetic children visiting this week, not all the kids had a medical condition and many campers came to give their parents a break and a chance to sort out issues in their own lives. Often these children needed a lot more TLC than the kids who had a medical condition they'd grown to accept.

She loved children—loved their unbridled enthusiasm, their abundant curiosity and the sheer joy they could get from the simplest things. Her work here kept her busy, but it also kept her sane, filling a big hole in her life, filling a need.

Nick fills a need.

Nick. A vivid image of sea-green eyes filled with the simmering heat of desire flooded her, making her swallow hard.

Two weeks had passed since she'd called at Riversleigh and visited Nick at home. Two weeks since he'd kissed her senseless, reducing her to a quivering mass of pulsating need that had driven every coherent thought from her head. She'd revisited that kiss every day from every angle, from every blissful touch. She'd lost herself completely—melting into his arms and giving herself over to the intoxicating way his mouth had roamed deliciously over hers, sparking trails of glorious sensation that had spun and wove, tantalising her until she'd vibrated with pleasure and yearned for more.

Pathetically, it had only taken the touch of one kiss for her to ignore every promise she'd made to herself. She'd caved in completely and returned his kiss with the fervour of a lust-struck adolescent and taken as much from him as she could get. She'd absorbed his touch, savoured his earthy taste and revelled in the cocoon of his arms, never wanting the kiss to end.

But as the pressure of his mouth had lessened and his lips had trailed gloriously along her jaw, the slight change in his touch had been enough for a tiny but rational fissure to pierce her desire-fuelled haze. Panic had immediately surged. She'd pulled back, half hating what she was doing but knowing it was the right thing.

No matter how she'd once imagined her life playing out, she knew that dream was dead and that getting involved with any man was impossible. She knew that to be an irrefutable truth just as she knew the world to be round. She couldn't offer a man the future he would want—a future that she longed for but knew could never happen.

That was why Anthony had trashed her heart and left her, and why all other men would eventually leave her too. No way was she ever risking her bruised and shattered heart again to such wrenching pain.

Instead, she threw herself into caring for kids because it was as close as she was going to get to a child of her own.

She opened the library door to shrieks of, 'Read this one, Kirby,' and four enthusiastic pre-schoolers mobbed her, each clutching their own choice of book. Laughing, she collapsed onto the bright cushions and beanbags and gathered the children in close. 'We can read them all. Let's start with this story about the hare and his nut-brown baby.'

Warm bodies snuggled in, heads rested on her shoulders and her lap, and podgy hands touched her. She breathed in deeply, knowing intrinsically that she needed the comforting touch of these children as much as they needed her time and care.

The loud clang of metal against metal roused them all from their fourth story. Kirby finished reading the sentence, placed a bookmark between the pages and closed the book. 'That's the dinner bell, gang. Let's skip to the dining hall.'

'I want to hop.' A small but determined five-year-old stood with her hands authoritatively on her hips.

Kirby smiled and adopted a mediating approach. 'We can do that too but maybe we should hold hands.'

With lots of giggles and squeals, they made their way across the quadrangle to the mess hall, where the girls' camp counsellor waited to take them into dinner. 'Wash your hands first.'

As the girls obediently lined up at the taps at the base of the stairs, the counsellor smiled at Kirby. 'Thanks for doing story-time. It gave me a chance to telephone their parents and reassure them that all is well.'

A real sense of community rolled through her. 'It's my pleasure. I think I enjoy the stories more than they do.' She glanced at her watch. 'But I'd better get going or else the supermarket will be closed and I'm getting tired of tinned spaghetti on toast.'

With a quick wave to the girls, Kirby ducked behind the old, grey, salt-weathered buildings and made her way back toward her car. She'd just pressed the auto-unlock button when she heard someone call her name and she turned toward the voice.

Hurrying toward her was Judy Dalton, the woman in charge of KC, her round cheeks pink with exertion. 'Oh, I'm so glad I caught you. Ben Hadley, one of the diabetic boys, has just vomited everywhere and he's looking a bit pale and wan.'

'Vomiting before dinner? Has he had his before-dinner insulin?' Kirby opened the boot and pulled out her medical kit, a thread of concern weaving through her.

Judy gave a quick nod. 'Yes, he'd just come up to sick bay to have it, which is why I left Phillipa with him, trying to encourage him to eat a jelly snake, and I ran to catch up with you.'

'I'm glad you caught me.' Kirby slammed the boot closed, hoping she could reach the boy before he had a hypo.

They jogged to the sick bay and found thirteen-year-old Ben lying on the bed, his face very white—even his freckles looked pale. Beads of sweat lined his forehead, dripping into his hair, and he'd pulled his legs up under his chin. Shaking, he gripped a large monometal bowl and promptly vomited into it.

'That's the third time he's vomited.' Phillipa quickly exchanged the bowl for a clean one. 'He can't have much more left in his stomach.'

Kirby pulled out her glucometer machine. 'I gather he wasn't able to hold down the snake.'

The woman shook her head. 'No, that came up too.'

'Hey, mate, sorry you're feeling sick.' Kirby knelt down beside Ben and put her hand on his forehead, her fingers hot from the heat radiating from his skin. 'Because you've vomited just after having insulin we need to give you some glucose to prevent a hypo. I'm going to put in a drip so you don't get dehydrated, and when your blood-sugar levels are sorted, we'll work out what's making you sick, OK?'

'OK.' The word came out in the familiar resigned tone that kids with chronic medical conditions often used.

'Finger jab first.' Kirby gave Ben a reassuring smile, quickly pricked his finger and carried out the glucometer reading. As expected, his blood sugar was too low. 'I'm going to give you mini-dose glucagon injection and then insert the drip.'

'My stomach really hurts.' Ben tensed up as a spasm hit him.

Kirby chewed her lip and swallowed a sigh. Vomiting in children could be due to so many different things— appendicitis, urinary-tract infection, meningitis. The list ran through her head as she injected the glucagon so the insulin had something to work on.

'Phillipa, can you please take Ben's temperature with the ear thermometer while I insert the IV?' Kirby handed the instrument to the woman and quickly primed the IV tubing.

'Thirty-nine point one.' Phillipa tossed the disposable earpiece into the bin.

'I thought he felt hot.' Kirby added an antipyretic to her list of drugs for Ben. Wrapping the tourniquet around his arm, she quickly found a vein, which was reassuring as often kids dehydrated really quickly. 'Hold still, Ben, it will be over in a moment.' She slid the IV cannula home and turned the drip onto a medium rate and gave him some Maxalon for the vomiting. 'Right, well, that combined with the rescue dose of glucagon should keep your blood-sugar level above five as well as keeping you hydrated. I've given you something to help the nausea and the fever but now I need to examine you. Tell me where your tummy hurts.'

'Everywhere.' Ben's voice broke on a sob.

She stroked his forehead. 'You poor old thing. I just need to have a gentle feel, OK?' Lifting his T-shirt, she started a gentle palpation of his abdomen, half expecting to find some guarding and rebound tenderness on the right side. Acute appendicitis presented with fever, vomiting and pain.

'Kirby.' Judy walked into the room, supporting a boy who was shivering violently. 'We've got another customer.' She laid the boy down on the other bed in the room. 'This is Cameron and he's diabetic as well.'

'I'm gonna puke.' Cameron heaved.

With the skill of experience Kirby managed to push a bowl under his chin just in time. She wiped his mouth and gave him a sip of water. 'When did you start to feel sick?'

'During dinner.' The boy laid his head back down on the pillow.

Kirby took his temperature. 'Thirty-eight five. You've got a fever, just like Ben. I need to check your blood-sugar levels, OK?'

'I can do it.' Cameron tried to sit up and fell back.

'Are you feeling dizzy?' Kirby asked the rhetorical question as she quickly pricked his finger. Deftly placing the drop of blood neatly on the stick, she inserted it into the machine. 'Two point seven. I'm giving you a glucagon injection into your thigh right now.'

But Cameron was too drowsy to reply.

'Judy, can you do a glucometer check on Ben for me while I insert a drip into Cam?'

Judy nodded. 'Sure. Do you think they've both picked up a virus? They're in the same bunkhouse.'

Kirby concentrated on locating a vein. 'I had thought

Ben might have appendicitis but his examination doesn't match up with that and now with Cameron I'm wondering if—'

Phillipa rushed in. 'I've got four more boys, all with the same symptoms.'

Kirby taped Cameron's IV in place, a sense of foreboding settling in her chest. 'Are they all diabetic?'

'Yes.'

She had kids dropping like flies. Running her hand through her hair, she marshalled her thoughts. 'Is anyone else at camp other than the diabetics starting to get sick?'

Phillipa shook her head. 'Everyone else is hale and hearty, chowing down to dinner as usual.'

She turned to Ben, who was more alert than Cameron. 'Ben, have you eaten anything today that didn't come from the KC kitchen?'

Guilt streaked across his cheeks and he dropped his gaze. 'Maybe.'

Kirby kept her voice light. 'I need you to tell me, mate, so I can work out what is making you and the other boys so sick.'

'I had…I ate a chocolate bar.' The mumbled words were barely audible. 'I'm sorry, I didn't think it would make me hurl.'

She patted his arm. 'I don't think a chocolate bar would cause you to be this sick. Did you eat anything else?'

The sick boy's gaze darted between Kirby, Judy and Phillipa, anxiety and fear duelling with a need to tell the truth. 'We…we sneaked out to the Greasy Spoon.'

Kirby recognised the name of the take-away shop

about half a kilometre away and suppressed a sigh. 'Who's "we"?'

He swallowed hard. 'Unit C.'

'And what did you eat?'

'Chicken and chips. The lady gave it to us cheap.'

A vision of hot food sitting in an old bain-marie for longer than the allowed time took residence in Kirby's mind. A cooling chicken would be the perfect vehicle for hosting salmonella. And the boys had the vomiting, nausea and abdominal pain that fitted the picture. She suppressed a groan at the thought of the diarrhoea that would inevitably follow.

She swung around to Judy. 'So we have six boys so far. How many boys are in that bunkhouse?'

Judy grimaced. 'Fourteen.'

'Fourteen?' She couldn't keep the rising inflection of horror out of her voice. Fourteen vomiting diabetics. Fourteen kids at risk of hypoglycaemia. Not to mention other members of the public who might have eaten at the shop. Her mind started to race with the logistics of dealing with this outbreak.

The hospital only had six acute beds and based on what had happened so far they could expect more than double the current number of cases. She needed to set up an isolation ward, get extra medical supplies from Barago and organise an urgent courier to rush samples to the lab for an accurate diagnosis. As Port's medical officer she had to notify the health department and shut down the Greasy Spoon pending investigation and testing. But most importantly she would probably be treating and monitoring fourteen really sick children.

Their care came first. How the hell was she going to divide herself up to meet every demand?

Judy and Phillipa looked at her expectantly. 'So what's your plan and how can we help?'

Nick dangled his legs over the edge of the Port Bathurst pier, a fishing rod in one hand and the other resting on Turbo's collar. The dog was crouched down, calculating how to round up the seagulls who hovered close by, ever hopeful of a free feed.

'Fishing is supposed to be relaxing, Turbo. You have to give in to the joy of sitting and waiting.'

Quizzical brown eyes met his gaze and Nick gave an ironic laugh. 'Yeah, well, that's the theory.'

Con Papadopoulos, one of his nursing-home patients, had told him that the pier at the turn of the tide was *the* place to catch dusky flathead. Fishing wasn't something that Nick had ever really done but right now he was looking for new experiences, looking for anything that took his mind off a blue-eyed, blonde-haired beauty with a smile that sent his blood racing.

Fishing didn't seem to be cutting it. Neither had cold showers, ten-K runs or fifty-K bike rides. No matter what he did, thoughts of Kirby roamed wild and free in his mind. He was used to getting what he wanted with women and the fact that she didn't want him in her bed ate at him.

Friendship. The word tasted bitter in his mouth. How could she only want friendship when their desire for each other vibrated palpably between them?

He reeled in the line for the fifth time to find the hook

baitless yet again. He sighed—so far he'd only managed to feed the fish and feed them well. He opened the bait box to try again and his phone vibrated in his pocket. Wiping his hands on his jeans first, he pulled out the phone, a crazy jolt of joy making his heart skip when he read the display. *Kirby*.

Kirby ringing at six o'clock when clinic was over and the evening was looming—perhaps she'd had a change of heart. Pressing the phone to his ear, he answered the call. 'If you're offering to take me out to dinner, I accept because not one single fish has landed on my line.'

'It's not a dinner invitation.'

The serious tone of her voice quickly dispatched all ideas of flirting and he immediately shot into professional mode. 'What's happened?'

'I need you out at Kids' Cottage—'

He cut her off, memories from his childhood flashing at him like a neon sign. 'I told you I don't work at the camp.'

'Well, today you do.' Her voice unexpectedly whipped him. 'I've got a suspected outbreak of salmonella poisoning and so far all the cases are diabetics.'

Hell! He raked his free hand through his hair as his pulse picked up. Sick diabetic kids. This was more than just maintaining fluids and electrolytes. This was complicated by either hyper- or hypoglycaemia. It didn't matter which way he looked at it, didn't matter how he felt about the camp, Kirby was right. This time he didn't have the luxury of choice. As a doctor he had to be there.

Forcing down uncomfortable memories, he sighed.
'I'll be there in ten minutes.'

'Make it five.'

The phone went dead, the silence deafening in its
censure.

CHAPTER SEVEN

THE sharp electronic beep of Nick's watch signalled three a.m. as he walked slowly and softly along the long row of beds, the old wooden floorboards creaking in protest as he checked all their patients. Low night lighting illuminated the beds along with the silvery beams of a waning moon and he didn't need to use his torch.

Every bed was predictably identical, although these beds with their laminated pine bedheads and built-in drawers underneath the mattress were a lot more flash than the old metal beds he'd slept on at similar camps around the country. The same brightly coloured doonas lay on each of the eighteen beds and fourteen of them had sick pubescent boys huddled underneath, fitfully sleeping. Four beds contained sick adults who'd also eaten at the Greasy Spoon, their pale faces looking slightly at odds with the 'superpowers' doona tucked under their chins.

Kirby had created an isolation ward in one of the dormitories in the grounds of KC and everyone affected by the outbreak was being treated here rather than at the hospital. It made sense seeing that he and Kirby had been frantic—treating children non-stop for the last nine hours. They'd just managed to go one full hour without admitting a new case and hopefully no one else in the community had eaten the contaminated food.

They'd divided the care of the patients evenly and both of them had been so busy they'd hardly spoken to each other all night, but he'd known exactly where she'd been in the dorm at all times. Her sweet scent wafted on the air and when she spoke to her patients he could hear her reassuring and gentle voice. An immature part of him wished he was sick so he could feel her hand on his brow and hear such care for him in her voice. He ignored the thought as he'd learned long ago to take no notice of errant thoughts generated by long hours and fatigue.

Kirby's manner with the kids was the perfect blend of caring mother and objective professional and he couldn't help but be impressed. *The cottage was a big drawcard for me to come to Port.* He wondered if he should talk to her about pursuing paediatrics.

Judy Dalton touched his arm. 'Phillipa and I are back from a break. I've just convinced Kirby she needs to take one and so do you.'

Nick looked up the dorm toward Cameron.

Judy followed his gaze, understanding on her face. 'I promise I'll call you if he needs you.' She gave him a gentle push. 'Go.'

'You've got my mobile number?'

She nodded patiently. 'You're not going to be far away and I've got your number plus my phone is on and charged. Worst-case scenario, I can yell really loud.' She pointed to the door and mouthed, 'Go now.'

Part of him felt he should stay but most of him wanted to take the chance of leaving the claustrophobic brown walls of the dorm. He hadn't had a break since he'd arrived.

'You OK?' Kirby greeted him as he walked into the kitchen, her voice soft.

'Fine.' Nick avoided meeting her far-too-observant gaze as he accepted the proffered mug of hot, steaming tea. Instead he stuck to the much easier topic of medical supplies. 'Has more saline arrived from the hospital yet?'

'Theo just rang and it's on its way.' She stifled a yawn but she couldn't hide the dark smudges under her eyes.

'You look completely whacked.' His hand tightened around the mug, tensing against the powerful urge to wrap his arms around her and pull her against him while he stroked her hair and let her sleep on his shoulder.

Her brows rose as her mouth twitched. 'I'd heard you had a way with words.' Laughter threaded through her voice. 'Now I can see why women lined up to date you.' She rested her chin against her palm. 'You look pretty exhausted yourself. How are your boys doing?'

'Fair.' He sipped his tea, welcoming the comforting warmth. Being inside the dorm had brought back far too many uneasy memories—massive homesickness, feelings of abandonment—and Cameron's grip on his hand and the baleful look in his eye had reminded him too much of himself at that age.

He leaned back and swung his feet up onto a chair. 'It's a fine line between too much and not enough insulin, and Cameron's levels keep swinging but at least he's stopped vomiting. I'll be a lot happier when Barago rings in the blood results.'

'Hypernatraemia is always a worry, isn't it?' She slid a covered plate toward him, a plume of steam curling up from the hole in the top of the silver cover. The aroma of garlic and onions filled the room.

He smiled at her rhetorical question that a couple of weeks ago would have been a real question. He was really pleased that she'd started trusting her judgement rather than second-guessing every decision. 'It is. We'll do another round of bloods at six a.m. and check everyone's electrolytes, including potassium.' He lifted up the food cover, suddenly hungry, realising it had been hours since he'd eaten.

She gave a quiet chuckle as she tucked into her spaghetti bolognaise. 'Poor Constable Masterton. This is his first posting after graduation and I think he came to Port hoping to crack an international abalone ring, and we've got him transporting blood samples between here and Barago.'

'Hey, he got to use the siren so he's happy.' Nick couldn't fault the way Port had pulled together to deal with this crisis. The paramedics had transported equipment, the nurses had all come back on duty and spread themselves between the hospital and KC, and now the camp kitchen was working all night keeping the staff well fed.

But it had been Kirby who'd organised everything. 'Three weeks ago I would have doubted you could have handled this sort of challenge but you've aced it. You're one hell of an organiser—I doubt anyone would have been brave enough to say no to you.'

'You tried.' She tilted her head and stared straight at him, her eyes lit with undisguised curiosity. 'I don't get it Why haven't you wanted to work here?'

Damn it, how had a compliment to her suddenly become all about him? He tried a flippant response. 'You love kids so I was giving you free rein.'

Her stunning eyes narrowed. 'You don't like kids?'

He willed his facial muscles to adopt a neutral expression. 'I don't have anything against them.'

A ripple of irritation skated across her cheeks. 'What sort of answer is that? I saw you in action tonight and you were thorough and caring so I know that you not wanting to work here has *nothing* to do with a lack of medical knowledge, unless…'

He caught the moment her mind made the connection and his stomach clenched.

Her forehead creased with an expression of complete bewilderment. 'Why wouldn't you want to work at a wonderful place like this?'

His sister Sarah's contorted face, her contracted muscles and wasted body beamed through his brain, taking him back twenty-odd years in an instant, the images clogging his mind. His heart hammered against his ribs as voices-past jumbled in his head, loud and discordant.

Your mother needs a break, Nick. This way everyone gets a holiday.

I hate it here, let me come home.

Sweetheart, we love you. Camp will be fun.

'Nick. Nick?'

Kirby's voice broke through the cacophony of sound as he became aware of the clink of the spoon against china. 'You've gone all white. Here, I've added some sugar to your tea.' She pushed the mug into his right hand and covered his left hand with her own. 'It's KC, isn't it?'

She'd done it again. For years he'd spent a lot of time with a lot of women and not one of them had read him like Kirby could. She managed to get under his guard every single time. Her warmth trailed through him, slowing his racing heart, calming him. He finally met her gaze, the pull of her concern drawing him in. 'Yeah, it's the camp, Sherlock. Not this camp specifically but all camps like it. I spent a lot of time in them as a kid.'

Surprise lit up her eyes. 'Not good memories?'

He laced his fingers through hers, the need to touch her overwhelmingly strong. 'If a kid wants to come to a place like this then, like you say, it's going to be a great experience.'

'But not for you?'

He shook his head. 'I didn't want to be there and I resented that I had to go.' His fingers brushed the back of her hand, absorbing her softness. 'My younger sister, Sarah, had severe cerebral palsy. She'd been born at twenty-six weeks, was blind, severely contracted and needed twenty-four-hour care. I was five when she was born and I remember the hushed voices, the strained and grey faces of my parents and grandparents, and an overwhelming feeling that everything had just changed. It was weeks before she came home and when she did, she understandably absorbed my parents' time.'

'But at five you wouldn't have understood.' Kirby's keen eyes shone with empathy.

'No. As a kid I was consumed by a feeling that I had

lost something huge but I didn't have the words to describe it. As Sarah got older and was permanently in a wheelchair, I realised she was never going to be any different and it was like a wound that never healed. Growing up I was both acutely embarrassed by Sarah and fiercely protective of her, especially if kids made crass remarks, but I just wanted to have a normal, healthy sister and be a normal kid. I craved a regular family, one where I could chase Sarah around the garden, tease her like a big brother is supposed to, and argue in the back seat during long car journeys.'

'And coming to camp just marked you as different.'

His head snapped up at the words that so aptly described what he'd been through. 'That's right. I always felt different. While my friends were off holidaying with their family or even getting to stay home and ride their bikes around the cul-de-sac, I was shunted off to camp.'

The vivid blue of her irises suddenly darkened. 'Or were you given the opportunity to have some freedom from your family?'

Her Pollyanna words gnawed at him, pulling at the child within. 'All I know is that had I ever been a father, I wouldn't be sending a kid to camp if he didn't want to go.'

'*Had* you ever been a father?' She leaned forward, her face earnest. 'You're thirty-three, with loads of time to become a father.'

He shook his head. 'Not after chemo, I don't. Chemotherapy doesn't differentiate between healthy cells and malignant ones, and it nukes sperm. One of the side effects is infertility.'

Her brows drew in, carving a deep V above her nose.

'I knew that. But surely you would have banked sperm before you started treatment?'

He folded his arms across his chest. 'I chose not to.'

'What?' Incredulity lay thick and heavy on the word. 'Why on earth would your doctors have allowed you to make that decision?'

'Allowed me?' Anger flashed inside him at her lack of understanding. 'I wasn't some naïve twenty-year-old, I was thirty-one and I knew what I wanted. I lived through my parents' unresolved grief after Sarah died so young and I saw the effect it had on their lives, felt the effect it had on my life. I want control over my life and I'm not taking any risks of having a disabled or sick child so a long time ago I made the decision that I didn't want to be a parent. Ever.'

Kirby abruptly pulled her hand out of his, her face flushing bright red and her eyes sparking with glints of pure rage. 'So you just tossed away a precious gift?'

Her fury rolled over him in ever-increasing waves, instantly putting him on the defensive. He stood up and walked around the table until he stood next to her. Drawing on every ounce of control he had, he managed to grind out a reply. 'Look, this was *my* choice and it has nothing at all to do with you.'

Her chest pushed in and out quickly, her breathing suddenly ragged. 'How could you?' Her voice rose, tinged with a maniacal edge, and her body shook. 'How could you give away your fertility, just like that, as if it was a disposable item?'

The thump of her fists on his chest caught him by surprise. He grabbed her wrists in self-defence, planning to set her back from him, but he caught a glimpse of her eyes and his breath left his lungs. Her raw grief knifed him, harrowing in its candour. What the hell was going on?

Kirby felt his vice-like grip against her skin and a surge of anguish poured through her. How could he have terminated his fertility? How could he have willingly given up the gift that had been stolen from her? Searing pain burned her chest, silver spots flickered against inky darkness and she heard a wrenching, guttural cry.

A moment later she became aware of soft-spun cotton cushioning her cheek and the reassuring pressure of Nick's arms holding her gently yet securely against him. His hands stroked her hair and his voice, low and mellow, caressed her ear. 'Breathe deeply, sweetheart, breathe, it will be OK.'

His calming voice, the tenderness of his arms and the heat of his body soothed her, and her anger ebbed away. A tiny part of her tried to hold onto it but the flames had been doused as fast as they had flared, and the only thing left inside her was exhaustion. Exhaustion and embarrassment. How could she have lost control like that? She valued her control—it protected her.

But today it had gone AWOL and left her totally exposed. She sucked down a deep breath and buried her barrenness back where it belonged—out of sight but rarely out of mind. With superhuman effort she dragged her head up from Nick's sheltering shoulder and stepped out of his arms. She pushed her facial muscles up into a wan smile and levelled her gaze at his left ear.

'Please accept my sincere apologies.' She splayed her

hands out in supplication. 'Sleep deprivation has obviously taken its toll on me but I promise you such an outburst won't ever happen again.' She turned toward the door. 'We better get back to the children.'

His hand caught hers, the grip firm. 'Kirby, two minutes ago you were hysterical. You're not ready to go back to the kids and right now they don't need you. Judy and Phillipa have everything under control and we can take a bit more time.' His keen gaze held hers, swirling with care and questions as his finger trailed down her cheek.

She tried to steel herself against the blissful sensations that coursed through every part of her. 'I'm just overtired.'

'There's more to it than that. I saw complete desolation in your eyes and I heard it in your voice. Tell me what's going on, I want to help.'

The empathy in his eyes, combined with the warmth of his touch, eroded her fragile façade and she closed her eyes for a moment, knowing that when she opened them she would have to tell him the whole truth.

She opened her eyes and strode to the freezer, hauling out two much-needed creamy vanilla ice creams covered in dark chocolate. If she had to bare her soul she needed comfort food. 'Here, catch.'

'Thanks.' Nick caught the confectionary, ripped open the gold foil wrapper, saluted her with the ice cream and then raised it to his lips, his mouth caressing the chocolate.

The memory of their kiss thundered through her and she bit down hard on her own ice cream, marshalling her thoughts. 'You can't help me but you do deserve an explanation, especially as I hit you, and I have *never* done that before to anyone in my life.' She gave a snort of derision. 'Not even to Anthony.'

He winked. 'Now, he might have deserved it.'

She managed a smile. 'You don't have to be this nice.'

He grinned at her—a look of pure magnetism. 'It's what I do.' He moved in next to her, his back against the freezer, his arm barely touching hers, and yet it pinned her with his support.

She bit her lip. 'I guess I start at the beginning. I met Anthony at a charity fundraiser for underprivileged children. He was ten years older than me, witty and entertaining, and he came from a large family, just like I did. We shared in common growing up in a chaotic household of kids, pets and love. He talked about how much he wanted to re-create those special times for children of his own and I knew exactly what he meant.'

A shudder ran through her. 'At least, I thought I did. Looking back, he actively chased me—flowers at work, helicopter rides to dinner and a whirlwind romance that culminated in his proposal three months later. He wanted to start a family straight away.'

Nick frowned. 'What about your career? Wouldn't waiting two years have been better for you?'

She dragged in a steadying breath, hating it that he could see so clearly what she had allowed to happen. 'Yes, but Anthony was nothing if not persuasive. He told me he was financially secure, and that he'd be a hands-on father and he'd support me to return to work to finish my training. I'd always seen children in my future so although it was all a bit faster than I wanted, I agreed that we'd start our family as soon as the ink was dry on the wedding certificate.'

'An old-fashioned honeymoon baby?'

She winced. 'Yep, but plans have a funny way of not working out. A few months before the wedding, in the middle of working flat out and trying to appease Anthony's mother, who wanted her son to have the full-catastrophe extravaganza, I missed two periods. I assumed I was pregnant and we were over the moon but...' She faltered, and took a bite of her ice cream, bracing herself for the words she really didn't want to speak.

'It's not unusual to skip a couple of periods during high-stress times.'

Nick's understanding voice encased her and she pushed on. 'If it had been that easy I wouldn't be standing here. When the blood-test report came back there were no signs of hCG.' She cleared her throat against the tightening sensation. 'I wasn't pregnant, my FSH levels were enormously high and my oestrogen was below the floor.'

'Premature ovarian failure.' He softly spoke the words for her as his hand slowly curled around hers. 'Are you sure it wasn't just a hormonal aberration?'

She shook her head. 'I prayed for that but I had a series of tests and for some reason my ovaries packed in at twenty-seven.'

'That totally sucks.' He rubbed his free hand through his hair, the silver strands on his temples glinting. 'So you and Anthony discussed adoption, right?'

She stared at him, her heart breaking. How was it that

this man in front of her, this man who didn't want children of his own, could see that there was another path available? Her breath shuddered out as she spoke the final indignity. 'Anthony refused to discuss egg donors or adoption. He blamed me for causing the POF, blamed my workload, my focus on my career—blamed me, full stop. I went into shock, unable to believe his reaction, but that's when I realised...' She fisted her hands, willing herself to stay strong and steady.

Nick's frown deepened but his voice was gentle. 'That's when you realised what?'

She bit her lip. 'That he didn't love me. That I was just the means to his end.'

'I don't understand.' Clear green eyes bored into her, searching for an explanation.

'POF exposed the truth about my relationship, which it turns out was a sham. I had invested all my love in something that didn't exist.' She rubbed her forehead with her forefinger, trying to marshal her thoughts into a coherent sequence. 'Anthony was older than me and from a large Italian family. I had no idea that he'd been promised a huge amount of family money when he produced a grandchild. Apparently, when I met him, his business was struggling and he needed a cash injection so he'd borrowed against this promise of money.'

Nick's sharp intake of breath sounded in her ears but she pushed on, just wanting to get the story over with. 'It turns out that he'd come to the fundraiser with the express purpose of meeting someone who loved kids and would fall for his charm and happily provide him with the child he needed. I was the bunny that fell but the moment he found out I was faulty goods, he replaced me with Lisa, who, it appears, is as fertile as a rabbit.' She blinked rapidly, hating her own weakness. 'Their first child is due in a few months.'

'He's a complete bastard.'

She gave a watery laugh. 'Yeah, he is.'

'So really POF saved you.'

Startled, she looked up at him, not believing he had said those words. 'Saved me? It stole everything from me.'

He tilted his head, his brows raised in question. 'It saved you from a loveless marriage, and that has to be a good thing.'

She rolled his words through her brain, thinking about everything she'd lost, and with sudden clarity she realised she didn't have a single regret about losing Anthony. But she had a suitcase of regrets about her future. She was damaged goods. Most men wanted their own biological child and POF had stolen her chance to give any man that.

Not Nick.

She immediately discarded the thought, not wanting to go there. That was just heartache on a stick. She wanted kids in her future and her infertility burned inside her, hot and painful every time she thought about it. But she didn't want to talk about her infertility with Nick. He didn't want children, he'd actively chosen infertility and he wouldn't understand. No, they were at opposite ends of that spectrum with an almighty and unbreachable chasm between them.

She tossed her head and gave him a tight smile. 'Anyway, that's the past, it's over and I'm in Port, working with kids and getting my fill that way.'

He squeezed her hand, his expression earnest. 'You could do foster-care when you've finished your GP training.'

He was trying so hard to help, trying to make her feel better, and it tore shreds off her heart. Yes, she could do foster-care and it probably would be great, but it would also emphasise what she'd lost. Like most women, she wanted a man who loved her and a family, and she couldn't ever have that.

Tears threatened, pricking the backs of her eyes, and she couldn't stand there one more minute or she'd burst into tears or, worse, she'd throw herself back into his arms. Neither was a good idea and crying wasn't a good look, especially after she'd already had one emotional melt-down tonight. 'It's something to think about but right now I need to think about the four a.m. round and so do you.' She dropped her wooden ice-cream stick into the bin and regretfully but crucially pulled her hand out from under his. 'See you out there.'

Nick watched her walk through the door—head erect, shoulders straight and hips swaying. The sexiest walk he'd ever seen, and she didn't have a clue. *Faulty goods, my eye.* That lousy ex-fiancé had stolen her belief that she was a gorgeous and desirable woman and after all she'd been through the least she deserved was to get that back.

She needed to know that she was all woman, one hundred per cent deliciously hot, and he was just the man to show her. He smiled as anticipation shot through his veins. Planning this was going to be fun—executing it even better.

CHAPTER EIGHT

KIRBY checked her watch, stretched and smiled. Five to six on a Friday evening and time to head home. After the drama of the salmonella outbreak, the rest of the week had been blissfully tame medically speaking, with straightforward consultations and only one tourist coming to grief. He now had a white cast on his leg— a souvenir to remember Port by and a reminder of the night he'd over-indulged at the pub.

Somehow over the last few days she'd managed to regain her equilibrium and had done a reasonable job of faking an 'Aren't we good colleagues?' persona with Nick. She hated it that she'd completely broken down in front of him and she knew that because of that one emotional outburst he now thought of her differently. She'd caught him in the act of a sideways glance a few times—he was probably panicking she'd break down again and was counting the days until the summer was over and he could get back to Melbourne and more sane company.

He'd never mentioned their conversation again but she kept revisiting the pain on his face when he spoke about his sister. She chewed her lip and sighed. Every-one had their own share of heartache.

Just keep moving forward one step at a time.

She quickly scribbled down a list of jobs for Monday, including a phone call to Melinda's oncolo-gist in Melbourne to get a treatment update. Then, gath-ering up her case histories and her bag, she headed out to Reception.

'Here you go, Vicki, all signed, notated and ready for you.' She dumped the folders onto the laminate counter.

'Thanks, dear.' Vicki's brown eyes bored into her from behind purple-framed glasses. 'So what have you got planned this evening?'

Kirby swallowed a sigh. Vicki asked her this question every Friday and never seemed satisfied with the answer. 'I'm picking up a new book from the newsagent's, grabbing a huge plate of seafood from the festival and then I'm going to sit on the deck, open a bottle of Barago merlot and watch the sunset over the ocean.'

And try not to think about Nick. Not think about how wonderful it had felt to be nestled against him, her head in the crook of his neck, his firm chest against hers... She pulled her attention back to Vicki, who had pursed her lips.

'Drinking alone, dear, that's not very wise.'

'But it's merlot so I can put the cork back in.' Kirby plastered on a smile and scooted to a safer topic. 'What are you doing this weekend?'

'My nephew, the lawyer from Melbourne—the one I was telling you about—arrived yesterday and is staying for a few days.' Vicki efficiently slotted the his-tories in the floor-to-ceiling filing cupboard.

'That will be fun for you, having a bit of company.' She knew how much Vicki missed her children.

The older woman nodded. 'Yes, but he won't want to spend all his time with his old aunt.' A cunning smile twitched the corners of her mouth upward. 'I'm a bit weary tonight and I'd really appreciate it if you took him to the jazz-and-seafood festival.'

Kirby tried not to groan audibly. Vicki had been very good to her and she didn't want to hurt her feelings, but on the other hand she really didn't want to spend her Friday evening entertaining her nephew, no matter how rich and gorgeous he was purported to be. Her mind trawled for the right combination of words to gently reject the suggestion but the creak of the front door opening interrupted her. Nick strode in, radiating vibrant good health with a broad smile on his handsome face to match.

An increasingly familiar surge of undisguised need immediately flared deep inside her and her buttocks tightened instinctively. He looked good. More than good—bronzed, toned and holding a toolkit, he looked liked her fantasy.

A well-known surfing-brand T-shirt caressed his broad chest and crisply ironed stone-coloured shorts clad his muscular legs, but her eyes zeroed in on his wet hair, which she noticed now had enough length to curl at the nape of his neck. He looked fresh, clean and sun-kissed and she realised he must have recently stepped out of a shower. A vision of Nick naked slammed into her, drying her mouth.

Nick raised the red metal box in his hand. 'Vicki, I was on my way past and had my toolkit in the truck so

I've fixed the wire door. It now closes properly and keeps the flies out, instead of inviting them into the waiting room.'

Vicki gave a cry of delight. 'Nick, you're wonderful. Talented *and* handy, and if I was thirty years younger, look out.'

Nick gave a deep rolling laugh, his eyes crinkling up with the ease of a man comfortable in his own skin. 'You would have been far too much woman for me, Vicki.'

She chuckled. 'Well, that's right, I probably would have—I wore out Roger, bless him.' She started pressing the buttons on the security pad. 'So, Kirby, if you come with me now, I'll introduce you to Andrew.'

Kirby thought she saw a ripple of tension cross Nick's shoulders but she didn't have time to wonder about that and it was probably just his muscles countering the weight of the toolbox. She *so* didn't want to spend the evening with Andrew and desperate situations meant desperate measures.

Ignoring every lesson she'd learned at her mother's knee, she prepared herself to lie. She'd make something up about a clinic problem and she fervently hoped Nick would just roll with it and not question her in front of Vicki. She'd apologise and explain it all to him later, after Vicki had left and she was off the hook from dating Andrew. 'I'm really sorry, Vicki, but Nick didn't just come to fix the wire door. I asked him to come in because—'

'The fact is, Vicki, she wants me, not Andrew.' Nick winked, his eyes sparkling with pure devilment. 'She's taking *me* to the festival.'

Kirby almost choked on the spot. His audacity was

unbelievable and a barrage of indignant words poured into her mouth, preparing to unleash her wrath. But they immediately clagged against her tongue as she realised none of them could be spoken without giving her away. Her lie neatly corralled every word, leaving her completely exposed and at its mercy. At Nick's mercy. What was he playing at?

Vicki's grin almost split her face and she gave Kirby a knowing look, one that said, *You're a sly one but he's as sexy as hell, so of course you want him.* 'Why didn't you just say that you and Nick are an item instead of hiding behind that silly story about drinking alone?'

Oh, great, now she looked like a desperate alcoholic. 'I—'

Nick slipped his free arm through Kirby's, his fingers firmly entwining with hers. He tilted his head, giving Vicki a serious look. 'We wanted to keep it quiet. You know what Port's like.'

Kirby could feel his body vibrating with suppressed laughter and it took every ounce of control not to kick him. Although Vicki could keep patient confidentiality, when it came to relationships, she was Port's biggest gossip. The moment her foot hit the outside step, this bit of news would roar through the town faster than a cyclone.

'Absolutely, Nick, I understand completely.' Vicki crossed the waiting room with a firm and decisive step and turned just as she reached the door. Tapping her nose with her forefinger, she beamed at them. 'You two have a lovely time. Your secret is safe with me.'

The moment the door banged shut Nick's hand tightened on Kirby's. 'Come on, we better get to this festival.' A wolfish grin moved across his face. 'After all, the entire town will be expecting us.'

She stared up at him, drawn by the look in his eye—laughter mixed with a simmering charisma. She should be furious with him, she should be vibrating with indignation at his highhandedness and she should be saying, *No, I'm not coming to the festival with you.* Instead, she followed him out the door, her brain stuck fast on the fact that the entire town would be assuming she was having sex with Nick Dennison while her body ached on the fact that she wasn't.

The mellow sound of a saxophone drifted across the air and Kirby fell back on the picnic rug. 'I couldn't eat another thing.'

'I'm surprised you managed that last plate of calamari.' Nick grinned as he leaned over her, sipping his wine. 'It's wonderful to see a woman with a healthy appetite, although more of my veggies wouldn't hurt.'

She gazed up him, taking in the way his thick chocolate-brown lashes brushed his cheeks, how his stubble creased along deep smile lines that converged into dimples, and how much younger he looked than he had a few weeks ago when she'd first met him. The last vestiges of his treatment had completely faded, leaving him more handsome than any man deserved to be.

He'd been attentive all evening in a casual way—slinging his arm across her shoulders as they'd wandered from stall to stall, feeding her samples of everything from prawns to oysters, and choosing the perfect local sauvignon blanc to match the delicious food. He'd made a point of holding her hand when they'd met the self-obsessed Andrew, and he'd teased her on and off all evening that she owed him big time for saving her from an evening of boredom.

Now he put his glass down and grabbed her hand. 'Come on, you'll feel better if you move.'

'I don't believe you.' She groaned as she let him pull her to her feet, enjoying the way his other arm snaked around her waist, holding her close.

'I wouldn't lie to you.' His eyes danced as he lowered his head and his voice rumbled against her ear. 'And I promise you, I'll make it worthwhile.'

Shimmering tingles raced from her head to her toes, streaking through her like wildfire and igniting everything in its wake until she quivered and she felt sure he would feel it.

'Hello, Doctors, lovely evening for it.'

She looked up through dazed eyes to see Doug Reardon tipping his hat as he walked past arm in arm with his wife.

Nick laughed and waved. 'A perfect evening for it.' He turned back to face her, shooting her a deadpan look. 'It's a funny thing but the whole town has been giving us indulgent looks all night.'

She rolled her eyes. 'I can't imagine why.' She broke away from him and started to walk, needing to move, driven by a need to leave the crowded foreshore park and get away from those knowing looks—looks that inferred something that didn't exist and never would. She headed out along the pier road, suddenly desperate to be home.

Nick fell easily into step with her. 'They like to see a couple in love.'

She increased her pace. 'We're not in love.'

'No, we're not.'

His words relaxed her. They weren't in love and the fact they both wanted totally different things out of life made them almost incompatible, but they laughed together and they were friends. *Think friendship.* A crazy laugh bounced around her head.

He stepped in closer so his arm touched hers and his heat soared through her. 'But we are in lust.'

His husky voice filled with desire brought her to an abrupt halt. She swung around to face him, her hands gripping her hips as she desperately tried to keep some distance. 'Speak for yourself.'

'I am.' His eyes, shaded by the fading light, flared with unconcealed desire. 'You're the sexiest woman I've met in a long time.'

Her heart hammered hard and fast as his sweet words rolled over her like honey. But she couldn't listen to them—she'd learned that words counted for little and these ones had heartache written all over them. 'You don't get out very often, do you?'

'I get out plenty.' He trailed his finger down her cheek. 'You're gorgeous, you're sexy and you're driving me crazy.'

She wanted to slam her hands against her ears to drown out his beguiling voice. 'This is crazy. We're colleagues, we want different things.' She started walking again with no clear direction, just letting her feet take her as her body buzzed with need and her brain raced with incoherent thoughts that tumbled chaotically over each other.

He quickly caught up with her, his voice insistent. 'Pretending we're just colleagues and friends is the crazy part. You want me as much as I want you.'

She strode along the road, hating it that she did want him so badly. Hating that he knew. Folding her arms across her chest, she forced herself to be the sensible one. 'I didn't know conceit was a tool of seduction. Is that how you've always got women to jump into bed with you?'

His hand touched her sleeve, his expression suddenly serious and his mouth curving into a wry smile. 'I've never had to try this hard with any woman. You've reduced me to begging.'

She stared at him in amazement. Raw need rolled off him, almost toppling her with its intensity. Deep inside her something cracked and she steeled herself against a crumbling sensation. 'It won't work.' But her voice sounded unconvincing.

Surprise streaked across his handsome face as if the thought had never occurred to him. 'Of course it will.'

'No, it won't.' She shook her head, trying to hold onto the last shreds of her resistance and common sense. 'You have your carefree childless life all mapped out, and that's the opposite of what I want.'

'You're over-thinking this.' He ran his hands down her arms, a touch gentle yet packing a seismic punch. 'This isn't for ever, this is all about now. It doesn't have to be complicated—in fact, it's pretty simple. I want you, you want me. It's summer, the season of being carefree, and we're both here for the summer so let's use this time we have together, use it for fun.'

His hand cupped her jaw, his expression suddenly earnest. 'Hell, both of us deserve some carefree fun after what we've been through. Let's wind the clock back to real carefree times and pretend we're sixteen.'

This is all about now. Tempting images bombarded her, collapsing all her worries about her future into a locked box. 'I was a very organised and responsible sixteen.'

His mouth curved up into a long, slow, seductive smile and his eyes twinkled. 'Then this is your chance to reinvent yourself.'

Reinvent herself? The thought tumbled through her, over and over, gathering massive appeal. She'd always been thoughtful, conscientious, a planner, and where had that left her? Shattered and alone. She was tired of worrying about what came next in her life so perhaps it was time to try something new, something just for her, just for a short time. Real life would intrude soon enough and knowing that they wanted such different things would protect her. Yes, this would be fun.

Bad idea. Very bad idea.

She instantly argued—no, it wasn't. Hell, the whole town thought they'd been at it like rabbits so why not do what was already considered a done deal? Standing strong against the constant barrage of need that burned inside her had worn her to a frazzle. Nick was right, she did want him. She wanted him so badly she throbbed with empti-ness. This was her chance to reinvent herself, take some-thing for herself. 'No plans, no future, just the summer?'

'No plans, no future, just the summer.' Nick held his

breath, watching the war of emotions on Kirby's face. From the moment he'd capitalised on her lie earlier and set her up in the clinic, the entire evening had been a gamble—exciting, enjoyable and totally unpredictable. He'd loved every minute of it and now it all came down to this moment.

Silently, Kirby stepped forward, looped her arms around his neck, tilted her head up and seared his lips with a kiss of pure hunger, devoid of any restraint.

Yes! Hot, firm and fast, the kiss thundered through him, and he instantly hardened while his head spun. His arms moved to pull her tightly against him but as abruptly as she'd kissed him she stepped away, turned and ran down the empty pier.

'Hey! That's not playing fair.'

Her laughter came back to him on the evening breeze. With sheer strength of will he managed to force enough blood back to his limbs so he could walk down the pier. As he got closer, the yellow light of the rising moon illuminated her hair, giving her a golden halo. An angel with a body for sin.

She threw him a crooked smile. 'What kept you?' Grabbing his hand, she quickly started jogging down the pier steps toward the moored boats.

A moment ago with the smugness of experience he'd thought he had her, but now he wasn't quite so sure. Somehow he'd lost control of the situation and now his planned seduction was unravelling in front of him. Nothing about Kirby was predictable. 'Where are you going?'

She didn't reply but kept walking, her feet slapping

against the boards of the lower pier. Dropping his hand, she hauled hard on a rope and then jumped down onto the deck of a yacht, its sleek white bow glowing against the dark water. She shot him a smile loaded with the promise of all good things. 'You said you wanted sixteen, so that's what I'm giving you.'

The fantasy hit him so hard he nearly lost his balance and pitched into the water. Staring down at her, he concentrated hard and managed to force out the words. 'I said carefree, not breaking the law. Are you allowed on this boat?'

She stared straight back at him, blue eyes swirling with a wildness he'd never seen before. Keeping her gaze fixed with his, she crossed her arms across her chest and hooked her fingers around the base of her T-shirt. Very slowly, she drew the clingy Lycra over her head and let it trail through her fingers until it fell to the deck.

The sonorous sound of a double bass and clarinet combo, carried by the breeze, and the steady slap of the water against the boat instantly faded as his brain emptied and every sense zeroed in on creamy white breasts nestled against a black lace bra. His pants felt tight.

She tossed her head back, the action full of sass as a curtain of hair swirled around her face and brushed her shoulders. 'So, are you coming?'

Probably. Letting go of every cautious thought, every shred of common sense, he jumped down onto the deck as Kirby disappeared through the hatch and into the cabin.

He found her skirt on the third step as he stumbled into the tiny space. 'Don't you dare go any further without me.' The words came out on a growl loaded with sexual frustration.

Laughing, she lay down on the tiny bed, a vixen smile on her face as she bent her knees and crossed her long legs, twirling one ankle at him. 'Well, hurry up, then.'

Somehow he managed to shuck his pants in the tiny space without banging his head. He lowered himself onto the mattress, supporting himself on his left elbow, his right hand trailing through her hair. 'A good lover is never rushed.'

'Is that so?' She raised her hand to his cheek. 'I've never met a good sixteen-year-old lover—they tend to be fumbling fingers, expired condoms, all talk, and mighty quick on the main event.'

He stilled, realising he wasn't as prepared as he'd thought. He'd planned to seduce her at his house. 'I don't have a condom.'

She bit her lip, the fun in her eyes instantly dimming. 'Neither of us really needs one, do we?'

Her bleak look pierced him—it didn't belong in their fantasy and the need to banish it consumed him. He traced the line of her jaw with his finger, savouring her softness and breathing in her jumbled scent of wildflowers and salt. 'Then we have the perfect fantasy, don't we? A stolen space and no contraception, but there is going to be one very big difference.'

'What's that?' Huge blue eyes absorbed him.

'The main event is going to take all night.'

The moment his mouth touched hers, Kirby gave herself up to him. Nothing existed except Nick—the pressure of his mouth, the graze of his stubble, his taste of salt and wine, and the scorching touch of his body against hers.

His deep kiss penetrated way beyond her mouth, his tongue eliciting a surge of response from every cell between her lips and her toes. And when he'd kissed her to the point where her mind had completely melted, he trailed kisses along her jaw, across the hollow of her throat and down to the lace of her bra. She was vaguely aware of his right hand under her back and a moment later her bra fastening was released, the cups falling away and her breasts spilling out.

She gazed into emerald eyes. 'You've done that before.'

A sheepish look crossed his face. 'I learned that technique at sixteen.'

But her quip morphed into a moan of bliss as his mouth closed over her breast, his tongue tracing her nipple, drawing it up into a hot, hard peak and sending spirals of white light thudding through her.

He lifted his head and grinned. 'I learned this technique a bit later.'

She caught her breath. 'I think you've refined it.'

He lowered his head again, this time paying close attention to her other breast. Exquisite shafts of tingling sensation—half pleasure, half pain—shot from her breast to a single point deep inside her. Gripping his back, she gasped in delight as her hips rose instinctively up toward him, needing to feel him hard against her.

His wicked laugh rained down on her. 'If you like that, then you might enjoy this.' His lips started to press hot kisses down her belly.

Every part of her craved to lie back and let him give

her what she knew would be beyond wonderful, but instead she grabbed his head to stop him, sinking her hands into his hair.

'Problem?' He raised his head, a questioning expression clinging to his cheeks.

'Big problem.' She'd fantasised about running her hands through his hair, pressing her palms against his smooth chest and exploring him in the same way he was exploring her, but if she let him continue, she'd miss her chance. Somehow she managed to get her liquid muscles to function and she wriggled out from under him, pushing at his right shoulder and laughing at the confused look on his face.

He rolled over onto his back, bringing her with him. 'I thought you would have enjoyed that.'

Straddling him, she leaned forward, her hair caressing his face. 'I would have adored it and I'm only taking a short rain-check.' She leaned back, her fingers flicking up the base of his T-shirt, pushing it up his chest, before pulling it over his head. Golden skin, taut abdominal muscles and a trail of dark hair that knifed downward from his navel assaulted her gaze and she sighed. 'You once told me I'd enjoy this sight. I hate it when you're right.'

The rich green of his eyes darkened. 'Gaze all you want, I'm yours for the night.'

Yours for the night. She hugged the words close. 'I'm done gazing.' She reached out, splaying her fingers over his heart and feeling the fast beat vibrating underneath her hands. A heart beating wildly and matching her own erratic rhythm—one of blissful anticipation mixed with unfulfilled need. 'I've wanted to touch you like this from the moment I met you.' Tracing his pectoral muscles, her fingers roved over the small patch of thickened skin—scar tissue from his treatment and the only flaw on a perfect landscape. Then she dipped and curved until she circled his nipple, tweaking it gently between her fingers.

His pupils dilated and his thighs stiffened underneath her. She laughed, loving it that she could get such a response from him. With a feather-light touch she continued downward, outlining the sinew and tendon of the solid pack of muscles and then trailing down to outline and cup the straining fabric of his jocks.

He bucked underneath her as a low growl left his throat. 'It's been a long time, Kirby, so if you don't want real sixteen…'

Her fingers caressed as she hooked his gaze. 'Can't you handle the heat?'

Challenge flared in his eyes and he immediately slid his hand down between them, sliding a finger firmly along the crotch of her panties.

Sensation exploded and her breath came hard and fast. She lost all focus on him, her body pushing hard against his hand, needing to rise on the surge of ecstasy that fireballed through her, leaving every part of her begging for more. 'Don't stop.'

'Sweetheart, I've hardly started.'

He flipped her over onto her back and using his mouth and hands he fuelled her already ragged need until every muscle deep inside her quivered, desperate to tense against hard flesh. She was past flirting, past banter, past pretence. She didn't care about anything except the driving need to have him deep inside her. 'Nick.' She almost sobbed his name. 'Now.'

Nick stared down at Kirby, her hair spread out on the bed, her eyes large and wide in her flushed face, and he didn't think he'd ever seen anything so beautiful. It had been so long since he'd been with a woman and she was driving him past control, but he wanted to give her this, she deserved it. 'Just enjoy, this one's for you.'

Her fingers sank into his shoulders with an iron grip and her eyes, wild with hunger, fixed with his. 'No, this one's for us.'

He'd dreamed about this moment for weeks. He slid into her with ease, as if he belonged there. She rose up to meet him, capturing him deeply, stroking him as he stroked her and they rose together as one, flinging themselves out to the stars, beyond the pull of reality.

CHAPTER NINE

NICK stood in waist-deep water, his back fiery hot from the sun, in total contrast to his belly where occasional trickles of icy Southern Ocean water chilled his skin, having penetrated his thick, black wetsuit. White, briny foam buffeted him and the sand under his feet moved as the tail end of each wave raced past him to the shore.

'Now!' Nick cupped his hands around his mouth like a megaphone, trying to make himself heard over the surf. 'Stand up now, Cameron.'

The determined twelve-year-old gripped the side of his board and launched himself from his knees for the fourteenth time in a row, his feet swinging forward to stand against the lumps of wax that roughened the surfboard. He stood, he wobbled, and he fell as the board soared skywards before slamming back down onto the waves, brought to earth by the black cord attached to the ankle strap. A moment later Cameron's head appeared above the waves, water streaming across his face.

'Do you want to take a break?' Nick motioned to the boy who'd been at it for half an hour.

'No.' Cameron shook his head and doggedly clambered back on the surfboard and paddled back out to try again.

Splashes of cold water unexpectedly hit Nick's back and he turned to find a laughing Kirby, body board hooked under one arm, scooping water and tossing it at him with the other. Her eyes sparkled vivid blue, matching the ocean, her face glowed with vitality and her full-length wetsuit clung skin-tight, outlining every sensual curve. Despite the icy water, his body instantly responded. Like it did every time he saw her.

Still splashing him, she continued moving forward until she stood next to him, her cinnamon-apple scent circling him, taking him instantly back to last night when he'd buried his face in her hair. *Buried yourself deep inside her.*

He splashed her back, laughter rocking through him at her joyful shrieks. A week had passed since the festival, a week of fun, hard work and the most amazing sex of his life. He felt alive in a way he'd never known before, different even from his life prior to getting sick. Colours were brighter, sounds more complex and his energy for work and his energy for Kirby bounded out of him.

She wrapped the body board's Velcro strap around her wrist, her expression filled with curiosity. 'I didn't expect to see you down here—I thought you said you had capsicums to pick.'

He gave a wry smile. 'I do, but when I called by KC the unit C boys cornered me and asked if I'd teach them how to surf.' He swung his arm in an arc. 'Today's conditions are perfect.'

'You called by KC?' Incredulity clung to the words, matching the surprised expression on her face.

He nodded stiffly. 'Judy asked me to talk to one of the boys.'

Her eyes widened. 'And you said yes?'

'Judy can be very persuasive.' A ripple of irritation mixed with discomfiture wove through him. He didn't want to examine too closely why he'd deliberately not mentioned Judy's call to Kirby, but the disbelief on her face that he'd got involved at KC unexpectedly morphed his irritation into a jag of indignation.

He tried to shrug it off because, if the truth be known, he'd been just as surprised as Kirby at the 'yes' that had slipped out of his mouth when Cameron had asked him to stay and help with surfing.

Two boys shot passed them, riding their boards expertly into the shallows.

'Great going, guys.' Nick raised his arms to shoulder height and held out both his thumbs above two closed fists.

Grinning widely, the two boys waved back before running back out toward the breakers, ready to try again.

'They're going really well. Perhaps I should ask you to teach me because I can never manage to get up off my stomach.'

'Ben and Steven are naturals.'

She threw him an arch look. 'And you're saying I'm not?'

He wasn't falling for that one. He moved his head close to her and whispered, 'You're amazing, beautiful and you have skills and talents in other areas.'

Her face flushed and he laughed at her blush. 'After last night I didn't think anything would embarrass you.'

She tossed her head, her plump lips forming into a

pout. 'You're totally wicked, mentioning *that* in daylight.' She turned away but a smile lingered on her lips as she stared out toward the horizon.

Nick longed to pull her into his arms and kiss her until her breath was ragged and she collapsed hard against him. But he was on duty and he could already predict the reaction he'd get from the group of pubescent boys if he kissed her, which would range from 'Oh, yuck' through to jeering sniggers.

'How's Cam doing?' Kirby pointed to the red-headed boy in the group of other wannabe surfers from KC.

'He's determined, I'll give him that, and he's almost got there a few times. He just has to find his centre and go with the movement rather than fighting it.' He cupped his hands again and yelled, 'Try this one, mate.'

She elbowed him gently in the ribs. 'You've got a bit of a soft spot for him, haven't you? That's why you're here.'

He bristled against her words. 'No, I'm here because seven boys tackled me to the ground and refused to get off me until I said yes.'

She rolled her eyes. 'Yeah, right. Come on, why not just admit it? You like the kid.'

He felt a muscle in his jaw twitch. 'No more than any of the other kids.'

'Yes, more than any of the other kids. During the salmonella outbreak and in the post-recovery check-ups I saw you taking a special interest in Cameron.'

He should have known nothing got past Sherlock, she noticed everything. In the last two weeks he'd recognised a lot of his twelve-year-old self in Cameron, but he didn't want to talk about it. Avoiding her gaze, he tried to sound offhand. 'He's had a tough year with his diagnosis of diabetes.'

Kirby tilted her head, as her eyebrows rose. '*And* his younger brother is severely autistic. I saw him in full flight the day Cameron arrived and it was pretty distressing for everyone.'

He let her words hang on the salt-tinged breeze, not wanting to acknowledge that he understood some of the stuff Cam was facing. Not wanting to risk getting close to the guilt that hovered around his heart whenever he thought of Sarah and how he'd lost her just when he'd been old enough to really understand.

Her free hand touched his shoulder. 'I think it's wonderful that you can help each other.'

Her words rained down on him, exacerbating the already swirling emotions that pulled at his gut, but it was anger that emerged from the melee. Hell, he didn't need any help! 'It's a surfing lesson, Kirby, that's all. It's a way of spending time before I return to Melbourne Central.' He shrugged off her hand, shrugged off her inference and waded out a bit further, shouting to Cameron. 'You can do this. Hands forward, knees in the middle of the board, paddle, paddle, now up!'

The boy planted his left leg forward and with a very wobbly stance rose up with his arms outstretched. The board nudged forward on the crest of the wave and scooted down the curve with Cam standing tall and proud.

Thirty seconds later the wave collapsed completely and Cam fell off, victorious. 'I did it, Nick, I did it!'

Nick slapped his palm against the boy's, an overwhelming sense of triumph fizzing in his veins. 'That was awesome. I'm really proud of you.'

Cam flicked water from his eyes, his achievement suddenly dimming on his face. 'I wish Dad could have seen me.'

The wistful words kicked Nick hard in the gut. He remembered those moments when his own father had been caught up with the care of Sarah and had missed out on seeing his successes. As an adult he knew his father must have hated the choices he'd had to make but as a kid Nick had never understood. It was yet another reason why he was never going to be a father.

He clapped his hand onto Cam's shoulder. 'I know, mate, but by Parents' Day next week you'll be a pro and you can show your dad then.' He hoped the weather cooperated and that Cam's dad could actually make it.

'Can you lift it a bit higher?' Kirby called to Nick, who stood high on a ladder.

'Like this?' His strong arms swung the large rope around one of KC's imposing brick gateposts.

Kirby clapped her approval, childlike excitement flicking through her. 'Perfect.'

Leaning sideways, his tanned legs locked in a solid stance and his muscular back taut with tension, he tied the KC banner in place so it hung high over the entrance.

With his back to her, Kirby took the chance to openly stare at him. It didn't matter that she knew every part of his body in intimate detail, she never tired of gazing at him, watching and loving the way his work-hardened body moved—poetry in motion.

The light morning sea breeze fluttered the red, blue and white bunting as a flock of fifteen pelicans flew overhead, their enormous wings slicing through the air with stately grace, as if giving their approval to the events below. Nick moved quickly down the ladder and walked over to Kirby, his face creased in a wide and mischievous grin. 'I now declare the annual Kids' Cottage fete open.'

She laughed. 'I think perhaps the celebrity patron does that in a couple of hours.'

'That'd be right. I do all the hard work and that other bloke gets the glory.' His grumbling tone was at odds with his twinkling eyes.

She stepped up to him, wrapping her arms around his waist. 'Are you feeling under-appreciated?'

He dropped his forehead down to touch hers. 'Well, I did risk life and limb at the top of that ladder.'

'So you did.' She brushed away a curl of his hair that had fallen across his eyes, loving that it was now long enough that she could do that. Leaning in, she pressed her lips to his, her mouth so familiar against his that it zeroed straight to the place that always made him shudder against her. She looked up and grinned. 'Feeling more valued?'

His eyes, sparkling in myriad hues of green, glinted back at her. 'Almost, but I'm sure I can take some more thanking tonight after this shindig is over.'

She loved teasing him. 'It's going to be a huge day and I'm sure you'll be way too exhausted.'

'Never.'

The word rolled out low and guttural, loaded with energy that swirled around her, pulling her in.

'Well, I might be. By the time I've done my time on the face-painting stall, read two books in the story-time tent and staffed the first-aid tent, I'll be ready for a long soak in the spa and a foot rub.'

A long, lazy smile moved into his cheeks, carving out swirling dimples. 'I'm sure that can be arranged. But meanwhile to keep your strength up and to make sure you actually stop for lunch, how about we meet at twelve o'clock at the barbeque tent? We'll both be ready for a hamburger by then.'

Warmth flowed through her at the suggestion. 'I'll be there. But what are you up to for the next few hours?'

He winked at her. 'It's a top-secret mission and I'd have to kill you if I told you so don't ask.' He then kissed her on the bridge of her nose and with a backwards wave walked off with his ladder.

She stood watching his retreating back, unable to keep a huge smile from her face despite the fact she was completely confounded by his caginess about what he was doing with his morning. He had moments of being deliberately vague and she suddenly realised it always happened when it involved the kids.

Just like with Cam and the surfing. He'd been great with Cam but whenever she tried to talk to him about it he sent up a towering brick wall between them and clammed up completely or changed the subject. She didn't get it. He obviously enjoyed the things he was doing at KC and was becoming increasingly involved with the children—he'd even arranged for someone else to man his Saturday market stall today and offered his help to Judy to be part of the biggest fundraising event on the KC calendar.

The annual fete was huge. All the favourite draw-cards were in place—the giant jumpy castle and a calliope playing carousel for the pre schoolers, the stomach-churning Rota and dodgem cars for the teenagers, the enormously high and long slide and a petting zoo for kids of all ages. Then there were the rows of white marquees, starting with the white elephant stall where one person's trash was immediately converted to another person's treasure. The handicraft stall was the domain of the Ladies' Auxiliary, where a year's worth of production was on display from lovingly knitted football teddies to layers of brightly coloured tulle used to create dolls, the ardent wish of every little girl's heart.

Kirby was never certain which stall was her favourite—the cake stall, with its fluffy cream-filled sponge cakes with passionfruit icing, home-made buttery shortbread in clear cellophane bags tied with gold curling ribbon, and deep-red raspberry preserves, or the quiet retreat of the Devonshire Tea tent, with hot tea, hot scones and lashings of Port Bathurst cream straight from the farm.

She quickly walked past a clown who was surrounded by a circle of fascinated children intently watching his hands quickly sculpt long thin balloons into animal shapes, and she took her place at the face-painting table. The crowd was building as every good fete attendee knew the tip was to get in early to get top pick of all the stock and be back at the beach by the time the sun got really hot.

Kirby angled the large market umbrella so it cast a large circle of shade over her and her customers, tied an apron over herself to protect her clothes from the paint and displayed her designs.

'I'd like to be a tiger, please.' An eight-year old girl with a helium balloon tied to her wrist held out her coin.

'One tiger coming up.' Kirby dipped her brush into the yellow and set to work, loving the delight on the kids' faces when she showed them their new look in the mirror.

The morning streaked past in a blur of faces, conversations and storytelling and by eleven-thirty Kirby had finished her morning's duties and was starving. With half an hour before she had to meet Nick she jammed her sunhat onto her head, bought a fruit smoothie and took the chance of exploring the fete before her afternoon duty in the first-aid centre started. Teenagers congregated around the stage, enjoying the Battle of the Bands, which was in full swing, and further over children cuddled in their parents' laps, squealing with delight as they raced down the bumpy slides.

That should have been me. Kirby sipped her drink against the lump that formed in her throat, trying to push the hollow feeling that pervaded her every time she saw families together. Looking for distraction, she headed toward the noisiest queue of shrieking and laughing children and as she got closer she realised most of the kids were KC campers who got to enjoy the fete too.

A form of scaffolding with a swing seat had been erected in the centre of a pool of water with a large painted target fixed behind it. The banner above declared, 'Dunk the Doctor' and Nick, wearing boardies, a rash top and a lifesaving cap, sat high in the chair.

Kirby blinked, unable to believe her eyes. The doctor

who'd been so adamant a few weeks ago that he was not working with children had put himself up as a sideshow attraction. By the look on his face, he was loving every minute of it.

First there had been his work with Cameron and now this. Her heart soared. They were having the best summer and he no longer held himself back from children. Perhaps what they both wanted had drawn closer together. Suddenly a daydream floated through her mind of Nick and herself surrounded by children. Adopted children.

Be careful, no plans—remember.

But she ignored the voice. Nick was nothing like Anthony. She and Nick shared a million things in common, including great sex and laughter.

She returned Nick's big wave to her and the huge teasing smile on his face, watching him as he leaned forward and called to the kid at the front of the line. 'I'm getting hot up here.'

'Do your best, Cameron,' Kirby called out. 'Take him out.'

Cameron grinned, straightened his shoulders and hefted the basketball he was holding above his head, aiming for the big black circle.

The crowd chanted, 'One, two, three.'

Cam threw the ball, putting his entire twelve-year-old effort behind it. It hit the target with accuracy, the chair tipped backwards and Nick somersaulted into the water with a satisfying splash.

The crowd roared, Cameron stood taller and Kirby laughed so hard her ribs ached.

A sopping wet Nick surfaced, water streaming off his handsome face, and he climbed out of the pool, immediately clapping Cam on the shoulder. 'Great throw, mate. Now go and get yourself a prize from Mrs Dalton.'

A glow of success emanated from the boy. 'Thanks, Doc. That was awesome!'

Cameron ran off and Kirby handed Nick a towel. 'I wish I'd known. I would have been here earlier with my camera.'

He slung the towel around his neck and gave her a wicked grin loaded with mischief. 'The local paper beat you to it. I'm next week's centrefold.'

Kirby shook her head in smiling bemusement. 'Is there any room next to that giant ego for me to walk beside you?'

'For you—' he put on a fake Italian accent '—always. But so you can walk close I'll just get changed out of this wet gear.'

'Meet me in the food line.' Kirby followed the aroma of barbecued onions and joined the meandering line, enjoying chatting to Jake, Gaz and Meryl while she waited, still stunned that Nick had got so involved in the fete. *He's got involved with the children.*

She'd just paid for the burgers when he arrived by her side, all tousled hair and glowing good health. She held out the ubiquitous white bag with the two twisted ears. 'Yours has the lot, including pineapple and beetroot.'

'Sweet.' He ripped open the bag and took a big bite from the burger.

'Hungry, are you?' Smiling, Kirby pulled some stray onion out of her bun and nibbled on it.

He pretended to be affronted. 'You try being knocked into the water fifteen times. It generates an appetite.'

They sat at a table in the shade of a grove of gnarled tea trees and Kirby neatly pulled open her white bag, dividing it down the seam line to make a mat for her hamburger. Nick had almost finished his and was eyeing hers when the music on the loudspeaker stopped and Judy's voice came on instead.

'Could Dr Atherton or Dr Dennison please come to the sick bay *now*.'

'Must be something more than a cold pack or a plaster can fix or Phillipa would have dealt with it.' Kirby stood up and started walking.

Nick picked up her burger and handed it to her. 'Eat and run. We don't need you getting sick too.'

They jogged to the sick bay. Jordan, one of the unit C boys, sat in the chair, his face alabaster white underneath a large trickling bloodstain. Phillipa had a gauze-covered ice pack on his head and looked up with relief as they walked in.

Kirby stepped up to the boy who looked so little and immediately felt for him, knowing he probably wanted his mother. 'Jordan, you poor—'

But he looked past her, straight to Nick.

'Mate, what have you done to yourself?' Nick immediately pulled on a pair of gloves and lifted up the ice pack.

'I ran into a pole.'

'Jumped out at you, did it?' Kirby opened up some saline, feeling slightly ignored. 'I think unit C is going to win the camp award for most admissions to the sick bay.'

'You wouldn't have let Ben run off with your prize,

would you, Dr Nick?' Jordan shot Nick a conspiratorial look that clearly said, *A girl wouldn't understand.*

'No way. I would have chased him down as well.' He bobbed down in front of the boy and shone a torch into Jordan's black hair. 'But you hit that pole so hard you've split the skin.'

'Skin glue?' Phillipa opened the medical kit, her fingers hovering over the tray.

Nick shook his head. 'It starts on his forehead but extends into his hairline so it's going to have to be stitches.'

'No way.' Jordan's eyes welled up.

Nick squeezed his shoulder. 'You'll have a manly scar and a good story to match it. I've got a few of those.'

'Have you?' Watery curiosity shone in Jordan's eyes.

'Yep. See this one?' He pointed to a faint line on his forearm. 'I fell off the top of the brick fence when I was trying to be Superman. I also broke my leg.'

'Did you have crutches and a cast?'

'I did.'

'Cool!' Admiration shone in the boy's eyes before dimming slightly. 'But I won't need crutches.'

'No, but you'll have a bit of a pirate scar, which is mysterious.'

Needing something to do now she'd finished her hamburger, Kirby drew up the local anaesthetic and handed it to Nick, who chatted away to Jordan about the current test cricket match, as if they were walking down to the beach for a surf instead of injecting lignocaine into his scalp in preparation for suturing. She watched him bring the skin edges together with tiny stitches, his brow furrowed in serious concentration, yet all the time trading sporting statistics to keep Jordan relaxed.

Deep inside her something ached—this was the man who so unalterably believed he didn't want to be a father. Couldn't he see he'd be great?

He snipped the black nylon, separating it from the final stitch, and dropped the needle into the suture tray. 'Phillipa will put a dressing on that and you won't be able to wash your hair for five days, which probably won't be too much of a hardship given your allergy to shower water.' Humour played through his words while the sound of latex snapped sharply as he stripped off his gloves and dropped them in the bin. 'You have to stay in sick bay for the rest of the day due to the bump on your head.'

Jordan slumped. 'But I'll miss the rest of the fete.'

'Yes, but you'll get ice cream and jelly and a personal visit from the celebrity patron.' Nick helped Jordan up onto the bed. 'He's a pretty famous runner and he might just autograph your camp book if you ask him politely.'

The boy settled back into the pillows slightly more happy. 'That would be great but can *you* come see me again later?'

Kirby caught the longing in the boy's voice. First Cameron and now Jordan. Nick had an easy way with these boys that generated respect and admiration.

Nick nodded. 'No problem. I'll drop by before I go home and I'll ring your mum and tell her what happened and that you're OK. Catch you later.' He gave the lad a playful punch before crossing the room.

'Here you go, Jordan.' Phillipa bustled about with gauze and tape.

Nick caught Kirby's arm and propelled her through the door. 'Come on, I'll buy you some tea and scones, I know they're your favourite.'

'Bye, Jordan.' She gave the boy a wave, before savouring the warm touch of Nick's arm through hers, and stepped out through the external doors. 'I felt a bit superfluous in there.'

'It was a simple suturing job and either one of us could have done it.'

'True, but I wasn't thinking about medical skills. You wanted to do the stitching and Jordan obviously wanted you to treat him.'

'Did he?' Nick looked surprised. 'I guess I've done a bit with that unit and he knows me.'

A bit? 'That would be the understatement of the day. You've done heaps with those boys in the last couple of weeks.'

The surprise on his face rolled into pleasure. 'I suppose I have but it's been fun and…' He shrugged his shoulders as if he couldn't find the right words.

'Gratifying?'

He nodded. 'Yeah, I guess it has been.'

She gave him a sideways glance, stunned that he hadn't made the connection between how he felt and the work he'd been doing at KC. 'You're really great with the boys. The way you talk to them and respect their growing independence, you're a natural.'

He cleared his throat. 'I don't know about that.'

'I do.' She spoke emphatically, the culmination of all her thoughts about him and the children unexpectedly forming into words. 'You genuinely like kids.'

He gave a wry grin. 'I guess I do.'

She smiled and hugged her secret daydream to her heart. 'Yes, you really do. I've seen you in action and you'd make a wonderful father.'

He immediately stiffened against her, his arm taut with tension. 'There's more to being a father than being able to chat to kids.'

'Obviously.' She stopped walking and turned to face him because this time she wasn't going to back away from the topic. 'But the thing is, you seem to really love being with them.'

'I love cats too but I don't have one.' His voice developed a chilly edge. 'My parents never recovered from the blow parenthood dealt them—spending so much time caring for Sarah and then losing her so young—and my life isn't suited to fatherhood. I don't want to be a father and I don't for one minute regret the choice I made.'

She stared into his eyes long and hard, looking for a sign that belied his words. 'Really?'

A flinty hardness she hadn't seen before glinted back at her. 'Really.'

A chill spread through her at odds with the heat of the day, spiking her like jagged shards of ice. Her daydream imploded, the faces of imagined children instantly vanishing.

Nick's hands suddenly cupped her face and he brought his mouth down onto hers in a kiss that rocked her all the way down to the soles of her feet.

He pulled back, his eyes loaded with the haze of desire. 'Summer fun, remember? This isn't for ever, it's all about now.'

She dug deep, burying her pain that he had no vision of her in his future, and she unearthed her sixteen-year-old self. 'In that case, you need to win me a doll on a stick.' She ran her finger down his shirt. 'And if you do, you might just get lucky.'

He gazed down at her, his voice huskily deep. 'How lucky?'

'Shelter-shed lucky.'

He grabbed her hand and marched her toward the shooting gallery.

CHAPTER TEN

KIRBY switched on the clinic's security and slammed the door behind her, pleased the long day had finally come to a close. The heat wave meant too many sunburned tourists suffering from heatstroke and dehydration, and the evening clinic had been full. She dumped her laptop and green enviro-friendly shopping bag that held her dinner—a can of chicken korma—onto the front seat of the four-wheel drive and then slid her key into the ignition.

The engine roared into life and she pushed the gear stick into first, preparing to turn right. *Home time.* But every part of her wanted to turn left and head out to Riversleigh, head out to see Nick and spend some time lying on the cool, mossy grass surrounded by ferns. Spend time making love with him.

She gripped the wheel harder and tugged right. She would *not* be needy. It was possible to go eighteen hours without seeing him, without inhaling that complex scent of soap, fresh pine and masculinity, and without feeling his strong arms around her, cradling her close.

Possible, yes. Enjoyable, no. Her mouth curved up into a private smile as she recalled his earlier goodbye kiss when he'd left the clinic at two p.m. He'd found her in the supply room, kicked the door closed and pinned her to the wall with the gentle caress of his entire body. His heat-filled gaze, filled with raw hunger, had shot through her so hard and fast that she'd almost orgasmed on the spot. She'd never experienced such powerful emotions from a man or for a man. It was wondrous, incredible and terrifying.

But it was also make-believe and she must remember that. This was summer frivolity, a summer fling. Nothing else, and she needed to focus on that. The summer would end, Nick would return to Melbourne City to his life in A and E and the lecture circuit, and she would finish her rotation in Port and get on with her single life that involved kids in some way.

But that was the future. For now, nothing serious was allowed to dent this time with Nick and she'd learned that at the fete. She'd pushed him to acknowledge how good he was with kids and he'd frozen on her. Knowing that, she now avoided all talk of children and as a result the last three weeks had been wonderful. Who would have guessed there were so many clandestine places for a couple to make love?

That would be sex. The realistic and grounding voice instantly reminded her that love was not part of this summer pact and it never could be. This time with Nick couldn't be anything but fun because ultimately, somehow and some way, she wanted children in her life and Nick didn't. That one thing was a huge gulf between them, impossible to bridge.

She bit her lip against the tug of concern and rounded

the final corner, catching sight of her tiny fisherman's cottage with its bright display of petunias, their purple and white heads waving welcomingly in the salt-laden evening sea breeze. Her stomach rolled over in pleasure. Nick's muddy truck stood parked out front.

She jumped out of the truck, grabbed her bags and opened the gate. Turbo's stocky form charged around from the side of the house, a stick in his mouth, a hopeful look in his brown eyes.

'Hey, mate, great to see you.' *Because if you're here, so is your master.* Kirby scratched the dog hard behind the ears. 'Sorry, there's not much room in my tiny garden for sticks.' She left the doleful dog and opened the front door, stepping into the blissful coolness that only a solid stone house could offer in midsummer. The pungent aroma of fresh basil immediately permeated her nostrils and her stomach growled hungrily. 'Nick?'

'I'm in the laundry.' His deep voice sounded muffled and far away.

'I don't have a laundry.' Confused and intrigued, she walked along the long central hall to the very back of the house where a lean-to had been added, probably over seventy years ago. She used it to hold her body board, bike and as a place to dry her wetsuit. Other than that it contained an old copper and a hand-turned mangle, and going by the cobwebs neither had been used to wash clothes in a very long time. Kirby, like previous tenants, spent Sundays at the laundrette.

She walked through the kitchen, passing her island bench, which groaned with fresh produce from Nick's garden. Pausing only to pop one of his plump and luscious strawberries into her mouth, she stepped down into the lean-to. 'What are you do—?' Heat roared through her.

A shirtless Nick, all golden skin and rippling muscles, with a tool belt strapped low on his hips, leaned over a shiny metal laundry trough, tightening a set of taps. Her heart hammered erratically as her breath came hard and fast. This was her fantasy, except he was real flesh and blood.

'Hey, Sherlock.' He put down his wrench and pulled her into his arms. 'You're later than I thought. Busy evening clinic?' His lips caressed her forehead as his tool belt pressed into her.

'Huge evening clinic.' She didn't care that a hammer pressed into her hip and a spanner imprinted itself on her belly. She leaned in, looping her arms around his neck, and breathed deeply. Kissing him long and lingeringly, she absorbed his taste, his touch and his boundless energy. A flash of white caught her eye and she reluctantly drew back, curiosity pushing her as she peered over his shoulder.

The old mangle and copper had vanished. Instead, a small white washing machine nestled snugly between the trough and a laminate bench, which had a power point fixed to its back board and two cupboards fitted underneath. High above the bench was an old-fashioned but very functional clothes airer suspended from the ceiling with a rope and pulley system so clothes could be aired and retrieved. Total surprise swirled through her, absorbing most coherent thought. 'What's all this?'

He turned, keeping one arm slung around her waist,

his face creasing in a wide grin. 'You needed a laundry so I traded vegetables for the reconditioned machine and bartered time in Jason's joinery to make the bench against keeping Jase supplied with tomatoes so he can make his famous Port chutney.'

He stepped forward and slipped open the top drawer under the bench and a small ironing board appeared. 'What do you think?'

'I…I'm speechless. I didn't expect… I…' Words failed her as her throat tightened. No man had ever done anything so thoughtful for her in her life.

A hint of a worried frown hovered on his brow. 'You do like it?'

Words couldn't come close to describing how she really felt so she kissed him hard and fast, hoping she wouldn't cry on the spot. She pulled back, breathless. 'I love it. Thank you. I can't believe you did this.'

He undid the tool belt, laying it on the bench, and then pulled on his shirt, which had been hanging behind the door. 'It's crazy for you to not have a laundry. I had a chat to the hospital board and they said if I wanted to do the work they had no objections, and you know how I enjoy working with my hands.'

She stepped in close, remembering exactly what his hands could do when they touched her body. She trailed her finger down the front of his shirt. 'I do know that and you're extremely good at it.' She couldn't keep the husky tone of desire out of her voice.

A flare of heat surged in his eyes but instead of pulling her hard against him, as she expected, he kissed her quickly on the cheek and grabbed her hand. 'Come on, that can wait. It's eight o'clock and I know you won't have eaten. I've got organic chicken with pesto and a home-grown salad all ready and waiting.'

She pulled against his hand, glancing over at the bench. 'What happened to being carefree, irresponsible and sixteen?'

His lips curved into a crooked smile. 'We've been sixteen a lot lately and right now I'm hankering for some long, lazy loving in a bed after a healthy meal.'

She stepped up against him. 'A bed? You're sounding like an old fuddy-duddy.'

His brown brows rose as his hands gently gripped her shoulders to keep a slight distance between them. 'No dessert for you until you've eaten all your veggies.'

'Is that a promise?'

'Absolutely.' The word sounded strangled as he moved toward the door, tugging her behind him in the direction of the kitchen.

She followed, surprised he hadn't wanted to christen the laundry but happy in the knowledge he wanted to have long, leisurely sex. She was totally up for a new experience.

Nick pulled the can of chicken korma out of the shopping bag and held it by the tips of his fingers as if it were poison. 'Seriously, though, you really don't take very good care of yourself, Kirby. When did you actually cook something decent to eat?'

'Hey, that has vegetables. Besides, I've been busy.' His words rankled but she appreciated where he was coming from. He'd faced a life-threatening illness and as a result treated his body with more respect than she treated hers. The horrible hot flushes that scorched her body twice a day might improve if she made sure she ate more soy and ate less processed food 'I promise to try harder.'

'Good.' But his expression clearly showed he didn't believe her.

She poured their drinks and set the table while Nick plated up the chicken salad, enjoying the camaraderie of being in the kitchen with another person. The truth was she hated cooking for one. Hated that no matter how hard she tried she always ended up with enough food for two, hated that she had to cook *and* clean up, but most of all she hated the silence that came with the meal for one. So she ate on the hop, standing up, or with a plate balanced on her knee, watching a movie, any way that didn't scream, *You're all alone.*

But she couldn't tell Nick any of that. She refused to admit her loneliness to him—after all, he hadn't signed up for anything more than sex and fun.

He's feeding you. He built you a laundry.

Don't go there, don't read more into this than there is.

But she disregarded the warning and let the words circle her heart, sending out fine connecting threads as she sat down opposite him. 'This looks sensational, thank you.'

His eyes sparkled with warmth as he raised his freshly squeezed glass of orange juice toward her and clinked it against hers. 'It's my absolute pleasure.'

She lost herself in his gaze as she forked some of the moist chicken into her mouth, letting the flavours of garlic and basil explode against her tongue. 'This is divine. I've never tasted chicken like this before.'

He nodded slowly. 'This is one reason why I grow my own food but I won't get back on my soapbox about it again tonight.' He drizzled virgin olive oil and balsamic vinegar over his endive and smiled at her as he ate his meal.

She basked in his gaze and asked him about his plans for the farm. With his fork waving, he enthusiastically outlined his success with some of the home-made anti-insect remedies given to him by the old Italian gardeners in the nursing home.

He asked about her day, laughed with her over her story about Meryl reducing the antagonistic, skull-and-crossbones-wearing, tough motorcycle rider into a compliant, polite and slightly scared patient with the flourish of a large glass syringe. From that point their conversation roamed wide and free, taking in the politics of health, the value of popular fiction and why it generated such rancour amongst the literati, and finishing with the importance of quality coffee on a Sunday morning. Kirby adored and savoured every single moment.

Nick drained his glass, scrunched his napkin into a ball and tossed it onto his now empty plate. 'Seeing as I've taken over your kitchen tonight, how about you take over mine on Friday? I'll have been harvesting all afternoon, ready for Saturday's market, so I won't be in the mood to cook.'

Something akin to pure happiness streaked through her as she pictured herself in his warm cosy home, sitting down with him at his huge farmhouse table and sharing eclectic conversation.

Be very careful—you're not playing for keeps. 'You'd let me loose in your kitchen to play with the Aga?'

He grinned. 'I think you'd be a perfect match for my kitchen.'

Perfect match. Recipes spun through her head as miniature castles rose slowly in the background of her mind. 'I'll ask Gaz to get me some prawns, mussels and calamari so I can make us paella. How does that sound?'

He stood up, walked around the table and pulled her to her feet. Gazing straight at her, a smouldering look in his eye, he spoke softly, his breath stroking her cheek. 'It sounds fine but I'm really more interested in what you have planned for tonight's dessert.'

'Let me think.' She leaned forward, nonchalantly trailing her forefinger along her bottom lip in a provocative gesture. 'Strawberries, cream and me.'

He shuddered against her and cleared his throat. 'I'll take it now but in reverse order.'

'Come with me.' Smiling, she took his hand and led him down the hall to her bedroom, glorying in the fact he wanted her so badly. She walked through the doorway, dropped his hand and slipped her dress from her shoulders. It cascaded down across her belly and pooled at her feet. She stepped out of it and turned to find him standing with his back against the closed door, his simmering gaze fixed on her.

A flush of need raced through her and instantly her breasts tightened as her body readied itself for him. She held out her arms. 'What are you doing over there?'

'Watching you. You're totally gorgeous, do you know that?' He walked toward her and pulled the clip from her hair, sending it tumbling down around her face. 'I've wanted to do that all day.'

She tilted her head back looking up at him. 'I've dreamed of this all day.'

He buried his face in her hair and she closed her eyes, wanting to block out everything except his wondrous touch.

The next moment her feet left the floor. He lifted her into his arms and swung her around before lowering her onto the bed as if she weighed nothing more than a child. The mattress moved as he lay down next to her and she opened her eyes to find him straddling her.

He gazed down at her, his expression a mixture of desire and decisions. 'Being sixteen has been fun but I want to show you what an experienced lover with all the time in the world can do.'

She grinned up at him. 'That sounds very smug.'

A dangerous glint shimmered in his eyes. 'I doubt you'll be disappointed.'

He lowered his mouth to hers as his hands travelled to places he knew made her heart race and her body lush with wanton hunger. She lost herself in his touch, craving it like a drowning man craved air and giving in to the most exquisite sensations she'd ever experienced in her life. Opening her body and her heart, she gave herself up to him completely and utterly, letting herself freefall into the glorious abyss of wonder in a way she'd never allowed herself to do before.

Much later Kirby lay in Nick's arms, the moonlight streaming in through the uncovered window, illuminating the white sheet that covered their naked bodies. His soft breathing sounded reassuringly behind her, and his exhaled breath tickled her neck. His promise of expert loving had hit every target. Her limbs now felt like hot treacle—thick and runny and deliciously unable to support her. She couldn't keep the smile off her face.

Before tonight their coupling had been hot, frantic and edgy as if they'd both feared they might never have another chance of being in each other's arms. And the moment the sex had been over they'd gone back to their respective homes or jobs, depending on the time of day. But tonight had been totally different.

What had Nick promised? Long, lazy loving, and he'd more than delivered. Her body, so overloaded with pleasure, now relaxed into his embrace, feeling like it had come home.

It's just sex.

It's way past sex. It's a new sparkly laundry, it's delicious food and conversation, it's companionship, it's having things in common, it's… Clarity sucked the breath from her lungs as she came face to face with reality. *It's love.*

Oh, God, she loved him.

Her hands gripped her temples, as if squeezing hard would change things. Loving Nick was dumb, stupid, senseless and a one-way ticket to heartache. They wanted totally different things from their lives so how had she let this happen? How had the protective barricades around her heart melted away, leaving her vulnerable?

But how it happened wasn't really important. The fact was it *had* happened and this was her new reality.

Nick moved in his sleep, his legs entwining with hers so his body wrapped around her, cocooning her completely. What would it be like to lie like this every night?

It wouldn't work.

The memory of the night on the pier flitted across her mind, complete with audio. *We're both here for the summer so let's use this time we have together, use it for fun.* Nick had his plans. *I don't want to be a father.* She wanted somehow to create a family so this summer together was all they could have, and then it was over.

Stop it now before you get in too deep. But she knew that depth was just semantics and she was already in way over her head. So she would do the only thing she could do and that was take and enjoy every last minute of the time they had left together, banking every experience to last her a lifetime.

The clock showed five p.m. and Nick switched off his computer ready to head home. It was the first afternoon he'd ever worked at the clinic but Kirby had looked so exhausted at lunchtime he'd sent her home to the quiet of his place for a restorative afternoon nap. Initially objecting to the idea, she'd finally compromised by insisting on cooking them dinner in his kitchen. It had turned out that, given the time, the recipe and the ingredients, Kirby could actually cook. He smiled in anticipation of the meal and the evening ahead—lazing on the couch with a full-bodied red wine and a full-bodied woman.

'Just before you leave, Nick, your mother is on line two.' Meryl's voice crackled down the clinic's intercom.

Son guilt immediately snagged him. Over the last few days his mother had left three messages on his mobile and two on his home answering-machine and he hadn't rung her back. He wasn't deliberately avoiding her, it was just he'd been really busy.

Busy having fun. Between the farm, the clinic, KC and Kirby his days raced past with lightning speed, as was his summer.

He pressed the button under the red flashing light. 'Hi, Mum, how's it going?'

'It's going very well, darling. You sound bright and happy.'

An image of Kirby, her golden hair spread all over his pillow and her face flushed with the joy of sex, thundered through him. 'You sound surprised.'

'Well, your father and I were a bit worried when we hadn't heard from you so that's why I'm calling you at work.'

'Sorry, Mum, I have no real excuse except things have been busy, but I should have called.'

'As long as you're well, Nick.'

He heard the strain in her voice and swallowed a sigh. He hadn't been fair to her, not returning the calls. She'd lost one child and had faced down the possibility of losing another. 'I'm great, Mum. Really, you don't have to worry about a thing.' He heard a sniff and a rustling of paper and something that sounded like the laugh of a kookaburra. That had to be wrong—kookaburras didn't hang out in inner Melbourne. 'What's up?'

'A couple of things. Melbourne City telephoned. They've sent you a letter and are waiting to hear as they're expecting you back on the first.' She hesitated for a moment and the silence strained down the line.

'Are you going back, Nick, or do you love the work in the country?'

He leaned back and gazed out the window, glimpsing the sweet curve of a wave before it broke over the reef. He leaned forward, tugging at his hair. 'I wrote them a letter last week confirming I'd be going back.' He just hadn't quite got around to posting it.

'As long as you're sure it's what you want, darling. You *do* seem to have embraced country life.'

You've embraced Kirby. He stood up abruptly, completely forgetting he wasn't on his mobile. The phone slid sideways, teetering on the edge of the desk, and he grabbed it just before it fell. 'Of course I'm sure it's what I want, Mum. It's my career, everything I've worked for.' The words sounded overly firm as they ricocheted back to him off the bookcase-lined walls.

'That's great then. So, seeing as you don't have too much time left down there, your father and I thought we'd come down to the farm for a couple of days and visit, if that fits in with you. Dad wants to fish and I'll take you up on the offer of berry picking.' Her smile radiated down the line. 'I quite like the idea of making my own raspberry jam.'

He ignored the selfish part of him that railed at the thought that a visit from his parents meant less time with Kirby. *They'd enjoy spending time with Kirby.*

He immediately pushed the thought aside as being completely untenable. He'd never actively sought to introduce the women he dated to his parents as he'd always moved on to dating someone else by the time he caught up with them again.

His gaze caught the date on the calendar—he only had a couple of weeks before he returned to Melbourne and Kirby had to stay in Port so there was no point introducing Kirby to his folks. Nothing about his time with Kirby was any different from his time with other women. *It's been all summer.*

He shrugged the voice away. Summer had a finite endpoint so despite this fling being longer than the norm, just like every other relationship, it would end. They wanted different things out of life so it had to end. He turned the desk calendar face down. 'It would be great if you and Dad came to visit. When are you coming so I can make sure you can actually get into the spare room?'

'Actually, darling, we're already here.'

A ripple of unease tightened every muscle in his body. 'In Port?'

The taunting laugh of a kookaburra vibrated down the phone line, followed by a familiar bark.

Turbo. All his blood drained to his feet. 'You're at Riversleigh?' His usually deep voice had developed a squeak.

'That's right. Your father has cleared out the spare room and Kirby and I have dinner cooking so we'll see you soon.' The click on the line sounded with precise finality as the line went dead, but not before he'd heard the delight in his mother's voice.

He groaned and sank his head into his hands. Since Sarah's death his mother had turned her full parenting attention on him and despite his dodging and weaving, and straight-up statements of 'It's not going to happen', she never wearied of her own position on the subject of him settling down. Meeting Kirby in *his* house would only have fuelled that desire and ramped up her expectations.

His plans for a long lazy evening vaporised. His carefree and easy summer had just got complicated.

CHAPTER ELEVEN

KIRBY sat outside on Riversleigh's veranda in the large and comfy rattan chair with her feet up on the wood box, watching Turbo round up the last of the chooks for the night and deny the foxes their dinner. Exhaustion clung to every muscle, making her body feel like it was made of metal and pinning her to the chair. She should be inside washing the dinner dishes, but Nancy and Michael, Nick's parents, had shooed her out of the kitchen and the thought of having to move from the chair was just too much.

Besides, Nick needed some time alone with his parents. His mother had been nothing but polite and friendly but Kirby could tell she had a thousand questions to ask Nick, starting with, *Who is this woman I found in your house?* Poor Nick—when he'd come home he'd looked more like he thought he was facing a firing squad than his loving mother.

If she'd felt less tired she would have stayed in the kitchen as a protective device, but the aroma of cooling lamb had made her feel queasy and she'd taken up the offer to watch the sun set.

Nancy and Michael were completely different from what she'd expected. Nick had painted her a picture of a couple worn down by trauma, a shell of their former selves. Instead, she'd met a vibrant and positive couple in their early sixties with a very close and loving relationship. When she'd taken the clean bed linen into the spare room, she'd found them with their arms around each other, and she'd noticed how Michael always seemed to touch Nancy with a caress or a pat when she passed him.

The squeak and bang of the wire door made her look up.

Nick strode down the veranda, waves of energy rolling off him, pervading the surrounding air. She swallowed—half moan, half groan. How could he be so gorgeously sexy and full of get-up-and-go when she just wanted to sleep for ever?

He walked straight over to her and bobbed down beside her, his hands resting on the arm of the chair. 'You OK?'

She gave a wan smile. 'I've been better. For some reason I'm really, really tired. I think the frantic pace of summer medicine has finally caught up with me.'

He plunged his fingers through his hair, leaving behind a trail of spikes. 'But you've just had two nights when you haven't been out on call so you should be jumping out of your skin.'

She stifled a yawn. 'I know, and up until yesterday I've been feeling really great, better than I have for a long time.'

No hot flushes. The thought popped unexpectedly into her head and she realised with a shock that it had been a while since she'd had one. Perhaps her body had finally adapted to menopause.

'You didn't eat much.' Faint disapproval hovered in his eyes before he leaned forward and kissed her on the forehead. 'You probably just need a good night's sleep and a hearty breakfast of free-range eggs.'

Her stomach heaved and acid burned the back of her throat. She swallowed against the bitter taste and thought of how much she wanted to be tucked up in her bed. She moved forward, preparing to stand. 'I'd better go home.'

Nick instantly shook his head. 'No way are you driving down that winding road when you can hardly keep your eyes open.'

The clink of crockery and the murmur of voices drifted out through the open front door. 'What about your parents?'

'We're adults, Kirby, and so are they.' A determined expression matched the set of his shoulders. 'How I live my life is up to me and I've told my mother she's not to read more into this than there is.'

Kirby chewed her lip. 'You told her we were a summer fling?'

His eyes crinkled up as a wolfish smile loaded with pure, unadulterated lust crossed his face. 'Something like that.'

A sharp jagged pain exploded out of the centre of her heart and she caught her breath, hating it that she'd let herself be this vulnerable. What had she expected him to tell his mother? That they were a couple who belonged together for ever? She blew out a long breath, blaming fatigue. No one was rational when they were exhausted and tomorrow after a long sleep she would be back to normal and able to enjoy their last couple of weeks.

'Come on, Sherlock, bedtime.'

She let him haul her to her feet and take her to his bed, savouring the warmth of his arms, as she gave in to much-needed sleep.

Nick had slipped out of bed an hour earlier, leaving a sleeping Kirby, and had gone for a run with his father up the fern-lined gully and along the creek. Swirls of morning mist lingered, trapped between granite rock faces, keeping the temperature lower than on other parts of the farm. Nick loved this time of day, when the air was slightly damp and cool before the sun blasted its summer heat into every nook and cranny. Turbo had joined them, beside himself with delight at having Michael running with them, and he'd bounded between them, not knowing who to run alongside.

Now showered, shaved and ready for breakfast, Nick had been surprised to find Kirby still in bed, the sheet pulled up over her head.

'Hey, Sherlock.' He gently shook the outline of her shoulder, the sheet warm to his touch. 'Time to get up.'

A muffled groan and a barely audible 'OK' came from under the covers.

He kissed the top of her head and breathed in deeply, never tiring of her familiar scent and savouring it while he could. 'I'll have hot tea waiting.' He left the room whistling and headed to the kitchen.

'Good morning, Nick.' His mother stood at the stove,

poaching eggs, 'I've made a bowl of fruit salad and the bread is just out of the oven so help yourself.'

'Thanks, Mum.' He plugged the kettle in and took the tea-caddy out of the cupboard. 'How did you sleep?'

'With all this country air I slept like a log until Turbo padded in, gave us his hangdog look and your father got up.' She removed the eggs from the stove. 'Seems like Kirby slept well, too.'

'Mum.' The word came out as a warning.

'I know, it's none of my business.' She scooped the eggs from their hot cocoons and transferred them onto a warmed plate but her shoulders had squared as if she wanted to say a lot more.

He let the silence sit, thankful that the kettle boiled quickly. Pouring the bubbling water into a fine china mug, he watched the way the fragrant tea leaves floated in the captivity of an infuser, every leaf a different shape. No wonder people thought they had a message. He glanced at the hall doorway. Still no Kirby.

He picked up the mug and walked into his bedroom. Kirby lay with her golden hair spread lankly all over his pillow, her face the same alabaster white as the pillowslip. A trickle of concern ran through him.

Putting her tea down on the bedside table, he instinctively placed his hand on her forehead, expecting to feel the burning heat of a fever. 'You look like you've come down with the summer virus that has laid low a fair percentage of Port. Is your throat dry and scratchy?'

Her voice, usually so lyrical, came out soft and flat. 'No, I just feel listless and blah.'

'Gotta love that technical medical jargon.' He smiled as he sat down beside her. 'Yesterday's tiredness was obviously your body fighting something. Do you have any neck stiffness?' Meningitis was always a possibility that needed to be considered and hopefully ruled out.

She moved her head from side to side against the pillow. 'No, but I've got a dragging pain down here that woke me up and bites me when I move.' She pointed to her right iliac fossa.

He blew on his hands to warm them up. 'I'm guessing you still have your appendix?' His fingertips pressed down gently.

'I do but— Ouch!' She bit her lip and stiffened in pain as he pressed a bit more firmly.

'Sorry.' He stroked her hair as a potential diagnosis came together. 'Dr Atherton, I don't think you have a virus.' He grabbed her shorts and T-shirt and handed them to her. 'Time to get dressed.'

'I just want to sleep.' The words came out on a wail.

Any other time he would have kissed away her pout but right now he needed to be the doctor. 'Kirby, I'm driving you to hospital for a full blood examination and an ultrasound. I think you might be taking a trip to Barago Hospital later in the morning to part company with your appendix.'

Kirby's foot hit the bottom step of the footstool as she struggled to wrap the hospital gown around herself, regretting that she hadn't grabbed a second one to wear as a coat. Not that Nick hadn't seen every part of her body naked, but that didn't mean she wanted to expose her behind as she hopped up onto the examination couch.

'Are you feeling dizzy?'

Nick's palm cupped her elbow, steadying her as she positioned herself on the narrow couch.

'Not really.'

He fixed her with a disbelieving stare.

'OK, sometimes, but that road into town from your place would make anyone motion sick. Mostly I feel tired with occasional jabbing pain when I move too quickly.' She pulled the modesty sheet over her legs and up under the gown.

When they'd arrived at the hospital, the staff had clucked around her while Nick had taken the blood sample, but now it was thankfully just the two of them in the treatment room.

'I've warmed up the transducer gel.' Nick grinned at her as he squirted the clear gel onto her abdomen.

'Thanks, but at 33 degrees in the shade it would probably have been OK cold.' She tried to joke but she just wanted to lie back and close her eyes.

He switched off the light so the images on the ultrasound screen could be seen more clearly. He tilted it so Kirby could see part of it. 'Let's see if this appendix has a reason to grumble.' His large hands flexed over the transducer and zeroed in on the appendix. The image slowly came into blurry focus.

'Hmm.'

'Hmm, what?' She couldn't really make anything out.

'Well, your appendix looks fine and healthy.'

Kirby shifted slightly, trying for a better look at the

screen, and a sharp, hot pain caught her as she moved. She immediately stiffened against it. 'Oh, but something really hurts.'

Nick's forehead furrowed and he gave her a wry smile. 'I guess I need to be Sherlock this time. You lie back and relax while I go hunting for the culprit.' He moved the transducer across her lower abdomen.

She tangled her fingers, turning them over themselves. 'You can rule out an ovarian cyst because that is *never* going to happen.' She lay back on the pillow, feeling sad and sorry for herself and hating it that she did.

Closing her eyes, she let Nick take over and be the doctor, and instead of second-guessing what was wrong she concentrated on feeling the smoothness of the transducer move across her skin, listening to the click and burr of the machine and trying to relax. *Hah!*

The transducer suddenly pressed down hard. She opened her eyes with a start. 'That hurt!'

Nick didn't reply. Instead, he leaned forward, staring intently at the screen, his knuckles gleaming white against the transducer. He moved it a fraction and pressed again.

A shaft of alarm sliced through her. 'What is it?' She struggled to see the screen.

Nick's face was in profile, his strong nose silhouetted by the light of the screen, his cheeks hollow. He didn't answer her, he just kept staring.

Real fear tore through her. 'Nick, what is it? What can you see?'

He captured the image. 'Two heartbeats.'

'What?' She struggled to her elbow, bewilderment

compounding dread and confusing her even more. 'You're nowhere near my heart.'

His Adam's apple moved convulsively in his throat as he turned the screen to face her. 'Here.' His shaking finger pointed to the fuzzy image. 'You're pregnant with twins.'

'I'm pregnant?' Disbelief rocked her and she stared so long at the screen that her eyes burned, but her brain had seized and wouldn't compute the image. Pregnant? That wasn't possible—she had the bloodwork and the letter from a Melbourne specialist to prove it to be impossible. She blinked three times but still the image stayed the same. Two tiny embryonic sacs could be clearly seen on the screen.

'I'm pregnant!' Sheer joy exploded inside her, making the New Year's Eve's fireworks display look like a dim light show. She sat up quickly, ignoring the jab of uterine ligament pain in her side, and threw her arms around Nick. 'I'm pregnant.' She heard herself babbling as euphoria bubbled inside her. 'I can't believe it...I never thought it could happen to me, it's a miracle...' She pulled back slightly, cupping his cheeks in her hands, gazing into his eyes as wonder and elation filled her to overflowing. 'We're pregnant! I love you and we're pregnant.'

'Against all odds, so it would appear.' Impassive emerald eyes stared down at her and his voice sounded hoarse as he removed her hands from his face and sat her back on the couch.

She grabbed his hands. 'Oh, Nick, I never thought I could be this happy.'

A muscle twitched in his jaw. 'It's hard to take in because, technically, we're both infertile.'

She nodded, her mind whirling. 'I know, and that just makes it even more of a miracle. For some reason I've ovulated and with twins perhaps both of my ovaries fired off at once.' Words poured out of her as her brain skipped from thought to thought as she tried to make sense of the most wonderful situation. 'And your sperm count, which should be zero, has obviously changed, and your body has somehow been able to produce at least two healthy swimmers.'

She laughed and kissed his hands. 'No one should ever underestimate the power of the human body to heal and reproduce. It must have been all that healthy organic food you've been feeding us.'

'Right.' A faint wry smile hovered for a moment on his lips as he tugged his hands from hers and crossed the room to switch on the light. 'We need to plan what we're doing.'

'Yes, there's so much to plan.' She couldn't stop grinning as an image of her future rolled out in her mind. Two bassinets in the front room at Riversleigh, a double all-terrain pram that could bump along the track down to the creek, with Turbo running close beside it, a baby snuggled against her chest in a sling, and Nick with his broad hand gently pressed against a baby's back, holding him nestled against his shoulder, fast asleep.

'Who's the obstetrician in Barago?' Nick started flipping through a health department folder, his fingers working so fast that the pages scrunched as they turned. A moment later he unexpectedly tossed it back onto the desk, the spine of the folder splitting as it landed with a loud crack.

A tiny stab of unease pierced her euphoria.

'Forget it.' Nick pulled his mobile out of pocket. 'I'll ring Jasper at the Melbourne City and pull in a favour so you can have chorionic villi sampling tomorrow.'

A sensation of cold jetted up inside her, quickly spreading into every cell and chilling her to the bone. 'I don't need to have chorionic villi sampling.'

His gaze, always wide and full of fun, now hooked hers, shuttered and resolute. '*Yes*, you do.'

She didn't recognise him. Nothing about his stance, expression or tone of voice was familiar. Sliding off the couch, she crossed the room, driven by the need to touch him and reconnect with the man she loved. The father of her babies.

Her hand rested on his forearm. 'Nick, I'm almost twenty-eight, not thirty-five. The risk of the procedure causing a spontaneous abortion is higher than the risk of a problem with the twins.'

'*No*, it isn't.' His hands rested on her shoulders, his cheekbones stark and stern. 'Kirby, I had heavy-duty chemotherapy and my ability to make sperm ended with that.'

Tension coiled off his body, threatening to knock her over, and as he blew out a long slow breath, the temperature of it almost scorched her cheek. She smiled up at him like she would smile at a child who didn't understand something pretty simple. 'But that doesn't matter because obviously your body recovered.'

He spoke through gritted teeth. 'The chance that the sperm was damaged is very high.'

She felt the muscles of her face move, felt her brows

pull down, and heard her quick intake of breath as his words penetrated her brain. She spoke as if in a fog. 'So you're saying the twins *might* have something wrong with them?'

His hands gripped her shoulders. 'That's exactly what I'm saying.' His tone softened slightly as his hands relaxed. 'Have the test, Kirby, and then we'll know. Our lives are going to be turned upside down by twins—we don't need them to be disabled as well.'

Her insides turned to ice as the room seemed to tilt. 'We don't need…' She heard the rising inflection of her voice, heard herself stop speaking, not prepared to voice what he inferred.

He pulled her close. 'Kirby, you have to listen to me. I've lived through this with Sarah and I watched my parents struggle for seventeen years with a grief that never healed. Hell, my mother still does grieve. Neither of us deserves that.'

His arms crushed her against him and she struggled to move air in and out of her lungs. For the first time ever she wanted to be—needed to be—out and away from his touch. She pushed against him and stepped back, wrapping her arms around herself to stop from shaking. 'Nick, these babies are a gift and I won't do anything that could put their lives in jeopardy.'

He threw his hand up in the air. 'Technically, with all the odds stacked against them, these embryos shouldn't even exist.'

Every part of her shivered. 'But they do.'

'Yes, they do.' He touched her arm, his fingers gently pressing into her skin. 'The least you can do is make sure they have a chance at a good life. Kirby, take the test.'

His words pummelled her hard and sharp like hail, unrelenting and shockingly painful. If he loved her how could he be asking her to do this? Asking her to risk her one and only chance at being a mother?

I don't want to be a father and I don't for one minute regret the choice I made.

All the air swooped out of her lungs as bile soared up, burning her throat, but she welcomed the physical pain because it hurt a hell of a lot less than the truth.

He didn't love her.

She'd been nothing more than a summer diversion now gone belly up.

He didn't want her or their children in his life, which was why he was asking her to risk everything and have this test. If the test showed there was a problem with the babies, he would ask her to do something that she couldn't do.

Her castles in the air shattered like crystal, falling down into a black abyss. There was no future as a loving couple and a family. But the children bound her and Nick together inextricably and his sense of duty would keep him in their lives, making him resentful and bitter.

She and the twins deserved more than reluctant duty. Tears pricked her eyes but she refused to let them fall. Taking in a steadying breath, she stood tall and made the hardest decision of her life. 'I release you.'

'What?' Nick ran both his hands through his hair, his fingers digging into his skull against the pounding in his head. How had summer fun turned into this nightmare?

Kirby wasn't supposed to love him. She shouldn't be pregnant—how the hell had that happened?

Wild sex with abandon. Pretending you were sixteen.

He wanted to roar and silence the voice in his head. Every logical part of him railed at the unfairness of the situation. Damn it, he hadn't taken a risk with pregnancy when there had been no risk to take. He raised his head to look at Kirby, trying to centre his thoughts. 'What are you talking about?'

Her jaw tilted up, the action full of purpose. 'I'm really sorry that *my* pregnancy has ruined your plans never to be a father so I release you from all paternal responsibilities.'

The pity and hurt in her eyes ripped into him and anger surged at her wilful misinterpretation of his request. He knew his obligations and he wouldn't walk away from them. 'That is *not* what I'm asking.'

'Isn't it?' Her brows rose into a perfect arch. 'It's nothing to be ashamed about—I mean, you've been more than upfront and honest about it. You never wanted children and you've never deviated from that line. This thing between us was supposed to be a summer fling, carefree and fun.' Her voice wavered for the briefest of moments. 'It was me who broke the rules by falling in love with you.'

He hated it that she was hurting. 'Kirby, you know that I resp—'

She shook her head and held up her hand to silence him. 'It's me who's always wanted children although I never expected them, so now we're at this impasse and there's no compromise. You don't want kids. I do. End of story.'

The image of Sarah's tiny contracted body, held upright by the head brace on her wheelchair, thundered through him. 'No, it isn't the end of the story, hell, Kirby, it's just the start.'

She tucked her hair behind her ears, the action decisive. 'I'm pregnant. Given my history, this might never happen again so no way am I risking the lives of these babies by having an unnecessary test. Come what may, I'm in it for the long haul.'

Memories of a parade of allied health professionals who'd visited his childhood home and yet hadn't been able to change a thing, assailed him. 'You have no idea what you're in for.'

She folded her arms. 'Yes, I do. I'm in for sleepless nights, heartache and worry, but I'm also in for joy, laughter and a journey into the unknown.' She raised her vivid blue eyes to his. 'It's called parenthood, Nick, and it's what I want. If it was a perfect world then you'd want it too.'

'Then have the test so we can have a chance as a family.' He heard the begging tone in his voice.

He saw the shudder race across her face, down her neck and shoulder, vibrating all the way down to her feet.

Her head came up, her jaw tight. 'We have a chance but you don't want to take it. Love doesn't come with conditions, Nick. If the world was perfect you'd love me and be prepared to take this journey with all its inherent risks.' Her eyes flashed with betrayal. 'And you would never have asked me to take the test.'

Her look seared him. He needed her to understand,

needed her to realise what she might end up dealing with. 'My parents took that journey.'

'And I don't see any regret on their faces. They're incredible people, so full of life.' Her hands extended toward him, palms upward, full of entreaty.

'You don't know anything about it, how it changed them. Their life, my childhood, it was no walk in the park.'

'But it wasn't all bad, was it Nick?'

Her quiet words drilled into him, winding back the years, taking him down into the black hole of grief and despair that he never wanted to visit again. 'Yes, yes, it was and I can't risk doing it again.'

She stared at him, a long look that started at his hair and finished at his feet, as if she was memorising every detail about him. Then she silently picked her clothes and bag off the chair, and hugging them close, walked to the door. 'In that case, we don't have anything left to discuss. Goodbye, Nick.'

The door closed with a loud but controlled and final click.

The roar of pain, frustration and anger he'd held in for half an hour exploded out of him as he thumped the wall with his fist, welcoming the bruising pain that radiated from his knuckles to his shoulder. How could she have just walked out on him? How could she say she loved him and then just leave?

A trail of guilt tried to carve a path through him but he refused to let it make a mark. They'd had an agreement and love hadn't featured in it. He pulled open the treatment-room fridge door and wrapped an ice pack around his fist.

Kirby had absolutely no idea what she was saying or doing, not a clue in the world. But he knew. He was the one with the first-hand experience and she should be the one listening to him. Damn it to hell, he should be the one making the decisions.

Running footsteps sounded in the corridor and the door swung open. 'Is everything alright, Nick?' Concern was on Meryl's face as she took in the ice pack around his hand.

'Everything's fine.' He picked up his keys with his other hand and stormed past her toward the clinic where at least his patients would listen to him.

CHAPTER TWELVE

SWEAT poured from Nick's forehead as he brought the axe down hard against the red gum, watching the splinters of wood fly high before spiralling down to the ground. The wood pile had grown over the afternoon and the kindling pile even more so as he'd taken refuge in hard physical work. Chopping wood was a lot easier than thinking.

When he chopped, his concentration centred entirely on the act of raising the axe and slicing it cleanly through the air, driving it down hard into the waiting wood. Creating kindling demanded precision cutting and was even better at keeping every single errant thought at bay. Keeping thoughts of Kirby at bay.

He hadn't seen her since she'd walked out on him yesterday morning. On autopilot, he'd gone on to work a full day in the clinic, but today Meryl had said she'd be back at work this afternoon so he'd only worked his usual morning, leaving before Kirby arrived. An hour ago a box containing some of his clothes, his tool belt and the shelf he'd planned to erect in her laundry had been delivered by courier to Riversleigh.

The sharp crack of splitting wood rent the air. Sending back the shelf was just crazy. She needed that shelf to store her iron and laundry liquids. She worked too hard to be wasting time hunting through cupboards looking for things, she needed to be able to easily reach up and grab.

She'll be washing baby clothes.

Thwack! The axe landed hard in the chopping block.

Fatherhood had never enticed him but for the last thirty hours he hadn't been able to think of anything else. His dreams had been filled with chasing kids along the beach, teaching them to surf, and he could almost feel the touch of his hand over theirs, holding the string of a kite.

Two children permanently incapacitated like Sarah. A dull ache throbbed near his liver.

She had to see things his way. He'd give Kirby a few days and then he'd go and install the shelf and try to talk to her again. Make her see reason.

Goodbye, Nick.

The finality of her tone hammered nails into his heart. He brought the axe down harder than ever.

'Planning for a long, cold winter, are you?'

He turned at his father's voice, wiping his forehead on the sleeve of his T-shirt. 'Technically it's autumn in a couple of weeks and the evenings can be chilly.'

Michael's brows rose questioningly. 'True, but I thought you were planning on being back in Melbourne then.'

He ignored his father's logic and kept chopping.

Michael's hand came down onto the axe handle. 'How about you give it a break, son, and come up to the house? It's far too hot to be out here and, besides, your mother's serving scones topped with her just-made raspberry jam.'

No, I don't want to. The petulant version of his childhood self stamped his foot in his head, but the unusual paternal expression in his father's eye, one he hadn't seen since he'd been eighteen, brooked no argument. 'Good idea, Dad. Come on, Turbo,' he called to the dog, and strode back to the house.

His mother had everything set out under the shade of the veranda, which caught the faint wisps of any passing breeze.

They sat down, drank tea, discussed the lightness of the scones—soda water apparently being the key—and the flavour and texture of the jam, which had set well.

He let the conversation wash over him, letting it drown out the constant argument in his head. He'd had every right to ask Kirby to have the test for genetic abnormalities, given the medical treatment he'd been through. He was the one being sensible. She was sticking her head in the sand and—

'…today, Nick?'

He heard his mother's voice. 'Sorry, Mum, I didn't hear what you were saying, I was too busy savouring your jam.'

She rolled her eyes and smiled. 'Of course you were, dear. I was asking if Kirby was feeling better today.'

'She's working this afternoon.' He spoke briskly as he sliced open another scone, not wanting to think about how she really was.

'Yes, but is she feeling better?' His mother's green eyes speared him with their intent.

His eye caught sight of the large transport box at the end of the veranda. 'She's well enough to organise a courier.' The resentful words came out before he thought to stop them.

His father refilled his mug with steaming tea and dropped a slice of lemon into the pale brown liquid. 'Why would she have sent you a shelf? It's not your everyday gift but, then, again, Kirby isn't your everyday woman.'

'What's that supposed to mean?' Nick snapped, wanting the conversation to just stop. If there was any sort of justice to the world he should be home alone, dealing with the mess that was his life, without his parents offering commentary.

His father smiled a knowing smile. 'Nick, for years you've dated a parade of women and none of them have come close to Kirby.'

'How would you know? You only spent one day with her!'

Michael leaned back in his chair, his body slack with relaxation as he sipped his tea. 'I don't entirely know, although first impressions are a strong indicator. But I do know you built her a laundry.'

'So?' *You're sounding very sixteen.*

Shut up.

His father shot him a smile full of superior understanding. 'So, that tells me that she's very special to you. I built your mother a kitchen once, remember?'

He did remember. Flashes of a summer long past flickered in his mind—a black-and-white chequered floor, the scent of freshly shaved wood and drying paint, his mother's arms wrapped tightly around his father's neck, the immense pride on his father's face, and Sarah's wide smile.

Tumbling in on the picture came his summer with Kirby—cooking together, laughing together and sleeping with her cuddled in close, and a sense of peace he'd never really known before.

Was that love?

Hey, you left out the sex. How could you forget the sex? His sixteen-year-old self sounded very bewildered as the images of shared times other than sex kept reeling on.

The ground seemed to tremble under his feet as a seismic realisation hit him. God, it was love. He loved Kirby. How had he been so stupid? He'd been so focussed on the glorious sex he'd missed the significance of the important stuff.

His mother leaned forward. 'And we're worried that our arrival yesterday, completely out of the blue, might have caused a problem between the two of you.'

I wish it was that simple. He sighed. 'It's nothing to do with your arrival.'

His mother touched his knee, care and concern clear in her gaze. 'Then what's the problem?'

He'd held it in for a day and a half, letting it eat away at him, and he couldn't do it any more. 'She's pregnant.'

Utter confusion swam across Nancy's face. 'But I thought you weren't able to…' Disappointment chased the confusion away, leaving only sadness. 'Oh, I see, it's someone else's child.'

Every part of him raced indignantly to Kirby's defence. 'No, Mum, you've got it wrong. The twins are mine.'

Ignoring his parent's collective gasp, he ran his hands

through his hair. 'I came to Port for wellness, remember, to get my health back. Ironically, it appears it came back with a vengeance and that's the problem.'

His father put down his mug, every part of his body alert. 'But you do love Kirby, don't you, so exactly where is the problem?'

How had his father worked out that he loved her when he'd only just realised it himself? A sigh shuddered out of him. 'There's a chance, due to the chemo, that my sperm may be damaged, but Kirby and I have very different views on how to deal with this risk.'

He dragged in a breath and raised his gaze to his parents, knowing they would understand. 'She's not like us, she has no idea what it's like, living with a child like Sarah, how shattering it is, and how you never recover from something like that.'

His mother sat stock still, her fingers clasped in her lap. 'Is that what you think? That my life is shattered and I've never recovered?' Unreadable emotions raced across her face. 'Yes, Sarah's arrival changed me from the naïve young woman I was, but life would have made that happen anyway. Sarah made me a stronger person, Nick, she made me a fighter and she made me...' She caught Michael's hand. 'Made us realise what was important in our lives. I miss her every day but I don't regret a moment.'

His mother's words, so unexpected, fell like lead weights, stunning him. 'But I remember you crying. I remember you getting so angry sometimes...' He tried to align his feelings with his mother's but nothing matched and he was left feeling as if he'd been hit.

Nancy gesticulated as she spoke. 'I was angry at the system, Nick. At how hard we had to fight for everything so Sarah and other children like her could have the best life they could. But I was never angry at her being in our lives.'

His father nodded. 'We know things were tough for you, Nick, and we're sorry, but that's why we were so keen for you to go to those camps so you could be a normal kid for a few weeks every year without any constraints.'

Or were you given the opportunity to have some freedom from your family? Kirby's soft voice sounded loud in his head. His gut twisted, being pulled in different directions. How had Kirby been so wise and how the hell had he misinterpreted things so badly?

Michael continued, 'For some reason you've only remembered the difficult times with your sister and you've forgotten the love she so freely gave us in the years she was with us. You used to play with her and I'd hear you both laughing.'

But it wasn't all bad, was it, Nick? Kirby's voice lanced him, making him hurt everywhere. When he thought of Sarah the first image that came to mind was her contracted and wasted legs peeking out from under the tray of her wheelchair, followed by the familiar surge of pain.

He closed his eyes and tried again. He saw Sarah smiling in the kitchen and then a faint and muffled sound bite of her squeals of delight as he raced her down the driveway in her wheelchair slowly pushed aside the sadder thoughts.

Memories stirred in Nancy's eyes. 'Nick, do you

remember, whenever we danced, Sarah would try and sing?'

Nick gave a wry smile. 'Half the time she sounded better than your singing attempts.'

'Hey, I can do a wonderful rendition of "Hey Big Spender".'

'Nick's right. I love you but you're tone deaf.' Michael laughed and dodged his wife's playful hit.

His mother's laughing face suddenly became serious. 'Nick, no one puts their hand up for challenging events but you've fought cancer and won. You've been a loving brother to a girl who loved us dearly and gave us so much for the short time we had her—both those things have made you the strong person you are.'

Michael cleared his throat, his grey eyes filled with empathy. 'No one can give you a crystal ball but avoiding experiences in case they're not perfect is not a way to live your life. You've fought too hard for your own life to do that.'

We have a chance but you don't want to take it. If you loved me you'd be prepared to take this journey with all its inherent risks.

His head pounded so hard he thought it would explode. He'd faced cancer head on but he'd hidden from the most important thing in his life. He'd been so blinkered, so stupid. He'd convinced himself he didn't want to be a father but this summer that conviction had taken a pounding.

He pictured Kirby's face and pressed his fingers hard against his temples. He'd hurt her more than anyone deserved and in the process had risked losing the love of his life and his future family. He'd risked *everything* that could make him happy.

He had to talk to her. He had to tell her he loved her, had to. *Move!* He stood up abruptly, the plate on his lap falling with a dull crash onto the wooden boards. 'I have to go.'

'Of course you do, son. Good luck.'

Michael's heartfelt words underpinned his fear— that he'd realised everything too late and Kirby would refuse to forgive him.

Kirby reluctantly shut the clinic door, needing to pull it hard against a sudden gust of wind. She glanced up at the lead-grey sky where dark clouds streaked past, full of threatening intent—the sunny day had suddenly come to an end. As she pocketed her key, she caught sight of the ocean now dark and menacing with white-caps that collided against each other, sending spray high into the air. Kirby could picture all the holidaying families quickly gathering their possessions, disman-tling their sunshade beach tents and scurrying home to play board games and read books.

She started to walk home, her feet dragging against the pavement. Although her afternoon at work on almost no sleep had taxed her to the nth degree, and her fatigue made her feel like she was wading through mud, walking home was preferable to driving as it delayed her arrival by a good fifteen minutes. She'd wanted to stay at the clinic longer but Vicki had pointed out there were no patients, and had wanted to lock up a bit early.

Her stomach rolled and she decided to walk to the

supermarket and buy more ginger tea and dry biscuits. Anywhere was better than being at home, where evidence of Nick's presence declared itself in every room from the repaired window sash to the immaculate laundry she couldn't bear to use.

He didn't love her.

She swallowed hard and fast against the pain. For five or six glorious minutes yesterday she'd thought she'd been given the world. She'd thought she'd been blessed with a man who loved her and a long-desired family to share with him.

But she'd got it all horribly wrong. Nick didn't love her and without a cast-iron guarantee that the children would be perfect, he didn't want them either.

She bit her lip. *Focus on the babies.*

She had two children to plan for and that was what would get her up every morning and keep her going through every day. She had to finish her time in Port and then decide what to do next.

A rumble of thunder vibrated in the distance, interrupting her thoughts, and on the spur of the moment she changed direction and walked along the pier. She'd always enjoyed watching the way a storm blasted across the ocean, Mother Nature unleashing her fury and reducing humans to pawns in her path. Today she wanted the wind to buffet and whip her, she wanted the salt to sting her cheeks and make her eyes water, but most of all she hoped against hope that the gale would blow all her pain away.

The fishing fleet hadn't sailed in the late afternoon as usual. Instead, the boats bobbed crazily at their moorings, safely away from being tossed against the pier. Only Gaz's boat remained and she waved to him as he prepared to sail out to his buoy.

'Crazy weather, Doc. You should head home.'

Waves crashed against the white wooden pylons, the vibrations racing through her body. Her stomach lurched and her nausea surged almost as strongly as the waves, but she'd rather be out here that inside her cottage. 'I've always enjoyed a good storm.'

But the wind caught her words, carrying them up and away, and Gaz just gave her a grin and a salute as he concentrated on his vessel.

A few large drops of rain started to fall, but were immediately whipped sideways by the wind, denied the right to land. Kirby stared out to sea, her eyes seeking the flat line of the horizon, but the waves prevented her from seeing it. Something caught her eye. She squinted but could see nothing but waves.

She peered again and caught a flash of yellow. Her stomach dropped as adrenaline poured through her, making her shake. She'd recognise that distinctive striped colouring anywhere. One of KC's inflatable dinghies was being blown out toward the reef. She sprinted across the pier yelling, 'Gaz! Wait!'

The fisherman didn't respond.

With every ounce of effort in her she screamed again. 'Help!'

He turned.

Waving her arms, she ran toward him. 'There are kids out there in a boat.'

He didn't hesitate. 'Hop on.' Throwing her a life-jacket and the satellite phone, he swung the boat away from the pier. 'Ring the police and let them know.'

A seed of panic sprouted inside her. 'Is this the best boat for a rescue so close to the reef?'

He tilted his head, his face sobering. 'I guess we'll find that out, won't we?'

Nick breathed a sigh of relief as he pulled up outside the clinic. The drive down from Sheep-wash corner had been horrendous, with rain lashing the ute so hard that the windscreen wipers on full tilt had scarcely made an impact. He killed the ignition, jumped out of the car and ran to the front door, rehearsing for the thirty-sixth time what he was going to say, which started with, 'I've been the biggest jerk' followed by, 'Please forgive me' and finished with—

His hand failed to move the handle. He looked up and read the after-hours sign directing people to the hospital. Damn! Five o'clock was early for Kirby and Vicki to have gone home. Perhaps they'd been caught up at the hospital.

He strode through the rain, rethinking how he would talk to her now she was in a more public place. The automatic doors slid open and he came face to face with Meryl and Constable Masterton, worry lines etched on their faces.

Meryl hurried toward him. 'Thank goodness you're here, Nick. I've got the air ambulance on standby and Theo's just left for the pier with the road ambulance so you must go now with the constable.'

Nick tried to keep up as she shoved the bright orange emergency worker's overalls and protective jacket into his arms.

Meryl gave his arm a squeeze. 'Gaz is a very experienced seaman. I'm sure they'll be fine.'

His confusion immediately transformed to anxiety. 'You're sure who will be fine? What's going on?'

Two deep lines made a V at the bridge of the nurse's nose. 'Didn't you get our message?'

He immediately patted his body, feeling for the distinctive rectangular shape of his phone and realising he'd not picked it up again after changing out of his work clothes. He'd been too distracted after finding the box with the laundry shelf in it.

The young constable put his hand on Nick's shoulder, gently pushing him back toward the doors. 'We just got an emergency call from Dr Atherton. She and Gaz are attempting a rescue of a KC dinghy with kids caught in the storm.'

'In Gaz's boat?' Incredulity became fear. The fishing boat could negotiate the narrow reef entrance in calm to medium rough weather, but in a storm like this it just didn't have the manoeuvrability. An image of the boat floundering against the rocks, its wooden beams splintering, slugged him so hard he lost his breath.

Kirby.

The twins.

He couldn't lose them, not now when he'd just worked everything out. Not now when they didn't know he loved them all as much as life itself.

You drove her to this. If you hadn't been such a jerk she would be tucked up in your bed, safe. Like a geyser, guilt shot through him, ramping up his fear into a hot and terrifying beast. He spun around, catching the police officer by the jacket. 'What the hell were you thinking, letting a pregnant woman out in weather like this when it's your job?'

The constable staggered back as Meryl grabbed Nick's arm. 'Nick, stop it. We have no idea how it happened, but it has.' Sympathy filled her eyes. 'We love her too and she's in good hands.'

He dropped his hand and muttered an apology as he hauled on his coat. 'I don't care what the policy is, I'm going out with you on the police boat and *nothing* is going to stop me.'

Kirby could barely keep her balance as the boat rocked violently, every weathered board creaking terrifyingly loudly. The binoculars' lenses fogged as rain poured over her, trickling down the too-big sleeves of the anorak, but she didn't care. All she could think about was finding the dinghy.

The storm had darkened the sky to the levels of dusk, making visibility tough, and Gaz had turned on the bright fluorescent night-fishing lights, but so far she hadn't been able to sight it again.

Gaz's hand's gripped the wheel, his knuckles white as he scanned the sea. Kirby knew he was as worried about the threat of the reef as much as he was about the children. She couldn't think about the reef and how boats always came off second best. She couldn't think about the risk she was taking, the risk she was putting the twins into… She stifled a hysterical laugh—she'd wanted Mother Nature to drive all thoughts of Nick away but she hadn't quite envisaged this.

Yellow caught the edge of her eye. She looked again. 'There!' She waved her arms and pointed as the dinghy rose on a wave, disappearing almost as quickly into a deep trough.

Gaz steered the boat according to her directions as waves washed over the bow, completely drenching her. Kirby pulled the life preserver off its holder, checking the knot that secured it to the boat.

As they got closer she recognised two terrified boys from Unit C huddled in the bottom of the dinghy. *Thank goodness.* She waved her arms out wide, hoping Lochie and Matthew would understand that it meant she could see them as all her words were captured by the wind.

Gaz yelled out instructions. 'Kirby, I need to keep the engines running so we can avoid the reef so we'll have to go past twice, getting one boy at a time.'

She nodded her understanding, hating it that one boy would have to wait longer than the other before he was safe but knowing it had to be that way or all lives would be at risk.

The waves pounded the boat, pushing it inexorably toward the reef, while the engine throbbed hard against them, desperately attempting to counter the relentless pressure. The dinghy was only three metres away but it could have been have been three hundred.

'One at a time.' She yelled the words as she hurled the life preserver out like a Frisbee to the waiting boys. As it arced in the air an almighty wave cascaded over the dinghy, picking it up as if it was a feather before upending it and tipping the boys into the foaming sea.

Kirby's scream was trapped in her throat as her brain

went into automatic and time seemed to slow down. She scanned the water for bobbing boys but she couldn't see a thing.

'I have to bring her round,' Gaz yelled from the wheelhouse.

The rope in her hands tugged. 'Wait.' Using everything she had in her, she pulled.

Lochie's terrified face appeared in the trough of a wave, the life preserver around his middle.

'Kick, mate, kick.' Leaning over the side, being hammered by the waves, Kirby managed to haul him on board.

Almost dropping him onto the deck, she checked the bare basics—that he was conscious and breathing. Broken bones or anything else would have to wait. 'Get into the wheelhouse. I have to find Matthew.'

Gaz had brought the boat round to avoid the reef and for a moment she was completely disoriented. Where the hell was Matthew? She stared at the dinghy, hoping he was clinging to its upturned form, but all she could see was yellow and black plastic.

'Look!' Gaz's arm pointed and she swung around.

The distinctive blue and white police boat was rapidly getting closer. *Thank God, more eyes.* But would they arrive fast enough? It took three minutes to drown and two minutes had already passed.

The white lights from the fishing boat lit up a small area but with salt-stung eyes and driving rain it was hard to see anything at all.

And then she saw it. A boy, face down in the water. Not moving.

She snapped her neck left and saw the jagged outlines of the reef. She swung back the other way and saw the police boat with its reinforcements had almost reached them.

At that moment she knew exactly what she had to do. Grabbing the life preserver, she dived into the roiling water and swam toward Matthew.

CHAPTER THIRTEEN

'No!' Nick's heart stalled in his chest. He was unable to believe his eyes as Kirby dived over the side of the boat. The love of his life and the mother of his unborn children had just disappeared into a raging sea before he could fix everything between them.

'Aidan, over there!' He pointed with an extended arm, his eyes never leaving the water, willing her to appear above the waves.

The smaller police boat moved quickly, able to change direction more easily than the larger fishing boat. White foam swirled around them, decreasing visibility, but adrenaline and raw fear had acutely honed Nick's eyes.

Bright orange bobbed up ten metres away and then disappeared behind a wave. 'Throttle back, she's over there.'

The constable skilfully brought the boat in close and Nick saw Kirby, her arm around a boy's neck, tilting his head up using the pistol grip and maintaining him in rescue position. Then her other arm shot straight up in the air—the international sign for rescue.

Thank you. Thank you.

'I see her, Nick. You get them on board.'

'Kirby, over here.' He leaned over the side, holding out a long pole.

She kicked hard and her free hand gripped the pole. A wave covered her and she came up spluttering. 'Take Matt. He's not breathing.'

Nick wanted to pull Kirby into the boat, feel her heavy in his arms to really know she was safe and unhurt, but triage left no room for feelings. Matthew was his first priority. 'I'll take him, you use the ladder.' He reached down and with Kirby's help heaved the lifeless boy out of the water.

He laid him down on the bench, clearing his airway and checking his carotid pulse. Nothing. Tilting Matt's head back and closing his nostrils with this fingers and thumb, he covered the boy's mouth and blew in two rescue breaths.

Behind him he heard the emergency radio and Aidan instructing Gaz to return to Port, heard the request for the air ambulance and confirmation that Lochie was un-injured, just cold.

The boat rocked, jolting him sideways, and he deliberately fell to his knees. Placing the heel of his left hand on the boy's breastbone and interlacing the fingers of his right hand, he immediately started cardiac compressions. 'Come on, mate, come back to me, you can do this.'

A sopping Kirby knelt down beside him. 'I'll breathe.'

He wanted to say no, he wanted to say, *Wrap yourself up in a blanket and just keep warm, look after yourself and the babies, you're a patient too*, but Matthew needed both of them.

They settled into the pattern of thirty compressions to two breaths. He remembered the first day they'd met and how she'd been doing mouth to mouth then as well. He caught her gaze and right then his own heart wanted to stop.

Kirby's clear blue eyes, usually so full of warmth and what he now realised was love, were harrowingly empty. Although she was so physically close to him that their hair almost touched, he knew without a shadow of a doubt that she'd left him emotionally.

'We're five minutes out of Port.'

Aidan's firm, controlled voice reassured Nick about extra help for Matt but not help for himself. He'd hurt Kirby too much, asked her to do the unthinkable, and had pushed her past the point of no return.

Matthew vomited.

Kirby immediately turned him on his side and cleared his airway and checked his air entry. 'He's breathing.' Sheer relief permeated her words.

'Matt, can you hear me? Matt?' Nick shook the boy, whose eyes fluttered open for a moment. 'I'll get the oxygen.' He managed to secure the small tank so it didn't roll and he carefully placed the mask over Matt's face.

'And Gaz, is he OK?' Kirby moved to stand.

'He's coming in behind us, Doc. Don't you think you should have a blanket around you? You're shaking.' Aidan reached up with his spare hand, grabbing the space blanket from the storage cupboard. Ripping the package open with his teeth, he shook it out and by using his knee to control the boat he wrapped it around her shoulders.

'Thanks.' Kirby smiled at up the young constable, gratitude shining on her face.

That's my job. Nick, halfway through checking Matt's pupil reactions, wanted to knock Aidan Masterton sideways. Damn it, he should be taking care of Kirby but absolutely nothing about the last few hours was going the way he'd planned and he had an aching suspicion that no matter how hard he wanted it, the situation wasn't going to change.

Kirby sat wrapped up in flannel pyjamas and a dressing gown, which seemed ludicrous in summer but she just couldn't get warm. Meryl had supervised her having a warm bath, had fed her hot chicken broth and now had tucked her up under a doona with a heated wheat pack at her feet.

'Kirby, I rang the hospital and Matthew's doing well at Barago. He's conscious and alert, which is wonderful, and Lochie is fine with a few cuts and bruises which will heal in no time. Considering what could have happened, it's a wonderful result.' Meryl clucked around, adjusting her pillows. 'You're sure to get a bravery medal for today.'

'I just did what anyone else would have done.' *Saving Matthew had been the easy part of the afternoon.* Working with Nick on the police boat had been the hardest thing she'd ever done.

Nick. The clock struck seven and she swallowed a painful sigh. Nick would have returned by now from escorting Matthew to Barago. Would have returned to Riversleigh. She took a big slug of her chai tea, welcoming the scalding liquid in her mouth. She really had to stop thinking about Nick and what he might or might not be doing because he'd made it clear he didn't want to do anything with her and the twins.

Meryl stood back with her arms crossed. 'So are you sure you'll be OK? I can stay longer.'

Kirby smiled. 'Thanks, Meryl, but I'm fine. Nothing that a good sleep won't fix.' But she felt the lie clean down to her toes.

The caring nurse hesitated as if she was going to say something else but then thought better of it. Instead, she picked up her bag and tucked it under her arm. 'In that case, ring me if you need anything and I'll see you tomorrow. Sleep well.'

Kirby listened to her retreating footsteps against the floorboards, heard the familiar squeak of her front door opening and waited for the banging thud of it closing. Instead, she heard voices—Meryl's strident accent along with a deep rumbling baritone she'd know anywhere.

Nick.

She simultaneously went hot and cold but before she had time to put down her tea and move from the couch he was standing in the doorway of her living room, sucking the air from the space and filling it completely with unusually restrained energy. 'Hello, Kirby.'

Hey, Sherlock. He used to greet her with dancing eyes. This serious greeting rammed home how much she'd lost and she wanted to dive under her doona and ignore him and the whole horrible situation. Instead, she held her head high. 'Hello, Nick.'

He rocked back on his worn boots, his hands jammed into the pockets of his jeans. 'How are you feeling?'

'I'm fine.'

He nodded slowly. 'That's good.'

She hated this. Hated the chilly air of politeness that now sat between them, suffocating all the passion and fun that had once connected them with every look and word.

He swallowed, hard, his Adam's apple moving quickly. 'And the twins? No problems there?'

A spark of anger surged up through her paralysing grief. 'No. Swimming generally doesn't disturb a pregnancy if that's what you were hoping to hear.'

He swayed as if he'd been punched. 'God, Kirby, is that what you think of me? That I'd wish for a miscarriage?'

His ragged words shocked her and she sought clarity. 'Yesterday you said—'

'Yesterday I was an insensitive fool.' In two strides he stood before her, staring down at her, his eyes filled with contrition and regret. He knelt down next to her. 'I'm so very sorry.'

Her hand tingled to touch his hair, to pull him close and soothe the devastated look from his face, but too much was unresolved and too much hung in the balance. 'What are you sorry for?'

His eyes flared with scorn for himself. 'For hurting you, for only telling you I respected you. God, what a pompous idiot I was.' He ran his hand through his hair, tugging at the curls at the nape of his neck, his expression begging her to understand. 'Until I met you I'd never been in love and even when it was banging me hard over the head I didn't get it. I didn't recognise it.'

He put his hand over hers, his touch gentle and warm in sharp contrast to the desolation in his eyes. 'But, Kirby Atherton, I love you. I was on my way to tell you when I heard you'd gone out in that storm and when I saw you dive into that water I knew right then that if you died, then part of me would have died too.'

I love you. She wanted to laugh, she wanted to cry as his words caressed her, stark in their truth, calling to her to believe. But after yesterday some doubt lingered. 'You love me? Why do you think you love me?'

His lips twitched up into a knowing smile. 'Because I built you a laundry.'

Her heart sang—he really did love her. She wanted to throw her arms around his neck, bury her face in the crook of his neck and feel his comforting arms around her, but still she held steady because too much was at stake and loving her might not be enough. 'But the laundry isn't finished.'

A sombre expression captured his face. 'No, it isn't. I have to enlarge the ceiling airer and it's missing a shelf and two nappy buckets.'

She held her breath. 'Two nappy buckets?'

He nodded, his smile now wry. 'I'm told that twins generate a lot of washing.'

Her heart hammered wildly in her chest. 'Are you saying you want to come on the journey with me no matter what might happen?'

'No matter what, with all its inherent risks.' He gripped her hands tightly. 'You were so right and I was so ridiculously wrong. Growing up, things were not as black as I remembered them and I now know that my parents survived and grew closer. So, come what may, we can and we will survive and grow old together. I love you with all my heart, Kirby. Will you have me along for the ride of our lives?'

She looked down into green eyes filled with uncertainty but backlit with a love so strong it almost took her breath away. Her palms cupped his cheeks and she lowered her mouth to his, claiming her man and giving her answer in her kiss.

'I'm taking that as a yes.' He grinned up at her. 'I know we have a lot to discuss, like where we're going to live, how you're going to finish your GP training and how you feel about me returning to Melbourne Central. Not to mention which hospital is the best one to have these babies, and most importantly how to restrain my mother from taking out a paid advertisement in the Melbourne papers announcing she is going to be a grandmother.' His smile changed to a more serious expression. 'But while I'm down here on my knees I need to ask you one more thing. Will you marry me?'

Her squeal of delight said it all.

EPILOGUE

TURBO bounded out of the four-wheel drive, his bark one of pure pleasure as his feet hit the gravel drive of Riversleigh.

The Dennison family was back for the summer.

A blond-headed boy ran straight to the back of the vehicle, opening the rear door and clambering onto the bumper bar. 'Dad, where did you pack the fishing rod? I'm going straight down to the creek.'

'No, we're going swimming first.' A girl with vivid green eyes and a determined expression pulled at her brother's legs. 'Aren't we, Daddy?'

Nick raised his brows at his eight-year-old twins, both of whom had spent most of the last two hours of the drive asking, 'Are we there yet?'

He gave them a teasing grin. 'Actually, I thought we might spread the manure first and get things ready to plant the lettuces.'

'Oh, Dad!' The wail of dissension was deafening.

'Let's get the car emptied first.' Kirby lifted an eager William out of his car seat. At four, unlike his older siblings, he loved to carry things in from the car.

Leaving Nick to organise the ferrying of gear, she walked up the straight path, the box hedges now at hip height. Sliding the heavy, flat key into the lock, she turned both the key and the handle and the door swung open.

The scent of fresh flowers and beeswax polish wafted out to meet her and she smiled. As much as she adored her Victorian home with its spacious extension in a leafy suburb of Melbourne, she loved the simplicity of the cottage and the way over a summer it deconstructed their city lives.

Sunlight filtered in through the windows, lighting up the old house, and the grandfather clock struck four. At the end of the hall she spied a ginger fluff sponge and a plate of sandwiches, sitting next to a vase of white and pink sweet peas on the wide Baltic pine table.

She called back over her shoulder. 'Hey, guys, work fast. Meryl and Vicki have made us cake.'

'Yes!' Like a whirlwind, Carter grabbed a box of food and ran up the steps.

'I love this place!' Melissa tore past her slightly older brother, crossing the threshold first.

Twenty minutes later the twins, with traces of cream still clinging to their lips, took it in turns to throw a ball to Turbo, who was starting to look longingly at the shade of his favourite tree. At ten, he'd slowed down some but he could always find some extra energy to round up the chooks.

Dark-haired William, trowel in hand and bright yellow gumboots on his feet, busily dug over the herb patch, holding up worms and slaters for inspection before dropping them back into the fragrant soil.

Kirby sat on the veranda with her feet resting on the worn bluestone step and her back against Nick's chest, feeling the regular and soothing rise and fall of his breathing, her hands in her lap resting over his. She still marvelled at how the touch of his hands made her knees buckle and her heart race.

She turned in his arms, slinging her own around his neck. 'It's great to be back.'

He smiled, his eyes sparkling with wicked intent. 'You're so right, Sherlock. We've got two months of long, lazy summer days and glorious nights.'

She laughed. 'With three kids?'

He winked and dimples carved into his cheeks. 'The fresh air exhausts them and they'll be in bed early and sleep like logs.' Tilting his forehead, he rested it on hers. 'Even so, I've made some plans that involve my parents visiting for a few days so they can get their grandparent fix and I've booked the same few days for us at an isolated beachside shack just down the road at Dolphin Bay. Complete beach frontage and no one else around for miles.' He grinned. 'I haven't visited that beach since I was sixteen.'

'Really?' Her fingers trailed down his cheek and toyed with the buttons on his shirt. 'Do you plan on reliving your youth?'

His teasing gaze faded. 'Hell, no. I plan on living my present, with you.' The heartfelt words spun around her. 'The last nine years have been brilliant and I wouldn't change a second, but I'm looking forward to the future.' He lowered his head, his lips grazing hers, full of love and simmering desire.

She answered his kiss, reaffirming her commitment to him and promising a summer of fun and sensual delight.

Tumbling arms and legs suddenly slammed into them as children wriggled and squished between them.

'Do you *have* to do that mushy stuff?'

'Yeah, you said we would go fishing.'

'Look at this big worm!'

Laughing, Kirby avoided the dangling worm and caught Nick's gaze. 'You wouldn't change any of this for a second?'

'Not one thing.' He swung William up onto his shoulders, grabbed her hand and slung his free arm around both twins, capturing them against him. 'Come on, you lot, hurry up. The Dennisons are going fishing and swimming down at the creek.'

Turbo barked his approval.

MEDICAL™ 2-in-1

Coming next month
SECRET SHEIKH, SECRET BABY
by Carol Marinelli

One night with surgeon Karim Zaraq leaves pretty midwife
Felicity Anderson pregnant! As prince of a desert kingdom,
Karim must propose marriage… But Felicity won't say
'I do' unless it's for love.

HIS BABY BOMBSHELL
by Jessica Matthews

When Adrian McReynolds becomes nurse and ex-flame
Sabrina Hollister's temporary boss, he discovers he's a father.
Adrian let Sabrina go once already, now this surprise dad is
back for good – and wants Sabrina as his wife.

HIRED: GP AND WIFE
by Judy Campbell

GP Atholl Brodie is determined to ignore his new colleague,
Dr Terry Younger, but not only are they working together –
she'll also be sharing his cosy cottage! And soon her
fragile beauty is melting Atholl's stubborn heart…

THE PLAYBOY DOCTOR'S SURPRISE PROPOSAL
by Anne Fraser

Caitlin knew Dr Andrew Bedi had a reputation, yet couldn't
resist his charm. When Caitlin discovers she's pregnant…
Andrew finds himself wanting to be husband and
daddy sooner than he thought!

On sale 4th September 2009

Available at WHSmith, Tesco, ASDA, Eason and all good bookshops.
For full Mills & Boon range including eBooks visit
www.millsandboon.co.uk

MEDICAL™

Single titles coming next month

PREGNANT MIDWIFE: FATHER NEEDED
by Fiona McArthur

Pregnant midwife Mia is expecting a new arrival to
Lyrebird Lake Maternity – but not a six-foot Adonis and
his son! Mia tries not to get involved with rescue medic
Angus, but he knows that, with Mia as his wife,
they could be the perfect family.

FOUND: A MOTHER FOR HIS SON
by Dianne Drake

Jenna never expected to work with the love of her
life again. Now, seeing how devoted Dr Dermott Callahan
is to giving his five-year-old son Max all the love and
care he needs, she wonders if she dare reach out
and risk her heart with them – for ever.

On sale 4th September 2009

2 FREE BOOKS
AND A SURPRISE GIFT

We would like to take this opportunity to thank you for reading this Mills & Boon® book by offering you the chance to take TWO more specially selected title from the Medical™ series absolutely FREE! We're also making this offer to introduce you to the benefits of the Mills & Boon® Book Club™—

- **FREE home delivery**
- **FREE gifts and competitions**
- **FREE monthly Newsletter**
- **Exclusive Mills & Boon Book Club offers**
- **Books available before they're in the shops**

Accepting these FREE books and gift places you under no obligation to buy, you may cancel at any time, even after receiving your free books. Simply complete your details below and return the entire page to the address below. You don't even need a stamp!

YES Please send me 2 free Medical books and a surprise gift. I understand that unless you hear from me, I will receive 5 superb new titles every month including two 2-in-1 titles priced at £4.99 each and a single title priced at £3.19, postage and packing free. I am under no obligation to purchase any books and may cancel my subscription at any time. The free books and gift will be mine to keep in any case.

Ms/Mrs/Miss/Mr _____ initials _____

Surname _____

address _____

_____

_____ postcode _____

Send this whole page to: Mills & Boon Book Club, Free Book Offer, FREEPOST NAT 10298, Richmond, TW9 1BR